THE SONS OF MARELLA WINDSONG

a novel

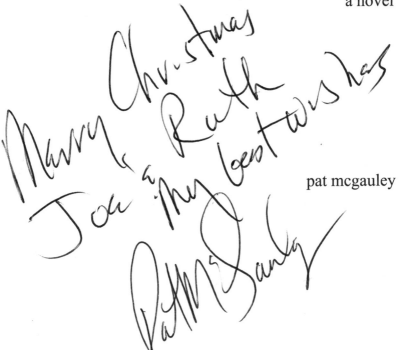

Merry Christmas
Joe & Ruth
My best wishes

pat mcgauley

a shamrock book

The Sons of Marella Windsong

Published by PJM Publishing
2808 Fifth Avenue West
Hibbing, MN 55746
Email: shatiferin@aol.com

Author's website: www.patmcgauley.com

Copyright: (Pending) est. November 2013
Library of Congress (EPCN) number: Pending
ISBN: 978-1-62890-103-0
First edition: November 2013

Shamrock Books from PJM are published by Bang Printing in the USA.
Cover design by Renee Anderson, Express Print One, Ltd.

DEDICATION

*Without the generousity of my son-in-law, this story
would not have been told. I owe my time in Florida and my
gratitude to Jim Otterbeck. Thanks Jim.*

ACKNOWLEDGEMENTS:

I am indebted to many people for their help with this story, some of whom I met casually at the Bois Fort or Fond du Lac Ojibwe Reservations and have no clear recollection of their names. In order to get certain character feelings, I read the works of many wonderful Ojibwe authors: Jim Northrup and Louise Erdrich come most immediately to mind. Ojibwe language teacher at the Fond du Lac Community College, Dan Jones, helped me with some language translations. Dave St. Peter, the President of the Minnesota Twins helped me with Twins organization and personnel questions. Rich Crosby provided the insights of a physical trainer. Gail Nevalainen edited the first rough draft and Sandy Bolf the second. Any and all punctuation errors are mine, not theirs. Renee Anderson at Express Print in Hibbing once again did the striking cover art.

Also, my family and many friends should be recognized for influencing the development of my fictional characters. An author is a thief–stealing traits and features and mannerisms from those around him/her without their being aware of the treasure they provide. The author uses whatever he gleans from people or places or events without permission or conscience. Some woman, or several women in my life experiences, gave me the stuff of Marella Windsong's personality. Trevor and Travis, her twin sons, and Florida entrepreneur Hector Munoz came from some of you as well. All are fictitious, but…their unique personas came from the back of my thoughts where all of you reside. Then again, some who populate this story are real. Terry Ryan of the Twins, for example, is a public figure that many Minnesotans would recognize on sight. I watched him pacing across the Hammond Stadium grandstand for nearly an hour one hot March morning in Ft. Myers and took the liberty of imagining his thoughts as he watched the young prospects on the field below us. The 'prospects' named in this story are also real people with the same hopes and dreams that Trevor Windsong had. Others with the Twins organization are real, too.

In most of my stories, the reader will find a reference to baseball and more often than not, that reference is to my beloved, and more recently, beleagured, Twins. Baseball has been in my blood since I could walk and talk. I love the game. And, although I've always wanted to do a genuine, 100% baseball story, too many people and too many other stories that needed to be told got in the way. Despite them, or because of them, I've created something that was even more fun for me to write. There is a fair measure of baseball in this novel but lots of drama and romance as well. I hope you enjoy reading *The Sons of Marella Windsong* as much as I enjoyed telling you their bittersweet story.

*"Every day is a new opportunity.
You can build on yesterday's success
or put its failures behind and start over again.
That's the way life is with a new game
every day—and that's the way baseball is."*

Bob Feller

1/ 'BRING IT ON!'

Wednesday: June 20, 2012

The rain whipped and slashed and pounded in torrents unlike anything the young man had ever experienced. Being out in this storm was foolish and he knew it, doing what he was doing bordered on sheer insanity, and he knew that, too. But when it was over, his Uncle Ben would be impressed with his feat. That was important; that was why he was so doggedly driven.

The gray sheets came in nonstop waves cutting his visibility to no more than twenty feet in front of his ATV machine. Nevertheless, he pushed the Honda four-wheeler to dangerous speeds. For him the adversity was like the ultimate challenge: 'Mother Nature' in all her fury against Trevor Windsong in all his daring. He would not let Her beat him in a duel of his own choosing. High-octane adrenalin pulsed in his veins. Trevor's teeth were clenched, his knuckles white and tightly gripped on his handlebars, his muscles as taut as bowstrings. The thrill of flying over a bump and landing on his back wheels brought a smile of satisfaction to his shielded face.

Trevor skidded to a stop at a fork on the winding trail of muddied dirt and slick gravel to get his bearings and wipe clean the fiberglass faceguard on his helmet. Twice he had felt the vibration of his cell phone tucked in his waist pack along with the keys to his truck and his wallet. He was completely in his element now and didn't want to talk with anybody. Not even Uncle Ben–not yet, anyhow. He spat a wad of Copenhagen, then tucked a fresh pinch of tobacco under his lip, then slid the round tin back in his shirt pocket. He cut short a smile and thought of how his mother would kick his butt around the block if she knew he was chewing. Mom was one tough lady and the sole authority figure in his world. No one commanded more respect than the woman who had given him life and love along with a strong dose of the courage and the drive that defined his nature. "Sorry, Mom", he mumbled his guilt under his breath, "Don't worry, I'm gonna quit this crap when football starts in the fall." His wind pants were caked with debris from the trail, his gray T-shirt was skin-clinging-drenched, his Honda ATV oozing mud like a happy pig. Pulling the shield back down and adjusting his red sweaty helmet, he let the chinstrap dangle…revving the engine to a scream, he spun out, resuming his reckless ride with characteristic abandon.

Within seconds he was back to forty on a straight section of the slimy trail that snaked along the swollen St. Louis River from Jay Cooke Park toward Carlton in northeastern Minnesota. What would have been a worthy challenge for a more experienced operator on a clear and dry morning became an Everest to be conquered for the headstrong youth. To Trevor Windsong, any opportunity to test his skills or his nerve was a 'bring it on!' test. Adding an extra dimension to his excitement was the unfamiliarity of the trail and its many precarious nuances. Twice Trevor Windsong had two-wheeled on a sharp turn and skidded dangerously close to mighty Norway pines that would have stopped his machine cold and thrown him like a rag doll into a thick tangle of brush. Once, he narrowly missed a protruding boulder and careened off a banked ridge without decelerating. That stunt could have dropped him thirty feet into the raging river below. Each scare only jacked his resolve to conquer the treacherous trail that would ultimately take him to the casino on the south edge of the Fond du Lac Indian Reservation, short miles to the north.

Trevor pulled his machine to a sudden stop; an uprooted birch tree blocked the trail and would have to be pulled to the side. Checking the time on his cell phone, he noted that he was running a few minutes behind his unreasonably determined goal and would be late for a meeting with Uncle Ben. The two men had planned to gamble a bit on the penny slots and have a light lunch together at the Black Bear Casino. Trevor cherished any and every opportunity to be with his uncle.

Trevor guessed that he was less than three or four miles from the I-35 underpass that would take him to Highway 210 and then into the casino's parking lot. Just as he had expected when checking his cell phone, the missed calls were from his uncle—not his mother. He punched 'Uncle Ben' in his directory...four rings, no answer. He left a message: "Hi Uncle. I'm wheelin' the trail south of Carlton. I'll probably be a few minutes late—hope you can find me some towels—I'm drenched." Ben would shake his head and smile when he got the message, Trevor thought. After all, Ben had lived dangerously when he was Trevor's age. Benjamin Little Otter had been a near-legendary stock car driver on the competitive northern racing circuit. Almost legendary! Ben broke his back in a collision ten years ago. Trevor was eight years old at the time, but remembered the rollover as if it were only last year.

Despite Trevor's raw strength, the young birch was wedged between two others and had a ton of soggy branches pressing it down. He yanked and tugged but the stubborn birch couldn't be dislodged more than a few inches in any direction. Frustrated to a wild flurry of cuss-words his mother would ground him for, he sucked up the minor setback. From the knoll where he was parked, he could squint and vaguely see the rocky outcroppings banking the angry river nearly fifty feet below. He remounted his machine, gunned the engine, and turned sharply into the thick brush above the fallen tree, then spun back onto the narrow patch of gravel. Despite the diminished and worsening visibility, he could see and feel that some of the trail's edges were washing out. Compensating, he leaned his Honda onto the higher side. Within minutes he was back on the attack, pushing precarious limits on a straight stretch of pine and aspen that bordered the narrow trail. He was determined to make up the three minutes of lost time. The rain continued to slash his shield and obscure his vision. Approaching another hairpin turn he decelerated, then suddenly squeezed the brakes...an overhanging pine bough slapped at his head as he skidded on the downhill curve twisting his unstrapped helmet to the side and blinding him for a fraction of a second...then he lost control.

2/ *TRAVIS WINDSONG*

Two hours north of the Fond du Lac trail, Travis Windsong, Trevor's twin brother played the Xbox 360 version of a *Minecraft* video game on his MacBook computer. His need for adventure was far more sedentary than that of his brother. The eighteen year-old was smiling with a satisfaction of his own; he had just bartered the trade of crude tools with a villager mob for valuable emeralds. A glance through the bedroom window reminded him to check the basement for water leakage. His mother had told him to check every hour or so. The sump pump hadn't been working and the rain had been nonstop since the previous afternoon. What was more important than taking the time to check for water, however, was the simple fact that his mother had told him to do so. Whatever Mom wanted her sons to do was the law in the Windsong household. Despite evidence of moderate flooding in low-lying locales outside of Hibbing where the Windsongs lived, the Iron Range area was not experiencing the drenching that was occurring in locations only fifty miles to the south.

Although a fraternal twin, Travis' nature had little in common with that of his more athletic and adventurous brother. Four-wheeling in the rain would be at the bottom of Travis' list of things to do on a summer vacation day. In fact, rain or shine, Travis spent more time indoors than outdoors, where his allergies bothered him. As different as the brothers were in appearance, temperament, and interests…the paranormal connection they shared with one another was surreal. Just when he was moving to a higher-level challenge in his video game quest, Travis was jolted so hard that he nearly fell from his chair. First his head split as if it had been struck by lightning. In that same instant, his left arm felt as if it were being ripped from his shoulder then smashed with a sledge hammer below the elbow. His wrist bent backwards as he tried to grip the corner of his desk. Grimacing with pains unlike any he'd experienced before, Travis screamed. Tears of agony were streaking down his brown face like the rain running down the windowpanes.

Pushing himself away from his desk with his good arm, Travis wobbled in sudden disorientation, then cried in agony once again. "Mom! Mom…where is Trevor? Mom…!" he appealed in desperation. Instinctively he realized something very bad had happened to his twin brother. He staggered from his bedroom toward the living room, holding his throbbing arm tightly pressed to his side. "Mom!" His plea, however, only echoed in the empty room. His mother wasn't home. His breath came in quick gasps as he fought against hyperventilating. As frightened as he was in the swirl of the moment, Travis cautioned himself against panicking: Something horrible had just happened, he would have to keep his composure…and do something quickly. He searched his memory ordering a clarity of focus: Fact– Trevor had left the house early that morning to visit their uncle Benjamin. Fact– Mom had told the boys that she would be working an overtime shift at her job. Fact– he had overslept this morning without seeing either his mother or his brother. Fact—although being on the verge of passing out he must get help, and fast! Despite the wrenching pain and initial stupefaction, details of his dire situation were becoming clear in his mind.

The digital clock on the radio resting silently upon the kitchen counter clicked 9:18. Trevor's mind raced, although Mom hated calls while at work…he must break her rule. He frowned, where was his cell phone? His eyes turned sharply to his left, focusing on the space next to a recent WalMart family portrait on the bookcase. The iPhone he shared with Trevor was gone from the shelf where the last user always placed it when they finished a call, the place where Mom put it whenever she found it lying somewhere else. Gone! The charging cord dangled from the outlet to the carpet. Naturally, Trevor had taken it along with him to Fond du Lac. The wall phone near the kitchen sink had been disconnected months before: Mom, always the economist, was convinced that two cell phones were all her family of three needed to be connected to the world.

Apparently, Mom's judgement wasn't as infallible as her sons had been led to believe. Travis knew that he needed to find help: Every moment was critical!

Looking outside from the open front door, the empty driveway confirmed what he already knew; both vehicles like both phones were gone. Mom had taken the Corolla to the HRA where she worked, Trevor had taken the Ranger pickup to the Fond du Lac Reservation where Uncle Ben lived. Travis was eerily alone and in excruciating pain—he needed to think quickly and clearly, but his head was becoming as mirky as the dark sky that swallowed the morning. Aside from the old widow across the road, the nearest neighbor was some distance away. He found his nylon jacket from the coat tree by the door and draped it over his head with his right hand. Twisting his body to cover himself shot the knife of pain deeply into his shoulder, nearly causing him to buckle over. Pulsating waves of pain were reaching his head now and he was feeling faint, unsettled, and nauseous. Yet, he realized that he couldn't just stand in the doorway and wish his situation were something different than what it was; he had to do something…had to find help. Moving onto the front porch, he was seized with a cramping queasiness. Struggling to keep his balance, Travis hobbled down the steps, one at a time, and into the slashing rain. Suddenly, the need to vomit was overwhelming…letting go of the railing he took three faltering steps before toppling over…the cool mud that splashed his face was the last sensation he would remember.

3/ FATHER MICKEY MORAN

"I felt the hand of God upon me…" Father Michael 'Mickey' Moran's eyes lifted toward the chandeliers adorning the ballroom's high ceiling as he stretched the truth of his recent experience by a few inches. Since childhood the priest had been prone to exaggerating experiences. "He wanted me to go there…to help others in need…to do the work that He had intended me to do all along—work that I had no idea needed doing." The young cleric, dressed casually in black slacks and a white Polo shirt, was addressing the Hibbing Rotarians at their Wednesday breakfast meeting in the historic Androy Hotel building. The Androy, once owned by his great-grandfather, held a special significance in Mickey's heart. Kevin Moran had been a titan in the annals of Hibbing's rich history. The refurbished main ballroom was pleasant, but as any old-timer would tell you, only a shadow of its earlier elegance. The Androy rose above the downtown commercial district as if it were the guardian and curator of all that occurred within its domain.

At times Mickey's audience hung on every word. His practiced narrative was informative, colorful, sometimes humorous, and enhanced by an embellishment of animated gestures. There was an obvious passion in the story he was sharing. The former Hibbing native's homecoming was proving to be both genial and enthusiastic beyond his expectations. It was a distinct pleasure to look out upon the familiar faces of former classmates and family friends from his formative years in the mining town. His brother-in-law, Kenny Williams, was seated at the front table next to Walter Harvey from the high school. At every glance his eyes caught the face of someone who conjured a pleasant, although sometimes distracting, memory.

Mickey's summer calendar had become rife with speaking engagements–from the Twin Cities to the Minnesota Iron Ranges. This morning's Hibbing breakfast event would be followed with a talk to a student assembly at the local high school, his beloved alma mater, at eleven. Afterwards, Mickey would drive sixty miles east to Hoyt Lakes where he would be the guest of the local Chamber of Commerce, and then, back to Duluth for a late meeting with his bishop. Three scheduled engagements on this day along with another on Friday at St. John's Catholic Church in picturesque Grand Marais, far up the north shore of Lake Superior, would be followed by more of the same in the next week.

The Catholic priest had slipped into his recent celebrity quite by accident—or, many had opined, by some stroke of Divine providence. Ordered by his bishop to begin an undetermined, mistakenly-reasoned, and ill-defined sabbatical in southern Florida, the headstrong and impulsive young priest decided to pursue his own agenda. Not only did he violate his vow of obedience, he did so with a well-concealed secrecy that had his usually unflappable bishop in a dither. As it turned out, however, his covert deviance resulted in an almost magical story of success. Miraculous success! In fact, what Father Moran was able to accomplish within a few short months in distant Florida not only placed him in the good graces of two bishops; it garnered deserved recognition from the Vatican in Rome.

The story of Mickey's selfless exploits in the destitute Hispanic community of TriPalms near Venice, in southwestern Florida, was the stuff of unbelievable fiction. The young priest had rallied a team of visionary developers that together had transformed an entire community—both physically and spiritually. The fact that Father Mickey Moran was a priest that made a difference in people's lives, also made for news—major news. In an era when the Roman Church often had to battle issues of deviant priests, cover-ups, and discipline failures, his heartrending story was a rush of fresh air within the Catholic community and beyond. Press conferences, speaking engagements, and an assortment of publicity events were becoming the stuff of his daily regimen. Mickey found himself on a fast track from an obscure parish priest in a tired old west Duluth neighborhood to a major voice for social activism.

Diocese of Duluth Bishop, Anthony Bremmer, shared his underling's limelight and carefully orchestrated the fallout publicity. Evidence of increasing numbers of Catholics attending mass (and receiving the sacraments) was an unmistakable windfall along with a healthy increase from Sunday's collection plates. A projected boost in parochial school enrollments was another benefit. Bremmer's struggling Saturday morning radio program on KDAL, 'The Bishop's Hour', was experiencing an ever-increasing audience and was securing new sponsorships from important community sources. WDIO television officials were seriously negotiating a pilot project they envisioned as 'Conversations with Mickey' for their religious programming obligations.

Upon his return from Florida, a consultation with Bishop Bremmer resulted in a reassessment of Mickey's role within the Diocese of Duluth's organizational structure. Unofficially and ostensibly, Mickey's newly created position was described as 'Native American Affairs Coordinator'. He, and others in the church hierachy, were of the impression that the spiritual revitalization of TriPalms could be replicated in some manner in this northern Minnesota diocese. The bishop was hoping to better integrate the five Ojibwa Indian reservations of his jurisdiction more intimately within the Catholic mainstream: a virtuous idea that woefully lacked in substance or structure. Nevertheless, to Bremmer and nearly everybody else, the creative and innovative young priest could accomplish things that his bishop could only imagine. Mickey Moran, it seemed, could do almost anything he set his mind and boundless energy to achieving.

Mickey's rendition of his 'TriPalms' experience in southwestern Florida, a story already familiar to most in his Hibbing audience, was nearing conclusion. His voice rose an octave and his satisfied grin enlivened the crowded room. "And, the new church currently under construction in TriPalms will be named St. Michael's. How flattering is that?" His enthusiasm was contagious. "I can't wait to go back there in December and see how the rehabilitation project is progressing and have the opportunity of saying the first Mass in the new church."

The caffeine was wearing off and Mickey's intense energy was losing some steam as he wound down his talk. The attractive young editor of the *Hibbing Tribune* caught his attention. "Will you be writing a book, Father?" That question had been raised at every event of the past two months.

"I really don't think that I'll have the time I'd imagine that it would take, Kelly." Mickey offered a smile that had been photographed a thousand times already this month and blinked at the flash from a nearby camera. "I'm going to be far too busy with my new position to do much of anything else." His answer caused his stomach to tighten; he had no idea of how he was going to achieve his, or the bishop's, expectations. His life had been turned upside-down since his return from Florida only months before. Everyone within the religious community, and outside of it as well, seemed to think that he could walk on water. Everyone, that is, but Mickey himself. His accomplishments in the Hispanic community of Florida were not likely to happen again– neither here nor anywhere else. Noticing the stir of chairs moving and bodies shifting, he glanced at his wristwatch: "How about one more question before I bow out with a quick closing prayer…?"

"Can you do it all again?"

The question Mickey dreaded more than any other hung in the space between him and forty expectant Rotarians and their guests inivited for this special event.

"That depends on the Boss up there," he gestured toward the ceiling. "I can only do His will…with the limited abilities He has blessed me with." Mickey's spiritual truth brought nods of approval. Had he given his audience the unmitigated truth 'It's not possible', he might have left his audience with frowns of disappointment. He knew in his heart and mind that the lofty expectations and the harsh realities remained countless miles apart.

The enthusiastic applause, along with a standing tribute, was heart-warming. "Please allow my blessing…" Mickey bowed his head: "Almighty God, I pray your blessings upon these my friends…"

4/ THE LAST MORAN

At times during his presentation, Mickey's eyes met those of Abe Atkinson. Abe was a local old-timer—probably in his late eighties or early nineties—with a memory as deep as the sagging furrows below his eyes. The grandson of a famous newspaperman, Abe was one of the few who knew the grit of Mickey's family roots—probably with greater depth than Mickey knew them himself. When Mickey had entered the building, Abe was one of the many Rotarians standing near the door to greet him and offer congratulations for past deeds as well as good wishes for those that lay ahead. Abe leaned toward Mickey's ear, cupped his hand, and said, "Never thought the last Moran would become a man of God." Mickey nodded and smiled but didn't understand the implication of the old man's seemingly inappropriate comment—*the last Moran!*

"Somebody has to do the Lord's work—I didn't choose Him, He chose me, Mr. Atkinson." Mickey frowned, making light of the old-timer's observation.

Atkinson's beige shirt was soiled, hair disheveled, and face stubbled. Mickey's memory was challenged by his appearance. Atkinson had always been as meticulous in his dress as he had been with his writing. "Hope you're doing well, sir," he said, as he moved toward Fred Zdon, a pharmacist who was standing nearby.

"The Moran men were unscrupulous and driven…I doubt if the same things will be said…" he heard Atkinson mutter from behind him. The man's last few words seemed to be doubt-laden, almost ominous.

Ignoring the old sage, Mickey greeted a former neighbor: "Great to see you, too, Fred. How's Mary these days…the kids. Did Zack get accepted to medical school at the U?"

~

The Morans of Atkinson's memory had enriched and embellished the history of the mining hub of Hibbing on the great Mesabi Iron Range of northeastern Minnesota through several generations. The mines surrounding the community—the Hull, the Rust, and the Mahoning to name a few of many—were massive and their footprints were deep in the earth. At the turn of the last century, the first of the Morans left their footprints in the red earth as well. Peter Moran was a ruthless entrepreneur with a vast financial empire that included lumber and coal operations, liquor distribution, real estate and commercial development. After Peter's untimely and controversial death, Kevin Moran inherited his father's fortune but chose to shun the flamboyant lifestyle that could have been his. Kevin, a philanthropist, along with his wife Angela, a nationally recognized artist, were like royalty in the flourishing community. Their son Patrick became a near-legendary peace officer and political activist during his lifetime. Patrick, known to all his friends as 'Pack', and his charming wife, Maddie, had one child—a son named Amos. Amos, like his grandfather, became an attorney of wide repute before his current semi-retirement. He, and his wife Sadie had a daughter Meghan, and son, Michael 'Mickey' Moran.

The early generations of the Moran family, along with the colorful history of Hibbing, had been chronicled in a fiction format by an obscure local author in the early twenty-first century.

~

Mickey's brother-in-law, Kenny Williams, greeted folks as the priest was making his way from the head table to the doorway. Kenny had asked Mickey not to mention his own role in the Tri-Palms story but his reasons for the request were vague: "This is your thing, bro," was what he said.

Mickey had respected Kenny's wishes during his speech. Still milling with friends, he felt the elbow tug of his brother-in-law.

"Well done, Mickey," Kenny beamed. "Everybody was with you." Mickey placed his arm on Kenny's shoulder, whispered "I hope so. Be honest with me, Kenny, did I come across as if everything was me, me, and more me? I hate when I do that. I really don't mean to come off that way."

"You can't possibly talk about what you accomplished without referring to yourself—no, you did quite well. Say...we can visit more later...I've gotta run...you ought to stop and say hello to your sister. Meg knows you're in town today."

"Hope to, Kenny...but, she must know that I'm on a tight schedule."

Mickey noticed Abe Atkinson waiting by the door and looking in his direction. "Kenny, do me a favor. Would you engage Abe over there," he gestured with a shoulder shrug, "in some kind of conversation so I can get out the door without his bending my ear again?"

Kenny puzzled, "I suppose...what's that about?"

Mickey didn't have any logical answer, "Nothing...thanks...see ya later."

5/ RAIN AND MORE RAIN...

Stepping outside the Androy onto the rain-peppered sidewalk, Mickey clutched his umbrella. Downtown Hibbing was awash in a downpour that hadn't let up since early on the previous night. The Sportsmens Café across Howard Street from the Androy building was only vaguely discernable through the silver-gray curtain between him and the dimly lit restaurant. He had an hour to himself before heading the three blocks to the high school for his next speech, and he hadn't found time to read either his *Hibbing Daily* or *Minneapolis StarTrib*. Failure to peruse a morning paper, like failure to get a good night's sleep, always left Mickey feeling a sense of deprivation and set his awaiting day noticeably akilter. He waited for a gap in the sporadic traffic and darted across the street, splashing in puddles and soaking his black loafers to his stockings and the bottoms of his trousers to below his knees.

Once inside the restaurant he found an open booth off to his right, the very same booth he had shared with his beloved grandfather, Pack Moran on many past occasions. A wave of nostalgia swept across his thoughts. In Mickey's youth, he and his idolized grampa had enjoyed many great conversations about good and evil and love and hate and being true to one's self. And, in the spring and summer, they talked baseball. The national game to both of them was centered on their beloved Minnesota Twins. The two of them, one old and wise, the other young and green, pondered those things that only a former cop, political junkie, and athlete like his grampa Pack could offer unique insights about.

"Just coffee please...black is fine..." he told the waitress wearing a Nora name-tag as he spread the local paper across the Formica tabletop. Before he could scan the front page, he felt the vibration of his cell phone in his pants pocket.

"Benjamin...what's up?"

Benjamin Little Otter was Mickey's close friend and coworker. A frown creased Mickey's forehead as he listened to Benjamin's urgent appeal. "Oh no!" Mickey could feel a stress growing inside his chest: "I can't! I'm really slammed today, Ben...I won't be...you've got to understand...no...no way...wish I could...but–" A reality split in his head like spring ice: Why did everything always have to be about Mickey Moran? About his schedule, about his commitments, about his 'gotta do's'?

Why was he the almighty and absolute priority? What was he becoming? In his forty minute speech that morning he probably used the word 'I' ten thousand times...I this and I that and I everything else. It was beginning to really trouble him. Why was he always so preoccupied...?

A long pause at Benjamin Little Otter's end...then a resigned

"Okay…I understand." Mickey's Ojibwe friend was signing off with an acceptance of Mickey's rejection…Ben swallowed hard "We'll catch up on things later…" his voice was subdued. "Okay…?"

Mickey shook his head: "No! Not later." His conscience cut like a knife in his soul: "I'll be there in an hour, Ben." Not only was Benjamin his close friend and coworker on a shared work assignment, he was a man that rarely asked for anything. Ben was one of life's givers.

Leaving a five-dollar bill and two unread papers in the Sportsmen's booth, Mickey raced back across Howard Street to his parked car, too consumed with the unexpected change in plans to realize that he had forgotten to retrieve his umbrella. In his Civic, Mickey pulled out his cell and punched in the high school principal's number. Emergency was one word that most people understood and were willing to make allowances for. Mickey promised the principal, Walter Harvey, that he'd reschedule the assembly as soon as he could. "I owe you one—big time!" he said as he buckled himself and tossed his phone onto the passenger seat.

The rain drummed upon the Civic's metal hood like a rock band on a quonset hut's roof as he headed down the quiet main street toward the beltline. He said a prayer for safe travel and for the injured boy Ben had told him about. When in need, or in doubt, or in a hurry for whatever reason, Mickey's mantra was always a simple prayer.

Crossing himself in the Catholic tradition, he conjured a mental image of his Lord: "Like everything I do, Lord, let my actions this day be of Your will—not mine, and may I render Your peace and Divine love to all…especially to strangers in need…amen."

The monotonous swish of the wipers was as mesmerizing as the stereotypical shrink's hypnotic sway of a pocket watch. He was more tired than he would ever admit. For months he had been losing his battle against his persistent foe– insomnia. Being in the claustrophobic environs of his car, with the windows closed, only added to the discomfort. Whenever Mickey accelerated over forty-five, his car began to hydroplane. The slick asphalt was puddled in every low spot—and there were many on the worn two-lane highway east of Hibbing. Looping off of the ramp from Highway 37, to the more heavily trafficked Highway 53, found him stuck behind a row of semis crawling along under fifty. In their wake were splashing waves of water, inhibiting his visiblilty even more, and adding a few additional ounces of tension.

Mickey hung well behind the trucks and resigned himself to making slow progress. The rain was getting thicker as he got closer to the port city of Duluth. He'd talked with Benjamin Little Otter twice since leaving Hibbing but was still uncertain about what his friend expected from him. It sounded to Mickey as if some relative or friend of Bens, he wasn't sure which, had been in a serious accident and had been taken to St. Mary's Hospital. Ben sounded very anxious and in need of support—spiritual and emotional–as he waited by himself outside the ER for any word about the condition of the young man. After bypassing the cutoff exit to Cloquet, Mickey tuned his radio to KDAL. Duluth was being inundated! *"Don't…I repeat…Don't travel into the downtown area or anywhere west of 57th Avenue. In fact, don't go anywhere this morning. It's very dangerous out there!"* The warning from journalist, John Gilbert, was emphatic. Callers into the radio station were reporting horror stories about conditions in their neighborhoods. One caller from far western Duluth had been rescued from the roof of his home by his neighbor in a motor boat: "The house– she's a goner—might even wash away into the river along with trees and debris like I ain't never seen."

Mickey's parish, St. Gerards, was in the west Duluth neighborhood of Benton Park. He called his housekeeper, Mary Alice, to check on conditions there. "Lots of our parishioners are suffering from this storm, Father. I've wanted to call but…" Mickey had told her not to call between ten thirty and noon as he would be in the high school auditorium and his cell would be shut off. "That corner of the basement has puddles, but nothing serious" she added.

Mickey's dog 'Torts' hated thunder, "How's my mutt doing? Will he go out and pee for you?"

"Not unless I go out with him, Father. Done that twice today. We're both wet and ornery 'cause of it. He's happiest sleeping under your desk, so I just leave him alone."

Mickey told her where he was going to be for the next hour or so and asked that she call if any emergencies came up. "I should be back sometime this afternoon."

~

As he approached the Miller Hill Mall on the northern boundaries of Duluth, Mickey's jaw dropped in astonishment. Off to his right was a lake he had never seen before. "Oh my God!" were the only three words that could describe what he was seeing.

~

Nearly fifty hours of rain, up to twelve inches in some areas of the long, narrow city, was creating a state of emergency unlike that of even the harshest of winter blizzards that Duluth was noted for. The picturesque San Francisco-like hillside that rimmed the central city from the Skyline Drive on the north, down to majestic Lake Superior below, was spawning raging rivers that were sweeping away anything in their path. The city's newly designed sewer systems along the hillside were failing miserably. Cast iron manhole covers were being flipped into the air like poker chips, as veritable geysers spewed raw sewage into the rushing rainwater. In many places sinkholes swallowed cars and roads buckled like toppled rows of dominos. The banks of swollen Lester and Tischer Creeks were so badly eroded that mature oaks bordering the stream were being washed away like matchsticks, clogging culverts and adding to the unprecedented mess. KDAL reported that an eight year-old boy slipped into a Proctor culvert and was carried several blocks underground before being rescued. Seals from the Duluth Zoo had been washed over a ten-foot wall and ended up stranded on the traffic artery of Grand Avenue. The seals would be safely recovered, but several of the zoo's barnyard animals would drown in the hollow that housed the zoo's many outdoor exhibits.

Some of the worst flooding occurred in far western Duluth, in the neighborhood of Fond du Lac, where the St. Louis River rose nearly thirty feet over flood stage. Neighboring Superior and Douglas County in Wisconsin were swamped. The flooding innundated Carlton to the north, and Moose Lake to the south, as well. The Red Cross and Salvation Army were establishing several temporary shelters for displaced families, as every resource was being brought to task in a valiant attempt to save endangered human lives.

(In the days following, Duluth Mayor Ness and Minnesota Governor Dayton would declare the city and surrounding counties to be natural disaster areas. The federal government would include three tribal nations, as well as the other adjacent jurisdictions in its disaster declaration two weeks later. And PETA—People for the Ethical Treatment of Animals– would demand that the Duluth Zoo be prosecuted for the animal deaths resulting from the flood).

6/ BENJAMIN LITTLE OTTER

Benjamin Little Otter had won a battle with his demon the night before but paid his price with a debilitating headache and sleep lost to his recurring nightmares. The haunting evil spirt, he knew to be his *Windigo*, took many addictive forms from drinking to chainsmoking and gambling, and had held the upper hand in its battles with Benjamin for too many years. Ben was on his seventh month of sobriety: two hundred and seventeen days! Quitting smoking was impossible, gambling was no more than a nuisance he could indulge without remorse. Before getting into bed, he had made the promised call to assure Lester that he was okay. Lester Hicks was his AA sponsor and the two men conversed at least twice every day. "Put on the sticker, my friend," Lester said. The sticker was a yellow smiley face that Ben affixed to that day's box on the calendar hanging on the bare wall across from the small pine-carved table near the kitchen window. The kitchen, like the other rooms of his small bungalow, was cluttered and in need of serious cleaning. So far, the twenty boxes of June were all clad in sun-smiling yellow.

~

The June Wednesday morning was wet and colorless. Benjamin Little Otter listened to the message from his sister in-law's son, Trevor. The time of the call was 8:12…the clock on the restaurant wall said 9:05. Trevor was late. Something was wrong. The large Ojibwe man, at six-six and two-fifty, shifted uneasily in the booth facing the entryway, scraping his ample stomach on the edge of the table, and wiggling the coffee cup and saucer. Every booth and chair that Ben had ever met was too small for him. Although physically intimidating, he was a meek man with a shallow voice that often forced people to step into his space in order to hear what he was saying. Yet Ben could hear a whisper from the other side of a room.

At the counter next to where Ben was sipping his coffee, two men were talking about the St. Louis River flooding in far western Duluth, "I think half of the city is gonna be washed into da big lake," the stout man with big ears said. "A few minutes ago dis trucker, he tol me that 210's been washed out south of here—left lots'a trucks stranded he tol me. Jay Cooke Parks' a goner, too."

"Yeah, I heard the same thing. And I heard some of doze zoo animals have got out and that they're running wild in the neighborhoods," said his bearded companion wearing a soiled Mack truck cap pulled down over his eyes. "This is the worst storm I've seen in my fifty-three years, that's for damn sure."

Big ears nodded agreement as beard stirred his coffee.

Benjamin's worry was furrowed across his broad forehead. What to do about Trevor? Give his nephew another fifteen minutes? Or, go looking for the boy? Making decisions had never been easy for the reluctant giant. He was good at following instructions but struggled mightily with giving them. The belief that 'to do nothing is to do something' was his preferred way of working through most situations. He'd tried to call Trevor's cell phone twice but got no answer. He didn't bother to leave a message. Then he tried to call Trevor's mother up in Hibbing, but got 'the number you have called is no longer in service': He hadn't ever thought to put her cell number in his directory. Whenever he called the Windsongs, which wasn't often, he usually wanted to speak with one of the twins. Instead he replayed the phone message from nearly an hour ago: "…on the trail south of Carlton…have some towels…" Obviously, Trevor was on his four-wheeler. In this weather, that spelled stupidity!

"Somthin's wrong Tammy." Benjamin placed his large hand over his coffee mug. "No more," he told the twentyish waitress. He stood and stretched to relax the tension in his back and shoulders, his giant frame casting a shadow over the two men only a few feet away. "I've gotta go find my nephew," he announced to all within earshot. "Somethin's very wrong," he repeated in a mumble as he headed for the door, then down the corridor to the parking lot. The asphalt lot was a under several inches of water. Benjamin sloshed through an ankle deep puddle, got his Ram pickup into gear and headed toward Carlton. Torrents of rain obscured everything beyond ten yards in any direction. Within minutes, he turned into a Mobil station where a local attendant in a neon yellow rainjacket

'Thanks for the truck', or an 'I'll be home at five', or the slightest kiss goodbye. Even a peck on her cheek would have jump-started her day. More than his brother, Trevor needed a man in his life and his uncle was that man. Although Benjamin would not be her first choice as a role model for her son, he was a good man at heart both decent and honest to a fault. When either son wanted to spend time with their uncle, Marella's only question was: 'Is he sober?'—her brother-in-law had been sober for quite some time. That was good—very good!

Turning south on First Avenue, Marella's concern momentarily diverted from Trevor, something was wrong with Travis, too. Always more restrained and less assertive, she could tell that he was experiencing great pain himself. The twelve-minutes younger twin was a totally different package. Reticent, studious, polite, and docile...he was his mother's opposite in nearly every way. She often wondered if he was a cut from his father—a man Marella hardly knew. Whenever a thought of Henry LaFrond crossed her thoughts, it brought with it a surge of anger. Her muscles tightened and her hands gripped the steering wheel so tightly that her fingernails stuck into the palms of both hands. An explosive fury was always close to the surface of the Ojibwe woman's disposition. Passing the WalMart store on the highway, she turned a sharp left through a red light and south onto Highway 73; her house was a left turn on Townline and a right on Anderson Road—three miles from the intersection she had sailed through.

8/ HANK LAFROND

Marella Windsong's anger was deeply rooted. As a child and as a teen, however, she had the easy nature and charm of her son Travis. Quiet, confident, and fun-loving, her friends considered her much more tomboy than Barbie. Her family lived in a small home, fronting on beautiful Lake Vermilion, on the Bois Fort Reservation. She grew up with a love of fishing, hunting, and autumn ricing in the many lakes dotting the northern Minnesota landscape. She also had a rich love of her Ojibwe heritage. The cute little girl became a pageant queen at area powwows when she was fifteen—by then, every boy in school had a secret crush on Marella Windsong.

As a seventeen year-old honors graduate from Tower High School, she enrolled at the Vermilion Community College in Ely with an idealism and optimism rarely evidenced in a Native American woman of her youth. She loved literature and wanted to be a teacher and wanted to learn everything she could about creative writing and expression. Before midterm of her freshman year she became disillusioned with her classes. As a state institution, graduation requirements included a repetition of basic mathematics, a four credit memorization-saturated biology course, and useless physical education credits playing pickup soccer. The lack of challenge in her coursework aggravated her psychologically and bored her intellectually. Marella brought her protest to the academic dean, Roland Dorsher, after the midterm exams. "I've already learned enough of this stuff in high school; I'm here to learn new things— college things. Things that I can sink my teeth into...things like regional history, psychology, and—more than anything else—literature! I want to be a writer like Louise Erdrich...I dream of someday being a voice for our people. I want to make a difference. I thought my tuition would be paying for things that would challenge me, enable me to grow."

The genial, gray-bearded dean smiled warmly; he'd recently read Erdrich's *Love Medicine* and could see some of that author's spirit in the young woman making her appeal. He encouraged her to take the matter before the faculty council after the semester break. "Get involved in the politics of college administration and curriculum so you can be an effective voice for other students with concerns like your own." A wise and judicious man, Dorsher knew that Marella knew that he was only blowing smoke: The faculty council wasn't going to change anything. The established coursework requirements at Vermilion College would be the same as those in all the companion community colleges– only the state legislature was going to make any changes. "Next semester you might want to take political science as an elective. Then you can learn the ins-and-outs of politics," Doctor Dorsher advised.

"I might just as well spit into the wind," Marella said, "But I'll think about giving it a shot nonetheless." Once outside and into the fresh air, away from the cramped and stuffy office, she allowed the reality of futile crusades to settle in. She would only get shot down by a group of academics who were so deeply ensconced in their subject areas that their views were too myopic to allow for any sense of objectivity. Nope! Marella would spare herself that embarrassment. Further, she had little interest in politics and would reject Dorsher's suggestion that she enroll in a political science class.

After a long walk in the crisp, pine-scented air, Marella felt refreshed and energized. She had allowed the frustration over her circumstance to become a self-focused ire. That was foolish. Somewhere she had read that 'those who anger you conquer you'…Somehow she must come up with a plan—a way to regroup her efforts, a way to make lemonade out of the lemons. As she let go of the anger, her mind cleared and the germ of an idea began to take form. Although not without consequences, there was a positive initiative open to her. Marella Windsong would shape her own education, not the Vermilion College faculty council! Why waste her efforts on losing a single battle when she had the moxie it takes to win the war?

With that thought, she turned back toward the adminitration offices. Inside, she met with her registration counselor. "Screw the degree," she told Susan Holgate, "sign me up for Western Civ, American Lit, Intro to Psych, and the two classes that Mr. LaFrond teaches next semester. That's eighteen credits that I will enjoy and, one day I hope, put to good use."

Holgate balked at the suggestion, "You'll regret…" Marella interrupted, "Regret what? Regret graduating with an Associate Degree? I don't think so. What I would regret is not getting the education I want for myself."

Marella flourished in the first weeks of her second semester. 'Hank', as Henry LaFrond insisted his students to call him, was easily her favorite teacher ever. She was taking two of his classes worth six credits—Minnesota Literature and Expressive Poetry—three afternoons each week. LaFrond was unstructured and spontaneous and his approach to subject matter was unconventional. "What do you think?" "Disagree with what I'm saying!" "Don't believe what you don't feel in your gut!" "Write with passion—pour out your heart and spirit without reverence for anything or anybody," These, and numerous other posers, were the stuff of his daily challenges in a classroom as animated as the man who orchestrated the lessons. In addition to her enjoyment of the diverse topics he covered, she became uncomfortably smitten with his good looks and intellect. The tall, slender teacher also played concert piano and wrote music in his spare time. "If any of you are interested in piano lessons, I will be offering them this summer," Hank LaFrond mentioned to his classes one brilliant spring afternoon as the poetry class met outside on a grassy campus hillside. "See me any time after class and I'll arrange an appointment on my schedule for June."

Marella was the first to sign up; she requested three lessons a week—preferably in the late afternoon after working her summertime day shift at the Fortune Bay Casino on the Bois Fort Reservation. Her freshman year flew by and her 4.0 grade point average placed her on the community college's 'Dean's List'.

9/ THE PIANO LESSON

The June afternoon was cool, gray and rainy. The first three weeks of summer break had been a monotonous blah: Work from seven until three at the casino, then return home to…not much of anything. Home was little more than a place where Marella ate and slept and kept her belongings. Sadly, her diabetic mother's lifestyle was a pathetic combination of recurring illnesses of every variety and the inactivity of her obesity. When Nelly Windsong wasn't lying around on the living room sofa watching soaps on TV with a bag of chips and a bowl of garlic dip, she was playing solitare at the kitchen table with a bag of nachos and a bowl of melted cheddar. Usually, when Marella got home from work or school, it was mother asking daughter "What are we having for supper?" rather than the other way around. From her mother's lack of ambition, Marella derived a powerful motivation to achieve, so that her life would not be anything resembling that of her mother.

Marella debated with herself on what to wear for her first piano lesson at Mr. LaFrond's studio in Tower, a short drive from where she lived. She had circled Friday and printed 'Lesson at 4:30' on her desk calendar. After trying on several outfits she chose to wear her favorite black tee-shirt with 'Anishinaabe' emblazoned in white across the front, a pair of stone washed jeans, and her black Nikes. When in doubt, she always chose to go casual. She decided not to wear any jewelry and skipped the dash of perfume that usually went out the door with her.

Hank LaFrond's 'studio' wasn't actually a studio at all. Instead, he conducted his lessons in the small cabin he was renting on Hoodoo Point Road outside of Tower. The property was pine-shadowed and generally unkempt: The lawn hadn't been cut in weeks, an old refrigerator with the door taken off rested near a dilapidated shed to the rear, and next to the fridge was the rusted frame of a tractor that seemed choked to death by thick brush. The gray drizzle of the afternoon only accented the dreary appearances of the neglected property. The heavy bamboo curtains on the bay windows were drawn. Marella knocked on the front door several times and was about to turn back to her car when Hank appeared. He looked surprised to see her but invited her inside: "Come out of the rain, Marella…what a pleasant surprise."

Marella, apparently more surprised than her teacher, stuttered in replying: "My lesson, sir…the piano…I'm here for my first lesson…remember? I signed up…"

LaFrond looked puzzled as he stepped away from the door and gestured for her to come inside, "Lesson?" he shrugged, repeating his invitation, "Do come in."

Marella stepped away from the door as LaFrond closed it behind her. The living room was small and dominated by a huge piano strewn with newspapers and men's magazines. A framed Van Gogh 'Poppy Flowers' poster hung atilt on one wall, a Lautrec 'Moulin Rouge' poster on the wall opposite. Classical music, Marella guessed to be Chopin, softened the space from Bose speakers on a makeshift stand of cardboard boxes in the adjacent kichen. The few furnishings were dated and worn and littered with junk mail. Mr. LaFrond, 'Hank', was wearing denim shorts and an oversized and half-buttoned white shirt with coffee stains, or something brown, down the front. Within three feet of him, she could smell his foul liquored breath.

This was not the well-dressed Mr. LaFrond who had been reciting poetry in his lively classroom only a few weeks before; this was a sloppy Hank LaFrond who had been drinking whiskey in a dingy little cabin on a dismal Friday afternoon. "What's the matter…you look shocked, Marella…it's that kinda day don't ya think…a little wine, music, and relaxation. And on top of all that, his grin was a crooked line across his stubbled face, "kismet has provided me with someone to share it all with. What do you say? A glass of Merlot?"

Marella shook her head, edging backwards toward the door.

" I came for my piano lesson, sir—my 4:30 appointment?"

LaFrond laughed. "I think you're one week off, sweetheart. It's next Friday if my memory serves me correctly," he slurred his words. "Don't worry, it's fine with me. How about I give you a freebee this afternoon?"

Marella cleared her suddenly dry throat: "No…that's okay, Mr. LaFrond. Next week will be fine. Even better…I've got other things to do this afternoon."

When Hank LaFrond put down his wine glass, his face contorted into a creepy smirk. "I think that's a crock of BS…yer not that dumb, Marella. I think you came to my place just to hang out. You're not the first…" What followed was the worst nightmare of Marella's young life. When LaFrond suddenly grabbed her shoulders, she pushed herself away with both hands, "No"–her scream of protest was barely audible as her voice was choked with fright. "Let go of me…you're drunk…I don't want this! You're mad if you think…"

LaFrond's resolve to force himself seemed bolstered by the smaller woman's resistance. "Loosen up, girl. I know you're gonna like it." His strength surprised her. As he pulled her forcefully toward him, she pushed away trying desperately to scratch his face and swing her leg toward his groin at the same time. Her knee only grazed the side of his thigh. LaFrond winced but kept his grip, "Don't get me pissed," he muttered as he managed to pin her shoulders against the wall.

The next thing she remembered was his mouth on her neck, his tongue on her ears. She felt her legs going numb. Then she felt his strong hands pressing into her lower back…then gripping her behind, forcing her body against his. "No! Please! Don't you dare…you animal…" The fire of her anger met the cold, hard, wood of the floor, her body went limp.

After her ineffectual struggles and vain protests everything became a blur. Her teacher's domination had prevailed…Marella

Windsong had been raped! Her mind spun with stupefied rage, her body ached as if she had been stomach-punched and crotch-kicked. She remembered hearing LaFrond's wicked laugh, "You got what you came for, sweetheart. Don't deny it." She knew that was a lie, she knew she hadn't wanted this to happen, she had said 'no', she had fought against him, she had pushed herself away…she had done everything she possibly could to stop him from undressing her…but when his hand went under her shirt her resistance might have melted away. She wasn't sure…the trauma had happened so fast and the bewilderment…and the pain… When LaFrond was spent, he rolled off of her and onto the floor where he passed out in an exhausted heap. Marella sobbed deeply. She wanted to hit and kick and scratch out the eyes of the man who had violated her.

Looking down on the half-naked man, Marella buttoned her jeans, and hooked her bra under the T-shirt torn from the neck to the sleeve. What a pathetic sight he was. The poet she had placed on a pedestal was a lowlife– nothing more than a lustful beast and sadistic drunk. She kicked him in the stomach and spit in his face before running out the door. The experience had been repulsive beyond belief and would leave lovely young Marella Windsong with emotional and spiritual scars that would never heal.

10/ 'UPTOWN' VINNY

Marella did not learn to play the piano that summer, or ever…and did not return to Vermilion College the following fall semester. LaFrond didn't return either. He went somewhere else. So did Marella. She packed a few clothes, said good-bye to her mother, hitched a ride to Duluth from a girlfriend, then took a bus to the Twin Cities. Once there, she met up with Vincent Bowen, a boy she had a crush on in high school—she was a freshman when he dropped out of school. Vinny, now twenty-three, was tending bar in a trendy 'Uptown' night spot in Minneapolis. Marella quickly became attracted to his uninhibited, undisciplined, and party 'til dawn lifestyle. And adding to the attraction package, Vinny was Ojibwe like herself. Short and stocky, he wore his long hair in a ponytail and had tattoos down both arms. He rode an '80 Harley Chopper, had a violent temper, and found his daily relaxation with vodka and pot. Vinny Bowen was a kind of fun than Marella had never allowed herself to indulge. Wild fun. The parties in his loft apartment on south Hennepin were the stuff of street talk. He was undoubtedly the worst person Marella could have hooked up with following the trauma she was running away from. In October, after about four months of party, play, and occasional abusive treatment, she knew. By Thanksgiving, Vincent also knew.

Vincent was blunt. "I ain't havin' no kids, Marella...this world's goin' to hell in a hurry and I don't want no kids of mine sufferin' through it. Sorry—that's it! Go home. Get a life. I'll help with the...you know, the costs and all that stuff."

She did go home, but Vincent didn't help with 'all that stuff'. Why should he? The twins weren't his. The twins were 'half-breeds' and that meant—by Vincent's definition—that his girlfriend, Marella Windsong, was a slut. Apparently, that's how most others defined her as well. Marella was ostracized, her sons shunned, their three lives challenged at every turn. Life back at the Bois Forte Reservation was like having an 'S' tattooed on her forehead. She moved to Cass Lake and commuted to Bemidji to work on getting a degree in sociology. After graduating with her BS, and before finding a job, her mother became seriously ill and Marella felt obligated to return to the Rez and help out with her care. She took a job she hated at the local casino and watched her mother lose her five year battle with the autoimmune disorder, lupus.

Although the twins tolerated school, their days and years brought frustrations that time and place could not resolve: Trevor because the sports teams from Tower-Babbitt were not competitive, Travis because he wasn't sufficiently challenged academically. But overcoming adversity built character, strength, and self-reliance. Nobody ever messed with the Windsong twins.

"My decisions have made your lives tough, and I've been a bitch at every turn," Marella confessed the candid truth on her sons' fourteenth birthday in 2008. "But you'll both be better men for it." By then, they already were mature for their age. Especially Trevor. Both knew there was a father out there—somewhere, but neither ever asked about him. Never, never!

It was in 2008 that Marella's estranged sister, Vanella Little Otter—everybody called her 'Nella'—was killed in a highly suspicious, and unresolved, hunting 'accident'. Nella had been having an affair with a man from the Mille Lac Reservation named Tomkins— Bad Brad Tomkins– to those who knew him best. Most folks were aware of what was going on between the two cheaters—including Nella's husband, Benjamin. Lila Tomkins, the defiled wife, told the authorities that her rifle discharged accidentally while their hunting party was chasing a wounded buck in the thick forest near Aitkin. The matter was never sufficiently investigated and never went to court. Nella's death left Marella with no family and her brother-in-law, Benjamin Little Otter, a tormented widower.

Marella's twin sons were all that remained and all that mattered in her life. She worked and she mothered and she worked and she mothered. Standoffish and reclusive, any man—and there had been many—who made any attempt to win her favor were met with a quick and conclusive rejection. Marella Windsong would have only two men in her life and those two men were her sons.

It was also in 2008 that Marella met a woman from Hibbing while attending a writing symposium at the Park Inn in Hibbing. Renee Tomatz was a social worker and community activist, and to those who knew her best, a saint. Renee's life was dedicated to those who were down and out and needed someone to help them get on their feet. Most never did, but Renee never quit on them. Marella had been writing poetry and journaling and volunteering on a project to identify wild flowers in the northern Minnesota woodlands. Like Marella, Renee was an alumnus of Bemidji State University. For reasons that Marella could never quite explain, she and the tall, insightful woman connected.

"You've got a degree in sociology and you're working in a casino? Marella, we've got to do better than that," Renee said. With Renee, it was always 'we'. Visiting one day over coffee, Marella confided her frustration to Renee. She complained that the education her boys were getting just wasn't what she wanted them to have. "I'm thinking seriously of moving back to Bemidji, it's best for my sons—maybe me, too." she said. "I've put myself in a box and find it hard to get back out."

Renee nodded, sipped her green tea, and smiled– her smile was more in her eyes than on her face. "We've got one of the best high schools in all of Minnesota right here in Hibbing," Renee bragged, "in both academics and athletics." Fortuitously, Tomatz was looking for someone to help staff the Family Investment Center she had founded in Hibbing. "What do you think about something like that, Marella? I think you need to venture out of your comfort zone. I think you're long overdue for a major life change—what do you say…willing to make a move?"

In the fall of 2008, Marella got a loan and purchased a home on Anderson Road, south of Hibbing, then began her new job at the Housing and Redevelopment Authority. Her two sons enrolled in the prestigious Hibbing Senior High School. For the mother and her sons, the move opened a new world of opportunity.

11/ ST. MARY'S HOSPITAL

Father Mickey couldn't remember a nonstop rainfall like the one he was driving through in his travel to Duluth. In the past sixteen hours countless inches had been dumped on the Arrowhead region of northeastern Minnesota, and no end was in sight. Thunder boomers raged above, a steel gray curtain loomed ahead, and the prospect of getting to the downtown hospital before noon was fading. Mickey's prayers for the safety of fellow travelers, and for those parishioners trying to cope with the widespread flooding, were mixed with prayers for the one injured young man that he'd never met. Mickey wondered about his motivations. On the one hand, he felt an obligation to help a friend who had selflessly helped him on countless occasions. On another, he hoped to be of some help to the boy and his family. But...mostly, doing something for someone else always made him feel good about himself. Which of the three was the primary reason he was making this trip? That question bothered him for a moment; then his thoughts meandered to something apart from, but connected to, his motivations. Had he become what he despised most in others, a selfish and egocentric person? Was the core of this morning's decision rooted in his need to do whatever best served his own interests: be it his narcissism or his self-righteousness, or...were both one and the same? For months, the young priest had been questioning himself, critiquing the purposes behind his actions...seeking a better grip on what made him tick. To Mickey, doing the right thing for the wrong reason was a deceit that corrupted the deed. . . regardless of what others may think.

Mickey knew that Benjamin Little Otter was the key to anything that might be accomplished within the Ojibwe Indian communities he had been called upon to serve. Was the reality that he needed Ben more than Ben needed him a pill he had to swallow? Or, was Ben the bridge from God that would enable Mickey to do His work? It was, he realized at some level, God's work and not his.

That concept, that truth, that mandate—more than anything—must sustain him and his every effort. A passing pickup truck speeding past him and spraying a thick splash onto his windshield, caused him to refocus on his driving and let go of the conundrum of his self-analysis.

Police were diverting traffic away from the Miller Hill Mall on the Duluth hilltop. Rampant flooding was extensive, a dire circumstance had become dangerous and potentially deadly. Blinking lights slowed him down, a drenched officer approached when he stopped behind a row of several cars. The cars ahead were being diverted as Mickey inched foreward to the patrol officer's cruiser that was blocking passage. "Sorry, sir…" the tall man squinted as if trying to place a face he knew that he should recognize. "You'll have to turn around or go back to Arrowhead Road. Can't let anybody drive into the city—downtown is a disaster area." Rain swept into the Civic's open window; the officer leaned closer…"Ain't you that priest…Father Mickey?"

Mickey nodded, "Yes, officer, I've got to get to St. Mary's. Emergency…"

The cop nodded, his expression was pained: "I'll see what I can do, Father."

Within minutes Mickey had a police escort down the city's eastern hillside. Closely following the flashing cruiser, he turned west on one-way Third Street. Passing through the intersections was like crossing a river and, at times, he felt as if his Civic would be swept down the sharp incline. It was nearly one in the afternoon but the charcoal-gray sky and plummeting rain made it seem like nighttime. Pulling to a stop in front of the cluster of towering brick hospitals, he put his clergy card on the dashboard where it could be seen and stepped out of his car without turning off the ignition. "The cops called ahead. I'll take care of it for you, Father. The keys will be at the front desk when you leave," said a hospital security officer standing under the canopy.

"God bless you," Mickey called over his shoulder as he rushed through the entry doors. Inside, an attractive young nurse met him and escorted him to the bank of elevators.

~

Benjamin Little Otter greeted his friend with a bear hug that lifted Mickey several inches off of the floor. "Thanks, Father. You didn't have to…" Benjamin said. His eyes were red-rimmed from tears already spent and others waiting. The giant of a man had an endearing sensitivity. He sniffled: "I'm better now that yer here. Din't think they'd let you down the hill. I heard everthin's blocked-up."

"The good Lord and some cops with big hearts was all it took."

"Ain't it like nothin' you ever seen out there? It's a miracle that we got my nephew up here. An absolute miracle!" Benjamin pulled his handkerchief from his jacket pocket. Tears returned to the big man's brown eyes, "I can't stop praying…there's nothing else I can do…just pray. He's—Trevor, my nephew, I mean…last I heard he's still in some kinda coma. That's all I know. He's in bad shape, Father. It's like…like every bone in his body is broke up. I saw bones pushin' outta his arm. I could hardly bear to look at it. He's lost lots'a blood, too." Benjamin went on to explain, in scant detail, the chain of events spanning the previous five hours. "It's a miracle. A man named Joseph was da first guy on the scene, he sez '. . . I got it from here…Benjamin'. Strangest thing, his knowing my name and all. Anyhow, then we wuz here. Somehow it all happened like I wuz in a fog." Benjamin's voice was fading as he sobbed, "Miracle…dat's all I can say…miracle!"

"Miracles do happen…just my getting here is a small miracle." Mickey calmed his friend, led him to a sofa, sat down beside him. "Try to relax a bit and tell me more about it, Ben. What happened?"

"I don'no. Dat's what I'm tryin' to tel ya, Father."

"Why not start by going back to the river where you found the boy–"

Benjamin swallowed deeply, cradled his large head in his large hands, bent forward with his elbows on his knees. "Okay...I wuz havin' coffee..." he chose his words carefully, beginning with the phone message from his nephew, followed by his search along the trail. "I saw dis busted helmet, den dis boot stickin' outta the rocks by the edge of the river...my first thought wuz that he gotta be dead. If Trevor wuzen't as tough as he is...God knows he'd be dead...but he's still alive...maybe barely alive—but hangin' on. Must'a hit his head perty hard, too. Blood was drippin' outta his nose."

12/ "TELL ME ABOUT TREVOR..."

Benjamin stood, walked to the small window on the south wall, parted the curtains, and peered outside. "Still rainin' out there." he said in the flat voice of stress. He returned to the sofa, sat down and folded his large hands in his lap. Before he could return to his description of the accident, a nurse came into the waiting room. She recognized Father Mickey at once. "Hello, Father, Mr. Otter...Doctor MacIver is still with the boy. I'm afraid there are no significant changes in his condition. You'll just have to wait...wait and pray." Her face was without expression, her voice without emotion. She was a lithe woman even in the baggy green scrubs she wore. Her white Nikes with a green swoosh looked new. Mickey guessed that she might have participated in Gramdma's Marathon, a prime summer event in Duluth. "I'll keep you both posted," she offer little more than a thin smile.

Ben didn't correct the nurse on his name, offered a dejected nod: "Thanks, ma'am. We'ze prayin' as hard as we know how to do. Oh...be sure to tell the doc we'ze prayin' fer him, too."

Mickey smiled, gave his friend a reassuring pat on the back. Benjamin was a good and thoughtful man—a simple and uncomplicated man as well. The gospels of Matthew and Luke admonished: *"Let them come to me as children..."* Truly, Benjamin exemplified that virtue of Christian faith and humility better than most of the holy men that Mickey had ever known.

Ben met Mickey's eyes: "The boy's gonna be all right...I just know it, Father. That guy, Joseph, he said so, too. If God was gonna take him away He'd a done it down by the river where I found'em."

Mickey reached across the sofa and took Benjamin's huge hand in his, "I can't argue that, Ben. God must have something special in mind for your nephew—for Trevor—He's not ready to take him home yet."

Benjamin squeezed Mickey's hand, smiled widely, and nodded. Words were not necessary to convey his sentiments of the moment. Both men allowed their emotions to settle inside– neither wanted empty words to fill the somber void of waiting without knowing. Each man contemplated how to convey solace and comfort to the other but neither quite found the thread. As close as the two men had become in recent months, however, Mickey was realizing how little he knew about his Ojibwe friend's family or background in general.

Mickey broke the long minutes of silence. "Tell me about Trevor. I can sense that the two of you are very close."

Benjamin's awakened beam was like the sun finding a gap in the bank of clouds. "Do ya follow sports much, Father?"

Mickey nodded, "Somewhat. I'm a big Twins fan more than anything else. Got that from my father, I guess. I went to lots of high school football and basketball games when I was at St. James in west Duluth. Some of my altar boys played on the Denfeld Hunters teams."

"If you'da kept up with high school sports you mighta heard of Trevor Windsong. He's been quite an athlete, since eighth grade when he moved to Hibbing– name's been in the sports pages quite a few times. Played for the 'Bluejackets', that's what they're called up there. His ma—Marella, that is–wanned him to have a chance to show what he could do on...what'd she call it..." his eyes brightened again with his recall of her words. " A 'bigger stage' that's what she said. It's worked out perty good. Fer his brother Travis, it's worked out pretty good, too. Now he, Travis I mean, he ain't into no sports, but he's gettin' a real good education in Hibbing. He can take lots of higher math classes there. Yep, moving like she did a few years back wuz da best thing she coulda done fer all of'em."

Mickey followed Ben's explanation. Being a graduate of Hibbing High School himself, he knew that the boys Benjamin was describing would have greatly benefited from being schooled there.

Benjamin continued, "Trevor's gotten some looks from college coaches. Travis has been takin' lots'a classes at the community college so he's gettin' a head start on a degree. Both of 'em...well, they make my life somethin' really special—they do. Each for different things, though." Benjamin voice swelled with a father's pride as he spoke of the two boys.

Mickey could see stress melting from the broad face of his friend as the approval of his nephew's achievements rolled off his tongue like a favorite song. He'd encourage Ben to keep talking in order to keep his mind off of what was happening with his nephew in the adjacent operating room. With his next question, however, Mickey struck the wrong chord. "You've never had kids of your own, Ben?"

Benjamin's dark eyes became brooding slits as his forehead furrowed in a twinge of discomfort or shame or some manner of distress. The question hung between them longer than it should have. Averting Mickey's eyes: "Couldn't," was all Benjamin wanted to say. Another long, quiet spell followed his single word. Mickey would wait until Ben picked up the thread or changed the course of dialogue.

Ben pushed himself up from the sofa again and began to pace with his hands clasped together behind his back. The mud on his shoes had dried but he left vaguely discernable brown tracks on the gray carpet. His broad shoulders seemed weighted with all the worries the world had pressed upon him. "Lots a stuff I ain't told ya 'bout, Father. Lots. Not that I'm ashamed or nuthin like that…you already know about the drinkin'…that's the worse part. But there's other things, too."

"You told me once that your wife died…tragically? But, nothing more than that." Mickey had never pressed Ben for details and he wouldn't do so now.

"True enough, I guess. Lawyers and courts, they sez Nella's death…" he cleared his throat…"sez it wuz all a bad fortunate accident. Others sez it wasn't dat at all. I don't think it wuz neither."

"Nella? Was Nella your wife?"

Ben nodded, "A good'nuf woman, sometimes did not so good things. Maybe it was me that caused her to…" Ben stood at the window for a long time. "I guess we weren't getting along so well."

Mickey was intrigued. His friend was usually a man of few words—very few words. Maybe he hadn't been asking enough questions. Every inquiry was opening another window into the psyche of Benjamin Little Otter. Mickey's notion that his friend was an uncomplicated man was going down the drain like old bathwater.

A different nurse—this one was short, under five feet and definitely not a marathon candidate—came into the room. She also recognized Father Mickey, nodded respectfully, then reported in a matter-of-fact manner: "The surgeons are still working on his arm and other injuries—some internal. He's holding up just fine—all the vitals are where they should be." Like the nurse before her, her round face didn't betray any emotion.

"Is he awake now?" Ben blurted the question. "I'm sposed to get back to his mother on what's goin' on here. She's on her way…"

"No he's not." The nurse stiffened her shoulders as if bracing her defenses against the towering Indian who dominated the small space, "That hasn't changed but the doctors aren't worried. There are lots of things going on. Either Doctor Brandt or Doctor MacIver will fill you in later—in an hour or two, I'm thinking." With that update, the nurse was gone.

Mickey stifled his urge to tell the nurse that a smile would add a soft touch to an otherwise brusque message.

13/ THE HOSPITAL VIGIL

In the O.R., orthopedic surgeon, Doctor Norman MacIver, worked along with Doctor Richard Brandt and a third doctor, assisted by a team of nurses, on the comatose young man. From the shoulder clavicle to the wrist, major bones had been fractured and intricate reconstruction was required. The humerus in the upper arm had a hairline fracture but would mend without surgery; repair of the radius and ulna would require rods, pins and screws. From a surgical perspective, MacIver had rarely seen worse: The shattered wrist posed a serious reconstruction dilemma unlike any he'd ever attempted to repair. For two hours he probed and cut, using a computer model that his nurse monitored on the screen above the surgical table. Of the eight carpal bones located in rows of four in the wrist, three were crushed beyond repair and had to be removed. The collateral ligament could not be reattached. MacIver improvised with efficient skill.

Of major concern to Brandt were the head and internal injuries—x-rays and MRI's would reveal the extent of damage from the boy's apparent concussion. No skull fracture was found. Fortunately, there were no discernable internal injuries beyond two hairline rib fractures. The two diligent physicians worked in tandem with the precision of experienced professionals.

Gurneys lined the narrow hallways as the hospital staff tried to cope with the overwhelming crush of flood related injuries. Children were given priority. MacIver had called for a neurologist to assist him but was told that the Windsong boy would have to wait his turn.

~

When the branch slapped his head, twisting his helmet, Trevor Windsong knew he was in trouble. Fractions of seconds were critical, instinctively he hit the brakes, then felt the complete loss of traction and control. He was off the trail and airborne and his machine was flying off beneath him...the river raged below. Shock preceded pain...a black silence overwhelmed everything else. Some time later he heard his name being called by a voice that assured him that he was indeed alive. He wanted to answer the ethereal voice but his mind and body were so numb that he could not respond. Later still, he felt a cold whiteness about him.

~

Tiring from his hand-wrenching pace across the room, Benjamin sat at the end of the sofa . . . not quite as close to Mickey as before. Body English told the priest that emotional exhaustion was a weight that even Benjamin's powerful shoulders could not carry too much further. With a number of lingering questions, Mickey would attempt to divert Ben's thoughts from apprehension to the less stressful place the two had been only a few minutes ago.

"You said that Travis is going to the U. next fall...how about Trevor?"

"How can twins be so different? Are they identical or fraternal?"

"Is their father in the picture?"

"What was Trevor doing down here if he lives up in Hibbing? Did he come down to be with you?"

"How often are you able to see them? What kind of things do you guys do?"

Mickey's questions came one after the other. Benjamin's answers were becoming more abbreviated; the inflection was gone from his voice. Somehow, Mickey sensed that there was something deeper and more painful than his memories of the woman he called 'Nella'—deeper than the reality of his not having kids of his own. If Mickey wanted to dig, he might uncover what it was, but…maybe another time would be more appropriate? That 'another time', however, would come sooner than later. Not only would Mickey learn of Nella's tragic and suspicious death, but also about the weld that joined Benjamin and Marella Windsong's relationship. Marella? Benjamin had said little about her and when he did, he spoke almost as if she held a power over him. If that had any measure of truth, any disclosure was a matter best left up to Ben. He wasn't going to prod any deeper.

"I've gotta call Marella again, Father. She's probably a nervous wreck." Ben had last talked with his sister-in-law just before Mickey's arrival at the hospital. "She must be getting close to Duluth by now…she said to expect her about two." His thick fingers punched his directory…he waited…when Ben talked his voice was a low murmur muffled behind turned shoulders. Mickey understood the body English—Ben wanted his conversation to be private.

Mickey was certain that Marella Windsong would not be allowed to get around the blockade and travel into the downtown area of the city as he had done earlier. Conditions were probably even worse now than they had been an hour before. He remembered the name of the officer who'd helped him get the escort. He extracted his cell phone from his shirt pocket and called 911: "I need to speak with an Officer McNulty…he's probably monitoring traffic up near the Miller Mall. Please, this is Father Moran and I'm at St. Mary's Hospital."

Mickey poked Ben's shoulder, asked to use his phone. Ben frowned, shrugged, said "Hold on…" to the woman he was talking with.

Mickey hurriedly introduced himself to Marella and explained that she should ask for an Officer McNulty when she reached the roadblock. "Tell him that I've asked that you get through." For reasons he had pondered before, Mickey found himself attempting to give the impression that he held influence over situations great and small. Why did this ego thing keep cropping up? Why did he feel a need to impress people…why this woman…this stranger that he had never met?

If Marella was impressed, her next few words were not what Mickey might have expected. "Okay…Ben still there?" was all that the woman had to say. Mickey passed the phone back to his friend. When Ben was finished his conversation he sat quietly for a moment, as if he was collecting his thoughts. Heavy thoughts.

"Don't get the wrong impression, Father." Ben's hands fidgeted with his tourquoise ring for a long moment, then slipped his cell phone back into his jacket pocket. "Marella…well, she's different. I mean, she's always had a tough time…" Ben looked away, then back to Mickey. His eyes narrowed. "I've told her about you—and our relationship," his face flushed. "I mean…like, our project…you know—that's all I've said. Anyhow, omething' tells me you ain't gonna like her. Most people don't. Leastwize, not at first." Another long pause, then a deep breath…"B'fore I tell you any more 'bout Marella Windsong, let me tell you what we're up against with this project of ours." Whether consciously or not, Benjamin had changed the drift of their discussion.

Mickey's jaw dropped. Ben's 'let me tell you' came out of left field. "What?" was all he could say.

14/ 'DOOFUS'

Months before, Ben had agreed to be Mickey's 'first lieutenant' in Bishop Bremmer's new Indian initiative. A position he agreed to take with great reluctance. For the past two months he and Mickey had floundered in their attempts to find the right initiatives to get a program off the ground.

Mickey puzzled at the cast of Benjamin's eyes and the unusually somber tone of his voice. "If you know something I don't know please give it to me straight-up, partner. I can see something in your eyes...tells me you're worried...or...?"

"Okay, maybe I am worried...maybe I'm somthin else." Benjamin leaned forward on the sofa, focusing on the door opposite of where they were sitting. He took a deep breath: "I still ain't gettin' it, Father. I mean...this thing we're 'sposed to be doing." There was a noticeable agitation in his voice. "Nobody else I've talked with is gettin' it neither. I went up to Bois Forte last week like ya asked me to; stopped by my cousin Meryl's place, then spent part of the afternoon at Marellas in Hibbing. I've never been 'specially close to Meryl, besides he drinks too much—makes me awfully uncomfortable, ya know. Then I been talkin' it up at the Rez, with some of the elders down here. They ain't, none'a them, much interested in any church stuff. Make's me feel stupid just talkin' bout it, makes me wanna have a drink or two—that's how bad it gets! My friend Lester...well, he tells me there's lots of bad history with Catholic missionary folks—way back he sez. I don't know what to say 'bout that stuff."

Mickey nodded. His recovering alcoholic friend battled his disease daily. "I know it's hard, Ben...the drinking, I mean. As for the history I'd be more than willing to meet Lester or any of your friends and talk about that stuff. He's right to a degree...lots of things were pretty lousy...

Ben shrugged, turned his face toward the window. He cleared his throat and met Mickey's eyes. "They all got that letter the bishop sent to em; the one that…you know…one that introduced me and you as some kinda Catholic lassons to the tribe."

Mickey nodded, "liasons" he corrected then wished he hadn't. Benjamin was self-conscious about lack of education and limited vocabulary. Likely, both were factors in his reluctance to be involved in the new program. Ben's scowl flashed across his face but was gone in an instant.

Mickey wanted to apologize for interrupting, but doing so might simply add salt to the obvious wound. Instead, he said: "You know it wasn't my idea to send out that letter, Ben. We've talked about that being a mistake more than once before. And I, neither of us for that matter, had any input on the contents." The priest had told the bishop that any mass mailing would have all three of them starting out on the wrong foot. He was emphatic; such a letter would only be giving those who bothered to read it a false impression. "We don't want to come across as missionaries," he protested to no avail. His disagreements with Bishop Bremmer were ongoing.

The letter from the Diocese of Duluth office had been sent two weeks earlier and had introduced Father Moran as the newly appointed 'Reservation Liaison'. "Please welcome him with the love of Jesus and in the spirit of our beloved Saint Kateri," the bishop had written. Sister Kateri Tekakwitha, the daughter of a Mohawk father and Algonquin Christian mother, was the first Native American to be canonized by the Catholic Church. Mickey had asked Benjamin to follow up the mailing by visiting with a few people he knew on the Reservations—just to get a sense of their reaction to the bishop's gesture. "Try to find out if they were offended in any way or encouraged to want to become involved in some way."

Benjamin's eyes averted, when uncomfortable he fidgeted with the turquoise ring on his large finger. "They din't like that letter. Said it was a lot of bullshit…Sorry, Father…that's their word, the elders and other folks, I mean. Meryl and Marella felt 'bout the same. Lester said 'Good luck' with that can'a worms. I don know what else to tell ya, they got the right to say what they feel."

"Mrs. Windsong called it bullshit?"

"And more. Oh, by the way, she'd burn yer eyes if you ever called her Missus. She ain't never been married and she ain't never gonna."

"Well, I agree with her—with all of them for that matter. It was a pile of crap. I didn't want any introductions and I told the bishop that. He went ahead and sent it out anyway—regardless of my objections. I wanted to make any necessary introductions my own way—just you and me and a cup of coffee in the kitchen. Without any fanfare." Mickey's concurrence and disappointment fed Ben's sense of justification.

"What else?" Mickey probed, "I feel like you're still holding something back."

"Okay, I'll give s'more of the truth. I'm warnin' it's gonna hurt some to tell ya. They, lots of folks up at Bois Forte…they said the same thing that my friends on the Fond du Lac Rez have been sayin' all along. They said you, and yer bishop, are in cahoots." He cleared his throat, "Ya know what I mean?"

"No. You'll have to explain that. Cahoots?"

"Yeah, I will. They think bot of you guys wanna get some of the casino money we got. They don't trust nobody, you included, Father. Nothin' I can do about that. I can tell'em yer a good man— which I done many times—and that you don't want nobody's money…but I can't make 'em believe it."

Mickey understood his friend's dilemma. "I get it. They've had more than their share of bad history in dealing with white folks like the bishop and me. Your friend Lester was right about some of the missionaries that came before us—and, probably most Christians in general. Trust is a fragile thing…very hard to piece together once its been shattered. I suppose I'd be a little paranoid myself."

Benjamin nodded at the reality. Thoughts were slowly forming in his mind. He wasn't cut out to be any kind of evangelist and that was how he perceived his association with Mickey and the bishop. "Hate to admit to it. But...I can't do this no more, Father. It's like a pair of pants that's too big and makes me feel like a...what's that word you used to describe that politician on TV...? 'member that guy?"

Mickey laughed, "*Doofus*, is what I think I called him."

"I don't wanna be no *doofus*, Father."

"Me neither." Mickey had been uncomfortable with this assignment from the beginning. Maybe he had too much confidence in himself. Notoriety is like a fine wine, it's warm and pleasant and tastes so good but it is dangerously intoxicating at the same time. It blurs one's perception of things and makes good judgement difficult. In Florida things just seemed to fall into place for him. He simply went with the flow, nothing pushy or intrusive, and gradually wonderful things began to happen. Trust and respect mostly. This new scenario, however, was too contrived and too convoluted. Meetings at the bishop's residence coupled with a few workshops on Ojibwe culture hadn't accomplished much of anything. He, far more than Benjamin, needed to establish a rapport, credibility, and a trust relationship within the tribal communities. The best way to do so was to become a part of their unique culture, to quietly assimilate. He keenly remembered the difficulties he encountered when first he attempted to integrate himself within the Hispanic population of TriPalms, an enclave of diverse Spanish nationalities near Venice in southwestern Florida. That experience found success because he had faith: Faith in God and faith in himself. Only the first half of that formula was firmly in place now—but as his untethered faith confirmed–that was the most important half.

Sometimes wisdom comes from the mouths of those one least expects. What Mickey struggled with, Benjamin grasped with ease. "Folks down there in Florida, they was pretty much all Catholics, Father—you said that yerself, din't you? If that's so, then they'd think a priest is somethin' special. Makes things an awfully lot easier, I'd hav'ta say."

Mickey nodded absently, he was too lost in his own thoughts to give Ben's insights the attention they deserved. His friend's thoughts were lost.

"Maybe I should find a place in Fond du Lac. Just move in and get to know the folks like a new neighbor…What do you think about that, Ben? Let folks know that we're not out to convert anybody— and, more importantly, that we're not out to get anybody's money. What do you think…?"

Ben had already said what he thought.

A gray-haired volunteer came into the waiting room with a pleasant smile and a decanter of fresh coffee. She walked with a limp and spoke with a strong Finnish accent. "How are you gentlemen doing? Any news from in there?" She gestured toward the closed double doors with the warning sign: 'Authorized Personnel Only'. She set the coffee and Styrofoam cups next to the stack of outdated magazines on the table. "May God bless your vigil and heal your loved one."

Her warmth caused Mickey to choke up. 'Loved one?' Mickey hadn't even met the boy. "Thank you, Ma'am. And may God bless you, and your work as well."

Benjamin nodded at the woman. Looking at Mickey, he shook his head, "About movin' to the Rez…I'd hav'ta think hard 'bout that, Father. My first thinkin', ya know, is it's not such a good idea as ya might think."

"Something you'll think more about, Ben?"

"I'll try. By the way, Father…ya' know that nobody seems to know nothin' 'bout the saint lady from the bishop's letter. I can't even announce her name…She a real Indian? American Indian, I mean? Like us folks here are?"

Mickey didn't even try to 'announce' or pronounce Tekakwitha for his friend.

15/ TWIN TELEPATHY

Marella Windsong found a parking place in the Third Street ramp attached to St. Marys Hospital by an overhead walkway. She regarded Travis sitting next to her in his muddied clothes. Her son hadn't spoken much about his aching arm on the trip down. "You've still got a big smudge of dirt on your forehead, Trav, and some traces of vomit on your shirt," she smiled. "You're a mess but I love ya anyhow." His features were more delicate than those of his brother. If Trevor had his mother's spirit, Travis had her fine features. Marella often wondered if Travis had more of his father than of her in his genes. She also wondered what part of the equation his mother's nurturing played. Nature and nurture—a combination that had puzzled science for generations. "Are you sure you don't need to see a doc yourself, Trav?" She asked her son as he struggled to get himself out of his seatbelt with one hand.

"You know better, Mom. I'll be fine when Trevor is." He winced at the thought he had kept repressed in the back of his mind. What if Trevor never fully recovered? What if his brother lost an arm? What if he died? What would happen to him?

"You okay?" Marella regarded her son.

Travis forced a weak smile, "Lets go."

Outside, the rain continued in gray torrents and the streets running down the steep hillside were veritable rivers. The damage the storm was inflicting on the hapless city would take months to clean up and years to repair. Travis' arm had become more numb than painful, almost as if it had been tranquilized. He'd improvised a sling with a light jacket his mother had left in the back seat of the car. Both he and his mother knew the symptoms as well as it was possible to know them. Since birth the twins had shared telepathic and psychic connections—a rarity in the field of abnormal psychology, and a rarity with fraternal twins. When either suffered an intense emotional or physical experience, the other had identical, or incomprehensibly parallel, feelings. The boys had counseled with Doctor Colin Huber about their unique condition. The psychologist had shared the research of Dr. Cherkas at King's College in London with the boys, and given Marella a remarkable book by Guy Lyon Playfair titled, *Twin Telepathy*.

In her brief conversations with Benjamin over the past two hours, she'd learned only scant details of Trevor's accident and less about the extent of the boy's injuries. Without question, she realized that her son was lucky to be alive.

Since learning of the tragedy, Marella had prayed with an intensity that surprised her. Her prayers mitigated her ire over her son's irrationally inane behavior. Trevor should have known better than to be doing anything outside in this weather—much less attempt to travel on a remote trail with his four-wheeler. But, she reminded herself over and over– that was Trevor! Trevor—she knew better than anyone–marched to his own distant drummer. Travis did, too…in a far more settled manner. Maybe that explained a fraction of why the two boys were rarely in step with one another.

Although not a religious person by any definition, Marella possessed a unique spirituality. If her Catholic heritage was buried beneath years of apathy and skepticism, her belief in a *higher power* had never diminished—in the best and worst of times. Paradoxically, the Great Spirit of her forefathers had allowed her to suffer that traumatic afternoon with her drunken teacher. Yet, it was that same Spirit, or the God of Christians, that had blessed her life with her wonderful sons. If she could go back and relive that overcast Friday afternoon in Tower those many years ago…she would gladly endure that suffered ordeal again in order to have her twin boys.

~

"She'll be here any minute," Benjamin said nervously. He was tempted to remind Mickey not to make hasty judgments, but knew his friend to be a perceptive and empathetic man. Marella was prone to making harsh first impressions. "She'll be a nervous wreck and probably..." He let the thought drop without adding what she could be like when she was troubled.

Mickey swallowed the last of his tepid coffee. "Of course she'll be stressed. I wish we could tell her more about what's going on in there with her son," he nodded toward the doors leading into the OR. "I suspect that we're all going to be in the dark for quite a while longer."

Benjamin cleared his throat, "Don't come on too strong, Father. I mean...I'd be more comferble if you din't bring up our project...like I tol ya...she's not someone who'll warm up to a bunch'a Catholic stuff. Know what I mean?"

"What in God's name are you talking about, Benjamin?"

Ben hesistated, "When we was last talkin', me and Marella, she said she din't want any of that 'love yer neighbor crap' from me or you or the bishop or anybody else. She din't use cuss words but she was...you know, pretty—what's the word...?"

"Emphatic?"

"Yeah, I guess so. Anyhow you know what I'm sayin'"

Mickey nodded agreement: "Ben...you know me better than that. No. I'm not here to sell anything to anybody. I just want to offer any comfort I can. If she wants to pray, I'll..." He might have asked Ben: 'What in the world did you want from me when you called' but kept the thought to himself.

The door from the hallway swung open and both men stood. Mickey was taken aback by the youthful beauty of the dark-skinned, raven-haired, and slender woman who burst into the room like a wind gust. Marella Windsong looked more like a college sophomore than the mother of eighteen-year old sons. The young man in muddied clothes was a step behind and a full head taller than his mother. His left arm was tied to his chest with a navy wind jacket. Both wore the pained expressions of anxiety.

"Fill me in, Ben," were her first words—no hellos, no introductions, not even a glance at the priest standing next to her brother-in-law. "How is my Trevor doing?"

"We don know, Marella," he said. "We're both still waitin' to hear somthin…"

"He's been in there for hours, what's going on here? Where's a doctor? Where's someone who knows something that I can talk to?" Her voice was edged with anxious frustration. "For God's sake, I need to be told what they are doing with my Trevor!"

Ben looked as if he'd done something wrong. "This here's my friend, Marella…Father Moran. Mickey. He's come here to help if he can…"

Marella's dark eyes met those of the priest, "Heard about you, Father. Thanks for coming over."

Mickey nodded, offered his hand, tried to smile: "If there's…"

Marella interrupted Mickey, ignored his gesture, turned back to Ben, "Well…let's rattle some cages and find out what's happening. You know that patience isn't one of my virtues, Ben…who's the doctor in charge here? Let's find someone—now!"

Marella's obvious snub did not go unnoticed by the tall youth. "I'm Travis, Father, Trevor's brother…Trevor's *little* brother," he laughed to ease his own tension. The 'little' brother, at about six feet tall, was slightly taller than Mickey and had a slight build. His features and complexion were more Caucasian than Native American. His face and nose were narrow, his hair more brown than black and cut neatly short. Stepping toward Mickey, Travis offered his right hand, "Mom's kinda wound up tight right now, even stiffer than my arm right now." The boy's light observation came with a quiet smile and a half-laugh. Travis' voice and demeanor were pleasantly respectful.

Marella turned at her son's words, "Sorry, Father. Trevor's accident and the drive down in this rain, and not knowing anything—all this craziness has me awfully damn, I mean, darn frustrated. And, Ben…you know Ben, not much of a detail guy. I still can't piece what happened together very well. He says some guy named Joseph saved the day."

"He's pretty stressed out, too," Mickey said. "I honestly don't think he knows anything he hasn't already told us. His memory of events and sequences is shaky at best...I can't add..."

Before Mickey could finish his thought, Marella continued with hers... "We'll be fine now—me and Travis...and Ben of course. You must have lots of other things to do," she said dismissively.

Mickey's eyes narrowed: "Yes, I do. And, like yourself, I drove down to Duluth in this rain...not knowing anything more than that Benjamin wanted me to be here with him. And, I can get my head around frustration quite well. With my job, you see, I get a plateful of other people's pain and frustration every day. I don't know your son, Trevor, ma'am– but I do know Ben. And Ben wanted me to be here for him." His tone of voice was unnaturally sharp, "If Ben wants me to leave I'll be out the door in a heartbeat." He looked up at Ben standing beside and dwarfing the petite woman with an expression of pained disbelief on his face. "Ben...?"

Ben seemed at a loss for words. His eyes went from Marella to Mickey and back to Marella. Before he could speak, his jaw dropped in astonishment. Marella was crying! In all his years, he had never seen her cry. His wife often called her sister the 'ice woman'. Before Ben could react to Marella's breakdown, Mickey lunged for her. The priest had noticed a slight wobble and immediately sensed that she was losing her balance. When her eyelids slightly flickered and her jaw slacked, Mickey knew she was about to faint. Reacting quickly, he caught her by the shoulders before she collapsed and crumpled to the carpeted floor.

Without being aware of what was happening to her, Marella's hands gripped the priest's shoulders and she clung to the priest for long moments. Once she recovered her composure she blurted an apology of sorts: "I'm sorry...I lost it for a second...I don't know what happened...I've never..."

Mickey guided her to the sofa, helped her settle. "Stress can do that—you'll be fine. Just try to relax." He looked to Travis who was as surprised as his uncle. "Sit here with your mom, Son...maybe if you hold her hand for a few minutes she'll unwind a bit."

The boy nodded, sat beside his mother, gave her his free hand. Travis' pent composure, like his mother's, was wilting: "I'd like to say a prayer, Father...but I'm not sure how to begin. Would you help...?

Mickey blessed himself, placed his hands on those of the two Windsongs and began saying the *Lord's Prayer*—Travis bowed his head, tried to mouth the correct words but gave up after *'...thy will be done'*. Marella only watched the priest as he prayed for her son.

The tall, lithe nurse in white Nikes entered the room for the second time, "Father," she said a respectful tone, "Mr. Otter...and..."

Marella stood and spoke in a stronger voice, "I'm Marella Windsong, the boy's mother. Can you tell me what's going on?"

"It's going to be a while yet—but not too long. Let me assure all of you that the boy is recovering quite well. All things considered, it's rather miraculous. Dr. MacIver will meet with you in less than hour. We have a neurologist in the OR right now...please try to relax and be patient." She checked her wristwatch, it was approaching two o'clock. "You might even want to visit the cafeteria downstairs and get a bite to eat. There's time."

Ben smiled for the first time in quite a while. Marella shrugged: "That's a relief to hear. More details might have been appreciated—but..." She had regained her strength, "You must be starving, Ben." Looking at Mickey she added, "Let me get both of you something to eat. Father...a sandwich and chips or fries?"

Ben, who was always hungry, spoke, "I'd go fer some'a that myself, long with some pie if they's got some." He looked at Mickey, "Father...?" Then to Travis, "You gonna join us? Trav?"

Mickey wasn't hungry and shook his head, Travis did likewise:

"My stomach's still kinda queezy; I'll stay here with Father if you guys don't mind."

16/ TRAVIS AND MICKEY

When Ben and Marella left the waiting room, Travis attempted to stretch his left arm and bend it at the elbow. He grimaced, drew it back against his chest again. Looking at the priest he said "I'm pretty sure it will get back to normal as soon as my brother's surgery is done."

Mickey puzzled, "I don't understand."

To Mickey's astonishment, Travis explained the unique condition shared by the twins. "Never heard of such a thing, Travis. That's absolutely incredible."

Travis smiled widely, "I knew Trevor was going to be okay about twenty minutes ago. My fingers began to get some feelings back and my arm didn't hurt nearly as bad as it did before. My wrist is another thing…it really feels weird." Travis wasn't usually this open to strangers, but the priest gave him good vibes. "My mom told me some things about you on the way down. Said you've had some incredible experiences yourself."

Mickey confirmed the *doppelganger* experience that had been a major news story only a few months before. He and a man named Brian Slade were nearly identical in every feature. Their similarity led to an extortion scheme that captured national attention. "It was surreal to say the least. Brian and his sister Beth both work in this very hospital. Someone at the reception desk downstairs told me that neither is working today, but I'm sure that I'll see the two of them at some point while your brother is recovering."

Travis could only shake his head at the story Mickey shared. Being a twin himself, it was especially intriguing. Mickey answered a few questions, then said: ". . . Tell me more about yourself, Travis…and your brother, Trevor. Your Uncle Ben hasn't told me much…he did say that the two of you don't look at all like twins."

Travis laughed: "We don't even look like brothers. Trevor is lots bigger than me—and stronger, too. Mom uses the word 'thicker'…"

"But not smarter, right?"

"I tease him about that sometimes. Not that he isn't smart, 'cause he really is. But, he's…maybe a little less motivated than me and involved in lots more things outside of school." Travis went on to describe his athletically gifted brother. "Nobody ever messes with Trev. Once last year he wore his hair—his is much longer than mine—anyhow, he tied it up in a pink bow just to see what kind of reaction he might get. He likes to confront people sometimes. Well, on the second floor of our high school– by the study hall– another senior made a comment about the pink…all Trevor did was give him a stare. His stare is almost scary. Anyhow, Jimmy, the kid making the wisecrack, apologized right away. He was a big kid, too— played football with Trev. Anyhow, after that nobody said anything more. He could have put on a pink tutu that day and nobody would have risked teasing him about it." Travis paused a moment, "Don't get me wrong, Father…Trevor isn't a bully, nor a fighter. Not at all. Matter of fact, if he sees anybody hassling someone unnecessarily, he'll step in for the little guy. He's done the same for me more than once."

Mickey could picture the second floor scene Travis had just described. In his day the congregation of upperclassmen, mostly seniors, and mostly jocks formed what had come to be called the 'meat line'. That was the one place where guys stood around watching all the girls as they passed by before first hour classes in the morning. The girls all seemed to know that the meat line ogling was just a venting of adolescent testosterone. Some used the situation to their advantage, others took the western stairs to their classes, avoiding comments or evaluations. Mickey nodded knowingly. He was trying to get a mental picture of this talkative young man that didn't look like his twin.

Travis continued: "He can throw a baseball like a bullet and hit the cover off the ball. In football he's a power running back and a linebacker. In practice, nobody wants to tackle him when he has the ball. On defense, opposing runners almost always choose to run away from the position he is playing. He's been all-conference in both sports. I go to his games with Mom, but I'm mostly bored. I haven't ever been much involved in sports myself—except for playing catch or tossing a football in our back yard. Maybe I never got involved because I didn't want the comparisons."

Mickey hadn't been athletic himself in high school and could closely relate to what Travis was describing. He nodded, Travis went on: "I think mom is worried that this accident might cost Trevor a college football scholarship. But, then again, she's never cared much for football." Travis elaborated on Trevor's exploits and how the two of them rarely did much of anything together. "Sometimes we don't even talk to each other all day. Yet, we're really tight—I mean, we connect in lots of non-verbal ways. I'd do anything for him, absolutely anything…I'd give him my left arm if he needed it. And I know he'd do anything for me."

Mickey believed he had never learned anything when he was talking himself, and knew that he had a tendency to talk too much whenever he nosed into someone else's monologue. It was most enjoyable for him to relax and listen to what Travis had to say. While Travis spoke, he noticed that the boy was favoring his left arm much less than earlier—a good sign that his brother was healing.

"We're both southpaws, that's what mom calls us 'cause we are left-handed in everything. When I told mom that my left arm was aching she got kinda angry—don't know if angry is the right word, maybe uptight is better. Whatever word, both Trevor and me know when she's in that place and we keep our distance. You see, Mom's hot and cold—it's not often that she's in-between. I know she thinks that Trevor will go crazy if he can't use his left arm any more. She's right about that."

Mickey only nodded as Travis went on. Most of the time the boy's eyes were off in some distant place, but on occasion he met Mickey's eyes directly. It seemed to him that the boy was venting his own stress by talking. Travis made a half-laugh at something that crossed his mind: "Trevor can't sing a note, remember a joke, win a Monopoly game, and he hates to read...I doubt if he's ever finished a book." Other tangents from Travis' monologue:

-"I talk more than either Trevor or Mom—maybe both put together...

-"Ben's like the father we never had..." On this note, the boy grimaced slightly before continuing on...

-"When my uncle isn't sober, Mom won't let us visit him or have him up to our place...did you know he's an alcoholic...?

-"We're what folks call 'half-breeds' and Mom said that's like having two strikes against us in life...really pushes her button...it bothers her lots more than us..."

Five minutes became twenty, Travis switched gears: "What about you, Father? Not the doppelganger story...but family stuff. I know you went to school in Hibbing like Trevor and me...where did you live? What kinda things did you do when you were a kid? Oh, and what made you wanna be a priest? I'm curious about that. My mom used to be a Catholic...had us both baptized...but these days..."

Before Mickey could get into his 'stuff', Benjamin and Marella returned. "For you, Father," was all that she said as she handed him a small bag and a Styrofoam cup of chocolate milk. In the bag was a cinnamon-sugared donut. Benjamin offered Travis the same two items. "Still pouring like mad outside," Ben said. "Haf'a Duluth probly musta been washed inta the lake."

17/ COMPLEX SURGERY

Mickey had turned off his cell phone when he entered St. Mary's Hospital more than an hour before. Brushing sugar residue from his black slacks, he slipped his hand into his shirt pocket and retrieved his phone to check for any important messages. He hadn't taken time to call the City Clerk in Hoyt Lakes to cancel this evening's speaking engagement there. "Excuse me for a moment," he said, "I've got to make a call or two."

The woman who answered his call was not surprised: "Been expecting you to cancel. We're getting drenched here, too." Mickey apologized and promised to reschedule as soon as he could. Next he called Mary Alice Murray, his housekeeper at St. Gerard's Church. "Can you feed Torts his Iams, Mary Alice? I hope you've put him outside every so often—I'm gonna be tied up at St. Mary's for some time." Mary Alice assured him that both tasks had been taken care of. "You know that dog of yours won't go out in this rain, Father. He just cowers and whines at the door. I can see that you'll have a little mess to clean by the back door."

"I'll be careful not to step in it." Mickey noticed three missed calls, two from Amos, his father, another from the bishop. He also had a text message from the Cook County News Herald, the Grand Marais newspaper, cancelling his speech for the following morning.

He called his bishop first. Bremmer's secretary answered and buzzed the bishop. Bremmer picked up and spoke: "Heard that your talk in Hibbing went well this morning," the bishop paused, "also that you cancelled the school thing. What's that all about? Did they close the schools because of this rain?" Somehow, Bremmer seemed always to know Mickey's whereabouts, almost step by step, these days. There was a time not long ago when Mickey disappeared from Bremmer's radar. His Grace wasn't going to allow that to happen again.

Mickey explained where he was and why. "How are you folks

holding up at the Cathedral?" The bishop's offices were on the hillside across from Our Lady of the Rosary Cathedral on east Fourth Street—only a mile from St. Mary's Hospital.

The bishop followed his opening words, 'Lots of damage…' with a more detailed account of how the large property was holding up through the deluge. "Gives a person an insight on what Noah had to deal with. Someone should have had an ark over by the zoo in west Duluth." The bishop laughed at his remark, cleared his throat when Mickey didn't laugh, and continued, "Lots of flooding out west in your neighborhood I understand. Have you been keeping in touch?"

"Just checked in a minute ago, Your Grace." Mickey had heard of the zoo's

unfortunate tragedy on the radio, "I hope we can get through this without the loss of any lives," he said. Not wanting to rehash any storm stories, Mickey promised the bishop that he would visit the following morning before heading back to his parish rectory. "My event in Grand Marais for tomorrow has been canceled.

"I know. I was copied on the email. How long will you be tied up at St. Marys?'

"No way of knowing, Your Grace. I'm playing it by ear for now. I wouldn't be surprised if I'm here for quite a while."

Next, Mickey called his father and apologized for not stopping by that afternoon as he had promised to do. His parents, Amos and Sadie Moran, lived in the Home Acres neighborhood of Hibbing. "I know…I know…just couldn't get over, Dad." His father had been called at the last moment to testify in a property dispute at the courthouse and hadn't been able to make that morning's Rotary meeting.

"Kenny told me that he saw you cross the street to the Sportsmens afterwards and wanted to join you for a quick cup of coffee," Amos Moran said. "But, by the time he got his raincoat and got out the door, he saw your car heading down Howard Street toward the beltline."

Once more Mickey explained himself. "My friend needed me, Dad. I've gotta go where I'm needed most…and hope that I'm in the right place at the right time."

After some small talk with his mother, Sadie said: "Kenny picked up your umbrella at the restaurant. He'll get it back to you one of these days. Oh, and he says thanks for leaving the newspapers and a five dollar bill in the booth for him."

"I hope he didn't keep the five."

"You know he's a struggling architect, Son. Every little bit helps."

Mother and son shared a laugh, "Hope to see you soon, Mom."

~

Had Mickey been able to answer the questions posed by young Travis Windsong before their conversation was interupted, he would have recalled a wonderful childhood in the iron mining hub of Hibbing. As to his calling to the priesthood, he probably would have said that that decision was made for him when he was a twelve year-old. While snowmobiling on Sturgeon Lake near the family's cabin, Mickey's sled fell through a slushy opening that was hidden from his view on the ice sheet. Technically, he drowned. In drowning he touched the threshold of heaven. His near death experience and a heroic recovery from the lake was followed by a series of medical miracles at the Hibbing hospital. Prayers got him through the ordeal and prayers led him to every decision afterwards. In telling his story to Travis, Mickey might have related his own experience to that of Trevor Windsong's accident. More than likely, he wouldn't have drawn any parallels, nor would he have suggested that being dead, or nearly dead, would dramatically change a person's perspective on life. He would, however, have told the youth that the experience had moved him in a different direction.

~

Returning to the waiting room shortly after three, Mickey was just in time to meet Doctor MacIver, the surgeon who had worked on Trevor along with a Doctor Brandt for the past several hours. MacIver introduced himself to Mickey, "Very nice to meet you, Father. I've heard quite a lot about you..." The tall, dark haired man wore the stubble of a few days without shaving; his red hair was tossled. "...I've met Brian Slade a few times—and..." he laughed, "seeing you has made a believer of me." Mickey's double had put his once dysfunctional life in order and was enjoying his own unexpected notoriety.

The surgeon explained what had transpired during the lengthy and complex surgery. In using medical terminology like colles and scaphoid fractures, carpal bones and something called a distal radioulnar joint, his small audience was attentive and in a fog at the same time. Mickey nodded along with Ben and Marella as MacIver gave a full description of the rod and screw fixation on the radius bone; and realignment of bones in the wrist. While describing the wrist repositioning, MacIver said: "I had to do some things that I've never done before with some torn ligaments and crushed bones—I must tell you that Trevor's wrist was an absolute mess."

Responding to a question from Ben, the surgeon said 'yes' the boy was probably lucky to be alive, and from the boy's mother 'yes' he would recover, and from Travis 'yes' there had been a serious concussion. "He's an incredibly tough young man," MacIver added. "With some rigorous rehab he should be able to recover nearly all of his arm strength. And, I can only hope that his wrist will have a full range of motion after all the stuff I had to remove...like I said, the arm injuries were bad but repairing them was kinda routine, too. The wrist was—what else can I say—was really, really, busted up! That's going to be a 'wait and see' kind of recovery. I've got an excellent CHT–certified hand therapist—his name's Crosby, to work with Trevor. "

MacIver paused, stroked his stubbled chin; "I'd advise against any contact sports—especially football—in the future. I know that's going to be terribly hard for him to accept. One of the nurses has a son at East High; she told me that Trevor's one of the best line-backers in the whole region." He frowned, "Sorry about the foot-ball news, but I'm aware that he's a pretty good baseball player, too. Doc Brandt, who assisted me in all this, told me about that. Base-ball's still a possibility…if his wrist turns out the way I hope it will."

Aside from her few questions, Marella had been quiet through-out the briefing. Travis, whose arm was now hanging loosly at his side, asked about the possibility of Trevor's being able to throw a baseball in the future. "He's always been a lefty, you know. Hardly anybody could hit him–he struck out one or two guys every inning." Travis considered asking the doc about his own left arm but the pain was nearly gone.

"I hope he can hit, Travis," MacIver said with a slight chuckle, "or become a righty. I wouldn't bet on his ever being able to get back to throwing the way he did before. Mostly though, it's up to him. If he does the rehab regimen religiously…I mean if he really commits to doing it…who knows what might happen?"

18/ *TREVOR'S TEMPER*

Who could possibly know? Trevor Windsong's determination was the stuff of disbelief. By mid-July he was flexing his *new* arm, by mid-August he was lifting and curling light weights. Doctor MacIver and Jon Morrison, the PT and athletic trainer recommended by the hand specialist, marveled at the youth's raw strength, perse-verance, and attitude. "I'm gonna be one hundred and fifty percent when I'm done with all this," Trevor told Morrison after nine weeks of therapy. Lightheartedly, MacIver called him the 'Bionic Indian' while examining the arm and wrist he had reconstructed. It was late August, nearly ten weeks had passed. "I've never seen anything like it," he told Trevor. "Your ability to rotate that wrist I rebuilt for you is absolutely incredible—almost miraculous. I'm thinking that I'll want to submit a story on your surgery to *JAMA* (Journal of the American Medical Association); then we can both enjoy our sixty seconds of celebrity." Through the weeks of rehab, Trevor and MacIver were enjoying much more than a strictly doctor/patient relationship—they were becoming friends.

Trevor's trainer was another story altogether. Jon Morrison was a much smaller man than Trevor. The two of them were too much alike to share the kind of closeness that MacIver and Trevor enjoyed. Morrison had a 'no nonsense', 'in your face', 'push until it hurts and then push some more' attitude that would have served him well as a drill instructor at a Marine Corps training camp. If Trevor was headstrong and committed to a full recovery, Morrison was an inch or an ounce more driven. The trainer had no tolerance for complaints with his regimen, and snapped whenever he heard any of his patients say *that hurts!* In his training room was a poster expressing a simple cliché that had become his professional mantra: 'NO PAIN, NO GAIN!' Morrison was the strength and fitness trainer for several players with the UMD hockey Bulldogs and was familiar with Trevor's athletic prowess. "If I had your size and strength I'd take every advantage of it, Windsong." Morrison said early in one of the therapy sessions: "Don't whine that you'll never be able to play ball again. I hear any of that BS and I'll drop you like a dirty jock."

Marella Windsong, however, encouraged her son to find other pursuits—activities outside of sports. Although very pleased with Trevor's physical recovery, she remained very apprehensive about the more nebulous risks related to his head injuries. She had read enough about second concussions to make it clear to her son: "No more football!" In July she called Jerry Kill, the Minnesota football coach, to inform him that her son would not be a walk-on at the U. in the fall. Next she cancelled the scholarship offer from the University of North Dakota and contacted several other Division II football coaches who had been in contact with her son as well. Travis understood. He had read a story in *Sports Illustrated* about the recent suicide of one of his all-pro football icons, Junior Seau. Seau was only forty-three. Most believed that a series of concussions throughout his illustrious career had driven Seau to the brink…and beyond the brink.

With the advent of September, Travis Windsong was getting ready for his freshman year at UMD where he was enrolled under a Gates Millenium Scholarship. Although undecided on what his educational goals might be, he was keenly interested in computer programming and electronics. If Travis was excited about college, Trevor was wallowing in the depths of depression: "What am I gonna do, Ma? If I can't play football any more, and I have no interest in going to college– I've gotta do something with my life…something physical. Just doing book stuff would drive me even further up the wall." Although eligible for scholarships himself, and special loans and grants available to American Indian students, he had shown no interest in filling out the required application forms.

The three Windsongs were sitting around the kitchen table. "You're not going to hang around here and mope all day son—that's for certain!" Marella admonished Trevor, "And you know as well as I do that you're not likely to get a job in the mines or anyplace else up here on the Range. If you don't know the right people you don't have a chance." Since the boys had graduated, Marella had been antsy herself. She seriously wondered if she wanted to spend the rest of her life in a deadend job in Hibbing. Since Renee Tomatz's death, she had been in a funk of her own.

Trevor met his mother's dark eyes, "So what? You gonna kick me outta the house or something?" He pushed away from the table and stormed out the front door. Looking back over his shoulder he said: "Maybe I'll decide to live with Uncle Ben on the Rez. I can get a job down at the Black Bear Casino." Then, to give his mother a shot of her own medicine he added, "Maybe you need to get a life, too. You're just as stuck as I am."

~

The late summer afternoon was crisp and sunny. A gust of the northwestern breeze parted Trevor's long, dark hair as he began his daily run along the gravel shoulder of Anderson Road. Despite being cautioned against overdoing his training, every day he had been running three to five miles, lifting weights, and jumping rope to keep himself physically fit. Being outside in the fresh pre-autumn sunshine calmed his apprehensions, working himself into a sweat made him feel alive and well. Up ahead, a mud turtle crawled out from a row of cattails and began crossing the dirt road. As Trevor approached, the head and legs retracted. Noticing the trail of dust from an approaching car, he picked up the turtle and placed it out of harm's way near a cluster of cattails in the soggy ditch by the side of the road. A bald eagle, watching the scene from a dead branch high above the road, screeched its approval.

Trevor's outburst of minutes before was foolishly juvenile. He'd had weeks to think about what he was going to do and had come up with nothing. It wasn't his mother's fault that he was floundering, but he wanted to blame someone other than himself for all the lost opportunities. At times, he allowed his mind to drift back to the muddy trail that had almost cost him his life. Would he ever do such a dangerous thing again? He knew he would. The rush he had experienced from that tragic morning's challenge was better than anything he'd done before. Better than running for a long touchdown or pitching a shutout or scaling the walls of an abandoned open pit mine. How and where and when would he find his next challenge? Whenever he figured that out...he was going to be in the best physical shape of his life.

19/ THROWING ROCKS

Trevor realized that his mother deserved an apology. It wasn't her fault that he was floundering like a wounded duck in the fog. He remembered Doc MacIver advising him to open up more, let his feelings get out in the open: "If you allow yourself to slip into a depression you'll be creating a monster a fiend that will sap your spirit, pollute your mind, and lay you low. Get over it! There might be a silver lining to all this—look for it, be open for it." MacIver was a wise man; Jon Morrison, who offered an even stronger dose of encouragement, was a driven man. He'd been fortunate to have the two of them helping him to put his life back together. He had better not screw things up. He laughed to himself as a childhood nursery rhyme slipped into his thoughts, "*Humpty Dumpty...*" he recited the lines.

After turning back toward the house and picking up his pace again, he stopped to catch his breath and wipe the salty sweat that burned in his eyes. He'd probably pushed himself harder than he should have, but he could feel that his muscles were regaining their lost facility. Every third day he ran with ankle weights and fisted three-pound barbells—pushing harder than even his PT guy would have imagined or allowed. *But, now what?* That simple–yet so very profound– question had become his constant torment. Trevor was an eighteen-year-old high school graduate with noteworthy athletic achievements; certainly not the stuff of an impressive resume for much of anything in the world he faced. A part of him had outgrown the restraining forces of Hibbing culture, his support system was devoid of close friends, and his Ojibwe blood was like a magnetic force being denied. The pull of the reservation was undeniable...and his Uncle Ben was the only man he could trust implicitly.

Trevor broke his run, breathing heavily, thinking deeply. He'd talked with his mother about her Anishinaabe tribal heritage many times. Her pride in who she was had inspired a desire to be more 'in touch' with his own Indian roots. As a child, he had learned some of the language and enjoyed most of the tribal lore. When his mother called him her *Dakaasin,* her 'cool wind', he'd enjoyed it immensely. However, going to the Fond du Lac Rez where Uncle Ben lived was probably foolish thinking. He wasn't going to grow, or put himself together, in that environment. Despite his deep respect for his mother and his love for his uncle, the world he wanted was not their world. But, did the world he wanted—if he could define that world in any tangible way– want him? That was one of many conundrums he needed to reconcile.

Walking off his exhaustion, he stopped and picked up a rock. Gripping the stone with the fingers of his left hand, he eyed the dented and rusting Railroad Crossing sign about seventy feet ahead. He dug in his left foot, wound up, and threw. The stone ricocheted off the corner of the sign. Not bad. He'd once hit that very sign from this distance twenty times in a row—but that was before his accident. He picked up another rock, toed the dirt again, and rotated his hips into the windup he'd used so effectively with the Hibbing Legion team earlier in the summer and before his accident. This time the rock hit dead-center. He threw another, and another—he lost count of how many. Only once did he entirely miss his target and then only by an inch. What intrigued him the most was the facility of his left arm. Although still tight and sore, the more he threw the less he felt any discomfort. Still not satisfied, he wanted to try something his doctors had cautioned him not to do. Trevor uncovered a round stone about three inches in circumference and threw it with a downward twist of his reconstructed wrist. He watched in surprise as it curved sharply before striking the bottom of the sign. He tried the same wrist rotation again, this time with a stone a bit larger, and he aimed about eighteen inches above and left of the sign. Snapping his wrist he watched the rock dip and hook and strike the low-center of the sign. For the first time that day, Trevor Windsong smiled. "I'll be damned! I can turn my wrist almost ninety degrees!"

He turned back toward his house and ran with an emotional enthusiasm he hadn't mustered for weeks. The door slammed behind him as he strode toward the kitchen. Out of breath from the run, he panted his apology: "Sorry, Mom—my bad, didn't mean to get upset with you. Okay?" He leaned over to give her a kiss on top of her head and breathed in her fresh scent. His eagerness was unbridled, "I wanna borrow the truck and pay a visit to Mr. Morrison in Duluth. Not right now, but maybe in the morning—is that okay with you?"

Marella puzzled, she hadn't seen her son this excited in months. "What's up, Trev? You're lit up like a light bulb."

"Tell you later Mom." He turned toward his brother: "Travis, get that old catcher's mitt in the closet by the front door…and a couple of baseballs. I wanna play some catch—show you something really neat. I'll get my glove from under my bed and meet you outside in a minute."

Marella stood up, concern masked her face: "Don't be foolish and reinjure yourself, Trevor. I've got more medical bills now than I know what to do with. You'd better give Doctor MacIver or Mr. Morrison a call before you start throwing a baseball." Her words were as futile as trying to calm the breeze outside with a wave of her hand. Marella could only be pleased to see her usually somber and brooding son show this unexpected burst of enthusiasm.

~

"My God, Trev! That ball sunk like a lead balloon. How did you do it?" The two boys played catch on the lawn beside the house for nearly half an hour. The more Trevor threw, the stronger his arm felt. The less he favored his left wrist the more natural it felt. He remembered his physical trainer encouraging him to do everything gradually—in measured stages…'your arm will let you know what's safe to do' he had said. 'If you don't allow it to regain its full strength it's gonna atrophy on you, and that's the worst thing possible'.

"I've had enough," Travis said, my hand is burning."

"You caught me before my accident, Trav...how does my fastball compare to where I was then?" Trevor's rehab program had strengthened his legs and hips as well as his arm and he could feel the added force they provided as he pivoted on his left leg and swung into his delivery.

Travis laughed, "You know darn well, Trev. That fastball is actually whistling, and that...whatever you call it...dropball...or curveball– it's nasty."

20/ A BOOK AND A VIDEO GAME

Following Trevor Windsong's tragic accident and Duluth's unprecedented flood, each would be in recovery mode for long weeks that would become even longer months. Mickey was also in a recovery mode of sorts, serious sorts. His issue was about something far less tangible. He needed to get his *spirit* back! That same spirit that had enabled him to accomplish the things he had accomplished only months before in TriPalms, Florida. He realized that every circumstance of people, time, and place were very different...but he was the same Father Mickey Moran. Or, was he? Here he didn't need to build anything, he didn't need outpourings of capital, he didn't need blueprints or infastructure...what he needed was a way to capture the imagination of souls. His religion, like his race and his mission, were not in sync with a culture that had painfully learned life's spiritual lessons by the time they were kindergartners: 'Trust yourself and your people—blood runs deeper than water.' He was facing a far more difficult challenge now than before. His progress, if it could be measured in any way, had been a colossal disappointment. His suffering spirit needed to be rekindled.

While 'touring' and 'touting' his overly publicized achievements, he often mentioned... *"I felt the hand of God upon me..."*

As to whether that was entirely true back in TriPalms– in what seemed a lifetime before– he wasn't sure. In retrospect, he felt more certain of being receptive to letting his God lead him along. These days, it seemed, evertything had turned the other way around— Mickey was asking his God to bless what he was trying to do all by himself. He knew that his thinking was flawed, but he wasn't finding the means to make the changes necessary to correct the flaw. Even his thought of the moment was seriously flawed…all by himself wasn't true at all—Benjamin had been there, with him and for him, all along. If his friend felt defeated, it was Mickey's fault far more than it was Ben's.

Mickey had met with Indian studies scholars, studied books on Ojibwe history and culture, attended powwows across the region— all the things that he thought were logical preparations for his mandate to integrate the Native Americans from the five tribal reservations more meaningfully into the Catholic mainstream. Benjamin Little Otter had introduced him to his friends and his relatives but like Mickey, Ben was feeling underwhelmed and without direction. On more than one occasion, Ben had threatened to throw in the towel. "I don't know how to help you because I don't know what we're sposed to be gettin' done." At a relatively small Mille Lac's band of Chippewa powwow on Memorial Day, Ben said: "I could'n even begin to tell ya 'bout all the tradition and all the spirit of my people, but I never been to a mass half as powerful as a full blown powwow." Mickey would be hard pressed to argue Ben's observation; the somber drumbeats and the colorful dancing were truly mesmerizing. Ben added a stinger, "If a Indian ain't born into a Catholic famly, ain't likely he's ever gonna choose bein' a Catholic by hisself. Only way we'll get'em to goin' to mass is if we give'em somthin' they ain't gettin' from their tribe. What's the somthin' is, Father? I donno fer the life of me."

Mickey sensed that finding a place to live on the Fond du Lac Reservation where Ben lived would only add to his friend's growing disenchantment with their mission. Ben needed his own space. In an effort to get away from the diocese bureaucracy and his best friend, Mickey rented a small house on Three Birch Road on the Bois Forte Reservation near Lake Vermilion and Tower, about a hundred miles away from Ben, St. Gerard's, and the bishop. To his way of thinking, living among the Ojibwe people might enable him to build some friendships and create a sense of trust. His thinking, however, proved to be as flawed as all of his other initiatives. His off-and-on-again living on the Bois Forte Rez during the month of August was fruitless. Folks were friendly enough, even respectful, but they knew who he was and had a negative preconception of why he was there. He was the 'Bishop's Man', the 'super priest', the 'modern-day missionary', and none of those things fit into the Rez' mileau. It didn't take more than a few days for Mickey to realize that he wasn't going to find the kind of acceptance here that he had found in the Hispanic community of Florida. In TriPalms he came as a stranger who had simply helped out a boy in need of help. He didn't have any script or agenda—in fact, he had difficulty in convincing anybody that he was a priest. Most of the time Mickey wished that he didn't carry the baggage of notoriety with him everywhere he went. At other times he enjoyed the ego journey. He wondered at the meaning of Hamlet's famous quote: *'To be or not to be...?* "Lighten up," he reminded himself. "Give it to The One who can make it happen."

~

Shortly after his release from the hospital, Trevor had received a bubble wrap envelope postmarked in Duluth, but without any return address. Curious, and suspicious of anything that arrived unexpectedly, Marella watched as her son opened the package. Inside Trevor found a paperback book and a small envelope. "Let me see what you've got there." Marella said.

Trevor gave her a hard look. "It's addressed to me, Mom. For cripssake, I'll show you in a minute—after I've read the note for my-self." Without looking at the book's cover, he opened the envelope:

Dear Trevor:

I hope this note finds you doing well and in good spirits. Al-though I wasn't able to meet you while you were hospitalized, I did meet your brother Travis. He thinks the world of you. I've done some research lately, mostly in the Duluth Tribune's sports pages from the past year, and learned what I should already have known. I was most impressed with what I discovered about your athletic successes. Don't be discouraged, your skills will come back and you'll have many new, even unexpected, opportunities. I will keep you in my prayers...

Father Mickey

The book was titled: *'Native American Son': the life and sport-ing legend of Jim Thorpe*, and was a 2012 first edition. Inside the front cover was an autograph from the book's author, Kate Buford. Trevor's eyes widened, "Wow, this is really neat...and it's signed by the lady who wrote it, Mom."

Marella smiled, "Do you know anything about Jim Thorpe, son?"

"Heard of him, that's all. Wasn't he an Olympian...way back?"

Marella nodded. "Yes, he was. I'd like to read the book myself when you're done...if that's okay with you." Marella found it in-teresting that the biography's author was a woman. Although it was very thoughtful of the priest...she was suspicious of his motives for sending it. Was this gift some kind of ploy to get her son to go to church on Sundays?

Trevor had never read a book cover-to-cover in his life, but he read his new book through the night and into the next morning with-out pause. "Incredible! That's all I can say, Mom. Did you know that Thorpe was named 'the greatest male athlete of all time' by some major newspaper? The greatest ever!" His excitement was unabashed. "He played pro baseball and pro football at the same time…that's unbelievable." Trevor, the son of few words, actually gushed his wonderment!

Travis, sitting at the table across from his mother, smiled at his brother: "That was a news service, Trev, the *Associated Press*, that gave him that honor. I've checked *Wikipedia* and some other stuff about Thorpe on my computer."

"Nerd," Trevor teased. "I read the whole book—all four hundred and some pages! So there—put that in your pipe!"

"Took you all night and half a day to read, didn't it? Took me less than ten minutes to find out the stuff that was important."

"Okay boys…" Marella enjoyed the banter between her sons, and wanted to be a part of it: "Which one of you can tell me about how his reputation got smeared in the mud? The super screw-job 'they' gave to a national hero, an American Indian hero?"

Both knew about Thorpe's Olympic gold medals being taken away because of the minor technicality of his having played for a semipro baseball team before the Stockholm Olympics in 1912. "What a travesty," Marella said. It was what she didn't say that both boys already knew, what had been drummed into each of them for years: Indians have been getting screwed since the first white people almost eradicated their race from the face of the earth with their diseases. She smiled, "I'm glad you read the story, Trevor. Did you know that Thorpe had a twin brother who died at an early age?"

"Run that twin brother thing by me again, Mom. I didn't see that on *Wikipedia*. It kinda spooks me out."

Trevor grinned sadistically but didn't respond.

Marella leaned forward in her chair. "What else, Trev?"

"The story told lots of stuff about his life. Thorpe had a white father and Indian mother, from the Potato-something tribe in Oklahoma."

Travis giggled at his brother: "Potato tribe? Com'on Trev, you can do better than that. Try again."

Trevor returned his giggle, "Okay, smart ass…sorry Mom…see

if you can say it right– and spell it too, while you're at it."

Marella couldn't hold back a giggle of her own at Trevor's slip: "Let's hear it, Travis. If you can do both, I'll give you a dollar."

Travis worked his forefinger across the placemat in front of him, silently spelling the tribal name to himself, then reciting: "P-o-t-t-a-w-a-t-o-m-e...how's that?"

"Sorry bud...check it out if you want to, but I'm quite sure you left out an 'i' before the last 'e'."

Travis knew immediately that his mom was correct.

Two days later, Travis received a bubble-wrapped package from Duluth. Marella was even more suspicious as her son sliced it open. "Probably from your priest friend," was all that she said. It was. The note inside said:

Hi Travis:

I didn't forget about you. If you've already got this game, exchange it at the WalMart store in Hibbing. Hope you're getting ready for college—only a couple weeks away. I have a good friend on the UMD campus, his name is Father Mario—if you ever need help with anything he's a good guy to go to. God Bless...

Mickey

Rather than appreciating the thoughtful gift, Marella Windsong was quietly upset. What's that priest up to? Why such an interest in her boys? She wondered if the young priest was some sort of pedophile, then she bit her tongue. Rightfully or wrongfully, the media had warped the public perception of Catholic priests.

~

Benjamin was enjoying his space. While Mickey was trying to immerse himself in Bois Forte Rez culture, he was spending time with his friends at the Black Bear Casino near his home on the Fond du Lac Reservation. For the past two months he had been putting daily smiley faces on his calendar and driving up to Hibbing on weekends to visit Marella and the boys—mostly the boys—and mostly Trevor. The bond between Ben and Trevor was as strong as any father-son bond. Travis was a third wheel that didn't mind his Uncle's playing favorites. Since the boys had been given the gifts from Father Mickey, Marella had cooled toward her brother-in-law. "I don't know what you and your priest friend are up to, Benjamin…but I don't like it one bit. It seems to me like he's got some kind of power over you. I think he's a manipulator—do you understand what I mean by that? It's a gut-feeling…"

21/ A FAILING MISSION

In late August, Benjamin and Mickey met for coffee at the Fortune Bay Casino near the priest's rented house on the Bois Forte Rez. It was a long drive for Ben to make in his rusted Chevrolet Cavallier, and while waiting for Mickey to show up, he lost twenty dollars in the slots. His mood was sour, their project was at a standstill, and another meeting accomplished little. "What next?" Ben's question might have been Mickey's question. Aside from an impromptu meeting they arranged with some friends of Benjamins in Fond du Lac a week before, the two men had only talked on the phone a few times in the past few weeks. The Fond du Lac meeting, however, proved to be the best two hours the priest had spent since taking on his new assignment. Ben had introduced Mickey to Jim Northrup, Fond du Lac's most influential resident. Northrup was an award winning author, renowned poet, publisher, and a philosopher extraordinaire.

Northrup wore a floppy hat displaying a U.S. Marines emblem, a red t-shirt with the same emblem on the pocket, along with a distinctive necklace of beads and bear claws. Short and thick-bodied, the heralded author's straggly gray hair hung to his shoulders, and dark sunglasses rested on his broad nose. Mickey had read and enjoyed several of Northrup's books and purchased a signed copy of his recent title: *Rez Salute: The Real Healer Deal* before leaving. Northrup complimented Mickey on his achievements in Florida. "I wish there were more people like you, Father: people who help other people to help themselves. I'm a huge believer in the adage about teaching a man to fish." Later, however, the Indian sage cautioned, "The more you learn about us, the more you will find yourself in the dark. We're very complex people and very spiritual in our own native way. I don't think you can understand an Indian—oh, and by the way, I hate that word Indian and sometimes refuse to speak it. Where was I?" He brushed a strand of hair from his brow and fingered his goatee, "Oh yes, I don't think anybody can understand one of *us* if they weren't born one of *us*. Does that make any sense?" Northrup's emphasis on 'us' spoke volumes. Mickey was not a part of 'us'.

"Sorry to rain on your parade, Father, but…I think your bishop would be well advised to leave us to our own ways. Some of us are Catholics, some Baptists, and lots of other things. And that's well and good." Later Northrup said that an Indian who becomes a Catholic will always be an Indian first—if not, he's not an Indian at all!

~

The 'What's next?' hung between the two men as empty as a moonscape. Mickey had a headache from the rancid cigarette smoke of the casino and needed some fresh air. Benjamin needed an Advil for his headache. Mickey pushed away from the table where they were sitting, "Anything else, pardner?"

"Say another prayer together?" If Ben hadn't laughed at his comment, Mickey would have believed his friend was serious.

"Good one, Ben. Maybe less praying and more doing is in order. Maybe I'm fooling myself in thinking that prayer is the panacea for everything."

Benjamin let the word he'd never heard before fly by without questioning what Mickey meant by it. Instead, he considered his next words carefully, "There is somethin'. Father, I been thinkin' you otta explain yerself to the boy's mother. Marella…she's kinda angry. Thinks yer meddlin' where you shouldn't," Ben's face evidenced concern. "Maybe next time yer in Hibbing you otta make some arrangements to visit with'er. Clear things up."

Mickey nodded to himself. Maybe his keeping a distance from the Windsong family wasn't sending the message he had intended it would. After the hospital vigil, he told Ms. Windsong that he would be available to help in any way he could. He gave Marella his card and wrote his cell number on the back—something he rarely did. He had expected to hear from the woman—maybe a 'thank you' card or even an impersonal email—but he hadn't received any acknowlegement. The only way he could track the progress of Trevor's rehab was through Ben, and lately, Ben had become a man of even fewer words than in the past.

Mickey had always preferred the spontaneity of dropping in on folks to arranging an appointment. With an appointment, the other party would be prone to creating appearances and impressions in advance. He knew that Marella Windsong worked days and was off on the weekends. He knew that Travis hadn't started his classes at UMD yet. He knew the Windsongs' Anderson Road address…and he had been thinking about making a visit to his folks' home in Hibbing sometime in August. Perhaps the stars were in an optimal alignment…

~

"How about grilling your barbequed chicken on the Weber, Dad?" Mickey put his phone on speaker so he could scramble an egg as he talked with his father. "I've told you a hundred times that your chicken is the best there is!" Cleverly, he added a compliment to his 'invite me up for the holiday'. The following Monday was Labor Day. "If I'm reading my calendar correctly, next Saturday is the first of September and I'm off duty. That would work very nicely for me. What say you?" Mickey appealed to his father. A visiting priest from Cedar Rapids was staying with relatives in Benton Park and was willing to cover the Saturday afternoon mass. "Invite Meg and Kenny and the kids over to the house—and Gramma Maddie, of course. We can have a grand ole Moran get-together." Meghan was his older sister, and the kids were his nephew and niece—Matthew, twelve and Kathleen ten—Maddie was his recently widowed grandmother.

There was a long pause on his father's end of the conversation; Amos finally spoke: "We've been waiting to hear from you for weeks, Son. Almost the entire summer is gone!" Amos' voice had an emotive charge. "Is that job of yours so all-consuming that you can't find any time for your family? Your mother is, well—she's more than a little upset with you. Your lucky she didn't pick up the phone when you called, she'd have given you the third degree, and then some."

Mickey was guilty as charged and knew it all too well. "When you say 'more than a little upset' do you mean awfully damn upset, Dad?"

Amos offered a light laugh: "You said it, Son—I didn't. But yes. She's pissed!"

"That's serious," Mickey said. This wasn't the first time that he had been negligent and insensitive toward his parents and family members; and it probably wouldn't be the last. When he was wrapped up in whatever he was doing at the time he became extremely self-absorbed—maybe selfish was the better word. The fact that his lifestyle was locked into a world of perpetual motion was not an acceptable excuse, and his attitude that 'one's family is always there when and if you need them' would never sit well at home. "You're right, Dad—I'm wrong. Apologies, and more apologies, to both of you. I guess that I'm the big jerk with the

Roman collar in the middle of our family's portrait." He swallowed his remorse, "Let me take my deserved medicine and apologize to Mom. Think she can be okay with that?"

"She's ten feet away and knows that you're on the line. As you probably already know, she's not doing any cartwheels across the floor. Oh, by the way, Saturday's just fine with me—I'll leave the reunion idea up to your mother."

If Amos Moran had always been ice, Sadie Moran was fire. The two opposites had forged a marvelous marriage of nearly forty years. Amos was an attorney and skilled in the gray areas of negotiations and compromise, Sadie was black and white. "Hello, Son. Where have you been this summer? Since the funeral in May, I should say? I've lost count of how many weeks that is. Anyhow, I did see in the local paper that you were here in Hibbing sometime...I think it was in mid-June. Ah...yes, it's here on my calendar...the sixteenth it was. You called us on your way up from Duluth that morning if I remember correctly. But I can't remember seeing hide-nor-hair of you. Kenny said that he saw you at the Rotary meeting—but, that you were even gone before he could catch up with you. In and out of town like a phantom." Her voice was more hurtful than heated.

Mickey deserved a good chewing out and wouldn't try to defend himself with the excuses of a job that was consuming and frustrating him in near equal measure. "God bless your candor, Mom. I stand convicted." He would try to humor his mother instead of making excuses or trying to reason with her. "There once was a son who abandoned his family and became lost in the world. Then, one day long afterwards, he decided to return home to ask forgiveness for his folly. Upon doing so, word was sent to his father...and his father ordered his family's fatted calf be slain for a celebration."

Sadie couldn't keep from laughing, ". . . didn't the father say: 'My son who has been lost has been found'? Is that how the 'Prodigal Son' was welcomed home, Mickey?"

"You got it, Mom!"

"Did the story include the feeling of the wayward boy's mother? No, it didn't. She was pissed...pardon my word choice, but your father used it before I just did. And, I don't believe she attended her husband's 'love my lost son's' bash either."

Now it was Mickey's turn to laugh, "Story doesn't say how the mother felt, but in Seminary I learned that she was even more excited than her husband. She and her other son—the good and devoted and slighted son– probably had lots of wine that night."

Guilt, however negative in most respects, is a marvelous motivator. When Mickey finished his conversation with his mother, he called his Gramma Maddie to see how she was getting along. The loss of her husband only months before had been totally unexpected. Maddie was doing quite well and was delighted to hear from her only grandson. They remembered the funeral together and promised to keep more closely connected. "I get self-absorbed in all kinds of things, Gramma...but I remember you every time I say my prayers. If I don't call for a while, please call me. I have a very special place in my heart for you—I hope that you know that. Oh, I'm receptive to any prayers you might send my way, too."

22/ SUNSHINE

On the first day of September, Mother Nature of the North was dressed in resplendent clothing. Her display of pristine pine greens was accented with deep lake blues and the purple-reds of aged mining mountains that gave the Mesaba Range of Minnesota its unique splendor. The morning's brisk air teased a sunshine blessed and cloudless sky with a magnificence that promised all who lived within its aura a day of perfect serenity. Mickey said his morning prayers as he drove from St. Gerard's toward Hibbing. North of the city, he turned west on Highway 2, an historic old highway that crossed Minnesota as it stretched across the northern tier of states from Houlton, Maine to Bonner's Ferry, Idaho. The US-2 route he chose was a few miles and a few minutes longer than taking the four-lane that went through Virginia and on to Canada. But, this marvelous new day was going to be something special—he could feel it blooming somewhere deep inside, a place that he knew was there but could never quite describe.

Mickey was in high spirts as his thoughts drifted toward the Labor Day holiday celebration with his family in Hibbing. He prayed as he always did, for God's guidance—he repeated *'Thy will be done...'* several times, hoping that it would sink in once and for all. Mickey had been into himself too often and too deeply of late. His friend Mario had been telling him, 'don't try to push God's rivers...they flow by themselves'—Mario called the expression his 'ten-cent' solution. Mario's wisdom and counsel was a special blessing in Mickey's life.

As he turned north on Highway 73 at the Floodwood intersection, he felt the sun's rays through his window. He smiled, began to hum, then sing the lyrics from an old favorite song by John Denver...*'Sunshine on my shoulders makes me happy, Sunshine in my eyes can make me cry, Sunshine on the water looks so lovely, Sunshine almost always makes me high...'* Always enjoying mental challenges, Mickey wondered how many songs that he knew had the words 'sun' or 'sunshine' in their title. The Beatles, *'Here Comes the Sun'*, came first to mind; then Elton John's *'Don't Let The Sun Go Down On Me';* then, he found himself singing... *'There is a house in New Orleans they call the Rising Sun, And its been the ruin of many a poor boy, and God I know I'm one...'* His singing stopped abruptly as a logging truck pulled onto the highway in front of him. Mickey, quickly edging left and noticing that the oncoming lane was open for as far as he could see, accelerated past the oblivious trucker. Sunshine returned to his window and his thoughts.

Mickey remembered studying *'The House...'* in Brother Sebastian's seminary class on fine arts appreciation. The discussion was memorable. The country-rock song had unknown and richly historic origins: Some claiming *the house* was a brothel run by a notorioius French madame (real or fictitioius?), others that it was a prison or a jail. Many artists, from Woody Guthrie and Bob Dylan to Dolly Parton and others had recorded the bluesy song—some preferred narrating in the male perspective, others in the female. Dylan's was female. Mickey remembered the most popular version by the Animals in the early sixties.

Passing the turnoff to his left at Island Lake, Mickey remembered a tongue-twister from grade school at Assumption Hall, no one in his class could say the two words 'Sunshine Soldiers' ten times, rapidly and without screwing it up. He concentrated on the two words...with his best effort of many, he managed to recite thr phrase only six times.

Mickey checked his iPhone, the screen blinked three bits of relevant data: 9/01/2012; 8:45 am and 68 degrees. He considered calling Marella Windsong to see if it would be okay for him to stop by and visit on his way to his parents house—"Can't do that," he mumbled to himself. He would much rather just drop by and say 'hello' to her and the boys and hope that he wasn't being rude. Deciding not to call or stop by, he drove past Townline Road, the best connection to Anderson Road where the Windsongs lived.

On further thought, however, it was still early and the Windsongs had been on his mind lately. Mickey was sometimes prone to dithering when faced with idle time—to do this or that or maybe?—and, then going back to an original idea. Benjamin Little Otter had the same 'ride-the-fence' tendency and each teased the other about it. It was only 9:30, he had time to kill before noon, why not drop by and say hello.

23/ UNINVITED

Once in Hibbing, Mickey swung by the Sunrise Bakery at its new location behind the old depot and near the railroad tracks. The unmistakable aroma caught him a block before he pulled in front of the building. Inside he greeted familiar faces and deliberated over familiar bakery items, choosing from the assortment was a challenge. One thing was certain, however, he'd purchase a potica for his Gramma Maddie. Armed with his pastries, he backtracked south on First Avenue past the empty lot at 28th Street where an old church had been razed not long before. Vacant lots where buildings had once been were like missing teeth in a hapless smile. Hibbing was showing its age in more places than he realized. For a man still in his thirties, nostalgia should not be the heartbreak that it seemed to be. He found Anderson Road off of Townline and proceded to the address on the *TomTom* GPS attached to his windshield. He signed himself as he pulled into the driveway and parked next to a green Ranger pickup with an *'Indians discovered Columbus'* bumper sticker.

Travis heard the door chime from his bedroom desk where he was surfing the internet for textbooks he'd need for his college classes next week. He called out, "Mom…the front door…" No response. Licking frosting from his fingers as he finished the last bite of a fresh cinnamon roll his mother had baked earlier that morning, he looked up from the screen. He wiped his fingers on his pajama bottoms and called out again. "Mom! You gonna get the door?" A second and third ring had Travis pushing away from his computer and rushing into the living room. As he crossed the carpet he heard the droning shower from his mother's bedroom down the hall.

Mickey was about to turn away when the door opened on Travis. "Well…how are you, Trav…" his lame introduction was a perfect match to his suffered smile. "What are you up to, today?"

Travis' jaw dropped, nobody had told him the priest was going to come by today. He was barefooted, still wearing his pajama bottoms and a wrinkled '*Big Bang Theory*' T- shirt. "Gosh, I mean, good to see you." He pulled the door open wider, "Come in, Father...I'll tell Mom that you're here. Oh, before I forget, thanks for that game you sent—it's awesome, I play it all the time."

Travis crossed the living room in three long strides, called down the hallway to his mother...then he said "excuse me" and disappeared down the hall way. Mickey heard him knocking on a door, then heard the drumming of the shower stop. Travis'voice was muffled but Mickey sensed he was telling his mother that she had company. He didn't hear Marella's response. The house became as silent as a tomb, seconds that seemed like minutes told him that his timing was bad—even very bad! Mickey, standing awkwardly in the narrow foyer, stepped inside and put the box of sweet rolls on the lamp table by the door. The simply appointed living room was warm and tidy, Indian artwork adorned the walls and woodcarved animal sculptures rested atop a large bookcase on the south wall. A beautiful '*Dreamcatcher*' hung in the west window. The house smelled pleasantly of cinnamon and coffee.

Travis Windsong wore the sheepish expression of someone who had done something wrong and been caught: "I'm sorry...I mean, my mom's sorry, I guess," he cleared phlegm from his throat. "Anyhow she said that you should probably come back another time. I think she's in a bad mood this morning...it's probably better if..."

The door behind Mickey opened suddenly and before he could step aside a large young man stepped into Mickey, knocking him slightly off balance. "S'cuse me," the voice was deep, the muscular frame sweaty. The long-haired, dark-skinned man scrutinized Mickey. "You the priest?" Mickey was in his 'civies' wearing Levi jeans and a short-sleeved white cotton shirt with subtle green striping. The young man in running shorts and a sweat-stained tanktop towering next to him had to be Trevor.

Mickey extended his hand, "Yes. Father Mickey."

"I'm Trevor." The young man returned Mickey's handshake

without crushing any bones. "Kinda sweaty, I'm sorry. I've been running."

Mickey noticed the scars below the screaming eagle tattooed on his left arm, "How's the arm mending?"

"Getting better all the time," Trevor said.

"He says it's stronger than it's ever been, right Trev?" Travis beamed his pride in the bigger brother. "We've been playing catch every day and he's got more stuff than I've ever seen. I've had to add extea padding to my catcher's mitt.

Trevor nodded, "Say…thanks for the book. I read all of it."

Mickey found it hard to believe that Trevor and Travis were twins. Trevor was taller by nearly three inches, thicker in the torso, broader-shouldered, and had a noticeably darker complexion than Travis. An awkward silence was broken when Travis said, "Father Mickey was just leaving, Trev."

"Why?"

"Mom said for him to come by another time."

Trevor looked into Mickey's eyes. "Stay. Take a chair at the table over there," he gestured toward the small kitchen. "I'll get you a cup of coffee. Its fresh."

Travis shrugged his indifference, when Trevor spoke he usually listened; when Trevor wanted something, he usually gave it to him: Trouble and tension are minimized when one understands who is the alpha. Nevertheless, Travis' face wore a pained expression. "Trevor, are you sure…?"

"Travis, why don't you put out some of those rolls mom baked this morning—or have you pigged out on them?"

Travis shook his head, "Only two…Mom said I could."

"Okay. I'll go and tell Mom to come out and join us," Trevor kicked off his running shoes and was about to cross the carpeted living room.

Mickey cleared his throat, then met Trevor's cold eyes, "I really don't think I should stay…maybe another time is a better idea. I only wanted to…"

"Wanted to what?" The sharp question shot from the hallway. "See my boys, Father?"

Although unsettled by the woman's attractiveness as she stepped into the room in cutoff jeans and a yellow tank top, Mickey caught the inference immediately. Should he say 'yes'? To be honest, his main reason for stopping by was his insatiable curiosity: a curiosity that he never fully understood. But he had hoped to see what Trevor looked like and how he was recovering; and he had found Travis to be an engaging young man when they met at the hospital. Or, might he simply say that he was just in the neighborhood and thought he'd stop by? Saying that, however, wouldn't even be borderline believable—the Windsongs' home was out in the sticks. He felt trapped by a question that had no good answer…in a place where he had no good reason to be.

Marella spared him any further embarrassment, "Travis, you've got some school packing to get done today…Trev, I think a shower would be a good idea." Her eyes moved from one son to the other, "Now!"

There was no argument, the boys nodded to their mother, then to Mickey, and left the room. Marella looked satisfied that her order—and clearly, it was an order!—found obedience without question or protest. "Now…where were we, Father?"

Mickey could not help but vaguely remember a scene from *Moonstruck*: Cher was telling Nicholas Cage to do something, her glare being more potent than her words. That was it…! That was the distraction; Marella Windsong had both the features and the fire of Cher Bono. Mickey's voice was weaker than he would have liked: "I really don't know. I guess I was about to leave."

"But the boys wanted you to stay…have a cup of coffee, chit-chat…a little social time for the three of you. Am I right about that?"

"This isn't going very well, Miss Windsong. I can see that you are upset—and rightfully so." He carefully measured his next words before speaking them. "I also get the impression that you have some warped misconceptions about me. I'm sorry for the intrusion. I'll go now," Mickey turned toward the door. He stopped and turned back, met Marella Windsong's dark eyes, "I've been praying for Trevor's recovery and will continue to do so." He swallowed hard, "Don't take this wrong, but I think you have been blessed with great sons."

"Just a minute..." Her face softened, in a contrite voice, she said: "I have a tendency sometimes to overreact to things. I appreciate your prayers and respect your friendship with Ben. I guess you caught me at a bad time."

"My bad...I should have called. I'm sorry..." Mickey's words were sticking to the roof of his mouth. Maybe it was all the singing on his drive up to Hibbing that morning. "I've...may I call you Marella? I've..." I've what? Mickey forgot where his 'I'ves were supposed to be taking him...

She nodded as if she understood his discomfort and felt bad about it. "Next time—if there is one, yes...please do call." An almost imperceptible smile crossed her face. She offered her hand, "I enjoyed the Jim Thorpe story myself, Father. That was very thoughtful of you. Trevor eats and breathes sports, but he doesn't read enough. And Travis, well...you hit the nail on the head with a video game. Thanks."

As he was about to open his car door, he heard his name whispered from a side window, followed by: "Father...keep in touch, okay?" Mickey wasn't certain if the voice was that of Travis or Trevor. His first thought was that Travis had made the appeal, but in his heart he hoped that it had been Trevor—the Alpha. Why was that? He wasn't certain. He was certain, however, that Marella Windsong was watching him from behind the sheer drapes in the living room's window. Best for him to get in the car and go.

As he drove away, Mickey tried to analyze what had just oc-curred in the Windsong home as it was becoming a fading and dusty reflection in his rearview mirror. The conversation with Marella, if it was a conversation at all, had ended with her 'Thanks' and his 'You're welcome'. Simple and succinct! No coffee, no cinnamon rolls; no invitation to visit again. To use a baseball analogy, he felt as if he had a watched strike three whiz by and the ump had just sent him feeling empty and defeated to the bench. He laughed to himself. Most importantly, he had connected with the boys and was reasonably certain that he'd get another turn at bat. In one way or an-other he would certainly *'keep in touch'* with both of the boys. Hopefully all the Windsongs would enjoy the Sunrise pastries and his Gramma's potica that he had left behind.

The remainder of Mickey's September Saturday went swim-mingly well. Being with family was the best tonic for anything that ailed his wounded spirit. Not only did he enjoy each and every member of his family, he had an opportunity to watch his nephew play in a Little League 'all-star' game against a Chisholm team at the Bennett Park field that afternoon. Both Mickey and the boy's fa-ther agreed, Matthew was going to be a pretty fair ballplayer some day. "I don't know where he got all his athleticism," Kenny con-fessed, "I was the furthest person from any sports in high school." Mickey knew the Kenny Williams' story all too well. Were it not for the grace of God and the generosity of Amos Moran, his brother-in-law might have been living on food stamps in the HRA projects. Mickey's sister Meghan had survived some troubled years as well. Now in their late thirties, Kenny and Meg continually worked on a relationship that had teetered in times past.

To the delight of all, especially Uncle Mickey, the little slugger launched a pitch over the fence in deep left center field to break a tie game in the seventh inning. Matthew's younger sister Kathleen even gave her 'big bro' a proud hug after the game. What was truly special about her hug was that she did it in front of her girl friends who giggled without mercy.

~

In addition to his nebulous Tribal coordinator position, Father Mickey had been overseeing the closing of his last parish, St. Gerard's, located in Benton Park in far western Duluth. Since his return from the so-called 'sabbatical' in Florida and the notoriety that followed him, attendance and weekly donations had been higher than ever before—so much so that Bishop Bremmer was seriously considering keeping the parish alive. Not only that, the bishop had hired an architect to offer some remodeling specs for the old church. All the while, Mickey had his fingers crossed—not something most priests would admit to doing—that his church would come back to life. He told his parish board that he was praying for a 'New Lazarus'.

Mickey was committed to saying two masses every Sunday morning and two weekday masses as well. After spending a marvelous Saturday with his family, Mickey returned to the St. Gerard's rectory to prepare his homily for the following morning. On the trip from Hibbing to Duluth, Mickey caught up on his prayers, called his priest friend, Father Mario at the Newman Center on the UMD campus, and listened to the tail end of the Twins game at AM:610 on his car radio.

Considering the wonderful time he'd spent with his family, Mickey's prayers were unusually flat that evening. Tonight he seemed to have too many things floating around in his mind. The visit to the Windsongs topped the list, his and Ben's floundering attempts to generate any enthusiasm for their new assignment followed, and the news from his sister Meghan that she and Kenny and the kids were considering a permanent move to Florida was a footnote. He was happy for them, and sad at the same time. Sad in a selfish way. With his parents already spending nearly half the year in Naples in southwestern Florida, he felt he might lose his connection to *home*. Home was, and had always been, the two-story house across 37th from the Greenhaven School, in Hibbing's Home Acres Addition. It was too hard to imagine his family at *home* anywhere else.

As always, Father Mario, was a font of encouragement and support. Mickey's best friend and confidante in all matters religious, Mario had been his spiritual mentor since Mickey was in high school. "You gotta hang in there, Mick. Remember how you felt those first days living in TriPalms? Remember how you poured your heart out in frustration. 'I don't know what God wants me to do here' you said—over and over again. I think you're closing up, my friend. You're getting too much into yourself and not allowing God to work through you." Mario's inspired spiritualty never seemed to waver. "I know, it happens to me every now and again."

"I find that hard to believe," Mickey teased.

"No. It's true. I get frustrated with the youth here on campus and I want to change their ways of thinking and behaving—their 'too-secular-for-their-own-good' value system. It's hard for me to fathom how far apart our two generaltions seem to have become. Sometimes I want to grab them by the shoulders and shake out their demons. Then, my better self intervenes. Then I listen to that voice that reminds me to calm myself—to let go...then I can love them like I'm supposed to."

Mickey finished Mario's tirade for him, "I know...you let go and let God." He couldn't argue with Mario. He knew that, all too often, he wasn't listening to the right voices in his head, nor was he hearing the right intentions in his heart. "I'll work on it, Mario. Say, let's get together next week when you're free for lunch. I think you owe me. No, I *know* that you owe me." Mario laughed along with his friend, "I'll check my calendar and get back to you tomorrow," he said.

"Is your life that complicated? Let's think of eating somewhere that's more high-end this time," Mickey teased. "Wendy's is good but…?"

"Is there is any place left in Duluth where the two of us can eat without the 'Aren't you Father Mickey' interruptions, photo ops, and paparazzi everywhere? Your celebrity is beginning to wear thin on me." Mario enjoyed digging Mickey about being the 'most recognized priest' in the diocese.

"On second thought, how about your kitchen, Mario? A peanut butter and jelly sandwich with a side of milk will suit me just fine."

The Twins were in the process of blowing an 8-2 lead against the Royals in Kansas City. Both Joe Mauer and Chris Parmelee had homered but the woeful Twins pitching staff was collapsing—again! Mickey would never be able to explain why he subjected himself to the agonies of the past two Twins seasons. Masochism?

Back at the St. Gerard's rectory Mickey checked his caller ID: Benjamin Little Otter had called several times. He left Mickey a brief message only an hour before. "Gotta talk. See ya tomorrow, after mass. Don't text me." Benjamin never responded to text messages.

Mickey rarely sent texts or email messages anyhow. Too slick and too artificial. Mickey knew well enough that Benjamin had his demons. The lateness of the calls suggested that one or more of them were barking tonight.

25/ BENJAMIN'S CONFESSION

On Sunday, both the eight o'clock and ten o'clock masses were packed. The congregation at St. Gerard's was swollen with curious Catholics from throughout the city. At ten, the most crowded of the two masses, some cars had to park more than a block away, some 'worshippers' had to stand in the surrounding aisles of the sanctuary. Most of the faces Mickey spoke to during his homily and most of the hands he shook after mass were strangers. The 'reglars', as he called his legitimate parishioners, attended the eight o'clock mass. Mickey liked to begin his homily with a funny story to loosen up everybody, including himself. "Our Sunday School teacher, Mrs. Hannity, spoke to the children just before this morning's mass. She asked them why it was important to remain silent during mass. Little Grace Ann said, 'because people are trying to sleep'." He chided everyone to poke the person sitting next to them and make certain they were wide-awake and listening to his sermon. His story amused the congregation and got him going.

Being an Iron Ranger, Mickey was familiar with the rich history of organized labor. His homily touched on the struggles for decent working conditions and a livable wage in the iron mines, but balanced his observations with the equally important responsibilities of management in our capitalistic system. "In many ways it's like politics, the two sides must be able to compromise for the common good. Yet, knowing and doing are two different animals." Although he spoke without notes, his thoughts were well-organized and lucid. He ended with a favorite Confucius quote from Brother Thomas' theology class at the Seminary: "Choose a job you love and you will never have to work a day in your life."

~

Benjamin lingered in the shade of an ancient dogwood tree between the rectory and church, waiting for Mickey to finish the conversations with all his 'fans' on the sidewalk in front of the church. Ben knew that Mickey's enjoyment of celebrity had grown thinner with each passing week. Ben had also noticed that attendence at mass by his Indian friends was also much thinner now than it was before Mickey's suspicious departure to Florida just after the previous Christmas. The only Ojibwe family, the Desmonds—Chuck and Becky and their three children—were in attendance at the ten o'clock mass this morning. Ben was especially sensitive about Indian and White interactions. There was, and would always be, a cultural schism and the depth of that reality was becoming more apparent to him as the weeks went by. On the reservation, he had noticed that people who approached him just to chat about the weather, or tribal politics, or the casino's profits, were less likely to do so now than they had been in the past. Since his name had appeared in the bishop's letter introducing Father Mickey Moran and himself, Benjamin Little Otter seemed to have become a 'suspicious' person. He was becoming more ill at ease about that and was beginning to keep more to himself. His life was changing in ways that he had never expected and he didn't like it. Ben nodded at Mickey's gesture suggesting that he would be over in a minute. He snubbed a half-finished cigarette on the bottom of his shoe and placed the butt in his pants pocket.

Mickey wandered over to the shade, "Mornin' Chief," the nickname had always been one of affection between them. He noticed the pained smile on Benjamin's broad face, and the furrows lining his forehead—something wasn't right. "I got your message last night, didn't call back because it was kinda late. What's up my friend?"

"I gotta tell ya somthin' that really bothers me, Father." His voice was tight and his eyes were becoming moist.

Mickey's first thought was that Big Ben had fallen off the wagon. "I can tell something heavy is on your mind, Ben. Do you want to go inside and talk?" Heat and humidity hung in the Sunday morning air like a sauna door had been left open next to where they were standing. "I'm starting to sweat myself."

Ben shook his head. "That somthin' been botherin' me too long, Father. Gotta get it out sooner er later." It was rare for Ben to use a confessional tone when speaking with his friend—but his words seemed laden with guilt.

Mickey nodded, repeated his invitation. "Sure you wouldn't rather go inside?"

"No." Ben was standing awkwardly, nervously shifting his substantial weight from one leg to the other, "No here's fine." He looked away, up at the yellowing dogwood leaves, or the cloudless azure sky, or heaven? "I jus can't do this no more, Father. Whatever it is we're sposed to be doin', I mean. I get all stressed up and that ain't no good fer me. My AA sponsor, Lester—you met'em once, Lester Hicks…"

Mickey nodded without speaking.

"Well, Lester says it ain't no good whatsoever fer me to be doin' somthin' that drives me…well, not 'zakly crazy…but makes me anxious and all. I really hate to let ya down, Father, I know yoze been expectin' me ta help ya but I ain't done nothin' and I don't wanna be takin' no more money fer what I ain't doin'." Benjamin was being paid a minimal salary of $100 a week from the diocese as Mickey's 'assistant coordinator'. "Matter'a fact I got this stuff here. . ." he dug his large hand in the cargo pocket of his olive colored shorts and withdrew several uncashed checks and a wad of money. "I'm givin' all this back 'cause I ain't done nothin' fer it."

Mickey saw that there were some fifty-dollar bills in the wad, "No way. Ben…I love ya too much to take that…no way! I've been the one who isn't getting anything done. Don't blame yourself for what's been an albatross for both of us from the start. Please, Ben…won't you give it another chance—another month or two? Maybe we can still manage to come up with something that works. Another month?"

Ben shook his head emphatically, "Can't Father. My conscience won't let me. Sorry. I mean it—I mean I'm sorry and I mean I ain't gonna do it no more." He held the money for Mickey to take. "Please…I'd feel worse if you din't take dis money back. Give it back to yer bishop, or give it to somebody needin' a lil help."

Mickey couldn't cause his friend any more pain than he was already feeling. "Okay. But only if you give me a hug and promise to be my friend always, Ben." Mickey was even more choked up than Benjamin. "Love ya, Ben."

Ben was in tears, "I luv ya, too…" he stepped toward Mickey, leaned over and gave him the hug he had asked for. "But…maybe we shouldn't see each other no more…I mean, I won't be comin' by and don't expect to see you at the Rez neither."

26/ BISHOP BREMMER

October was another month dominated by seemingly endless presidential politics. All too often nasty politics! Unprecedented negative campaign ads suggesting that Obama's goal was to social-ize America in the mode of European countries, and that Romney was a rich guy who would take away the entitlements that America's poor needed in order to survive, were on millions of tongues. Char-acter assassination wasn't something new, but it was being taken to new levels. The televised debates were getting record audiences. Then, as if God were angry with it all, October's last days brought horrific Hurricane Sandy to the east coast! New Jersey and New York were hit the hardest; yet even that devastation would not over-shadow the upcoming election. In perfect accord with everything else, the storm became as politically volatile as it was tragic.

~

November arrived in northern Minnesota with an Arctic blast of cold that killed the last of the annuals in Mickey's small flower gar-den behind St. Gerard's and left a layer of frost on the windshield of Mickey's Civic. His Thursday agenda included a meeting with the bishop at ten, lunch with Father Mario on the UMD campus, and mid-afternoon cup of coffee with freshman Travis Windsong. The 'light duty' brought an easy smile.

Through a grapevine that Mickey had nurtured in Bishop Bremmer's office, he had been given a 'heads-up' on what to expect from His Grace. The bishop was going to announce a reprieve for St. Gerard's and expand Mickey's pastorial duties with his former parish. Also, there would be a reprimand with a veiled threat attached. Mickey had been *asked* to submit weekly progress reports on his 'Native American Reservations' project since Benjamin was given his 'leave of absence' in early September. Mickey's first report (one-half of a page in large typeface) suggested that he was formulating a new plan. His next report was even more brief, 'still working on a more aggressive approach', and his third report stated: 'I have terminated the lease on my rental house at Bois Forte and will be considering a new strategy to implement the objectives of the plan that is currently being prepared for submission'. That report, more than other business, was what had earned him an impromptu meeting and a mild reprimand from the bishop.

"I'm in a huge funk over this project," Mickey confessed to his bishop. "Nothing that I have tried to do has worked. I've arranged coffee socials in each of the reservations social halls, sing-along and karaoke concerts, attended every Indian cultural event from Mille Lacs to Grand Marais, scheduled lectures on the life and works of Saint Kateri as you suggested. The end result of it all has been little more than a 'nice to meet you, Father'. Last week in Cass Lake my Kateri lecture attracted eleven people who came—it seemed obvious– for the coffee and donuts. Noone had any questions or ideas about how to get a regular get-together going. When I asked if they would like me to come back in a couple of weeks, eleven pairs of shoulders shrugged. I've attended and offered prayers at several AA meetings on the Reservations and gone to pow wows wherever I can find them. I've even contacted Dan Jones at the Fond du Lac Community College about taking Ojibwe language lessons."

"Why haven't I seen any of this in your weekly reports, Father?"

"To be candid, most of all–I hate reports, Your Grace. Unless they offer something positive, that is. I've just told you in a hundred words what I've accomplished in the past four months. Ben Little Otter couldn't take it and I'm on the verge..." Mickey let the thought drop. His bishop wasn't some bloke from off the streets he could dump his troubles on—Bishop Bremmer was His Grace, and was deserving of Mickey's utmost respect. "Sorry," he mumbled, "I haven't been able to accomplish what you've expected of me. My heartfelt apology..."

"You're struggling, aren't you, Father? And I'm responsible. In retrospect, putting you on public exhibition wasn't such a good idea. At least not for you." Bremmer's smile was warm and genuine. "The diocese has had a windfall but our dear Father Moran has paid a price. I'm sorry for that. If you'd like, you have my explicit permission to scale back your speaking engagements—just tell Millie in the office and she will accommodate any schedule changes." Bremmer paused, "I'm offering this magnanimous gesture with some reluctance...as you know, the more you're 'out there' the better our receipts have been. I hate to admit how important those revenues are to our diocese—especially the vocations program we've initiated."

Mickey grinned, risked a bit of humor: "Do your realize, Your Grace, that you just called me 'your dear Father Moran?' I like that. Just to think...only months ago, I was 'that disgraceful Father Moran."

The bishop was taken aback, "Never disgraceful, Father—perish that thought. I was worried about you for sure...and frustrated to my wits end, but never once did I think of you as disgraceful. A poor choice of words, Father. How could you possibly think...?"

Mickey chose not to engage the bishop in an argument over semantics, 'shameful' might have been a better choice of words. "Sorry," was all that needed to be said.

Before leaving, Mickey promised to continue with the ill-fated endeavor, and to keep the bishop better informed with monthly (not weekly) reports. Yet, in his heart he doubted whether he would be able to accomplish much more than he already had. As Benjamin had often told him, 'We are a different people and we believe that you folks are responsible for much of that difference. You and me and the Pope himself can't undo what's already done'. Benjamin's insight, however, was best left unsaid.

Mickey's morning meeting with Bishop Bremmer had gone surprising well. Bremmer commented that he was looking forward 'with great anticipation' to attending the christening of St. Michael's Church in TriPalms in December. "It's an unprecedented honor for all of us, Father...I've been in contact with my bishop friend in Venice almost weekly about details. Bishop Cordoba is as excited as I am." Before granting leave and blessing his priest, Bishop Bremmer encouraged Mickey to immerse himself in his revitalized St. Gerard's parish. "Rather than spending only a small part of your time at St. Gerard's, I'd like you to become more involved in the daily affairs there."

~

A relaxing lunch at Father Mario's kitchen table was a perfect companion to Mickey's pleasant meeting with the bishop. In giving Mario a recap of his session with Bremmer, Mickey acknowledged his frustrations, "The bishop is kinda letting me off the hook on the tribal project without blatantly telling me that I've failed. But, the truth remains, I have failed—regardless of how hard I've tried..." He let it drop. Mario was his sounding board and understood his friend's anguish more than anybody else. "I hate to be a constant complainer, Mario. But...I guess I am."

As always, Mario assured him that the good Lord was hard at work in his life and that God would make clear the path he had chosen for Mickey. "You've only failed at something when your heart is so closed-up, and so cold with malice, that you wash your hands of it and turn your back to it. That's not gonna happen, Mick. You've told me too many times how deeply you respect these people. Pray harder, love more, and let God…" Mario's spirituality was contagious and Mickey left with a positive uplift. "You always pump me up, Mario. I don't know where I'd be without you."

"Enough of that, Mick. Give yourself some credit…you didn't have anybody but yourself down in Florida a few months ago." The two men hugged at the door, "Go in peace, my friend," Mario said. Mickey could actually feel those five simple words as he stepped out into the midday sun. It was no wonder that his friend was so deeply respected by those who knew him. In his ministry at UMD, and in his lectures throughtout the diocese, Father Mario was personally responsible for at least ten ordinations to the priesthood in his years there. His gifts of spirituality and insight were something that young people connected with.

27/ TALKING POLITICS

Mickey would be a few minutes early for his meeting with Travis Windsong in the Library cafeteria at the far corner of the sprawling UMD campus. It was a Jekyll and Hyde kind of day with the sun at his back and a brisk north wind in his face: the kind of day where you layered your clothing, wore warm gloves, and covered your ears. Mickey wore a hooded sweatshirt under his light jacket so that he could make an adjustment if or when conditions changed. He headed toward the building with his head down against the wind's bite. Being early, he'd be able to browse the library for a C.W. Lewis book that he hadn't already read and sign it out in Father Mario's name. To Mickey's surprise, the large man giving him a nudge as he stepped into the foyer of the library was Trevor Windsong. Trevor's face, obscured by dark sunglasses and a Vikings cap pulled down on his forehead, wasn't immediately recognizable. His voice, however, was: "Hey, Father…mind if I join you and my bro for a cup of coffee?"

Travis was late, giving Mickey his first opportunity to get to know Trevor. Trevor was in high spirits and explained what had been going on in his life of late. He explained that he was in Duluth for his four-month check-up with Doctor MacIver at St. Mary's. Everything was 'incredibly healed' according to the surgeon. "He actually used the words 'incredible' and 'unbelievable' more than once," Trevor beamed over his progress report. After his MacIver appointment, he had driven up the hill from the hospital to the campus for a second meeting, this with his PT guy, Jon Morrison. He received yet another positive report from his trainer. Trevor's dim world had been transfused with a dab of brightness that day.

Optimism was a stranger and Trevor didn't quite know how to cope with its presence. I didn't expect so much good news at one time—I'm still trying to take it all in. "Morrison was really surprised, he couldn't believe my conditioning." Trevor explained that he had been working part time at the Atlas warehouse in Hibbing loading and unloading furniture and spending a few hours at Any Time Fitness every evening. "I told Morrison that I had been pitching two or three times a week in the high school gym, too. He was kinda intrigued when I told him about how hard I've been throwing—and about my awesome sinker pitch. He didn't believe me, said I was exaggerating. I told him that was bullcrap. He's stubborn. Wants me to prove it—told me to meet him in the Saint Scholastica gym later this afternoon—about five. He said he'd bring a radar gun or something...I'm pumped—I've never been timed with a speed gun before."

Trevor's ten-minute update on the past two months was accomplished with minimal wordage– *'I'm pumped'* best characterized how he viewed his life at the time. Trevor invited Mickey to join him later at the gym..."See if I've got some Jim Thorpe in me," he laughed. When Travis arrived the three men had a wide-ranging conversation that included sports, academics, and politics. Travis was flourishing: His classes were stimulating, campus life was fun, and he had become active in the Students for Obama campaign. Trevor was sick of what he called 'political pollution' and had a different take on the better man for president than his brother. Regardless of their informed argumentation, neither would change the mind of the other. Mickey raised the question about the 'Marriage Amendment' on the Minnesota ballot—both supported gay and lesbian unions; both opposed required voter ID's.

"You're a liberal, Trevor, whether you know it or not," Travis injected.

Mickey, of course, differed with them on the marriage amendment but wasn't very persuasive. He was positive that both amendments would fail. According to Mickey, traditional values had dramatically changed in recent years as America moved toward a more secular society. The boys accused him of living in the past. "Values, schmalues...life has never been such a trip," asserted Travis.

"Who you voting for, Father?" Travis asked.

"That's none of your business," Trevor said.

Both, however, were curious. "He's probably an Independent," Travis offered. "Most Catholics are Dems, but with the liberal positions on abortion and gay marriage, I'd think that it's gotta be kinda confusing."

Mickey would use one of his favorite little witticisms, "I used to think I was indecisive, but now I'm not so sure."

Travis got it and laughed, Trevor only puzzled.

"Whatever! I can't wait until next Tuesday when all this campaign crap is over with," Trevor sighed his exasperation. Both Travis and Mickey agreed with his opinion and all three believed that rather than providing contrasting positions on the critical issues of the day, the political ads were dripping with the mud of character assassination.

Travis chuckled, "One of my professors suggested that Congressmen should wear uniforms, you know, like NASCAR drivers. That way we could identify their corporated sponsors."

28/ *A MAN NAMED MADIGAN*

Back at St. Gerard's in west Duluth after watching Trevor's workout, Mickey sat at his desk reviewing monthly bills and re-playing his afternoon with the Windsong twins. Of his many random thoughts, one cropped up a second and third time. On a whim, he picked up the phone on his desk and called his father in Hibbing. When Mickey's lovable mongrel 'Torts' heard his master's voice say "Hi Dad," he wandered from the sofa and curled up under the desk near Mickey's stockinged feet. Once comfortable he farted, looked up, then quickly averted Mickey's scowl.

Without waiting for a reciprocal 'Hi Son', Mickey continued: "Who's that guy you know who used to play for the Twins years ago?"

"If I'm thinking of the same guy as you are, he never played with the big club but had some success in the minors," Amos said. "But his name escapes me...Morgan, Milligan...something like that."

"Com'on, dad. You must remember him, I think he was a friend of Terry Ryan's? He used to get up to Hibbing every now and then. From Duluth...?" Terry Ryan was the General Manager of the Minnesota Twins and charged with the responsibility of rebuilding the failing franchise. The previous season, his first back in that capacity, had not gone well.

Amos Moran smiled to himself as a light went on his mind, "Pete Madigan! That's it. I was in the same flight as Pete in the Northwest golf tournament a few years back. He's not in great shape anymore and his golf game has gone south along the rest of him." Madigan was ten years older than Amos and had been closer to Amos' father, Pack Moran, than to himself. "He seemed to be awfully negative about the Twins back when I saw him last. Not the team as much as the organization—maybe both, I can't remember—been a while."

"It couldn't have been that long ago, Dad. Up until two years ago, the Twins were a playoff team."

"That's true enough. I remember Pete predicting a downward spiral when he was talking with some guys in the clubhouse after his round. He said that if they don't get some decent pitching they were going to struggle for a few more years. I guess that we all know that," Amos paused, reflecting back. "But…I think he had some other issues with the Twins. If you read between the lines of what he was saying, I thought that he must have had a falling out with the management. Anyhow, that was my take. Why do you ask?"

Mickey ignored the question, pressed further: "Does he still live in Duluth, or has he…?"

"In the summer months, I think—not sure, though. Someone said he was selling

his lake home on Pike Lake. But whoever said that claimed lots of things. Madigan told George Versich that he still did some scouting. Said he was following the kids in the Northwoods League, mostly the team from Duluth. Mort Sundvall told me that Pete's full of it…George felt the same when we talked afterwards. Who knows." (The Duluth Huskies were one of sixteen teams comprised of top-rated collegians aspiring to become pro ballplayers).

Amos paused, "Why? What's up, Son?"

"I'd like to talk to him. Just a minute, Dad…I'm *Googling* the White Pages on line…nothing in Duluth for a Madigan that I can see. Let me check the phone directory…I've got it in the drawer."

Expecting a long pause, Amos put a cup of cold coffee in the microwave, pushed the thirty seconds button, as he waited at the kitchen counter. He had been following what baseball fans called the 'hot stove league' since the end of the World Series. The Twins did need better pitching—would they be willing to spend the big money needed, or make a trade, to rebuild their woeful staff?

"Could you ask around and find a phone number or email address for me, Dad? I'm not finding anything in the directory."

"Check Ft. Myers on your computer, Son. He claimed that he's been spending most of the winter on a golf course down there. Hard to believe he's playing much golf, though—I think his handicap was in the high twenties."

"Didn't you just say that the two of you were in the same flight?'

"Lets not go there, Son," Amos tried to swallow a chuckle without success. "Anything else I can help you with? The news is coming on in a few minutes."

"If Madigan's only got a cell phone he'll be hard to locate," Mickey said. "Just a second, Dad...got it! Yep, he's there—in Ft. Myers. Thanks for the help." Satisfied with locating Pete Madigan's address and phone number, Mickey's excitement waned. "So, how have you and Mom been?" he footnoted the conversation.

"Fine, for the most part. My back's still giving me trouble...Mom's been busy taking the grandkids to one thing after another while your sister and Kenny do whatever it is that keeps them on the run all the time. Matthews's hockey has already started and Kathleen is in some sixth grade volleyball league. I don't know how Meghan will manage things when your mom and me are back in Naples and won't be around to help out with our taxi service."

"Don't make it sound like a chore, Dad. You both love it and you'll miss the kids like crazy when you're gone. That won't be too long now, will it? When are you two snowbirds heading south?"

"After Thanksgiving, as usual. Your Mom's already packed. Oh, by the way, you are coming up for Thanksgiving Day, aren't you?"

"Wouldn't miss it for the world," Mickey said. He hated clichés but used them as much as anybody else. What did 'for the world' actually mean?

29/ AN IMPRESSIVE WORKOUT

Trevor's session at the St. Scholastic gym that afternoon was nothing short of amazing! Morrison had timed Trevor's fastball in the high eighties. The Scholastica baseball coach, Bobby Young, had joined the group of hoopsters gathered to watch the impromptu workout. Young stood a few feet behind Travis Windsong, who was catching his brother. The coach was astonished at what he was seeing. One of the basketball players, with the name Olson on the back of his jersey, quit practicing free throws to watch the Indian kid pitch. Olson also played baseball in the spring. Seeing what was happening, he slipped away to retrieve an aluminum bat from his locker. When he returned he asked the Coach Young: "Can I stand in and take a few swings?"

"What do you say, Trevor?" Coach Young frowned at the idea. Trevor nodded, "Fine with me, sir."

After telling the eager jock that he could go ahead and give batting a try, Young found some catchers gear in a nearby locker for Travis to wear. Then he cleared the floor, sending bystanders to the side of the gym so no one would get hurt if Timmy Olson managed to make any contact with the pitches. It took a few minutes to set the stage for a live batting exhibition. After fouling a hanging curveball into the folded bleachers behing him, the lanky batsman cursed under his breath, then smirked: "Bring it on," he told Trevor. Trevor did. The expectant slugger swung and missed every ball Trevor threw. Timmy Olson shook his head: "Is this guy gonna play for us next spring, Coach? I've never seen anything like those sinkers he threw. Either I'm really bad or they are unhittable!"

The humbled batter walked toward Trevor and offered his hand, "You can play on my team anytime," he said. "Great job."

Coach Young was standing near Trevor's trainer. He asked Morrison, "Is that the same Windsong kid who busted his arm a few months ago?"

Morrison nodded without words.

"His stuff, that sinker pitch especially, is downright wicked."

Mickey wandered over to the two men. "Quite a demonstration wasn't it?"

"I'd say so. Father…I was thinking…if I were able to find some scholarship money…do you think…?"

"You'd have to talk to Trevor about that," Mickey said. "I have no idea."

Coach Young walked up to Trevor who was putting on his jacket and getting ready to leave the gym. "Is it okay if I see my AD about a baseball scholarship, Trevor? From Scholastica, you'd be just across the street from your brother at UMD?" Trevor's eyes showed little emotion, he looked to Travis who had just taken off his cather's gear, then to Mickey who was standing next to the coach: "I guess that's okay with me…I'd haf'ta talk to my mother first."

To Mickey, Trevor's response meant 'probably not'. Marella Windsong would find a way to 'rain on on Trevor's parade'. Another cliché!

30/ THE GIFT OF A CHIEF BENDER BOOK

Trainer Morrison and Coach Young left the gym and drove to the Bulldog Pub on Woodland Avenue to continue their conversation about Trevor Windsong, the young phenom they had just watched at the Scholastica gym. "I've been trying to remember a movie about a guy, a pitcher, that had an arm injury and when it was repaired he became much more effective. I think it was based on a true story," Morrison said. "But he was a much older guy if I'm remembering right."

Coach Young laughed, "Yeah…the guy's name was Morris, I think—Johnny or Jimmy Morris? Anyhow, he was like forty years old when he made a brief comeback—nothing spectacular, though. There's another big difference in these two stories if that's what you're getting at. Morris had already played and failed in the big leagues several years before he made his comeback."

"Really, then that story is a lot different than this Windsong thing. Apples and oranges." A light went on in Morrison's mind: "...*The Rookie*, that's the name of the movie. Help me...who played the pitcher?"

Young found the thread, "Dennis Quaid, I think—yeah, Quaid played Morris in the movie. He was good, had enough athleticism to pass himself off as a pitcher."

"I thought Kevin Costner would have done better– but Quaid must have been a jock before Hollywood. All-in-all, I thought the movie kinda sucked," Morrison said.

Coach Young agreed.

~

On the short drive back to the UMD campus to drop off the twins, Mickey suggested the three stop off at a popular pizza place just down the avenue from the Bulldog Pub. Both agreed with enthusiasm. Trevor quietly devoured most of the extra large pepperoni and mushroom pizza as Travis talked about the classes he was taking. "Freshman math is a snap. English 101 is the same stuff I had back in Hibbing. I took an advanced Spanish class as an elective, Jeeze am I lucky to have had a great high school teacher– I'm way ahead of most of the other kids."

When they were finished, Trevor finally entered the conversation. "I've been thinking, he said, "I don't really want to go to college now...maybe later. Maybe after I've had a chance to do some other things."

"You will ask your mother what she thinks about Coach Young's offer, won't you?" Mickey asked. "See what she thinks?"

Trevor gave Mickey a disgruntled look, "I don't tell my mom everything that goes on with me. And I don't need permission from any one to do things I wanna do."

Mickey might have suggested that Trevor's remark was inappropriate, instead he put up his hand in mock self-defense: "I'm not telling you what to do. Just asking." After the minor flare-up, nothing of any consequence was discussed. The forty minutes passed quickly. The trio left the pizzeria for Travis' dorm, and then to Trevor's pickup truck.

"Hope you'll keep in touch, Trevor," Mickey said as the young man stepped out of his car. "Let me know if I can help in any way."

Trevor gave him a strange 'help with what?' expression: "Yeah...okay, I guess." After closing the car door and stepping into the evening chill, he turned and rapped on the passenger window. Trevor's face creased into a faint smile, "Thanks for everything, I'll be in touch," he said.

~

On his drive across the long, narrow city, Mickey noted infrastructure repair work was still progressing months after the calamitous flood of mid-June. He wondered if Trevor's thoughts were as troubled as his own. He would have liked to help Trevor with life decisions that the boy seemed reluctant to come to grips with. Trevor was smart enough to do well in college and had incredible athletic potentials. But, the young man had built some rigid walls that kept him insolated from other people. In the short time that Mickey had known him, he could sense an edge on Trevor's personality that could cut him deeply if he tried to get too close. 'Don't meddle, Mick,' he reminded himself—knowing full well that he wasn't very good at simply watching things shape themselves without getting his hands in the mix. "None of your business," he told the face in his rearview mirror.

The next morning, Mickey stopped by a bookstore in the Fitger's Mall at the edge of downtown. He found the book he was looking for in the biography section. He purchased an iTunes gift card at the same time.

~

The following week, Trevor opened a package with no return address. The picture on the book's cover brought a smile to his face. Chief Bender, he knew, was a legendary American Indian pitcher and a distinguished Hall of Famer. What he didn't know was that Bender was born in Brainerd, Minnesota, and that he was the son of a white father and an Ojibwe mother. For a long moment, as he read the blurb on the back cover, Trevor Windsong had to swallow emotions and fight back tears. He went to his room and began reading a book he would treasure more than any other gift he had ever received.

The following day, Travis Windsong opened his campus mailbox and found a small envelope with no return address. Father Mickey must have sent something to his brother and wanted to keep things even. He laughed to himself and read the note:

Hi Travis: Sent Trevor a book and found something for you as well. Do you have any Dylan songs on your iPhone? If not...you might find something on iTunes. Enjoy. I'm living at St. Gerards out in west Duluth now –give me a call anytime. Mickey

Mickey's address and phone were written on the bottom of the note.

31/ MARELLA'S INVITATION

Mickey perused the *Duluth News Tribune's* account of the Tuesday election returns. As expected, Obama had carried Minnesota in his electoral vote rout of Mitt Romney. Obama's relection was no surprise but the margin of victory was. The Benton Park precincts surrounding St. Gerard's were largely populated by government dependents and voted overwhelmingly Democrat—as were Duluth and the Iron Range. Minnesota also voted 'NO' to an amendment that would define marriage as a union of one man and one woman.

Mickey could only lament the changing values of American society. For better or for worse, television entertainment would never again be like it was a generation ago. No more Nelson or Cleaver-like families would survive on prime time, nor would a Lucy or Carol Burnett, and…only reruns of Andy and Barney of Mayberry. If entertainment mirrored culture, it might be more and more of the Lindsey Lohans and the Kardashians and the Housewives of Orange County. For a long moment Mickey felt much older than his years. As he turned to the sports page, his phone rang.

"Father Moran?" Mickey recognized the voice on the other end of the line. "Yes…" the call gave him pause…he regained lost composure: "Yes," he repeated. "Can I call you Marella, or do you prefer Ms Windsong?"

"Marella works just fine for me." She cleared her throat. "First, I told Trevor to send you a thank-you note a week ago and I know he hasn't. He said he would write so I'm not going to hassle him about it."

"Well, it certainly isn't necessary. I just hope he liked the book."

"Liked is putting it much too mildly, he's reread it twice I think, and seems obsessed…no, not obsessed; but something I can't put a label on—maybe depressed or despondent? He's been more remote than I can remember, and he doesn't want me to read the story. Said it would upset me."

Mickey anticipated a deserved reprimand from the boy's mother. "I haven't read the book myself and I honestly don't know much about Chief Bender…but I'm sure the biography is…accurate. I'd hate to think…" He was putting himself in a box, "I'm sorry, I'll be more careful…"

"No, your intentions were noble. I'm sure the story is accurate and, I'm guessing, also quite profound. I did go on line and check some bio things. Bender's life was a tragic roller-coaster that didn't end well…I worry how a story like that might affect Trevor. He struggles, you know–" Marella took in a deep breath–"struggles with his own mixed blood. He's always kept his feelings to himself. It's like he's living behind his own defensive walls and doesn't want anyone to come inside and nose around. Do you know what I mean?"

"I do. He keeps his guard up…at least that's what I see." Mickey smiled at his earlier insights on the boy's reticent personality. "But I don't really know your son that well. My grampa, my late grampa I should say, was like that—kinda defensive, self-absorbed, like Trevor. When he was into his role as a cop—which was most of the time—he was very compressed, if that's the right word, he kept his feelings hidden from sight. Wouldn't let anybody get too close."

"Lately it's like walking on eggshells around here," Marella said. "And, with Travis away at school, my life has really changed. I miss him terribly—he's always been my buffer, my 'uplifter'. Travis sees the half-full glass…know what I mean?"

"I do."

"Anyhow, he'll be home for Thanksgiving, of course…and I really look forward to that." A long pause, "He called the other night and asked me for a favor." Another pause, "He asked me to invite you over to our house on Thanksgiving."

"That was thoughtful, I'd really enjoy that but…"

"I know, Father, I told him that you've probably already made plans to be with your family. But…I promised him I'd call and invite you over anyway."

Mickey ran a hundred thoughts across his mind in less than five seconds, "Yes, I have plans…but, how about if I stop by after I have dinner with my family? Maybe I could stop over for coffee or dessert or something?"

"That would be just fine. Trevor said he'd enjoy seeing you, too."

Her voice suggested a smile he could only imagine. "Let's

make it a date, then." Mickey bit his tongue—was that an appropriate thing to say?

"Great. Oh, there's something else. I don't quite know how to say it but…"

Mickey could recognize tension in another's voice from his years of experience in the confessional. He gave Marella a moment to collect herself.

"I've joined a prayer group. Indian women mostly. They meet on Tuesday nights over in Grand Rapids. Good people, many of them car pool from Cass Lake near Bemidji, some others from Leech Lake. I think most of the ladies are Lutheran, but some of us are Catholic. Anyhow, I did something I shouldn't have done without permission."

Mickey couldn't resist an interruption, "Something like dropping in on someone without an invitation?"

Marella laughed; "Nothing that bad, Father! Heaven sakes."

Her laugh was much softer than Mickey could have imagined–almost warm, and without any edges to it. His curiosity was piqued, he was having a 'normal' conversation with the woman Benjamin had called the 'ice lady'. He let her continue with her 'something' news.

"I told the ladies that I knew you…and that…maybe, just maybe . . . I could talk you into visiting our group sometime?"

"Oh…I'd be invited, then?" Marella caught his humor and laughed again. "Pick a date, Marella…I'll look forward to it.

~

After hanging up the landline phone on his desk, he paced the small rectory office. Was this simple invitation from Marella Windsong a breakthrough of sorts? Could it be something that might lead to something else? Pacing with hands folded behind his back was Mickey's way of slipping into a contemplative state. He said a prayer. "Lord, open my eyes to the opportunity I've needed in order to do the work you have entrusted to me." So far, he hadn't met anybody from the Leech Lake Band of Ojibwe…maybe this unexpected opportunity…?

He took three steps, then pivoted to his left, and took three more. 'Torts', sitting under the desk, turned his head with each of Mickey's turns; wondering what his master was so nervous about. The office space was small and cluttered and stale with age. For the past year Mickey had resolved to have it repainted and refurnished. He needed a brighter and more comfortable space to think and work in. He'd ask the contractors who were working on a bishop-approved church remodeling project next door if they could do a small add-on job in the rectory without busting his budget.

Feeling stifled inside, Mickey grabbed a light jacket from the coat tree by the rectory door, slipped into his Nikes, and before stepping outside into the brisk morning air, heard a whine at his heels. He took the leash off of the hook, attached it, and opened the door. As he sucked the chill deeply into his lungs, he felt his companion's protest—Torts had decided that he didn't want to walk outside after all. Mickey let the dog back inside and began a light jog down the street to loosen his limbs and open his mind to whatever needed to see the light of day. He continued saying his prayers but soon his thoughts carried him to other things—worldly things…

There was a phone call that Mickey had put off making. His reluctance was rooted in the fact that his meddling in other people's affairs had burned him more than once. He had scotch-taped the Peter Madigan phone number to the lampshade on his desk lamp where it served as a reminder. Why hadn't he asked Marella Windsong's permission to make that call while he had her on the phone moments before? It wasn't that he completely forgot—it was something else. Something best described as a 'gut-feeling'; such feelings did not require any justification. As he contemplated his decision not to make the call to Florida, he found his thoughts reversing direction. Acting on a curiosity wasn't really meddling—was it? If he were to glean something of value by taking an initiative, then he'd be in a better position to decide what to do about it. Share it, trash it, file it away for some future time?

The Benton Park neighborhood was quiet on this brisk Wednesday morning and Mickey had nothing on his agenda until an afternoon 'family counseling' meeting with a young couple in marital crisis and a parish council meeting at seven that evening. At some point he planned to call Benjamin and catch up on things; maybe the two of them could have lunch at the Fortune Bay Casino, only fifteen minutes from St. Gerards and a stone's throw from Ben's house. He hadn't talked with Ben in more than two weeks. But there was another call he would make first.

BOOK TWO

32/ PETER MADIGAN

Peter Madigan believed that his purpose in life had been wasted away years before. His defeated attitude, combined with his intimate relationship with Jack Daniels, were the stuff of a relationship doomed to bring him down. Added to the lethal mix was the added weight and general lethargy that went along with the booze, and you had the stuff of wanting to end it all. Lately, Pete Madigan had thought of how easily the .45 he kept in his bottom dresser drawer could give him that ultimate peace he wasn't going to find on this earth. He had just gotten off the phone with his estranged daughter Brenda, who seemed to be no better off than her father. She was trying to cope with a bitterly contested divorce, a job scaled back from full to part time, and a drinking problem not unlike that of her father's. Peter had agreed to send her some money to 'get through the month' knowing full well where most of it would be spent. But, who was he to judge his daughter's behavior or that of anybody else. The bottom line was quite simple: He still had some money—she didn't. He worried day and night that his savings wouldn't last much longer. He was living on a monthly social security check of $1800, his monthly bills were $1600, and he was dipping into his savings by midmonth. Every month!

Madigan had hoped to sell the once lovely cottage he had on Pike Lake, north of Duluth, but the mid-June storms had washed most of the steep bank that merged into a sandy beach, along with a stand of birch trees, down to the shoreline. To make matters worse, his insurance didn't cover the 'act of nature' damage to the landscape. Subsequently, his realtor had reduced the price to a point where he would be underwater himself—he owed more than the lakeshore property was currently worth.

In his youth, Pete's baseball skills were legendary. A dominating pitcher, he set high school records in strikeouts and shutouts that were unparalleled to this day. That was in '64 and '65, nearly fifty years ago. Several major league scouts had their eyes on him, but Pete was enamored with the American League championship team in his home state of Minnesota. The '65 Twins had made it to the World Series and nearly upset the highly favored Los Angeles Dodgers. Pete was a huge fan of Jim Perry, Jim Kaat, and Camilo Pascual—all Twins pitchers on that team—but he held a special admiration for Jim 'Mudcat' Grant, the ace of the Twins pitching staff that season. For the promise of an autographed Mudcat Grant game jersey and three thousand dollars, eighteen year-old Pete Madigan signed a minor league contract with his beloved Twins. He advanced rapidly through the system, making it up to the AAA affiliate Denver Bears in 1967. Ironically, Pete's career reached its peak in the Mile High city. Working on a shutout against Portland in the sixth inning, he blew his elbow. After three major surgeries and five attempts to make it back to the major leagues, Pete retired from the game he loved. He was only twenty-two at the time.

Fortunately he had made some friendships within the Twins organization and Calvin Griffith, the club owner, kept him on board in various capacities: doing some color commentary with Halsey Hall and Herb Carneal on the radio network, managing a rookie league team at Tinker Field in Orlando, and assisting with player development in various locations. By the 90's he was in charge of scouting for the Midwest region until he picked up a DWI in Peoria, Illinois. Since then, and for the past fifteen years, he had failed at jobs he could no longer remember.

Peter Madigan stared at the bottle on the kitchen counter top of his small condo on the third fairway of the Eagle Ridge Golf Club off the Daniels Parkway in Ft. Myers. He was behind in his association dues and was considering puting the two–bedroom unit up for sale in a soft market where he would lose even more money. The option of allowing the place to go into forclosure even sounded better than trying to sell. Either way, maybe he'd be better off going back to Minnesota for good and live out his remaining winters in the snow and subzero temperatures. He had been born in Duluth, graduated from East High School there, and always enjoyed spending the summer months up north. Back when he had money in the bank, he belonged to the Northland Country Club on Duluth's North Shore and hobnobbed with the rich and famous of the port city. He had outgrown Duluth in his twenties, and Minnesota in his fifties. Florida had the year-around sunshine and Minnesota too many gray days. As he contemplated going back he realized that he wouldn't fit there any better than he did here.

Pete looked away from the temptation across the room. Two weeks of sobriety would go for naught if he succumbed. He sipped the tepid coffee instead, slipping deeper into the consuming melancholy of self-pity. He had turned sixty-five the previous March, a day he wouldn't soon forget. He had been invited to dinner with Jerry Bell, an old friend and a top official with the Twins organization. After checking his mail and finding nothing more than a utility bill and an ad from the Fuccillo Kia dealership in nearby Cape Coral, he broke down in tears. No birthday cards. Not a one! Not from his daughter Brenda, not from his former girlfriend Susan (who never forgot a birthday), none from any of his golfing buddies, nothing from his closest friend back in Hibbing, a cop named Pack Moran. Angry and saddened by the loneliness he felt that day, Peter poured a tall glass of whiskey and sobbed—who gave a damn about him, anyway. A second glass straight up, then a third…and in the late afternoon he passed out. When he awoke at nine that evening, still groggy and suffering a bout of acid reflux, he remembered his dinner invitation from Jerry Bell. The memory of that day from months before still gripped and tore at his stomach.

Peter Madigan was close to tears again and the bottle was inviting him to find oblivion. Then…his phone rang.

~

Father Mickey Moran couldn't pass on an opportunity to meddle! His penchant for getting involved in the affairs of other people was always motivated by the best of intentions—but…too often his interventions weren't viewed as kindly or caring and too often they didn't end up as well as he had hoped. He called these altruistic attempts to 'make things better' a *'priest's privilege and duty'*; the bishop called them *'being nosey and uncalled for'*. Occasionally, he got his nose into places where it didn't belong and either embarrassed himself or the church he served. Most recently he had followed up on a malicious rumor that the daughter of a parishioner had been engaging in untoward behavior. Concerned, Mickey paid her a courtesy visit just to 'see how she was doing' and invite her to join a Catholic women's guild at St. Gerards—a priest's privilege and duty for sure. Sarah Donovan, a gossip-mongrel from the Benton Park neighborhood, saw him enter the young woman's duplex and word went rapidly around the community that Father Moran was seeing 'that immoral woman'. As it turned out, the woman— Penny Trigg—was not involved in anything beyond doing housecleaning for some wealthy families on London Road. Although both Mickey and Penny got a 'kick' out of the local misinformation, Bishop Bremmer did not.

Mickey punched in the numbers he had written down and taped on the lampshade. The afternoon exhibition Trevor Windsong had made in the St. Scholastica gym the week before was still fresh in his memory. If he was going to be seeing Trevor next week, after a Thanksgiving meal with his family, he'd like nothing better than to bring some good baseball news along with him. In addition to helping out where he thought the Windsongs would appreciate his thoughtfulness, Mickey enjoyed surprises.

After the fifth ring, Peter Madigan picked up his phone, resting only inches from the bottle he had placed on the lampstand next to his worn sofa. He was about to have one—just one—drink to settle his nerves.

He mumbled a 'Thank God' to himself as he lifted his cell phone instead of the bottle. Turning his back from temptation, he walked out of the living room and into the kitchen, as far away from Jack Daniels as possible. When Father Mickey introduced himself to Pete, the old man smiled for the first time in days. Pack Moran's grandson, the Duluth priest...maybe God was watching over him today. "Say, Father," Pete said, "I've gotta apologize for not making it up for your grandfather's funeral last spring. I was involved in some business down here and just couldn't get away," he lied. To admit that he didn't have the money for an airplane ticket was an unthinkable admission. "A wonderful man, Pack. One of the 'real people' I liked to say—nothing pretentious about that guy." The two men shared Pack memories for several minutes.

Mickey broke the ice, "Mr. Madigan, my dad gave me your number and thought you might still have some ties with the Twins. He told me that the two of you golfed in the same flight a while back."

"Yeah, your dad kicked my butt...I mean, if I remember...he beat me five and four in the match. Amos is golfing better than I remember—or I'm much worse."

Mickey withheld any comment about Madigan's golf and felt it was time to get to the point of his call. "You still with the Twins, Mr. Madigan?"

Pete had expected the priest would be asking for Twins tickets or an autographed baseball, things that in the past he could easily take care of. He lied a second time, "Oh yeah...still connected with the team, not as closely as before, but still keep myself in the loop, so to speak." His one and only identity with folks back home was his former associations with the Twins—he would cling to that mistaken perception like a lifeline.

"Great! I'm sure you get calls like this all the time, but..." Mickey went on to sing the praises of Trevor Windsong. "How does one go about getting a 'look-see' with a Twins coach or a talent scout? I mean, is there someone you know who would be willing to take a look at the young man? I'm sure that he'd put on an impressive show. Matter of fact, Coach Young at Scholastica thinks the boy's got some awesome stuff."

How does one say 'no' to a priest? Madigan wondered. He wished he still had a legitimate contact with somebody in the Twins system, but he didn't. He hadn't talked with Jerry Bell since he stood up the Twins official back in March. He didn't even know what staff might be down in Ft. Meyers this time of year. Pete Madigan hadn't been honest so far, maybe another half-truth wouldn't hurt. "Might be kinda hard to send someone up there to take a look—you still in Duluth?"

Mickey briefly explained what he was doing for the diocese, then suggested: "What if I were to take the boy down there, to Ft. Meyers. To the Twins' Lee County training facility? I'm planning to be down there just before Christmas anyhow."

Pete Madigan searched his thoughts for something to say—something to discourage the priest without actually offending him. When in doubt, he usually chose the wrong thing to say. "Sure…that shouldn't be a problem at all. Around Christmas time? Yeah…I could probably arrange something." Madigan silently thanked God for the timing of the priest's request. Nobody would likely be around the sports complex during the Christmas season. The top brass didn't usually arrive until February when the Twins opened their training camp. "Probably be best for everybody concerned if we get it done before the first of the year," Pete suggested.

Mickey tried to keep his enthusiasm in check but failed: "You pick any date near Christmas and we'll be there!"

Pete Madigan was up to his ears in stress. He looked back to the lampstand and the bottle smiling back at him. "Say, Father…how about I take a look at the lad myself? Don't mean to toot my own horn, but I was a pretty good scout in my day."

"That would be fantastic." Now Mickey was stressing, was he

getting in over his head? He hadn't even talked to Trevor about any of this—and, even more importantly, he hadn't talked to Marella Windsong. Once again he was putting himself in an awkward situation. He would be honest: "Mr. Madigan, Pete, I must tell you that I haven't broached the possibility with the boy or his mother yet. I know Trevor, that's the boy's name, would like to show off his stuff, but…?"

Silently, Peter Madigan hoped that the boy would back down or the mother would put a kibosh on the priest's plan. That would spare him a ton of embarrassment. In a pinch, however, he might be able to bribe someone on the grounds crew to let them into the complex where he might be able to stage a sham workout. "I hope you can work things out…" he lied again.

Now, he badly needed a drink. More than badly, just one…half a glass. No more. On the bookcase near his television set, he saw the picture of himself and his daughter, Brenda, standing on a rock in Duluth's popular Canal Park. Lake Superior, splashing large waves over the rocks, and splendid sunshine were a perfect backdrop for a snapshop. His girlfriend, Susan, took the picture and shared that wonderful day with Pete and Brenda. He had his arm over his daughter's shoulders, she was a smiling and happy young woman—the picture had been taken three years ago, before her divorce, at a time when Brenda drank lemonade and diet coke. A time when Pete and Susan were together and happy.

"One last thing before I let you get away…" Peter said, "I'd like to ask a favor of you– but I don't want you to feel obligated in any way." In his own awkward manner, he asked Father Mickey to look in on his daughter Brenda. "She's going through an awfully tough time." Pete was certain that the priest would understand her situation. "Since her divorce, I think she's been drinking more than she ought to." Peter Madigan had another pang of conscience: "Father, let me be more candid…my daughter is pretty close to rock bottom with her drinking and her depression." Had he been even more candid, he would admit to being in the same place, only two thousand miles and fifty degrees Fahrenheit to the south of Proctor, Minnesota, where Brenda was living.

33/ A LETTER FROM TRIPALMS

Mickey found Benjamin Little Otter sitting by himself in the Black Bear coffee shop located off the lobby in the large, crowded casino. A decanter of coffee rested like a copper centerpiece on the narrow table, a pair of menus were set at right angles. Ben was wearing his lumberjack plaid shirt and a green John Deere cap. He was intent, running his large index finger down a column of classified ads of the morning paper. Mickey stepped behind him and pulled the cap down over his friend's eyes.

"What's that?" Ben turned in his chair, lifted his brim, looked up, "Hey...yer lookin' bright-eyed this morning. What's the big news yer itchin' to tell me 'bout?"

Mickey explained everything about the gym exhibition at St. Scholastica the previous week and his conversation with a Twins official down in Ft. Myers. "I'll– I mean both of us– will be going down to Florida next month for the dedication of the new church in TriPalms. Don't say no because I won't hear it. Now I need some advice, my friend." Mickey explained that he had arranged a tryout of sorts for Trevor. That's if...well, it's a pretty big 'if'...because I haven't talked with Trevor yet—nor his mother. I'm praying that everything will work out." He looked at the big Indian across the booth for a reaction. "What say you? Think they will be interested? Willing to take a shot at it?"

Benjamin shook his huge head, brushed a strand of black hair from over his eye, smiled: "Sounds ta'me like yer gonna do it regardless of what I think." He frowned, 'Good luck. Las I heard, Marella tossed ya outta her house." His laugh was deep and sincere, yet as always, pleasant to Mickey's ears: "You've won over the boys, though. Travis says yer 'cool', Trevor...well, Trevor—he ain't much on compliments of any kind...he says yer different from any priest he's ever heard of. That's pretty good comin' from him. Oh...he a'ready tol me about the pitchin' thing the other day. He's been keepin' in touch pretty reglar."

"Well, maybe things have chaged a bit. Maybe it's my turn to laugh now. What I didn't tell you, Mr. Little Otter, was that Marella called me...yes—she called me! I think it was the night before last. Anyhow, she invited me to visit with a prayer group she's joined up north."

Benjamin's jaw dropped, "I find that perty hard ta believe, Father. That don sound nothin' like the Marella I know. I don think she's called me in...gosh, I can't member when that might'a been. Weeks?"

"Maybe I'm a bit overly optimistic, Ben, but I think the prayer group invitation is a break-through of sorts. For the first time I'm not butting-in, I've actually been invited somewhere, even welcomed. How about that? And speaking of invites, I'm going to stop by her place next week—Thanksgiving Day. For, better hold on to your chair now, an *invited* visit. I like that word—invited. What do you say to that, Benjamin?"

"Yer on a roll, seems to me. See, ya didn't need me to help with things, did'ja? Yer better off doin' things by yerself."

"Listen, my friend...and get this through your thick head...without you, none of this happens. Without you I would never have taken this position; without you I never would have met the Windsongs; without you I'd be much less of a person and priest than what I am. Ben, don't always short-change your self. I hate when you do that! You're a good man. A very good man! Honest and trustworthy and..." Mickey's emotions welled inside, "Okay, enough of that. Pick what you want on the menu—it's on me this time."

"It's always on you, Father. I ain't never bought you so much as a cup of coffee. How 'bout you let me this time? Those nice words you gave deserve it."

Mickey's 'yes', brought a satisfied grin to Ben's face.

"Now, tell me who you know up in Cass Lake…or Leech Lake. That's territory we need to visit one of these days."

"You ain't never givin' up are ya?'

~

Back at the St. Gerard's rectory, Mickey put out the dog, filled his water bowl, and checked his mail. A blue, card-sized envelope stood out from the bills and ads. Whenever he saw the Venice, Florida postmark, his eyes lit up. He recognized the handwriting on the envelope to be that of Maria Olivio from TriPalms. Maria, a freshman at Florida Gulf Coast University, wrote him a letter almost weekly with news about her family, her college coursework, and things going on in the community. Often, her little brother Miguel sent a note along with her letter. Maria was doing well, but thought that her last test in Biology was only a B. "The teacher didn't ask any questions about the things I studied." Mickey remembered saying the same things about his instructors in college and seminary. "I'm going to see him about that, Father. I've become more assertive than you might think—not in a bad way, though." Lovely and reserved, Maria was so filled with life and hope these days. Mickey couldn't stretch his imagination far enough to picture an outspoken Maria Olivio. His thoughts filled with happy memories of his time in TriPalms. Each day was a day closer to his return visit only a few weeks away. All that Maria would say about the new church was that it was lovely and nearly completed: "Everybody is so excited and can't wait to see their wonderful *padre!*" Maria had told him in an earlier letter that Mr. Munoz, Mickey's dear friend in TriPalms, had told everybody not to forward any photos of the church to Father Moran. Hector Munoz was determined that the church and the planned activites be a Christmas surprise for the priest. Nobody would ever think of disobeying the wishes of Mr. Munoz.

Miguel's one page note reminded Mickey of the boy's greatest wish: "I still want to be a priest like you someday." His P.S. said: "I hope you can bring 'Torts' along with you." 'Torts' had been a stray dog that the people of TriPalms fed and tolerated for years before Mickey's arrival. Torts was 'Tortuga', a shaggy, shedding mongrel, appropriately given the Spanish name for a turtle because he was lazy and slow of foot. For some reason the dog had attached himself to Mickey, and the folks of TriPalms thought it was only proper that he go to Minnesota with his adopted master.

Only last week, Mickey spoke with his 'teammates' in the Tri-Palms revitalization project—Larry Wheeler, Hector Munoz, and Bishop Cordoba of the Venice diocese. All agreed that he would be amazed at the progress that had been made in the months since Mickey had returned to his duties in Minnesota. Cordoba's involvement went far beyond TriPalms and into other Hispanic enclaves, from Venice to Everglades City in southwestern Florida. What Father Mickey had started quite by accident (or Divine intervention) had become a model for other immigrant communities. Catholic businessmen, religious leaders of other denominations, and church congregations themselves were being pressed into the rehabilitation efforts: "We've got generations of ignorance and general neglect to try and make right. All of us as Christians share in that responsibility." Cordoba's appeal spread throughout the diocese.

Back home in west Duluth, another church and community was experiencing a spiritual epiphany of its own. Upon the news that Bishop Bremmer had given their historic church a reprieve of sorts, the St. Gerard's parish council had committed most of its meager treasury to a major renovation. Mickey had corralled some 'high rollers' from throughout Duluth (and some benefactors from his previous St. Francis parish in Brainerd) to bankroll an addition to the church that would house social activities and a new playground in the vacant lot across the street from the church.   With Father Mickey as a permanent fixture in the parish once again, monthly revenues were inching upward. Bishop Bremmer was planning a multi-parish bazaar at the DECC on the Duluth waterfront to raise additional monies for the St. Gerard's rehab and for the vocations fund he kept privately. Mickey once told his friend Mario that…"I know our bishop is a spirtual guy, but Bremmer would have been a whiz in the world of finance."

To that, Mario said: "What makes you think he isn't already?" Over the years, Bremmer had done investment wonders with the diocese finances. He's got some shrewd contacts on Wall Street.

34/ SPEAKING OF SAINT KATERI

On the Monday and Tuesday prior to Thanksgiving, Mickey notched a pair of modest achievements. His meeting with Pete Madigan's daughter Brenda revealed issues that her father must have either been unaware of, or failed to disclose. The woman was living in an apartment in a rundown woodframe house across from the Powerhouse Bar on Fifth Street in Proctor. Brenda was a mess! Her life was out of control. At first hostile and belligerent, she gradually softened, then had an emotional collapse. "Help me," she finally pleaded. "My broken and depressed father doesn't give me anything but a few dollars now and then, my womanizing ex won't return my phone calls; nobody gives a damn whether I live or die."

"I do. God does. That's why I'm here." Mickey persuaded the mid-fortyish woman to contact his friend Benjamin and to join the AA group that Benjamin belonged to in Cloquet. He promised Brenda that he would keep in touch with her and keep her in his prayers. At the door as Mickey was leaving she took his elbow, "There's something else…my dad is a drunk, too. I love him despite everything…" she paused to consider her next words. "Do you know that he's really not much better off than I am? He's even burned all the bridges with his beloved Twins–they no longer want to have anything to do with him."

Mickey left Brenda's apartment with a sinking feeling. Now what? If Pete Madigan was a fraud and a liar...he was betting on a crippled horse. Back at the rectory, while checking the phone messages Mrs. Murray had left on his desk, he did some soul-searching. Should he get back in touch with Pete Madigan now...or wait until he had an opportunity to talk with the Windsongs in a few days? If Madigan was a has-been, there was still enough time to find someone else who could help with making connections. A week or two ago, a sports program personality had interviewed the Twins' President about the 2013 Twins—a man by the name of Dave St. Peter. St. Peter sounded like a straightup guy. The radio man, Paul Allen, asked tough questions and St. Peter handled them with clarity and conscience.

Mickey got a familiar whiff before feeling Torts curl up and nudge his feet under the desk. He looked down into Torts' big browns, "Excuse yourself for goodness sakes," then he laughed. Torts always brought back memories of his brief time in Florida. "You wanna go back home for a few days, old dog? You miss Miguel and all the TriPalms kids?"

Torts simply drooled and lapped his nose with his tongue as if to say, 'whatever.'

~

On Tuesday afternoon, Mickey took Highway #2 north to Grand Rapids, where he would have dinner with Father Gregory at St. Joseph's Catholic church. After that, he'd meet with Marella Windsong's prayer group in the adjacent school. Marella, wearing a burnt orange sweater over a white blouse, designer jeans, and stylish black leather boots, stood out like a rose among a patch of cucumbers.

She introduced Mickey to the group of nearly forty—mostly women. Normally the group consisted of no more than twelve, but the visiting priest from Duluth was an obvious attraction everywhere he went. Mickey spoke about Saint Kateri, who lived and died more than 300 years ago. She was the daughter of a Mohawk father and an Algonquin Christian mother. She grew up in a place where there was great hostility toward Christians. He spoke on her devotion to prayer, teaching prayer to children, and helping the sick and the elderly. "She had a purity of heart that raised her up to the communion of saints, and is a role model to all of us—women and men, red and white, Catholic and Protestant." Mickey answered questions before praying with the group and joining them for coffee and cookies afterwards.

Before returning to Duluth he spoke briefly with Marella and a friend of hers from Hibbing by the name of Janette, who had a son serving with the Marines in Afghanistan. He promised Marella's friend that he would keep her son in his prayers and assured Marella that he prayed for her sons as well. Marella offered Mickey a box of cinnamon rolls as he headed for his car: "They're even better than the ones you missed out on back in September. These are filled with gratitude for the good things that you do." Mickey nearly lost his balance and dropped the box at the compliment–he decided not to mess up a pleasant 'good bye' with any baseball meddlings.

35/ PLANNING A ROAD TRIP

The days and weeks between Thanksgiving and Christmas fly as if they are in a hurry to get to a new year and start over again. Every third or fourth day, Mickey was in communication with someone back in TriPalms, Florida. Most often he was given an updated project briefing by either Larry Wheeler or Hector Munoz. Both men, however, were careful to explain things in general terms without divulging much in the way of specific information. Larry had been the first to plunge himself into the renewal project with his commitment to construct a community building for the predominantly poor residents of the crowded and decrepit Hispanic community. Munoz was an entrepreneur and an unsatiable whirlwind. Coordinating the sacred christening ceremonies for the new Catholic Church was Bishop Cordoba. At last count, eight priests from the Venice Diocese would participate in an elaborate procession that would begin the required blessings.

The ceremony in St. Michael's Church would be televised and broadcast to an overflow crowd in the new community building and into the huge tents erected outside the church for the occassion. Bishop Bremmer from Duluth would co-celebrate with his friend Raul Cordoba in the December twenty-second dedication. The planning was meticulous, the anticipation beyond measure. Mickey's host family, while he was living in TriPalms, were the Olivios. They, along with their neighbors, would be hosting a social on that Saturday evening, "You must bring your guitar, Father...we will all be in a mood to sing along," Maria had written in a recent letter. The memories of his time in TriPalms flooded him with emotions that tightened his throat—emotions that would be even greater when shared once again with those he loved.

On Friday, December 14, Mickey cried along with millions of Americans. In the small Connecticut community of Newtown, a tragedy of unthinkable horror struck at the very heart of this great country. A deranged killer forced his entry into the Sandy Hook Elementary School and gunned down twenty children, most of whom were only six years old, before taking his own life. In all, twenty-six were killed including the boy's mother and school personnel. Mickey remembered his time at St. James parish in west Duluth. Pictures of the elementary children he taught on Wednesday mornings while he was there flashed across his mind's eye. How any rational person could look into those beautiful little faces and kill was beyond comprehension. Mickey prayed for the families, the community, the school…and for the soul of Adam Lanza, the twenty year old who killed those innocent children.

~

Mickey's conversations with Pete Madigan, the alleged Twins official, were less frequent and much cooler these days. Although Mickey had given everything to God, his optimism had been dampened by Brenda Madigan's revelation that her father's career with the Twins was history. He kept that information to himself. When they talked, Peter was always gracious and couldn't thank Mickey enough for his intervention with his daughter. Brenda had completed her first month of sobriety in her Cloquet AA group. Benjamin Little Otter had offered to be there for her at any time—night or day. Pete Madigan continued to assure Mickey that everything was in order, but when pressed for particulars, he offered less than scanty details. "Not to worry, Father, I'll give your kid a good looking-over; you've got my word on that!"

Peter Madigan's 'word' was highly suspect. When explaining what he was doing for Trevor to the boy's mother over homemade pumpkin pie on Thanksgiving evening, Mickey was candid. "I can only hope for the best." Trevor was quietly excited, asked a few questions, and focused mainly on his mother's reactions to the priest's idea. Regardless of anything his mother might decide, Trevor's mind was made up—he was going to go to Florida 'come hell or high water!' Travis showed the most excitement of the three Windsongs sitting around the table. He would be on semester break in December and had never been south of the Twin Cities in his life. It was agreed that he would travel along and that the three men would share with the driving. Without pushing too hard, and with good weather, they could easily make the trip down to Florida in three days.

Travis was a font of questions: "How far are the beaches from where we'll be staying, Father? Will it be a lot warmer—like in the seventies, down there in December? Will any of the Twins players be around to watch Trevor? Will I be able to use my Spanish in this place we're going?" What intrigued Travis the most, however, was the Thomas Edison-Henry Ford museum in Ft. Myers. "I've checked out the museum's webpages and it sounds like an awesome place. Promise me we'll find time to visit there."

Secretly, Marella was hoping for an invitation to make the trip along with her sons—even if she would have to drive her own car. She had plenty of vacation time built up and had managed to save some 'rainy day' money after paying installments on Trevor's medical bills. She hung on Mickey's answers to Travis' questions. Mickey sensed Marella's interest. His parents would already be down in Naples for the winter and would be honored guests at the mass and reception following—and they had lots of room in their Naples home—if...? He had already asked Benjamin to go down to TriPalms as his guest, and Father Mario was going to drive down as well—why not Marella, too. He'd enjoy sharing his special day with as many friends as possible.

The boys went to bed around ten, and Mickey stayed for 'one last cup'. Marella talked about her prayer group. "They thoroughly enjoyed your talk and your prayers. Since your visit we've added four new members." Mickey was pleased and thanked her again for the invitation–and the delicious cinnamon rolls "I'm hoping to get up to Cass Lake after the holidays...maybe I'll meet some of your friends again."

It was getting late as Mickey fidgeted with his wristwatch. Mickey pushed slightly away from the table. "Well…" his yawn was genuine, "I'm keeping you up pretty late and I've got some driving ahead." He stood. "Duluth and my bed are about ninety minutes away and I hate driving Highway 37 in the dark." Mickey bit his tongue, what a stupid way to verbalize that he was very tired…'my bed is ninety minutes away'. . . What connotation did that have? He didn't see any reaction from Marella and added, "I'm always expecting a deer to leap out of the woods in front of me." At the door, he paused: "Let me throw something out for you to consider…but don't feel obligated in any way…but…if you'd like to join us on our mini-vacation, you are more than welcome. Your brother-in-law is coming along…?" Mickey framed the invitation in a question.

Marella's jaw dropped, "I'd love it," she stammered without so much as a moment's thought. "I've got vacation time and money put away—oh, Father, thank you so much for the invitation." Mickey had not seen such emotion before. She leaned toward him and put a soft kiss on his cheek. Her face immediately flushed: "Oh…my gosh– I didn't mean to do that, Father—I'm so sorry, I'm so embarrassed."

Mickey laughed, made light of the situation, "Happens all the time, Marella. My irresistible charm is almost legendary in these parts."

~

Tony Angelo was an assistant groundskeeper at the Twins' Lee County training facility. He was one of the few in the organization who hadn't written Pete Madigan off as a lost cause. Angelo was conflicted; he didn't want to be part of any scheme that might cost him his job, but he was the father of five kids and short on cash this

Christmas. "For fifty bucks, sure. I can't see any problems with letting you in the gate. Nobody's around these days anyhow. Half hour or forty five minutes shouldn't bother anybody." Angelo would open the back gate to the south practice fields and let them use the facilities they needed. There were pitching mound enclosures between fields one and two in the minor league complex. A meeting time and place were agreed upon.

36/ 'WHY ME, LORD?'

The trip to Florida was an adventure for all six travelers. Crossing Wisconsin from Superior to Madison, Mickey and the twins (and Torts) rode together in Mickey's travel-worn '98 Civic. Father Mario had borrowed a 'Town and Country' van from a parishioner and had ample room for most of the luggage. Benjamin and Marella rode with him. In Madison, the arrangements changed and the boys rode with Father Mario while Ben and Marella (and Torts) rode with Mickey. Had a vote been taken, Torts would have been dropped off just outside of Hibbing—the dog was 'gassy' and the car windows had to be rolled down every few miles. The third rearrangement, south of Rockford, Illinois, had Mickey, Mario, and Benjamin in the van, allowing Marella to drive his Civic with her sons and Torts as passengers. Everyone got to know everyone else quite well. Torts was the only passenger that didn't change cars and those who rode with him were left with his sheddings on their clothing and an unpleasant burn in their nostrils. After more than seven hundred miles, the travel wearied Minnesotans spent their first night at a Motel 6 in Mt. Vernon, Illinois.

Mickey treated his troupe with two large pepperoni pizzas, one sausage and onion, and one 'house special' with everything on it at a local pizza shop. Afterwards, Mario nudged all seven of them inside a small ice cream shop next door and insisted that each have a cone—his treat. Travel weary, tired, and stuffed with too much food, sleep came easily to all but Mickey. Mickey had mistakenly ordered coffee after his meal; and secondly, Mario who shared his room, was a mild snorer; and lastly, Torts was having flatulence attacks at the foot of Mickey's bed. Before turning in, all had agreed to meet in the motel lobby at six-thirty in the morning.

In the early afternoon of the following day, the two-vehicle tandem passed through the country music mecca of Nashville. Trevor marveled at the football stadium off to the right of the heavily traveled highway where the professional Titans played. Travis, leaning over his brother at the rear passenger window, was awed by the incredible urban skyline dominated by the distinctive architecture of the ATT Building's antenna towers. Travis gave his fellow passengers an informed report—gleaned from his iPad–on the history and tradition of the 'Grand Ole Opry'. Two hours later, everybody delighted at the mountains banking the rim of Chattanooga in far eastern Tennessee.

"Chattanooga was was the gateway to the heart of the Confederacy," Father Mario said. Being an avid Civil War history enthusiast, he delighted in the feelings of 'being there...where it all happened back in 1863'. "Col. Horatio Van Cleve and the Second Minnesota Regiment fought valiantly in the Union's victories here." He pointed toward the fifteen-hundred-foot-high escarpment of Lookout Mountain on their right." The Rebs held that position. The fighting there and at Missionary Ridge up ahead was intense and lasted for more than two months. General Grant came to Chattanooga and took charge of the armies there..." During Mario's history lesson, Travis asked relevant questions while Trevor listened to his music.

At the eastern edge of Chattanooga, they pulled off the highway for a 'potty stop'. Torts could only go about four hours without risking a bladder incident, and Benjamin about the same without having a nicotine attack. Each morning at the motel, and again at the gas stops, Marella filled her thermos with coffee and purchased peanuts, Twinkies, and granola bars for everybody to munch on. While Mickey was taking Torts for a walk, Benjamin slipped off by himself to enjoy a Marlboro, and the others found a picnic table and enjoyed snacks in the shirtsleeve December weather of Tennessee.

Late on the second day they traveled through the canyons of Atlanta—unfortunately, they were caught in late rush-hour traffic. Passing through the megalopolis took more than an hour. Marella and Benjamin, traveling with Mickey at the time, were breathtaken at the enormity of the southern metropolis. Travel-wearied once again, they spent their second night in Perry, Georgia. The 'home stretch' on day three was brushed with marvelous Florida sunshine. Late on Thursday afternoon, the six travelers arrived in Venice.

Mickey's busy schedule would begin the following Friday morning with a meeting and 'grand tour' of the revitalized TriPalms community with Hector Munoz and Larry Wheeler. "Just you, Father Mickey...we don't want to sound snobbish, but we're...so anxious and so proud...we want to share first impressions with our beloved friend from the northern tundra," Larry said.

∼

Before dinner at the bishop's residence in Venice on Friday evening, the Minnesotans spent an hour on the sugar-sandy Gulf beaches of Venice. Marella and Father Mario went on a shelling trip along the shoreline, filling plastic sandwich baggies with colorful shells; Travis and Benjamin went for a dip in the chilly waters; Trevor jogged along the shoreline by himself. Mickey watched them all enjoying the bountiful sun and glittering, blue-green Gulf from a railing on the historic Venice Pier. He felt truly blessed with the friendships of his companions and for the reasons they were with him here in Florida. The words of a favorite Kris Kristofferson song meandered through his thoughts: *"Why me Lord, what have I ever done to deserve even one of the pleasures I've known...Tell me Lord, what did I ever do that was worth love from you and the kindness you've shown...* " His eyes misted with pent emotions as he hummed the melody to himself.

In the early evening, before dinner with the bishop, the group watched the dramatic setting of the sun; the wonder of seeing the golden orb drop out of sight on the western horizon brought goose-bumps to all and applause from the hundreds of others along the railings of the Venice Pier.

37/ MR. HECTOR MUNOZ

Of the many people that Mickey had known in his thirty-four years, Father Mario and Hector Munoz were the two people he admired more than any others. His connections with Mario were the stuff of spirituality and sincere friendship. His ties with Hector were ties of admiration and respect. The tall Cuban was a legendary humanitarian in southwest Florida, a self-made millionaire, and a role model for every Hispanic he touched through his philanthropy. More than any single person, Hector was the driving force behind the building of the new Saint Michael's Church in TriPalms: First he went through the myriad of Catholic bureaucracy for approval, then he conceptually designed it, and finally he built it. He accomplished all of this in seven whirlwind months.

After parking his car on the newly blacktopped road leading into TriPalms, Mickey approached the tall man wearing the crisp *Zegna* white shirt and the pressed *Banana Republic* khaki slacks that were his trademark outfit. With a smile that matched the Friday morning sunshine, Mickey greeted his friend. "Hector...it's wonderful beyond words to see you again." The two men met at the new sign marking the entry to TriPalms: '*Where Sunshine and Spirit Come Together*'. The brightly painted wooden sign stood twelve feet from corner to corner and pictured three palms bowing in the wind with vivid sunrays behind them. Mickey hugged the man, despite his knowledge of how uncomfortable displays of affection made Hector feel. To his surprise, Hector reciprocated the embrace and smiled down into the eyes of the shorter man. "It's so good to have you back, if only for a few days, Father. *Dios le bendice! Amigo.*"

Mickey thanked him for the blessing, "I can't wait to see all that you and Larry and the folks down here have done."

"A labor of love, Father. Our sign expresses our feelings quite well, don't you think?"

Mickey nodded, "It's simply perfect! Colorful and uplifting— what a change all this is from my first visit here in what seems…my friend…almost like a lifetime ago. Say, I've been told that you're living here in TriPalms now. That surprises me." Hector could afford to live anywhere he wanted and build a house as big as he wanted. His business interests and timely investments over the years had earned him a ranking somewhere at the edges of the *Forbes 'Fortune 500'.*

"I was hoping that you, and the boys you brought along with you, might stay with me—I've got two bedrooms and baths and a pair of roll-away beds."

"Haven't I told you, our little Minnesota contingent has expanded to six, Hector. The boys will be staying with their mother in Venice—they've already checked in to a motel there. You'll probably meet them, along with Mario and Benjamin, later today or tomorrow for sure." Mickey shielded his eyes from the bright eastern sun. He realized how much he missed the sunshine that blessed nearly every day. The things about northern winters that bothered him the most weren't the cold and snow, rather the seemingly endless stretch of days without seeing the sun. "Well, my friend…I'm ready for the TriPalms tour that you promised me," Mickey said. "More than ready…I'm anxious!"

Hector gave an exaggerated bow, "The grand tour begins right now. We'll be taking my pickup. Hope that's okay with you."

"Just fine, Hector."

Hector's voice took a playful tone: "Have you ever played pin the tail on the donkey?"

Mickey puzzled at the strange question. "Yeah…when I was a kid. Why?"

"Because I've brought along a blindfold, Father. I want you to see your church before you see anything else that's been going on in TriPalms these past few months."

Once inside the white Dodge Ram 1500, a blindfolded Father Mickey imagined the first turn onto Calle de El Cid, where the gas station and HME (Hector Munoz Enterprises) maintenance shops hugged the road; and then, what seemed like another three blocks onto what he remembered to be La Calle Decimo. Hector's clever idea allowed Mickey's imagination to generate pictures and memories. "I think I know exactly where I am right now," Mickey said.

Hector chuckled, "Another block, Father. Can you remember the worn-down-to-bare-dirt field where the kids played soccer?"

Mickey's mental picture was vivid. "How could I ever forget? Yes I remember. My goodness there are so many wonderful memories here that I get choked up. The kids made me play goalie because I couldn't keep up with them. And, how fondly I remember the sing-along concerts we had there." Mickey's wide smile loosened the blindfold but he caught it in time and retied it behind his head. "I'm going to walk up and down every street in TriPalms before I leave—say hello to all the folks."

Although Mickey couldn't see Hector's face, he knew the tall Cuban was enjoying the experience as much as he was. Hector spoke: "You'll love the new fenced-in soccer field, it's been relocated to a site down by the river; not far from where I'm living. Our friend Larry added the athletic fields to the community renewal designs shortly after you left for Minnesota. Believe me, our kids have great pride in having one of the best soccer and baseball fields in this area. They take good care of it, cut the grass, trim the shrubs, even scrub the bleachers every so often. You'll be amazed at how green our little town has become."

"Then…what's happened to the old field?"

Hector's laugh was hearty. "You'll see for yourself." Hector eased to a stop, "Just a minute, Father, don't take off the blindfold just yet. I'll help you get out of the truck."

Mickey could hear someone nearby clear their throat, then a child's giggle, "I'm feeling kinda strange, Hector…what's going on out here?"

"One second…" When Mickey was safely out of the truck and the blindfold was removed, Mickey saw the gathered crowd. There must have been a thousand people crowded into the newly surfaced public square and down the narrow streets radiating outward. In the front row, closest to where he was standing, he saw the Olivios: Alexi and his wife Carina, Alexi's brother Alberto and his family. Mickey beamed and his heart caught in his throat as the first person rushing toward him was little Miguel Olivio, fully five inches taller than Mickey remembered from the previous March.

"Father, you are home again," the ten year old said in high pitch. "Welcome, we love you." He tugged Mickey's elbow, "Did Torts come with you?" Mickey nodded, lifting his eyes in total wonderment. For once in his life, Mickey was absolutely speechless. Walking slowly behind Miguel was his lovely sister, Maria Olivio, her silky dark hair shining in the sun, her white smile radiant, her striking emerald green dress clinging to her slender body in the wind. "I've worn your favorite color, Father…" she smiled self-consciously as she approached with her arms open. Mickey accepted the hug from Marial, then gave not-so-little Miguel an embrace as well: "My family," Mickey said, "My wonderful second family, God bless you all." Mickey shook a hundred hands before Hector intervened. "Later, everybody, please," he said. Just his few words brought a hush from the crowd. Hector had deliberately situated Mickey to the side of his truck so that the new church remained behind them at all times, and he stayed close beside the priest in case Mickey attempted to turn around. "Are you ready, Father?"

"Ready? My gosh…yes, I'm ready."

"Okay, you can turn around now."

37/ ST. MICHAEL'S CHURCH

Mickey held his breath for a long moment before turning around. In that moment he said a simple prayer to himself, "Thank you, my Lord, for blessing my life in so many ways," then he turned. What struck Mickey first were the lovely Imperial Palms rising high above the lush flower gardens bordering a brick walkway toward the church. The trees stood like an honor guard at attention for the arrival of a dignitary. Lowering his gaze, Mickey's jaw dropped at a sight he could never have imagined. Nestled in a veritable jungle of vegetation stood the Spanish Mission-styled church of St. Michael's with it's brown-stained native pine bell tower rising to the height of the palms. Atop the tower, a massive golden cross glimmered in the eastern sun. The stucco facade was cream colored, the woodwork around the windows a dark green, the ornate doors a heavy oak. Mickey was breathless. Tears filled his eyes. "It's beautiful…it's the most beautiful church I've ever seen." On cue from Hector, the bells chimed for the first time, inciting a huge round of applause from more than two thousand clapping hands enhanced with shrill whistles, and hoots, and jubilant shouts.

Hector took Mickey's elbow, led him on a wide inlaid brick walkway toward the front entry, passing two small fountains—one on either side—then through the lushly appointed grounds and toward the back. The Cuban wanted Mickey to enjoy the exterior before opening the doors to the sanctuary. The crowds stayed some distance behind allowing the two men their private moments. Hector pointed up: "Bishop Cordoba contributed these beautiful stained glass windows, had them done in a place called Winona, in your state of Minnesota." On his first steps toward the church only moments before, Mickey had been impressed by the two multi-colored, rectangular windows, one on each side of the large entry doors. Along the east side of the building were four more, and behind the church—in what would be the altar area were two additional windows matching those in front. "A window for each of the Apostles," Hector said.

Looking beyond the back of the church, Mickey saw an extended garden area with statuary of Mary and Joseph. "Unbelievable," Mickey said—over and over again. Mickey knew of Hector's love of plants and flowers and realized that this area had to be very special to his friend. "I've never seen such splashes of color, Hector. I can see your fingerprints on everything."

Stopping to admire the windows on the west side of the church, Mickey repeated his praises: "These are absolutely beautiful, Hector. I wish Bishop Cordoba were here to see them with me right now. I'll have to thank His Grace as soon as we're done with our tour."

"You'll be able to do that sooner than later. I think he's inside—waiting to greet you himself."

Mickey's eyes teared, "And you, Hector, I just can't thank you enough. I don't have the words…you designed this magnificent church, every bit of it—outside and inside– didn't you?"

Hector smiled, "Truth be told…I offered the conceptual ideas, your brother-in-law, Kenny Williams, had most of the architectural wherewithal. The two of us have spent hours together by fax and text and phone. He's really good—really good! Larry Wheeler and his construction crew, obviously, did the lion's share of the actual construction."

Mickey shook his head in disbelief, "I had no idea! My brother-in-law was doing all this right under my nose?"

Hector nodded, the men's secrets had been honor-bound. Taking Mickey by the elbow he said: "Are you ready to open the front doors, Father? A few more surprises are still waiting for you."

"Everybody is going to see me crying, Hector…I'm already completely overwhelmed and I haven't even been inside."

"You won't be alone on that score, Father. I'm crying on the inside and hoping to keep my tears hidden there for a while longer. I'm ready if you are."

Inside the church, Mickey was greeted first by the two bishops—Bremmer had flown from Duluth to Ft. Myers the day before—and he, along with Bishop Cordoba had driven over to TriPalms from Venice earlier that morning. Mickey's parents, Amos and Sadie, were next in the receiving line, then his sister Meghan along with Kenny, and Father Mario who had slipped into TriPalms while Mickey was blindfolded. "Oh, my God!" Mickey was in tears. "My dear God in heaven…I'm absolutely overwhelmed!" The handsome young contractor, Larry Wheeler, stepped toward Mickey and offered him a fresh handkerchief. "Looks like you could use this, my friend." The two men, friends since childhood, hugged affectionately: "Later, the two of us can do a little tour around town. Just you and me—no Hector," he said while poking the tall man at Mickey's elbow.

"You'll be astonished at what can be accomplished without you down here slowing everything down," Larry teased. Both men laughed at the reference—Mickey was best at watching, Larry at building. Larry Wheeler's construction company had done, and continued to do, most of the TriPalms infrastructure work as *pro bono* contributions to the revitalization effort.

After the round of greetings inside the church, Mickey was welcomed with another round of applause. His closest TriPalms friends were waiting patiently beyond the special guest receiving line in the crowded sanctuary.

Following Mickey's church tour would be an afternoon's reception in the new community building. With so many well-wishers, that event would consume much of the afternoon. Mickey's hand was sore from all the handshakes, and his eyes ached from all the camera flashes. The 'Community Center' building, across the street and south of St. Michael's Church, had been the first element of the TriPalms renovation. Outside that building were a swimming pool and neatly appointed flower gardens that the TriPalm's women tended with care. Attached to the main structure was a conference room and library. On a tour of the community with Larry Wheeler later in the afternoon, Mickey could see the ongoing construction of curbs and gutters, water and sewer lines, and upgraded housing everywhere in evidence. "Unbelievable!" was the only word that worked—over and over again–for Mickey on that special day.

39/ CELEBRATIONS

The first mass at St. Michael's Catholic Church would be a celebration of the last Sunday of the Advent season. Mickey had contemplated the skeleton of his homily for months, but hadn't put flesh to its bones until early that Saturday morning while everyone was still sleeping. His emphasis would be on God's creation of an Eden out of a vast emptiness, and would suggest that God, in his infinite goodness, wanted to accomplish something similar here in Tri-Palms. He would find time to run his ideas past Mario for fine-tuning later that morning. He and Mario had availed themselves of Hector Munoz' hospitality and slept on rollaway beds in the small living room.

The night before, the three men grilled steaks on the patio outside Hector's modest home and shared a sixpack of Corona beer. The manufactured ranch-style house rested on the bank of a narrow river that fed into the Myakka, and not far from the new soccer complex. "It took me a while to get comfortable here in TriPalms, but it's working out well," Hector said. "With so much work related travel these days I suppose I could hang my hat almost anywhere. Might as well be with folks I care about, folks that are like family to me." Hector had no family of his own. He'd always believed that he would never be able to balance family responsibilities with work ambitions—one or the other would have to pay too great a price. And, over the years of building his businesses, he had become rather comfortable with his bachelorhood. If he were a lonely man, nobody would ever have known it. He kept his personal life under wraps, maintaining a privacy that no one had ever violated. Mario found Hector to be everything Mickey had told him: A generous and committed Christian who had his values and priorities in perfect order and balance. "Building this beautiful church probably means more to him than to anybody else—and that includes you, my friend" Mario had told Mickey before both retired the night before. "This world needs a few more men like him."

Two miles away, Marella, Ben, and the boys were staying at the Venice Palm Motel on Tamiami Trail, where Amos and Sadie Moran had reserved four extra rooms for Mickey's friends. Mickey's parents along with Mehgan and Kenny had driven up from Naples earlier that day. The two families hosted a seafood dinner at Sharky's on the historic Venice Pier for the Minnesota foursome. Amos was especially interested in chatting with Benjamin Little Otter. Being an attorney, Amos had wide connections in the legal community. His former law clerk—a man named Ross— had been involved in the investigation of the alleged 'accident' in which Benjamin's wife had been killed. Not surprisingly, Ben felt the matter had been resolved—rightfully or wrongfully didn't make much difference to him anymore. Amos complimented Benjamin's attitude, "I wish there were more people like yourself, Mr. Little Otter, people who were willing to let go and get on with their life. Most men don't have your gift of fortitude."

Ironically, Sadie saw the same Cher beauty in Marella Windsong as did Mickey and commented to that effect: "If I didn't know better I'd expect Nickolas Cage to join us at the table, all dressed up as if he were taking her to the opera." Her reference was to a familiar scene from the popular movie, *Moonstruck*. Meghan laughed, "Exactly! If your hair were curled, I think you would be a perfect doppelganger."

In agreement with his wife, Kenny Williams added, " We'd have another Mickey and Brian Slade story on our hands." His reference was to Mickey's near-double from Duluth, and the myriad of complications that situation had inspired. Marella knew Mickey's story well enough but hadn't seen *Moonstruck*; she vowed to do so when she got back to Minnesota.

~

A procession from the soccer field along the riverbank to Saint Michael's Church moved slowly under threatening skies with wind gusts that bent the newly transplanted palms on either side of the route. More than a thousand men, women, and children walked the four blocks along narrow Calle de Varna to the intersection where the Community Building and town square gardens bordered the church. Bishop Cordoba led the procession and opened the heavy oak doors to the flower-adorned sanctuary for the first celebration of the Eucharist. Although complete in every other detail, several rows of pews had yet to arrive, so folding chairs from the community center were borrowed to fill in every available square foot of space. The sanctuary would eventually seat 220 worshipers, and perhaps, another sixty on occasions when standing room was necessary. Somehow, nearly four hundred packed the church for this Saturday afternoon's christening mass.

In a rare exception to established Catholic protocol, two bishops assisted a priest in the special concelebration of the mass. Father Mickey was more nervous than at any time he could remember. And local TV affiliates were present to capture his every anxious expression. Knowing that all eyes and three live cameras were upon him, Mickey's face ached from the perpetual smile that camouflaged his anxiety. Under his breath he was praying for both composure and an extra dose of confidence to carry him through the celebration.

During the Gospel reading, a clap of thunder caused hundreds of eyes to look skyward. Only a flicker of power outage interrupted the sound system during the reading. There would be agonizing discomfort to follow, however. An opening ceremony without a glitch of some kind is said to bring one year of bad luck to all who participate. Saint Michael, from his vantage far above the storm, would never allow bad luck to vivit those participating in the celebration but he did allow the lights to dim occasionally. When the Archangel's back was turned, however, the air conditioning system would go out completely.

Bishop Cordoba's welcome was as congenial as the bishop himself. He thanked Father Mickey for 'getting him off his duff' and initiating long overdue diocesan reforms. His reference to his 'duff' brought embarrassed laughter from the older women of the parish. "This beautiful new church is a tribute to the young Minnesota padre who was sent to do God's work in our midst. And it is evidence of what one, well-meaning Christian can accomplish, when his mind is set to a task." He did not, out of respect, mention Hector Munoz' name. Hector shunned any recognition and all manner of publicity.

Bishop Bremmer was thoughtfully brief in his comments. "Let me assure all of you that the prayers of our Duluth Diocese will always be with our new friends in TriPalms," he said after praising Father Mickey's vision.

Father Mario, who had planned to speak for about five minutes on his perception of *'commitment to Christ'*, chose instead to simply introduce Father Mickey Moran to an audience that already knew him well: "Let it suffice to say that we are all blessed with his friendship…"

Even with the windows and doors open, the heat inside the church was rising beyond ninety degrees. A perspiring Mickey stepped to the pulpit, raised his eyes to the ceiling: "I think Saint

Michael wants to remind us all of what's down there," he pointed both index fingers toward the floor, "and has chosen this, of all days, to make his point." His spontaneous remark and the applause it inspired broke the ice and led him nicely into his homily. Mickey had been careful in conceiving the theme of his sermon to avoid the *I's, Me's,* and *My's* as much as possible. His first exception came early: "I have learned, painfully at times, that I can accomplish nothing, absolutely nothing...*nada...cero...rien*...without the hand of my Lord and God." Almost as if by a small miracle, the AC fans came back to life...Mickey paused for effect; "Would you believe me if I told you that I just asked God to cool things off a bit?" More applause echoed throught the sanctuary. As if on key, a blast of sunshine lit up the stained glass in the twelve windows of the vibrant new church, casting a multi-colored aura to the space. Perhaps the hand of God was truly upon the young priest on his special day.

~

After nearly two hours, the ceremony concluded and the crowds filed from the church, community center, and overflow tents— where hundreds watched the celebration of mass on live TV—and were making their way to the soccer field for a community picnic. The earlier clouds had vanished along with the thunder and lightning storm of the afternoon. Tents encircled the field. Covering the linen-draped tables were trays of every imaginable food: From tacos to burritos to Millie Wang's egg rolls, from BBQ ribs and wings, to the American staples of burgers, brauts, and hotdogs. Nachos, chips, homemade salsas from mild to nuclear, and countless desserts were placed adjacent to the main tent on Rue de Sol Street on the eastern perimeter of the community. Separated by a gazebo from the foods were a pair of beer tents housing kegs of Corona and Budweiser beers. In the center of the field was a rented Merry-go-Round and enormous air-inflated play areas for the children. South of the prefabricated stage were the horseback riding rings, volleyball nets, and beanbag tossing games. The event's planners had included something for every person of every age, including a bingo tent with a dozen tables and a $1000 grand prize.

The highlight was to be an early evening sing-along concert featuring Father Mickey with his Martin guitar, and to the surprise of all, Bishop Cordoba's accompaniment on a few of the tunes with his Hohner chromonica.

To the delight of everyone, Mickey opened with the question: "Does anybody here remember the words to *Michael*?" The response was a thunderous 'Si .. Si .. Si' so Mickey, along with thousands of voices began *"Michael row the boat ashore...hallelujah..."* From ten minutes of *Michael* repetition, to the ballad *Tom Dooley* and then to *'He's Got the Whole World in His Hands'*...the sing-along was rocking! Mickey had taught the lyrics to so many in the TriPalms community when he had held the sing-alongs in the past; the singing was a nostalgic experience for all.

40/ FLOWERS AND BIRDS

Exhausted from an all-night celebration, Mickey roused himself at 5:30, awakened Mario and hoped that a cold morning shower would perk him up. After shaving and dressing, he could smell the aroma of coffee wafting from down the narrow hallway; Hector was already up and about. When Mickey entered the kitchen he found Mario and Hector at the table in deep conversation about landscaping and birds of all things. Mickey pulled out a chair for himself.

"I've planted a lot of Bouganvillea, my favorite shrubbery," Hector was explaining. Mario shook his head, "Hard to believe you have all this color in December. When Mickey described TriPalms to me he implied that it was a barren wasteland. St. Michael's Church looks like it has been placed in the middle of a tropical jungle—all of this in just a few months time. It's hard for me to believe."

"We can transplant huge, mature trees—some of them forty feet tall, and mature shrubbery as well—and expect them to flourish. An empty lot can easily be transformed into something lush with a skilled crew in a good day's work."

"Incredible!" Mario said. "You must be pretty good at it, Hector."

"I do take pride in my landscaping. My reward is the birds that it attracts. I love to watch the birds."

Mickey joined the conversation, "What are those birds with the white bands on their wings and tails?"

Hector smiled, "Mockingbirds, Father. Mockingbirds like to nest in Bouganvillea, and I like mockingbirds. They truly do mock the songs of other birds. I've got cardinals in the live oaks outside and they wake me every morning. And...the mourning doves— probably my favorites. If you think about it, all are like the flutes and ocarinas in God's marvelous symphony along with the violins of the wind and the thunder of the drums." Hector laughed at his corny analogy, "I get carried away sometimes, Father."

Mickey cleared his throat, "Not at all, Hector. That was rather profound. What's an ocarina anyhow?

"If I remember correctly, it's a Chinese flute of sorts...some are quite shrill."

"I hate to break things up, fellas, but I must–bathroom's yours Mario– Hector's mine for a few minutes." He checked the clock, gave Mario a wink: "We're on for the eight o'clock mass, pardner. Better get a move on."

A grin crossed Mickey's face as he took Mario's chair opposite Hector. He appraised the Cuban without commenting. A long moment passed between them.

"Yes...I take it that you have something to say?" Hector Munoz puzzled. "What's so amusing?"

Mickey knew Hector to be a man of custom and convention. The businessman wore a freshly starched Zegna white shirt every day—Mickey had never seen him in any other color and had never seen him wearing a tie. Along with the white shirt he wore crisply creased Banana Republic khaki slacks. "You look very nice this morning, Hector," Mickey said. "I like the shirt and pants combination."

Hector burst out laughing, deep and throaty. "My Sunday best, Father." Hector actually giggled at his comeback and got Mickey laughing along with him. Mickey was one of the few people who could needle the tall Cuban. Hector settled himself, "I like Mario very much. We've been up since four, talking about everything from predestination and the deteriorating morality of a secular society, to Florida's flora and fauna—he's a very knowledgeable and insightful man."

"And birds—I must have missed the heavy stuff."

"You did."

"Yeah…Mario's okay, I guess. That is, he's okay for someone who hates birds and music."

Hector bent over in laughter. "I hope you're kidding."

Mickey shared in the mirth of the moment. "Just kidding, of course. Mario's been there for me since I was a teenager–through thick and thin. He, along with my guardian angel, have kept me mostly on the straight and narrow."

Hector was quiet for a long moment, musing on something. Mickey refilled both coffee mugs and returned the carafe to the counter. "I like all of your friends from Minnesota. I hope to get to know them a little better at the picnic this afternoon." At the concert the night before, Hector had sat with the Windsongs for a time; then the Olivios who were joined by Benjamin Little Otter. For a good part of the evening they all seemed to be having a wonderful time together. Hector smiled, "I enjoyed Travis quite a lot. Quite the talker that young man. He's bright, too. With that combination I think he's going to do well for himself. And I wasn't alone. Seems like the Olivio girl, Maria, enjoyed him, too. I guess they had a lot in common with being college freshmen and all." He looked away, his expression changed, "His brother Trevor, he's quite a different personality—they're almost more like polar types than twins. For some uncanny reason, he reminded me of myself when I was much younger: Very serious for his age, headstrong, searching…seemed very pensive, deeply into his self and his private thoughts. He listened to what everybody had to say with a passion that I could see in his eyes. To my untrained eye, it seemed as if he was processing what everyone else had to say, reconciling their thoughts and ideas with those of his own. He hardly said ten words himself."

"I couldn't have described Trevor any better than you just did."

"If you hadn't told me anything about him, I would have known that he was an athlete by the way he carried himself."

"I'm still trying to get my head around Trevor. He's a challenge to say the least. Ben says that he feels closer to Trevor than to Travis for the same reasons you just mentioned. Ben's the strong, silent type—a heart as big as yours, Hector. He says Trevor accepts me, 'Thinks you're okay' is the way Ben put it."

"I'd say that 'okay' is a ringing compliment coming from Trevor. I guess the apple doesn't fall far from the tree; the boy's father didn't say more than five words all evening either. Yet, I could tell that he was having a good enough time. I even caught him singing along with everybody more than a few times. When he stood up…my gosh, he's a giant of a man."

"Just a minute. Did you say the boy's father—Benajamin?"

"Yes, the huge man sitting next to Marella. Benjamin. The boy's father…why?"

"Hector, I'm afraid you are mistaken. Benjamin is the boy's uncle. He was married to Marella's sister some time ago."

"I just assumed. Ben and Trevor, they are both such large men." Hector scratched his head, "Then, where is the boy's father? Marella's husband?"

"Heaven only knows who the father is, and there has never been a husband. I've asked Benjamin that same question, he say's nobody knows any of that aside from Marella herself." Mickey became pensive himself for a long moment, "Marella's quite a mysterious woman. I've struggled with getting to know her…"

"Let's go, amigo!" Mario said as he strolled into the kitchen smelling of Irish Spring. "We've got a mass in half an hour. And I'd guess we'll have another full house to inspire."

Hector checked the clock, "You'd better get going. I'll only be a few minutes behind you guys."

~

Mickey told everybody that he and Trevor would be leaving the picnic early in the afternoon, but he didn't offer any details about why. "Should be back in a few hours," he said. He had called Peter Madigan after mass that morning and confirmed that they were on for the afternoon. Madigan told Mickey exactly how to get to the Lee County complex from off of I-75. He suggested that they avoid taking Highway 41, "It'll take half-an-hour longer from Venice if you go that way. Take the Daniels and Cape Coral exit, instead— then go right for two miles or so. You'll want to go left at the Nine Mile Cyprus signals. You should be able to see Hammond Stadium off to your right. Drive through the parking area…I'll meet you at the gate by the beige building on your right."

~

The Sunday picnic was another huge affair. This fete was a celebration for the TriPalms community in general and for the generous financial support provided by the Morans (Mickey's parents—Amos and Sadie) and the Wheelers in particular. Like the concert the night before, it brought everybody back together for another celebration—the finale of the three festive days. TriPalms not only had its new Catholic Church, but the bishop had introduced its new priest, a youthful Puerto Rican named Father Juan Garcia Cabrerra. The picnic was a welcome of sorts for Father Juan, as well as a farewell to their beloved Father Mickey. Once again, the new soccer field was alive with music and ethnic foods, and games and merriment. Mickey and Larry Wheeler found time to slip away after mass and walk the streets of TriPalms.

With typical enthusiasm, Larry pointed out the changes already made and those yet to come. A miraculous transformation was in progress. "It all reminds me of the mustard seed parable," Mickey observed, "The good Lord planted the tiny mustard seed and allowed it to sprout into a gorgeous tree."

While everybody celebrated, Trevor and Alberto Olivio (Maria's uncle) played catch in the shade along the west side of the Community Center. Hector had introduced the two men the night before. Alberto had been a catcher in the Dominican Leagues years ago and was delighted to be asked to give the youngster a light workout. After twenty minutes, the two men rejoined the picnic. "I was impressed," Alberto told Hector. "His release point isn't consistent yet, but that's just a matter of muscle memory. He's quite good!"

"Alberto doesn't give compliments," Hector later confided to Mickey. "The boy is not simply good—he must be very good."

41/ "... YOU, MR. MADIGAN, ARE A LIAR!"

The drive south on I-75 from Venice to Ft. Myers took about forty minutes. Quiet mintues. Trevor had asked his uncle Ben to come along, and Marella decided to join the three men as well. Travis had decided to stay behind. "You guys have a full car as it is," Travis justified. Maria Olivio smiled approvingly at his decision to hang out with her family and friends. Madigan's suggestion that he take the interstate over the Tamiami Trail (US#41) was proving to be a good one. Traffic was light and moved at nearly eighty miles an hour. Mickey had allowed plenty of extra time for the trip. As he passed the North Port exits and south toward Ft. Myers, Mickey tried again to engage the others in casual conversation. Nobody, however, had much to say. It seemed to Mickey as if everybody had thoughts of their own to mull over. From the quietude of their private worlds, each watched the passing scenery without question or comment. The vista from the Punta Gorda bridge raised some eyebrows, but nothing in the way of conversation. Mickey explained how the lovely city had been devastated by Hurricane Charley back in 2004, "Folks here almost had to start from scratch with the rebuilding. It's turned out well. Tourism is booming here again."

The Sunday traffic on Daniels Parkway was thicker than Mickey remembered. The port city was growing rapidly and its transportation infrastructure was challenged to keep pace. He followed Madigan's directions and pulled into the Lee County complex, parking his car near the building Pete Madigan had told him about. Mickey was ten minutes early. One car was parked in a palm-shaded area off to his left. A short man in navy shorts, flipflops, and a green tank top got out of the car and headed toward Mickey. "You Majican?" he said.

"No, I'm not Madigan," Mickey said, immediately realizing that the mistaken name and identity as bad omens—more than likely this was going to be an unfortunate experience. "You don't know who Mister Madigan is?"

"No, sir." Despite yellowed teeth, his smile was engaging. "Angelo…he call me dis mornin'"

Mickey shook his head, who was this man? Who was Angelo? What was going on? "Madigan should be coming any minute," he told the confused man. Mickey prayed under his breath that they wouldn't be stood up. He offered the darkly tanned man a hand shake, "You are, I mean your name…?"

The man introduced himself as Francisco: "Tony, Tony Angelo…well, he couldn't make it here this afternoon. He's da ground crews boss guy. I'm called Punch, I work some with Tony when his crew is short. He tol me to open things up for ya'all today. Din't say why, tho." Punch walked over to the gate and opened the lock, "Com'on in, you guys. Ooops, and yer lovely lady, too."

Two miles from the ball fields, Pete Madigan's head throbbed with stress. He had to wait nearly half an hour for Sergio Zahn, a golfing buddy, to find his catcher's glove in a storage bin buried in the back of his two-stall garage. Zahn was confused about what was supposed to be going on with this charade of Madigans, but had agreed to help out Pete for a case of beer—if, and only if, it wouldn't be for more than an hour or so. When Madigan turned off of Daniels Parkway toward Hammond Stadium, he reminded Zahn, "Just agree with everything I say, okay? I might have to do some BS'ing, make these folks think I'm a big wheel with the Twins. Okay?"

Sergio had a small problem with that. "Just be a yes-man to what you say and catch fer this kid? That's easy enough for you to say, but I'm the one that's gonna look stupid. I ain't caught a base-ball in years. You told them I'm legit, Pete? They're thinking I'm an instructional catcher with the Twins team?"

"Shuddup, there they are, waiting for us. Don't forget that I want you to say 'yes, Mr. Madigan'—no more no less. Got it?" Pete pulled in next to the group clustered together near the gate. He recognized Father Mickey, not the woman or the two huge men. The short guy didn't look like Tony Angelo; he muttered a profanity under his breath. "What the…?" Then he noticed that the gate was already unlocked; there was still hope he could pull this off. Pete adjusted his Twins baseball cap and brushed cigarette ashes from his yellowed Killebrew replica jersey, then stepped out of the car and approached Father Mickey with his hand outstretched, "Great to see ya, Father."

When Mickey smelled liquor on Madigan's breath, his suspicions were confirmed. Everything began sliding downhill from the quick introductions at the gate. "This here's Sergio Zahn. Says he's a little rusty today—hasn't caught a prospect for me since…probably back in August."

Zahn forced a smile, offering a weak: "Yes, sir, Mr. Madigan" as if on cue.

Mickey doubted that Zahn, a man of nearly sixty with longish gray hair and a belly that hung over his belt, had caught anybody since August of seventy-something. He shook the man's clammy hand. While Marella scowled and Ben moved well off to the side, Trevor was jogging along the cinder pathway to loosen up. "Where we s'posed to go?" the groundsman called 'Punch' asked. "Nobody tell me nothin' at all.'"

Mickey excused himself, pulling Madigan off to the side. His expression added bold italics to his few sharp words: "What's going on? You've been drinking, and I'm very confused, Madigan. This isn't what you promised…"

Madigan's face reddened, "Just a brandy for my sore throat." Forcing a smile, he parried the accusation, pointing an index finger toward the playing field, "That the boy you told me about?" He lit a cigarette, blew his first drag to the side. His hand was shaky, his eyes averted.

Mickey fumed, "You've duped me into believing this was going to be a tryout…it's a sham and you, Mr. Madigan, are a liar. What am I supposed to tell my friends? We've come all this way…"

"Oh, oh…!" The exclamation came from either Sergio or Punch who were standing awkwardly with Marella and Ben. "Madigan…!"

Mickey turned around, a Lee County Sheriff's vehicle was pulling up near the gate. The door opened: "What's going on here, folks?" The officer who stepped out of the cruiser was every bit as big as Benjamin; his badge ID read Farley.

Everyone looked to Madigan, whose face had turned from three shades of red to ashen, as he stepped forward. "Just touring the grounds, sir…some folks from out of town," the Killebrew-jerseyed man mumbled as he stamped out his cigarette.

"Sorry folks, but you're trespassing. I'll have to ask you all to…"

"Just a minute," Madigan said in a voice pitched high with anxiety. "Wee'rre here with the grounds guy, he just let us in and…" his stress and embarrassment were causing him to slur his words. He looked from the cop to Mickey, and back to Farley; he'd try to pull an ace from somewhere up his sleeve, "Jerry Bell, he's top brass with the Twins, anyhow he told me there was no problem with our being here."

Officer Farley had no idea who Jerry Bell was. "That may be, but if he gave you permission to be here, someone with the Twins organization would have let our department know about it in advance. That's the protocol. I can call Mr. Ryan if you'd like—he's the GM with the Twins– and check it out. I think I saw his car parked over by the stadium a few minutes ago." Ryan was Terry Ryan, the General Manager of the Twins organization.

Madigan's white face turned back to red and then to a shade of purple. "That's okay. Won't be necessary. Sorry for the inconvenience, sir. We'll just go…" He turned to Mickey. "There's a ball field in the park near my place—only fifteen minutes from here. We can go over there and…"

Now all eyes were on Mickey. He swallowed hard, looked from Trevor who wore a confused expression to Marella who wore a scowl. "I'm sorry. I think we've been had. Mr. Madigan hasn't been honest about all this…and he's been drinking. Probably best if we head back to Venice and the picnic."

Trevor, in a sweat from his running and stretching, brushed past Mickey and grabbed Madigan by the shirt, "You lied to Father?"

Farley stepped toward Trevor, "Just a minute, young man. Don't–"

Marella took Trevor's sleeve, "Let's go Son. We don't want any trouble."

Trevor glared at Madigan, then Farley, and let go of Madigan's shirt. "Dirt bag," he said in Madigan's face. "You can go to hell." Then he stepped back and walked toward Mickey's car.

"Be careful, young man," Farley warned. "You're flirting with assault charges." It was his turn to be confused: "Who's Father? You a priest?" Farley looked at Mickey, dressed in shorts and a gray Minnesota Gophers T-shirt.

"Yes, sir. Father Michael Moran...visiting here from Minnesota..."

Madigan's eyes began to tear. "Officer, this is all my fault. Father Moran has nothing to do with this... I apologize." He was breathing heavily, "Will you give me a minute to call Mr. Ryan at the stadium and explain things, sir?" Befuddled, and clearly remorseful, the old man struggled to regain an ounce of composure: "Can you find me a number for the Twins office over in the stadium? Please."

Farley sensed the old man was on the edge, "You folks stay right here while I run over and find him myself. First, let me jot down all of your names and your business here." He pulled a small tablet from the shirt pocket of his uniform.

"Can I go with you, sir? I know the names of these folks...and I know Mr. Ryan. I can explain things to him." Madigan was determined to save face with his guests at all costs. He had met Terry Ryan on a few occasions and always found him to be a straight-shooter. There was a thread of hope, however thin, that he could still pull this off.

Officer Farley looked at Father Mickey and the others, "That okay with you folks? We won't be but a few minutes...that's if we can find Mr. Ryan."

42/ ALL IS WELL THAT ENDS WELL

Twins G.M. Terry Ryan was leaving the Hammond Stadium office with his newly hired bench coach, Terry Steinbach, when Officer Farley and Pete Madigan approached. "Afternoon Officer," Ryan said. "Merry Christmas."

"Same to you, sir. Sorry to bother you, but I think we have a situation…" Farley was about to explain.

Ryan's face puzzled, "Madigan? Pete Madigan?" He squinted at the man trailing the officer. "Is that you or…?"

Madigan's knees almost buckled. "Yes…yessir," he offered his hand. "We've met before."

Terry Ryan smiled at Steinbach, then the other two men. "Pete here was quite a pitching prospect years ago. Gosh…when was that, anyhow?" He didn't wait for anyone to answer, "He blew his arm back in the days before we had all the new, sophisticated surgeries. He's worked with the Twins over the years," Terry Ryan explained. The G.M. had a memory of names and faces that rivaled any computer. "So, what brings you guys here? Some kind of trouble?" He looked toward the tall officer.

Farly shrugged without speaking.

"Can I speak with you…privately, for a moment, sir?" Madigan said as he held the handshake of Terry Ryan.

Ryan excused himself to the others and took a step off to the side. "Sure. Not a problem. What brings you here, Pete?"

Pete Madigan poured out his heart to Terry Ryan for two minutes. Terry gave him a pat on the back, turned back to the officer. "Everything's cool, Mr. Farley. I'll see that the gate is locked when we're done. I guess I had forgotten, but we've got a young pitcher to look at this afternoon. Thanks for everything."

Ryan explained what Pete Madigan had just told him as he and Steinbach drove the short distance to the training building near the minor league practice fields. "A GM's job is 24/7," he said. "I've gotten so much heat about our pitching this winter that I'd drive to

Tallahassee on Christmas Day to see a prospect."

When Terry Steinbach was introduced to Mickey and the others outside the clubhouse, Trevor's excitement could not be contained. "Can I have your autograph, Mr. Steinbach?" Steinbach grinned, "Sure. First, let's see what you've got young man. I'm a bit rusty, but I'd enjoy catching for you."

Terry Ryan led the group down to the pitching pens near the stadium, unlocked a storage room door, and retrieved a bucket of new baseballs. "Loosen up a bit before you do any throwing young man. We'll find a place to sit up there," he gestured toward the bleachers behind a row of 'bull-pen' mounds.

~

Trevor Windsong's demonstration had Terry Steinbach smiling. The former Oakland Athletics and Minnesota Twins catcher borrowed Zahn's old catcher's mitt and crouched behind the plate to receive Trevor's pitches. "Let's see you throw from the stretch position," Steinbach suggested. Trevor complied. His fastball was not quite as sharp, but his slider pitch was as effective from the stretch as from the full windup. Terry Ryan, stone-faced and deep in thought, sat on the edge of his seat for the ten-minute workout. "That'll do it, guys. I've seen enough." Ryan stood. He had seen some minor, and correctable, glitches in Trevor's delivery, but the boy's slider was something to marvel at. He turned to Mickey sitting next to him, "He's just out of high school, you say? Up in Hibbing?" Terry Ryan searched his memory for the name Windsong. Then it clicked, he had been given a heads up from his old friend and roommate, Rick Tintor, months ago. He'd make some calls later that evening. Assuming that Madigan was agenting for the prospect, he suggested that Pete and he talk after the others had left. "I'm interested. I like what I've seen, Pete."

Pete Madigan hadn't been in such high spirits since...probably since he was a kid with a golden arm of his own. That morning, before heading to the ball fields, he had prayed that he'd get through this episode without a major embarrassment. In his wildest imagination he could not have expected anything like what had just happened.

On the walk back from the bullpen, the two Terrys—with Trevor between them—lagged behind the others. Steinbach put his hand on Trevor's shoulder, "Nice job. I was telling Mr. Ryan that your ball sinks like nothing I've seen since Rolle Fingers back in Oakland. That's major league stuff in my book."

"Thanks." Trevor tried to smile but his emotion made his face too tight to form the expression. He was walking with two men that he'd seen on TV many times and the feelings he tried to process were things of disbelief. Trevor Windsong, shoulder to shoulder with two of baseball's iconic figures. Who would have ever thought…? He didn't know what to say or how to react to the compliment.

Ryan and Steinbach talked in subdued tones about the workout, but skirted the topic of what Trevor's plans for the future might be. Not knowing any details about what Pete Madigan and his priest friend, had arranged Ryan assumed that Madigan was probably an 'agent' of some kind.

"Where do we go from here?" Terry Steinbach asked his boss.

Ryan slowed his walk, "So…what do you think, Trevor?"

Trevor couldn't answer the simple question because he didn't have a clue as to what was going to happen next. He was stuck in a fantasy world without any idea of how to get back to reality. "I guess…I guess that you'll have to talk with Father Mickey and Mr. Madigan," he said. "All I know is that they arranged for this tryout with you guys. That's really all I needed to know."

Before leaving the complex, Terry Ryan and Pete Madigan agreed to meet after the holidays. Trevor, seeking Mr. Ryan's advice, was told to continue the workout regimen he was on and cautioned against any throwing outside in the cold temps of northern Minnesota. "You could do damage to your arm and we certainly wouldn't want that to happen."

Ryan promised to keep in touch with the lad. He stepped beside Benjamin, took the tall Indian's elbow: "Mr. Windsong, would you be kind enough to leave me your phone number and address?" Once again, there was mistaken identity. "I ain't Mr. Windsong, sir. This here's the boy's mother."

Marella, still nursing her suspicions and feeling left out of what the men were up to, reluctantly put down her name, address, and phone number on a slip of paper provided to her by Mr. Steinbach. "I don't want you sending a lot of junk mail…and I'd appreciate if you would speak to me before talking with my son about anything."

Trevor fumed inside, but held his tongue over what his mother had just said.

"You've got my word on that, Ma'am." He gave a frowning Trevor a firm handshake: "I'll be in contact with your mother soon."

Mickey thanked Pete Madigan, "Whatever it was that you said to persuade Mr. Ryan to join us surely turned out nicely for everybody. Thanks. I'll have to confess that I was just about ready to get back in the car and head back up to Venice," he admitted.

Madigan was beaming, "I don't know if it was your prayers or mine, but it all turned out pretty good. We'll keep in touch about where we go from here, okay?"

Mickey wasn't sure how to interpret the *'We'll'*. "I think it would be best if I call you. Okay? Ms. Windsong might have different ideas for her son than either you or I might have."

For Peter Madigan, the afternoon was an epiphany of sorts. He would never drink again. And he would begin putting his life in better order. Upon returning to his home he made a call to his daughter Brenda. Some ice needed to be broken: "If you can get away for a week or two, I'd love to have your come down here and hang out with your dad."

43/ "STOP THE CAR!"

The sun was setting over the dark and rolling Gulf as the four Minnesotans drove north to TriPalms. Despite the great exhibition at the Lee complex, the passengers were even more preoccupied with their separate thoughts than on the trip down. Mickey's attempts at levity floated like bowling balls in the quiet car. Trevor tossed the Steinbach autographed baseball from one hand to the other as if to express his boredom or repressed anger. Marella wore an expression that was even more difficult to interpret. Mickey was certain that Marella's comment to Terry Ryan was troubling them both. Ben half-dozed in the passenger seat.

Trevor broke the silence as they passed passed through Port Charlotte. "Why did you do that, mom? Why did you make me feel like a little kid in front of everybody?"

"Later, Trevor."

"No. Not later. I asked you a question here and now."

"This isn't the time or place. We'll be back at the motel soon."

Trevor's jaw tightened as he turned away in a boiling frustration. Under his breath Trevor muttered what Mickey discerned to be 'bitch'. Glancing in his rearview mirror he noticed that Marella winced, she had heard the expletive too, but chose to say nothing. Instead of initiating any confrontation, she turned her shoulders and stared out of her window as well.

After several miles, Marella got Mickey's attention away from a classical music station he was listening to on low volume. "What time are we leaving in the morning, Father?" Her voice pitched higher than natural; the edges of her tension could not be disguised.

"When everybody's ready, I guess. Hopefully early," his reply was nonchalant despite the tightness in his throat. "Regardless, we'll probably be going through Atlanta during a Monday rush hour—I dread that."

Marella flashed a diffident smile, "I'll get everything packed tonight so we can be ready when you are—however early." As pleasant as she wanted to sound, her voice remained tight. Mickey could tell she was hurting from something deeper than her son's rebuke. He could feel a welling tension of his own—below the surface of things, there was trouble brewing.

While passing by a North Port exit on I-75, the lingering tension finally cracked. "I ain't going home!" Trevor turned toward his mother, gave her a defiant glare. "There's nothing there for me any more, least not now."

Somehow, Marella had expected something like this to happen. From the first time Mickey mentioned this trip she had had an unspoken apprehension that the experience would be life-changing for her family. It was a vague notion, but it was as real as the sunrise and as ominous as a storm front. From the first time Mickey had mentioned the vacation opportunity, she had tried to modify the initial elation of a road trip with the interesting young priest and her sons. Nothing exciting had brightened her life in…she couldn't remember when. Father Mickey remained an enigma she hadn't quite figured out yet. Marella believed that she had to be there for whatever it was that was going to happen. If Mickey hadn't invited her, she would have asked to go along. Despite some preconceived apprehensions, so far there had been considerably more excitement than reasons for concern. That was going to change.

Marella regarded her angry son, forced a smile, then her face iced: "We'll see about that."

Trevor was not about to challenge his mother in the priest's car. "Yeah…we'll see, won't we…?" he mimicked the edge to his mother's threat and turned back to staring out his window.

Ben was as stressed as anyone else in the car. He tried to make small talk about anything but baseball. "Atlanta's huge," he said from somewhere out of the blue. "Ain't it, Father? Lots bigger than Duluth and Superior together, I'd hav'ta say." Amused by Ben's comparison, Mickey glanced in his rearview mirror and nodded. "Bigger than fifty Duluths, I'd guess."

Ben smiled, "After that we will go to Chattanooga...then Nashville. Right? Or, is it the other way around?"

"Very good, Ben. Now, can you name any three states we'll be traveling through—not counting Florida, on the trip back?" Levity was sorely needed and silent Ben was coming to the rescue.

Ben's face widened from a thin smile to a full grin, "I know'em all, Father. Betcha five on that." He had just seen a Georgia license plate on a passing car.

"Okay, you're on."

Benjamin said, "I'm gonna go backwards...Minnesota..." he laughed out loud, "you didn't say I couldn't count that." He continued, "Wisconsin and Georgia. That's three! You owe me five."

Even Marella seemed to be enjoying the diversion. She leaned forward in her seat, willing to let go of her tension for the moment. "There are three more, Ben, besides Georgia. I'll give you another buck if you can name any one of those."

Ben scratched his head, took his time. From the car window he looked for some license plate clues. He saw an Ontario but held his tongue. Then he blurted: "Michigan?"

"Sorry. Not Michigan. One more wrong guess and you're out."

Ben missed with Iowa, then Ohio. Trevor, temporarily out of his funk and not enjoying being left out of the banter, said: "Five bucks if I can name all the states backwards or forwards, Father?"

"You got five bucks you can cough up, Trevor?" Mickey challenged. "Try backwards—that's what's coming up tomorrow."

"Ready...Florida, Georgia, Tennessee, part of Kentucky, Illinois, Wisconsin, then Minnesota."

Marella clapped, Ben smiled approvingly from the back seat and met Mickey's eyes in the mirror: "...he nailed 'em, din't he?"

~

By the time they reached Venice it was dark. The tension seemed to have abated. Mickey had promised Hector and Larry that he would meet them at the picnic and say his 'good byes' and 'thanks' to everybody. "We're all going back to the TriPalms picnic, right?" he said.

"If it's okay with you...no...I've got packing to do. Trevor will help me. You go right ahead, Father, without us. Ben, why don't you go, too," she added. "Would it be out of the way for you to drop Trevor and me off at the motel, Father?"

Mickey felt the familiar tension of impending conflict working a painful spasm from his shoulders to the back of his head. "No problem at all," he said, then glancing in his rear view mirror he saw Trevor grit his teeth.

"I'll go with you and Ben, Father," Trevor snapped.

"You will do exactly as I tell you to do, Trevor. We'll both be getting off at the motel, Father."

"Stop the car," Trevor shouted. "I'm getting out."

Mickey froze, the two Windsongs had put him in the middle of something that didn't belong to him. Or, did it? "Trevor, how about we all talk at the motel. Settle this little disagreement there. Okay?" Mickey's tone was as appeasing as he could manage as Trevor unbuckled his seat belt. "Trevor..."

Trevor pushed open his door, Mickey checked his speedometer...his speed had dropped to thirty. "Don't, Trevor. Please..." his foot eased down the brake pedal..."We're only two minutes from the motel."

Defiant, Trevor pushed the door open wider. Mickey was down to twenty, "Please don't do this, Trevor."

"Just pull over. I'll get out."

Benjamin reached across the seat and grabbed Trevor's right arm. "Close the door, Trevor. This minute!"

The door closed.

~

At the picnic grounds, Travis had just finished dancing with Maria Olivio when he felt the hammer strike the back of his head. "Oh no...Good God..." He clutched his head and doubled over in pain. Maria was bewildered by the grimace that crossed his face, "What's wrong, Travis? What just happened to you?"

Although Travis rarely had the experience of extreme tension transference, he recognized it immediately. "It's not me," he said. "It's Trevor."

Maria's face contorted, "What do you mean?"

Travis clenched his eyes, rubbed the back of head for a long minute as if squeezing out the pain. "Trevor's in a bad place right now. I can feel it." He took Maria's hands in his own, "You see, we have this weird connection..." He went on to explain.

44/ CONFRONTATION: MOTHER AND SON

When in doubt about what to do, say the three-word prayer: 'Help me God'! Mickey did. His first thought was 'blessed are the peacemakers...' He crossed over Highway 41 and entered the motel parking lot. "Before we get out of the car, lets every one of us do some talking—you included, Benjamin. I know that it's been a long few days and we're all a bit frazzled...but..." Mickey searched the three faces for acknowledgement.

"I'll talk with my son, thank you. You've done enough already, Father."

Mickey puzzled, "What do you mean by that, Marella?"

Instead of answering, she opened her passenger door opposite Mickey and turned to Trevor, "Lets go inside, Son. No public displays are necessary."

For a moment, Mickey saw a 'help me' in Trevor's eyes. The boy sat rigidly, staring at something in the darkness beyond the car.

Marella tugged at his sleeve, "You can thank *the Father* and say good night, Trevor."

Mickey hadn't been called 'the Father' for some time. There was something confrontational in Marella's tone. He let it go.

Trevor spoke, "You can't boss me around, Mom—not any more. I'm eighteen. I can do what I want with my life."

Marella bit her tongue, looked from Trevor to Mickey. "I've never had my son speak to me like that before. Where did he get that attitude from, Father Moran? This 'I can do what I want with my life' crap. Who pumped his ego to the point where he can tell his mother to f—off? Not from Ben, I'm sure of that. Not from any man I know." She stepped out and walked around the front to the car to the back door where Trevor was sitting. "You can get out, too, Ben."

Ben squirmed in his seat, shook his head as if agreeing with Marella. He opened his door but didn't step outside.

"What has Father Moran been telling my son, Ben?"

"Nothin' I know about," Ben said in a weak voice. He was so torn his mind and body were near paralysis.

"Okay…let's not blame Father or anybody else." Trevor pushed himself out of the door, "We're both out now, Mom. The two of us can talk right here. Get this settled. Let Father go back to the picnic and see his friends." He looked at his uncle, "You can go, too. Travis is stuck there without a ride." Trevor's words were more command than useful suggestion.

Mickey joined mother and son on the driveway, hoping to step between the two of them before they locked horns. "Just a minute. I hate confrontations, hostility. Can't the two of you resolve this?— give each other a hug or something? I know you love each other too much to…"

Mickey had chosen the wrong words.

"What do you know, Father? Where have you been all these years while I've been raising my two boys? Is that the kind of counseling you offer in order to resolve issues—or what did you call our disagreement? *Hostility?* What are you suggesting? That we hug one another and make up? If so..." She shook her head in unmitigated disgust.

Ben finally stepped out of the car, put his large hands up in a defensive posture, "That ain't really fair, Marella. Father doesn't want you guys to be fightin', that's all. I don't neither."

"This doesn't concern you, Ben, butt out! " Marella snapped. Tears welled in her eyes, "You've ruined my family, Father...that's what you've done. Maybe not intentionally—I don't know. But since you showed up, what—a couple of months ago? Anyhow, my boys have changed. I'd appreciate if you'd just step out of our family picture once and for all."

Mickey felt badly misunderstood, but not defeated. Trevor was looking at him for some kind of support. Ben's eyes beseeched him to say something. "Marella...I don't think you actually believe what you've just said. You're angry...and we all say things in anger..."

Marella screamed: "Listen to me. All of you. You are trespassing in my space, my role as parent, and I won't allow that. I'll call 911 if I have to."

Just then, Mickey's cell rang. "In a few minutes," he mumbled. "We've just arrived back at the motel now," He put the phone in his trouser pocket. "Just Hector, wondering where we all were."

An awkward moment had all four of them standing as if frozen in place. What needed to be said or done? Mickey was about to apologize for whatever he'd done wrong and get back to TriPalms for his 'good-byes'—it was already after nine. He looked from Marella to her son, then to Ben, and back to Marella. "Well, I guess...I'm not the peacemaker I'd hoped to be. Is there anything else before I leave. . .?"

Trevor unexpectedly saved the moment when he stepped over to his mother, gave her a hug. "I love you, Mom." The two of them, Trevor a foot taller than his mother, rocked back and forth in their embrace. Trevor raised his head, "You guys go ahead. I'll stay here."

~

Everyone still lingering at the picnic grounds wanted to know how the 'try-out' in Ft. Myers had gone. Mickey gave glowing reports. Mario standing nearby pointed to his wristwatch. The goodbyes, however, would take nearly another hour. The last to leave were Mickey's parents and the Wheelers, who were driving back to Naples together. The last good bye would be the hardest, "Hector," Mickey's eyes were moist. "I'm at a loss for words, my friend. Everything you've done for me...for all of us."

Hector had sensed that Mickey was 'out of whack' since his arrival an hour before. He knew something wasn't right but was certain that it wasn't any disappointment with the TriPalm events of the past few days. "What's wrong? Don't go without telling me. I won't sleep if there's something I can do..."

"It's nothing. Really nothing. Believe me."

Hector would not be put-off, "I know better, Father. While you were away, Travis came up to me and said that something wasn't right with his brother. He was positive and asked if I would call and check on things. What's that about? You should tell me, maybe I can help?"

Mickey had to be honest with his friend. He explained the confrontation to Hector with Ben and Father Mario listening in. Benjamin nodded in agreement with all that Mickey said. Hector seemed very disconcerted as he listened. A man of deep empathy, his heart hurt for both the mother and her son. Travis and Maria Olivio were sitting under a cluster of palm trees saying their goodbyes.

"So, that's how I left it. I think Trevor defused things for now," Mickey said.

Mario and Ben collected Travis and headed to Mickey's Civic, twenty yards away, allowing Mickey and Hector a few final moments. As Mickey was giving the tall man a hug, his cell phone rang...

45/ A LAUNDROMAT ON EAST VENICE

"He took off!" Mickey told Hector as he kicked at the grass in frustration. "His mom had taken a shower and laid on the bed to watch some TV until Travis got back. She thought everything—the tension and all—was over. She fell asleep."

"When she woke up—no Trevor?"

"Yep. She's an absolute mess right now, Hector. Doesn't know what to do, where to look. I told her we'd be back to the motel in ten minutes."

"Give me your phone please, I want to talk with her," Hector insisted. Mickey punched the call return, handed Hector the phone.

Hector walked a few feet away. He was on the phone for about five minutes, listening more than talking. Turning back toward Mickey, he said 'goodbye' and returned the phone.

"What was that all about," Mickey asked.

"I told her not to worry. I'll find Trevor."

"That's all? You were on the phone for half an hour," Mickey exaggerated. "Did she say what I'm supposed to do?"

"Take Travis home, that's all." When Hector was in deep thought you could only imagine the wheels turning in his mind. "You might not be getting an early start in the morning, Father."

"That's the least of my concerns at the moment. I feel as if I'm to blame for all this and I don't quite know why. I wish you'd tell me what Marella told you so I had some idea about the reception I'll get when I bring Travis back."

Hector smiled, put his large hand on Mickey's shoulder, "I think you know she's miffed. She told me what you just said—that's all; obviously, she's worried."

"And...that would be about a one minute conversation. What else did she say?"

"And she thinks your friend, that baseball guy in Ft. Myers, is a sleazebag—never heard that expression before but it sounds horrid. And she won't allow her son to have any dealings with him again—for as long as she lives. She said the distinguished looking man from the Twins was sincere enough. That's about it."

Mickey knew Marella meant Terry Ryan. He shook his head: "You said 'miffed'...would pissed-off be a better way to describe it?"

"Miffed more than pissed, I'd say—such vulgar language, Father! Hector's smile was genuine, his hand on Mickey's shoulder comforting. "I think she's already told you, or implied, that she isn't comfortable with your relationship with her boys. Anyhow, she's overwrought at the moment and is saying things she doesn't really mean." He took Mickey's elbow and walked with him to his car.

"Thanks, Hector. I'll keep you posted."

"You'll be seeing me again shortly. I'm following you to the motel. For some strange reason...I think she trusts me. Said she wants to help me find her son."

~

A Venice squad car was parked in the motel lot when Mickey arrived. Marella was talking with two officers, the taller one was jotting down whatever Marella was telling him. The short officer with a large belly hanging over his thick gunbelt, and his cap tipped back on his head, was asking the questions. As he approached, Marella gave him a cold look. "That's the priest I told you about," she pointed.

Mickey heard the comment, raised his arms in mock-surrender..."I didn't do it," he said, hoping to defuse the tension. Both cops looked at him as if he was looney.

"You Father Moran?" The short officer barked with assumed authority. "C'mere, let's hear what you have to say."

~

Hector Munoz had connections everywhere. Connections that were so private and personal that he would never divulge their names to anyone else, even the police, under any circumstance. Some of his most valuable contacts were street people and gang-bangers who were indebted to him for any number of favors he had provided: A job for an unemployed uncle, groceries for a family that needed food, a doctor who would make a house call to a sick grand-mother…the list of compassionate deeds went in every direction, and into every corner. His first call went to Tug Vargas who owned a tattoo parlor in Venice. Next he called Randy J's unlisted number. Lucy was a dealer who knew the street culture better than anybody. The former hooker lived in nearby Sarasota, but had tentacles reaching from Clearwater to Venice. Lastly, he called Inspector Bradford of the Bradenton police department. Hector was confident that one of these calls would give him a lead to follow up on. Trevor Wind-song was a conspicuous young man and probably wouldn't have traveled far from the motel on the busy highway. Unless! Unless he hitched a ride—the streets of Tampa were less than an hour away. Tampa was a megalopolis.

Within ten minutes, Randy J. called. "The guy yer lookin' for just went into a laundromat on East Venice and Seaboard, north side of the street. Want me and Impy, he's that bro of mine you lended money to; 'member that? Anyhow, do ya want us to detain him? Looks like he'd be a handful for just one of us."

"Not necessary. I'll be there in five, just keep him in your sight. Let me know if he goes somewhere else…okay? Thanks Randy, I owe you one."

"Hell, man…you ain't never gonna owe me nothing,"

~

Trevor sat in the shadowed corner of the empty laundromat eat-ing a Snickers candy bar and sipping a Pepsi from the vending machines and seeming to be in deep thought when Hector approached. "Can I join you, Son?"

Startled, Trevor dropped the candy in his haste to stand up and defend himself. He recognized the tall man from the picnic but couldn't remember his name. More relaxed, he sat back down. "Okay, take a seat, I'm not gonna stop you." He gestured to the chair next to the one he had been sitting in and sat down himself. He averted Hector's eyes, "Mom send you to find me? I thought she'd have the police lookin' all over town by now."

Hector sat beside the young man, said nothing for a long minute. "Police won't do much of anything for twenty-four hours or so. You're an adult and they would respect your right to go as you please—at least for twenty-four hours or so."

Trevor's smile was slight but he liked what the tall man had told him. "Yeah, that's what I told my mom—I'm eighteen, I'm an adult."

Hector let Trevor collect his thoughts for a long minute. "Let me know when you're ready to go back to the motel."

Trevor was relieved that this tall man in the white shirt had found him rather that the priest or Benjamin or someone else he knew. He stood, offered his hand, "I'm Trevor, but I guess you already know that…what's your name?"

Hector introduced himself and shook hands.

"Is she really mad? My mom, I mean."

"More concerned than mad, I'd say."

"I wasn't gonna run away or nothin' like that. Just needed to get away and think some things out. Cool down."

Hector understood. "I know the need for space. How's the 'thinkin' going?"

"Mister Munoz…I know what I need to do…and my mom's not going to like it one bit. But…"

"But she can't stop you. Is that what you were going to say?"

"She can't–really. That's gonna be hard for her to swallow.

She's always had control, you know what I mean? Now things are different. I told her there's nothin' back home for me now. Nothin' at all."

"How about we all—you and me and your mom—talk this out. Maybe we can come up with something that works for all of us," Hector suggested. He had some options in mind that might resolve things. "What do you say?"

"You gonna take her side?"

"No. I'm a neutral party, Trevor."

"You got kids of yer own?"

"No. Why?"

"Just wondering. Can Father Mickey be a part of what we talk about? He's fair-minded."

"I'm okay with that…but we'll have to see if your mom is. At the moment, she's…well, she's kinda upset with Father Mickey. But I agree with you, he's about as fair-minded as anybody I know."

46/ HECTOR MUNOZ AND TREVOR WINDSONG

When Hector drove into the lot in his black Escalade it was nearly midnight, the police were just leaving. Marella was the first to spot Trevor through the heavily tinted windows. She raced to the door and pulled it open…"Are you okay, Trev? I've been worried sick…"

"Yeah, mom. I'm fine," he settled into his mother's tearful embrace. "I'm fine. Sorry I caused such a big deal. Mr. Munoz found me…I wasn't running away…I would have come back here in another hour or two. Just wanted to be by myself."

Hector joined the circle with Benjamin, Mickey, Mario, and the boy's mother. Marella dried her eyes with the sleeve of her terrycloth bathrobe, "Thank you, Mr. Munoz—Hector. It was so very kind of you."

Hector nodded without comment. Even in her disheveled and

emotional state, Marella Windsong was a beautiful woman.

"Let's get this over with," Trevor said. "Can we go in the room and talk?"

Marella nodded, "All of us?"

"I'm okay with that. We're all in this...this whatever-you-wanna-call-it...together, aren't we?"

~

Inside the small motel room, Marella sat on the bed beside Trevor holding his large hand in hers. Benjamin, more comfortable with conflict-avoidance, decided to go into the adjoining room and watch TV with Travis: "I'll keep an eye on Travis" he announced. Proactive behavior was not typical to Benjamin but his hasty retreat would spare him from any involvement in what he imagined might become a tense discussion. Mario chose to take a walk outside and get some fresh air. "It's too nice to be inside right now and I've got some prayers to catch up on. I'll join you all in an hour or so."

Mickey broke the uneasy silence from his chair near the bathroom door, "I'm going to apologize for...for whatever it is that I've done to offend you, Marella." He met her sharp gaze, then turned his eyes toward Trevor sitting beside her. "I'm sorry...to both of you. Would you like me to leave?"

Before his mother could respond, Trevor said, "No. Of course not. And, I don't know what you have to feel sorry about. Taking us all on the trip to Florida? Sharing your parties and all with us? Making arrangements for me to show off to Mr. Ryan and Mr. Steinbach? You've been more than generous to all of us and I, for one, am grateful. I've never seen so much of the country and visiting the Twins training grounds—my gosh, that's like...like dream stuff for me. Thank you very much, Father." Trevor, a young man of few words, had shattered the mold—both Mickey and Marella were almost dumbfounded to hear him say so much at once and express himself so clearly.

Marella swallowed the reality, but didn't add a thanks of her own. She placed her hand on Trevor's knee, "If it's that important to you I don't mind if Father stays. And Mr. Munoz? Do you want him to be involved in our issues, too?"

"Absolutely, I like him." Trevor met Hector's dark eyes. "It was pretty cool how he found me and let me decide what to do, what I wanted to do– without being pushy." The boy's emphasis on 'I' did not go unnoticed. Marella winced.

Hector nodded, his face as stoic as ever.

Another long pause, "I guess I started it all so I'll say what's on my mind," Trevor said. He went on to elaborate how his confidence had been given a huge lift by Mr. Ryan and how going home to the cold weather where every kind of training had to be done indoors was pointless. "In a month or two I'd want to come back down here anyways. That's when the Twins players come down for spring training." He turned to his mother, "Mom I'm not disrespecting you...I'm only respecting myself by wanting to try my own wings."

"I understand all that, Trevor," she gave his hand a squeeze. "I know you love me. But...what are you going to do when we've all gone back, Son? You know we can't stay down here. I don't think you've given this much thought. You can't live in some motel in Ft. Myers. I don't have that kind of money, and besides, I'd be a thousand miles away and worried sick."

Mickey turned to Hector as if on some unspoken cue. Without regard for costs, Hector could make any arrangements he wanted to–and Mickey's intuition told him that he wanted to do something. "Can you help us out with this, Hector? Any ideas?"

Hector was most comfortable when he was standing on his feet and in motion. Abruptly, he stood and surveyed the small room to appraise where he might be able to pace. There was no easy route so he turned from Trevor to Marella. "Marella," he chose to be personal in his comments, "I'd be more than happy to help of you'll let me. I have a business or two down here and a house with plenty of room for two people. I'm willing to give Trevor a job and have him live with me at my place. That's until his baseball stuff is resolved and we have a better handle on things."

Hector met Trevor's stare, then Marella's: "I'm strict. I won't tolerate misbehavior. I do travel quite extensively, but when I'm away from TriPalms, I'm confident that everybody there takes care of everybody else."

On the trip down to Florida, Mickey had told Marella about his deep respect and admiration of Hector Munoz. She remembered him saying that he was one of the finest men he had ever met and how he would trust Hector with his life. For reasons that confused her, she felt that trust...and a curious attraction for the tall, hand-some Cuban. He was easy to talk with, successful and stable, and...again, he was quite handsome. Hector's proposal was a so-lution that she could be comfortable with. "That's a very generous offer, Hector." His first name, rather than the more appropriate Mr. Munoz, came out without her intending it to. She looked at Trevor, then up at Hector standing behind the chair that Mickey occupied in the back of the room. Her next words, she knew, would change her life forever. "I would be okay with that..." she said, then turned to her son. "Trevor...the decision is yours to make."

47/ MINNESOTA JANUARY BLUES

Mickey sat in an empty pew facing the altar. It was early on a January Sunday morning and the church was dark and cool. Be-yond the rattle of the windows a heavy wind howled, while inside the sanctuary of old St. Gerard's, he listened to the creaks of age. It was as if the old building was protesting the subzero cold in a voice from the depths of its soul. He regarded the paint-splattered scaf-folding along the walls and the thick canvas drop cloths along the floors. His once doomed church was well into the early stages of a major renovation project. The air smelled of fresh paint and plaster. He closed his eyes in hope that his tangled thoughts might turn into prayer. But, his spirit seemed as frigid as the weather outside.

He hadn't slept well the night before, nor had he slept much the night before that. His insomnia of months before had returned, and along with it—a sore throat. He knew the symptoms well, the sore throat would be followed by a tight cough, then the suffering congestion—three days coming in, three days of misery, and three days of gradual recovery. Nothing he might attempt to do: liquids and rest, the numerous over-the-counter remedies in his medicine cabinet, nor bowls of chicken noodle soup, were going to make much of a difference. His hectic pace since well before Christmas had undermined his resistance to whatever was going around. A near epidemic flu virus had become a national concern, and Minnesota was one of the most contagious states. Half of Benton Park, in far western Duluth, was sick with colds and flu or a crud that fell somewhere in between. Offering the chalice of wine at mass as well as encouraging the handshakes when extending a 'sign of peace' had been suspended.

The past month of 'coming down' from his Florida 'high' had left him in a peculiar spot—a *'what am I supposed to be doing?'* mental atrophy, where any definition seemed too elusive to grasp. He hadn't seen Ben in nearly two weeks, hadn't talked with Marella since the group had returned to Minnesota, and hadn't even heard from the bishop in several days. In his last conversation with Hector, Mickey had learned that Trevor was doing well. Hector wasn't one for a lot of detail and Mickey didn't press for details. The only two people he had been in contact with on a near-regular basis were Father Mario (the two had talked almost daily for years) and Travis Windsong. He and Travis had met for coffee or lunch more than a few times. The boy was energized and steeped in campus life and…Mickey believed, very fond of a young woman back in Florida. "We text a lot but that's nothing like hearing her voice on the phone," Travis had confided. Mickey smiled to himself at the thought. Mickey, however, found himself wondering if things would have been better if he'd gone to Florida for the TriPalms festivities by himself. His life would certainly be less complicated than it was now if that had been the case. The events of the TriPalms reunion had been widely covered by the Duluth-Superior and Iron Range media, giving Mickey's celebrity another bounce. His feelings about all the renewed and amplified publicity were mixed.

At the center of Mickey's insomnia was his troubled self-perception. He both enjoyed and despised the 'ego trip' that had come to characterize who he was. Father Michael Moran had allowed himself to become 'Mickey' to everybody—like a carnival attraction wearing many different hats: *Father Mickey the adventurous priest, the miracle man, the reformer, the 'new face' of Catholicism,* and Father Mickey the parish priest. Strangers still flocked to St. Gerard's to hear him speak, shake his hand, have a picture taken with him after mass–nearly half of his phone calls came from groups who wanted him to be their guest at a meeting. Bishop Bremmer, the man that had reined him in and resettled him in St. Gerard's only weeks before, now wanted him back on the circuit and doing more of the PR things that perked the image of his beloved church. And, not to go unnoticed, much of Mickey's popularity rubbed off on His Grace at the helm of the Diocese of Duluth. Mostly, however, people in the pews meant bucks in the basket. TV and radio ads for the 'Catholics Come Home' campaign were renewed. If the bishop and the church bureaucracy were enamored with Father Mickey, Father Mickey was not enamored with himself.

Mickey's 'passageway' to prayer was clogged with all the superfluous *self* stuff this morning. Mickey had showered and dressed at four that morning, and had consumed four cups of 'rise-and-shine', black and strong, Arco Coffee. Despite the chills and overall lethargy, he felt hot-wired. His thoughts were bouncing off the walls of his mind like ping pong balls despite an after mass agenda, that was without commitment for the remainder of the day. He considered a drive over to the UMD campus for a visit with Mario, or Travis, or both. Or, perhaps, he might make a trip up to Hibbing to visit with his sister Meghan and her architect husband, Kenny. Kenny had hinted that there was something 'kinda confidential' that he wanted to talk over with him. Kenny and Meg were fun to be with. More than the two of them, however, he especially enjoyed spending time with a nephew and niece who adored him in the way that only children can. In Hibbing he might even visit his widowed Nana, Maddie Moran. He hadn't been up to his hometown—only seventy miles away– since Thanksgiving; two busy months had whisked by since then.

And, Marella Windsong lived in Hibbing. Their parting after the two-day trip back from Florida had been cool. A 'thanks for everything' and a weak invitation to 'keep in touch' were all Mickey could remember when he dropped her and Travis off. Why had he expected more? Marella had her life, he had his…and now, her two kids had theirs. The disconnect shouldn't really bother him. After all, little more than six months before he hadn't even heard of the Windsongs, now he seemed preoccupied with them. Why was that?

The scattered thoughts and feelings bouncing across his mind were not a compatible mix with his mass preparations, nor for the homily he hadn't given much thought to during the past week. The past week? Where had it gone? What had he accomplished since the previous Sunday? Mickey racked his memory for something of importance from seven lost January days. Morning masses, a luncheon talk to the Catholic Women of Duluth at the Damiano Center on Monday, the Rafinski funeral on Tuesday, religious education classes on Wednesday and an evening dinner-speaking event with the Hermantown Elks, Thursday was a blank, and a parish council meeting on Friday. What else? He hadn't done one spiritually gratifying thing in the past—how many hours were there in seven days? He computed the math in his head—168 hours! What did that say about his priesthood? His relationship with God? His personhood?

This Sunday was the *Third Sunday in Ordinary Time* on the Catholic calendar. Luke's Gospel for the mass was profound—one of Mickey's favorites. Yet he didn't know what he was going to say about the beginning of Jesus' ministry in Nazareth of Galilee, His own 'home town'. What element of the story would he focus on— the bold proclamation Jesus gave to His synagogue audience: 'I am the one', 'the fulfilment of Isaiah's prophecy...' or would he get a step ahead of that compelling story and suggest that Jesus' popularity of the moment was about to get trashed. What had he said in last year's homily? Then it struck his memory like a wrong chord on his guitar: Nothing—last year at this time he was on his 'sabbatical' run, somewhere in Florida. He remembered having been even more lost and struggling with his self and his priesthood back then.   Mickey closed his eyes once more and tried desperately to pray. This time, his mind was able to shut out all the distractions.

48/ THE RICH AND THE POOR

Trevor Windsong was discovering a world that he found almost too difficult to comprehend. For his first week, Hector had assigned him to a landscaping crew with one simple instruction: Learn what to do from those who are doing it. His foreman was a short man with a thick mustache named Pedro—Pedro something, a name in Spanish that Trevor didn't catch—Pedro who the other men simply called 'boss' or *jefe*. Pedro drove the truck and told the men what he wanted them to do. The other five men in the crew were experienced in using the equipment, spoke little or no English, and kept in perpetual motion. On his first day, Trevor was given a heavy *Echo* backpack blower along with earplugs, then a shrubbery trimmer that droned like a chainsaw. Obviously, he was to blow cuttings and debris from the streets, sidewalks, and driveways with the wand, and trim hedges evenly. The noise of both machines was deafening and, even with the muffling earplugs, his head throbbed and his nostrils burned from the exhaust of his machines. He hated the blower and envied the riding lawnmower jobs the others were given. Day two was spent unloading heavy bags of mulch, spreading the mulch, and crawling in the dirt planting flowers and shrubs. Everything was either noisy or boring. And…it was hot! Although the January heat was suffocating, he was required to wear thick green cotton coveralls with long sleeves. Salty sweat dripped from his brow, into his eyes, burning and blurring; wiping it away only seemed to make it worse. Whatever his assignment, *Jefe* was never too far away and always watching without expression. The small man's eyes were hidden behind aviator sunshades under the shading brim of a safari helmet. Trevor wondered if the bossman could read his anger as he studied every movement.

On the third day he went out with another of Hector's crews, this being a cement and interlocking paving stones contractor. Mostly he unloaded paving bricks and heavy concrete blocks for the driveway to a guest house that was under construction at the far end of the mansion's property. If the truck driver had parked ten feet closer to the job, he would have had some shade and much less distance to where he stacked the bricks. He was the 'new man' and as such did the heavy grunt work. Trevor, however, kept his frustrations to himself while avoiding association with his workmates. At the end of the day when Hector Munoz inquired about how he was doing, Trevor's response was simply 'okay'. Both were men of few words and cherished their personal privacy. In the evenings, Hector worked on his ledgers or read, mostly biographies, and Trevor watched TV or listened to music on his iPod. The matters that Trevor most wanted to talk about were things that Hector, being a wealthy man himself, might not be comfortable with. So Trevor kept them to himself.

During the first week, Trevor's crew had worked in the Mission Valley Country Club area of north Venice. The second week they traveled out to Casey Key, off the Gulf coast, and then worked a job in Boca Grande on Gasparilla Key. Trevor was not prepared for what he saw in those worlds of affluence and privilege. Mansions like castles, Bentleys and Massarati automobiles, yachts half as long as a football field, and every trapping of wealth imaginable. How could anybody be so rich? Rather than being struck with wonderment, Trevor was struck with outrage. He kept his feelings inside, allowing them to fester and gnaw at him constantly.

Hector was a perceptive man. For the first two weeks he abided Trevor's privacy without any attempt to pry. As he had agreed to do, he called Marella Windsong on Wednesday and Sunday evenings and gave her a report on 'how things were going'. Trevor talked with his mother briefly on each occasion, explaining his days and answering his mother's questions with: "Okay", "Not bad", or "No problem". For his part, Hector looked forward to his calls to Hibbing more than he would care to admit. Marella was a beautiful and spirited woman. Mysterious. And her voice had a lilt and timbre that was as unique as it was alluring.

Marella Windsong's days were empty now. She often sat on the beds in the boys' room and remembered happier days–days when she had a family to nurture. Her empty nest was her personal hell and she wasn't coping with that reality very well. She looked forward to Wednesday and Sunday when she spoke with Travis at UMD in Duluth and Trevor in Florida. Her conversations with Hector Munoz were pleasant, too. Hector was soft-spoken, kind, generous, and intelligent. Marella admired intelligence more than any other quality—that, and a sense of humor. Hector, however, didn't seem to have much of a sense of humor. Despite that, the tall Cuban had many other admirable qualities...and, he was quite handsome. There had been several occasions during the Florida trip when she caught him looking in her direction. And, she thought, he had caught her doing the same. For an hour or two during the Saturday night concert, she sat next to him...even sang along with him. She liked his white teeth and the crisp white shirt he wore; she liked his clean-shaven face and the soft scent of his cologne. Benjamin had told her that Mickey had told him that Hector had never married. Why had this seemingly wonderful and successful man never married? And…more importantly, how could a man like Hector ever be interested in an ordinary and mundane woman like her? Was there an attraction on his part, or was she simply imagining things? In the past, other men had found her to be quite attractive…but, that was some time ago. Now, just over forty, perhaps she had resigned herself to being single and alone. Perhaps? Maybe?

Marella knew there was one person that could, if she asked him to, serve as a 'go-between' of sorts in getting to know Hector Munoz better. Marella laughed to herself, and at herself. What foolishness! She could never ask. Yet, maybe if he were to volunteer some information? No, that wasn't going to happen, she hadn't talked to him since returning from Florida. How many times had she wished that she hadn't been so accusatory, so rude, so incredibly ungrateful? She remembered the deepest cut of all: "Why don't you stay down there where people think you can walk on water?" Marella wouldn't beat herself up any more—what's been done is done! 'Get over it', she reminded herself whenever the guilt surfaced. "Don't beat yourself up," she said into the boys empty bedroom. "Life goes on. It is what it is!" She hated both clichés, hated herself for using them. "Get up and do something," was a much healthier attitude.

~

The Sunday afternoon was blustery and much too cold to be outside for more than a few minutes. The weather service had issued a 'wind-chill advisory' for all of northern Minnesota. Marella had gone to an eight o'clock mass at the Immaculate Conception church, done some grocery shopping at Super One afterwards, and returned home to shovel drifts of snow from the front porch to the driveway. Weekends had never seemed so long and she virtually 'killed' time by finding household chores to do. She had never before ironed sheets, her inlaid oak laminate floors shone from cleaning, tabletops were dust free, windows were nearly invisible. Laundry and ironing and everything else that once took hours every weekend, now could be accomplished in a fraction of the time. If only it weren't so cold outside, she might cross-country ski along an old deer trail behind her house this afternoon. If only...

Marella eyed her cell phone resting on the kitchen countertop near the coffee pot. She wasn't expecting Travis to call until the late afternoon or early evening, Hector and Trevor closer to seven. What to do for the next five hours? Who to call? She microwaved her last half-cup of coffee, returned to the front window to watch the snow continue drifting over what she had shoveled earlier. She contemplated putting on her warm clothes again and reshoveling the sidewalk and the front of the garage door. No, that could wait until the wind died down. Turning back to the kitchen she considered her limited options: Maybe...she hadn't baked in weeks. She had a new recipe for peanut-fudge bars and all the ingredients in the cupboard. When she was bored or out of sorts, Marella often thought of food, snack foods, chocolate! The calories, however, were powerful inhibitors. "How silly is that?" she scolded herself, "My God, woman, you haven't gained a pound since high school..."

Her cell phone rang...

49/ TRAVIS, PETE, AND BEN

Travis put the finishing touches on his letter. He felt that a hand written letter was far more personal than any email or text message he might send. Besides, his phone plan charged extra for every text message. Mostly, Travis was writing because he had always enjoyed the feeling of a pen put to paper. Since junior high school, Travis had kept a diary. Sometimes he would make an entry every day for several weeks; at other times he would find a week or two had elapsed without his adding anything. Lately, letters had been replacing journal entries. The two highlights of his week—aside from an 'A' in his advanced computer-programming class—were the letter with the Ft. Myers, Florida, postmark and the Saturday night phone call. If they talked or skyped with each other every day, both agreed it might be too much. In his letter, Travis had confessed that 'after I talk with you I'm unable to get any of my schoolwork done…' then he asked the obtuse question of a boy in love but unaware of it: 'Why is that, Maria?'

When spring break came, in about five weeks, Travis was hoping to make another trip to Florida. He had enough gas money in his savings account and a dependable Toyota pickup truck. His only hurdle was his mother. Travis wondered to himself if he really needed her approval. He wasn't brash like his brother, nor was he as self-confident—but, he was eighteen. Travis and his mom, although opposites in most ways, had a solid relationship—a more tranquil relationship than she had with Trevor. Since returning from Florida, Travis had only talked with Trevor once and he felt like their bond was loosening. Was that good, or bad? At least there hadn't been any 'transferences' in weeks—aside from an aching back from time to time.

Relationships that simply 'happened' when he was younger were perplexing Travis now. His feelings for Maria Olivio, his disconnect with Trevor, his disgust with so many of the personal habits of his roommate, Gary Arthurs. The next time he visited with Father Mickey he would ask for the priest's perspective on these matters and others. Also, he was curious to find out if it was important that he get his mother's permission for everything he did—not so much the little things, but…

~

Peter Madigan was both confused and encouraged. In his last conversation with Mr. Ryan, Pete was informed that the Windsong family had expressed their wish that the Twins have only one contact person regarding Trevor's future. That contact person was an investment manager named Hector Munoz from Venice. On the other hand, Mr. Ryan had expressed an interest in employing Peter to do some scouting in the Gulf Coast League that summer. Further, a week ago, Jerry Bell had called him…'just wanted to say hello, see how you're doing, Pete'—Bell made no reference to any bad feelings over being stood up for dinner the previous spring. "Stop by the complex when you're in the neighborhood," Bell had cordially invited.

Sobriety, and the AA meetings he was regularly attending, had given him a sense of self worth that he thought had been lost and gone forever. He was beginning every day by attending mass and going to the gym to work out. While his spiritual self was growing, his waistline was shrinking. He was beginning to like the person that looked back at him in the vanity mirror. An uncle who lived in Columbus, Ohio, had died in November and left each of his four surviving relatives with a tidy sum of money. Pete couldn't remember the last time he had seen his eccentric uncle Robert, and had not been informed of the man's failing health or any details regarding the long past funeral arrangements. The tidy sum was $23,000. The frosting on Pete's recent 'cake of good fortune' was twofold: A legitimate offer on his Pike Lake property north of Duluth had been forwarded to him, and his daughter Brenda, had not only found a new job, but she was seeing a man who 'respected her'. Maybe she and Daryl Solen, the new man in her life, would come down for a visit in the fall. Life was good for Peter Madigan. He made a mental note to give Father Mickey a call and to thank him for…for opening a door of opportunity for him.

~

For Benjamin Little Otter, however, life had taken a wrong turn on the way back from Florida three weeks before. The trip wasn't a good experience for Ben. The big Indian had been the object of children's insensitive gawking and taunting, 'Geronimo' some had called him. Ben took the horseplay in stride, even did a little dance for them during the Saturday night sing along. What hurt the most was watching all the others enjoying themselves while he hung mostly in the shadows of everything going on around him. And, his habit of smoking tended to isolate him from his traveling companions. More than once he had been tempted to make his way to the beer tents. Why had he agreed to come in the first place? He knew he would be the 'third wheel'. With every pleasant gesture, and there were more than he would admit, he felt patronized. When asked by one of the visiting clergy: 'What are you doing here?' he shrugged and said 'I don't really know.' Even Mickey had been too busy with his own agenda to pay him much attention.

Back home at Fond du Lac, Ben slipped into a funk. During the long, gray days of January he hung around the Black Bear Casino for hours on end, playing the penny slots and drinking countless cups of coffee. He'd lost his appetite and wasn't sleeping well. One night he bought a pint bottle of cheap whiskey and locked the front door to his small bungalow. For nearly an hour he stared at the bottle, locked in a mind-game—*who was stronger*? In anger, he smashed the bottle in the kitchen sink and washed down the brown liquid. The smell of the booze nearly drove him crazy. He called his AA sponsor, Lester Hicks, and told him what had just happened. The two men prayed together. After that experience, Ben spent most of his time cutting and splitting wood for the stove in his small basement bedroom. Time in the forest, away from people, gave him a semblance of peace.

Mickey had called a few times, mostly just to say hello. Respecting his friend's resolve, Father Mickey never mentioned getting back together to work on their 'project' and Ben didn't inquire as to how things were going. Ben had little to contribute to their infrequent conversations. One sunny afternoon, as Ben was splitting and stacking firewood near the shed behind his house, a stranger wearing a white thermal coat wandered over to where he was working.

"Can I give you a hand, Benjamin?" The man was vaguely familiar and knew his name. Yet, people he knew rarely called him Benjamin.

"Nah, I gotta get some exercise, ya know."

The man lingered as Ben split another log. "How's Trevor doing, Benjamin?" the man asked.

Taken aback, Ben said, "Jus fine an dandy. He's been livin' down in Florida these days. Wouldn't be s'prised if he's playin' baseball with the Twins one day." Ben always felt the buoyancy of pride when speaking of his nephews.

When someone knew his name and he didn't know theirs, Ben felt an awkwardness. To ask 'Who are you?' seemed offensive, seemed to make the other person less of an equal, so he simply conversed as if he knew who the person was. "Yep…he's doin' mighty fine, I'd haf'ta say."

"Last I knew he was in pretty bad shape, busted up from that accident down by the river," the man said.

"You got that right…he surely was." How did the stranger know that? Was he one of the doctors? Or…?

"You don't know who I am, do you, Ben?"

Ben rubbed the sweat from his brow and unbuttoned the top two buttons on the thick plaid jacket he was wearing. He'd have to admit that he didn't. "Yer familiar…yet, these days I ain't got so good a memory."

"I'm the fellow that helped you get Trevor to the hospital."

Ben's memory of all that had transpired during the trauma of that rainy morning had never been clear. He looked away for a moment, leaning his axe against the stack of wood, trying to pull a name out his memory and match it with the face. Then it came to him, "Joseph"! He lifted his head to thank the man…

Benjamin Little Otter thought he was losing his mind. The man was no longer there.

49/A PEEWEE HOCKEY GAME

"When was the last time you watched a PeeWee hockey game?"

Marella recognized the voice immediately, smiled. "What kind of question is that, Father? You should know that Trevor never put on a pair of skates in his life. And, Travis doesn't have much interest in sports of any kind. So…probably never."

"Its not a question at all…actually, it's an invitation. An inept invitation at that."

Marella's forehead wrinkled, "Invitation? I don't get it."

"I'm nearly in Hibbing, just passed the Silica Fire Station on Highway 73. I've mangaged to wrangle an invitation to watch my nephew, Matthew, play hockey at the Memorial Building in half an hour. You've met his parents—remember Meghan, my sister, and her husband, Kenny?"

"I can't believe you're driving in this snow."

"It's either my love of hockey or my love for Matthew—I get the two of them mixed up. No, truth be told, I was bored sitting at home in the rectory with nothing to do and no one to do it with. Mario's tied up today and…I guess I don't have many friends to hang out with."

"Sounds familiar. But it's gotta be a bad case of boredom for anyone to drive in this weather."

"Promise you'll never tell a soul that I said that—the being bored thing, I mean. A priest must never be bored—Rule number three in our 'Practical Priesthood Manual'."

"What's rule one?"

"A priest must never drive his car in bad weather—unless it's an emergency."

"So you consider going to a kid's hockey game as an emergency?"

"A potential emergency. Hockey can be a dangerous game. Played on glare ice, by kids with lethal sticks…almost anything can happen." Both laughed at the same time. Mickey added, "Seriously, the weather was just fine when I left Duluth. It started snowing over the hill and began getting thicker near Floodwood. I'm following in the tracks of an SUV and I'm almost to Hibbing already."

Marella was still puzzled, "I see…and…did I miss something?"

Mickey apologized, "I'm sorry. I'll bet you're wondering why I've called."

"I am."

"Well, long story short, if you'll join me for Matthew's game, I'll buy you a hotdog or a cup of hot chocolate…maybe even both. It'll get you out of the house for a while and enrich your cultural awareness—you can't be a Hibbingite without a basic knowledge of hockey…so, what say you?"

Marella was both surprised and pleased in equal measure. "What if I wanted a burger and a Coke? And nachos if they sell them?" her laugh was soft.

"Okay, a burger is possible. Nachos? Let me think about that."

"I'll put on my face and be ready in ten minutes." She put away her phone without thinking of how people might perceive her being with Father Mickey. If everybody in this small town didn't know everybody else, they all knew Bob Dylan, Kevin McHale, and Mickey Moran. As she did her eyebrows in the vanity mirror, the thought of other people's thoughts brought a smile to her full lips. So what!

~

For Mickey and Marella, the ice of nearly a month was finally broken. The Sunday afternoon hockey game was fun. Hot dogs and Pepsi, sitting with Meghan and her daughter Kathleen, and watching Hibbing's kids beat Grand Rapids by three goals made for a wonderful time. And, watching Mickey's speedy and shifty nephew, Matthew Williams, score two of Hibbing's goals was frosting on the cake. Kenny was one of the bench coaches for Matt's team, keeping the lines together so swift changes could be made on the fly.

In the lobby, as the group waited for Matthew to pack up his gear, several people stoped by to say hello to Father Mickey. Marella was surprised that many of the parents, some of whom were well known in Hibbing, knew who she was. "You look lovely, Ms. Windsong," from the wife of Jim Rauker, the president of the Wells Fargo Bank. "How are your sons?" from Jennifer Berklich, the owner of a floral shop on Howard Street. Her daughter was a classmate of Trevor and Travis. "I heard that Trevor has recovered from that accident. Will he be playing ball next summer?" From Andy Saccoman, an architect whose son played goalie on Matthew's team. Marella relished her unexpected popularity.

Afterwards they all gathered at Meghan's house to watch the end of a pro football playoff game. Meghan made a batch of sloppy joes and put out a variety of nibbles—crackers and cheese, mixed nuts, and chips. Mickey's niece, Kathleen, went next door to hang out with her girlfriend, and Matty opted to play his Madden's football game on the computer upstairs. Although a stranger to hockey, Marella knew football fundamentals and strategy quite well and enjoyed the game as much as the men. "Interference!" she shouted as a Bronco receiver attempted to catch a Peyton Manning pass. "That guy would have had it if that defender wasn't all over his back."

"That's Decker, he's from Minnesota, played at the U." Mickey added an aside to impress the others.

"Did he play for Jerry Kill?" Marella asked. Kill was the second year Gopher's football coach that she had met when the coach had visited her home to talk with Trevor about being a 'walk on' at the U.

Neither Mickey nor Kenny knew the answer but were impressed with the question.

At six, Mickey and Marella excused themselves. Marella was expecting phone calls and Mickey had to drive back to Duluth. Meghan implored her brother to stay overnight, "The roads will be bad with all this snow. You can leave early tomorrow morning of you need to."

Mickey declined. "Too many things to take care of yet tonight and an early mass in the morning. I'll be fine, I'll take 53 instead of 73—it's probably much safer."

In thanking Mickey, as he opened his car door in the Windsong's driveway, Marella confessed that she hadn't done anything fun in years—"Today was good, relaxing, fun! I loved every minute. Thanks." Mickey couldn't believe it, "I thought you were having fun in Florida."

Marella shook her head. "I enjoyed the experience, *enjoyed*. It was all new and interesting."

"But?"

"But I was very tense, I guess. I never quite knew where I fit into the scheme of things. Feeling out of place was one thing, but the debacle with that sleaze in Ft. Myers was another—enough said. I can't believe you couldn't see it, my stress level, I mean."

"I guess I was too wrapped up in myself to think enough about how anybody else was doing. I hate to admit that, but I do…I always seem preoccupied with myself."

"You think that makes you different? Heaven's sakes, we all do."

"I suppose."

Marella nodded, smiled. "Have you ever felt like a shadow person? I mean, like you were an unnoticed nobody in a crowd of people?

Oh, and there were crowds...almost everywhere you went down there. I don't mix well in crowds of people."

"It was hectic...and, yes...people were everywhere." Mickey might have admitted that he loved the crowds and enjoyed being the center of attention. But, that was something he could confess to Mario and very few others.

"And then there was Trevor's episode," Marella said.

Mickey didn't comment. That was a can of worms best left for another conversation. He diverted,"I find it hard to believe you felt unnoticed?"

Marella nodded, "Well, I spent a lot of time with my brother-in-law. But, Benjamin is so low-key I have to check his pulse every so often," she laughed along with Mickey. Even my boys were wrapped up in other things and hardly had time for doing anything with me. I felt dull, too." Her eyes averted and she swallowed hard.

Mickey saw that her dark eyes were focused on something beyond this place and time. It was cold and snowflakes sparkled and danced in the headlamp beams of his idling car. "It was all so new and so interesting, and I couldn't believe the beautiful weather..."

"But?"

"Oh, I'm sounding like a chronic complainer. It was all very generous of you." Marella's eyes found Mickey's, "I thought your friend, Father Mario, was nice. Very nice. I felt as if he was the only one who could tell that I was feeling kinda low."

"Well...I don't think Mario was the only one concerned about you."

Marella puzzled. "Well, everyone was very nice—I mean...your parents, Meghan and Kenny, the Wheelers, the Olivios...everyone! And they all think the world of you, that's for sure. As your guest I was certainly a person of interest and treated as such...and...Travis make quite a splash with everyone."

"I think you've missed someone, Marella." Mickey gave a subtle wink, "That tall, dark stranger? One my dearest friends in all the world?"

Marella knew exactly who he meant but her forehead furrowed and she shrugged her shoulders, "Who?"

Mickey broke out laughing. "I'm sorry. It's not funny, but it is amusing. Of all the people you met over that weekend you only forget to mention one of them. How strange is that?"

"Oh…Mr. Munoz?" A long pause, "I thought he was very *nice*. And his offering to take Trevor into his home—well that was an *incredibly nice* gesture. Yes, I'd have to admit—he was especially kind for a relative stranger."

Mickey didn't comment. Mildly embarrassed, Marella continued by repeating herself, "Yes, I couldn't agree more; Hector was very nice. . . but I didn't really get to know him very well."

"Nice…you mean kind and polite *nice*? That's a pretty mellow adjective, Marella, don't you think?" Mickey was good at reading people's faces and mannerisms and discerning things that were not said. And, he loved to tease. He could read emotions in a person's eyes and their subtle facial nuances—and, even more clearly, he could hear it in another's voice. Marella fidgeted with the hood of her green and purple Columbia jacket. "Yes…kind and polite, and every bit the gentleman you said he was on the trip down."

Mickey smiled, "A gentleman in every way." He would be very careful and respectful of Hector's feelings. The two had talked on several occasions since parting ways a month before. He also knew that Hector and Marella talked with one another quite often. "Hector and I talk from time to time and he always asks how you are doing. Not just in passing…Hector, more than anyone I know, has a powerful sense of empathy. He knows how dramatically your life has been changed by everything. He hopes and prays that Trevor does well—and Travis, too. And he hopes that you are coping—is that the right word, Marella…coping?"

50/ HECTOR'S STORY

When Hector called later that evening, Marella was much less reserved than usual. In previous conversations she and Hector talked mostly about Trevor and his work. Both were inhibited about sharing details about themselves. Tonight, Marella shared the enjoyable day she had had with Father Mickey and his family. "Have you ever seen a hockey game, Hector?"

"As a matter of fact, no. As a kid in Cuba…"

Marella giggled, "I forgot about that. I suppose ice cubes were as close as you came to an ice skating rink."

Hector laughed. "Ice cubes were for the very wealthy who lived in Havana, not for farmers on the southern coast where we lived. Anyhow, you asked if I've ever seen a game? Not really…a minute here or there when I surf the TV, but I have been meaning to see a game in live time. We have a pro team down in Estero, not too far from here…and a huge new arena."

Marella's enthusiasm was contagious. For the first time she heard Hector Munoz actually laugh. And, for the first time there were no awkward pauses. He didn't know much more than hockey was on a sheet of ice with sticks and a round thing called a puck. His questions about the game were an amusement to both. "I didn't know much before this afternoon, either," Marella confided. "But if was fast and fun, and these little kids on Matthew's team did a lot of banging into each other—mostly by accident I hope. It's a good thing they have plenty of protective equipment."

After exhausting their hockey knowledge, there was a lull. Hector picked up the lost thread with some good news to report. "I'm seeing some really positive changes in Trevor these days…"

~

After his first two weeks, Trevor Windsong began opening up a bit. The two men were sitting in Hector's small living room—

Trevor was perusing a *Sports Illustrated* magazine, Hector playing Backgammon in his iPad. Trevor asked the one question that would lead to another, then another…"How did you get to be so rich?"

Hector was amused at the unvarnished inquiry: "I can't make a long story short, Trevor. Are you okay with that?"

Trevor nodded, putting aside his magazine, "I'm not going any-where," he said.

Hector grinned, "You asked for it. I started setting goals for myself at an early age, shortly after my sister and I settled here in the States. Goals like good grades in school and having a savings account of my own." Hector explained how, as an eleven year old he found an old lawn mower near a dumpster in Ft. Myers. Living across the alley from his family was a mechanic who knew how to fix the engine and Hector asked for his help. "That's one important lesson I learned: Ask for help when you don't know how to do something." Hector sold the mower for his first six dollars. At twelve he learned how to detail cars, "I was determined to be more detailed than the other detailers; I even used a toothbrush and Q-tips when cleaning the dust from every nook and cranny of the interior. A very wealthy man gave me a twenty dollar tip. The man's name was Burns, Walter Reed Burns. I saved it and I saved every dollar I made after that, detailing Mr. Burns Rolls Royce every week—often when it didn't really need it. "I told him that he could save money by only cleaning his car when it needed it. He said, "I'm making an investment in you–not the car!' When I was fifteen, my uncle had me help with a wallpaper job he was doing. So I learned how to do that, too. By now, I was continuing to do odd jobs for my generous benefactor, Mr. Burns—not only washing his cars, but doing some outside painting, cleaning his garage, things like that. When I told him that I could do stuff inside, too…he asked what that might be. He knew that I could paint, so I told him that I could also do wallpapering.

"I remember Mr. Burns laughing, 'I'll tell my missus about

that'. He did. Weeks later, when he said 'Give it a whirl' I tore out some old wallpaper in a back foyer of their house and hung some new wallpaper for Effie, his wife. She was delighted. Am I boring you yet, Trevor?"

"Not at all," a rare smile escaped from the boy. "Where did you learn how to do wallpaper stuff?"

"From my uncle, Eduardo Munoz—my surrogate father here in the States."

"Okay. So you're a teenager who can wash cars and do wallpapering. I'm getting the picture."

"Well, by the time I was seventeen I had saved twelve hundred dollars. My friends were buying fancy cars and pickup trucks, I bought an old Mack tow truck. My neighbor and I got it running pretty good. You can imagine how much razzing I got about my wheels. But their wheels were for fun and mine were for business. My first high school date was a girl named Claire...she was also my last high school date. Claire just didn't appreciate going to a school dance in a tow truck." He laughed to himself at the memory. "Now, tell me when to stop, Trevor. I can do this story in installments."

Trevor actually chuckled while shaking his head. "Did you get a good night kiss?"

"Not even close!" Hector continued. "Mr. Burns had a business partner named Frank something-or-other. Frank was married, but he wasn't a monogamous type of guy—you know what I mean?"

"He fooled around?"

"Yes. Anyhow, Frank and this 'other' woman, had partied too much and Frank went off the road down near North Port. Frank called Mr. Burns from a gas station–said he was in trouble. Mr. Burns called me: 'Still got that tow truck, Hector?' Well, I picked up Mr. Burns and the two of us saved Frank a world of embarrassment. I never asked Mr. Burns if this Frank guy quit all his cheating and drinking after that."

"That was none of your business, right?"

Hector nodded.

Hector went on to explain how Mr. Burns gave him seed money to purchase a small lawn and landscaping service in Bonita Springs. "I had just turned twenty-one when Mr. Burns got me a contract to do some work in a new, high-scale gated community called Emerald Pines in Sarasota." Hector's first company did well and that led to the purchase of another. "Then I asked myself, 'why purchase flowers and shrubs and sod when I could grow them yourself'? That's when I began purchasing land. Next, I asked myself 'why should I pay to have my equipment serviced when I could do that by myself as well'?" Hector went on to explain how one thing led to another and another. "It always takes money to make money," he said.

After fifteen minutes, wide-eyed Trevor asked the one question that had been at the core of his discomfort. "Why do people build castles to live in?"

Hector had an incredible memory and the insight of a self-made man. He had been picking up on the little things Trevor had been saying when the boy came home from work. And he had talked regularly with Pedro, the crew foreman, who informed him: "The boy stews a lot...the only two bad things I ever saw him do was the times when..." Pedro told Hector he saw Trevor spit on the tire of some guy's Masseratti and when Mr. Grant up in Boca gave him a dirty look for blowing leaves in his direction, the boy had given him the finger—'behind the man's back, of course' Pedro added.

Hector anticipated Trevor's not-so-subtle distaste for wealth. "Everybody has a story. Remember that mansion on Casey Key, the one with all those fancy turrets?" Trevor did. "Well that's Mr. Burns' house. I wanted you to see his place and the best way to see it was to have your crew trim the shrubs and all the little things you do to make a customer's property look attractive. I think you did the mulching and weeding around the entire house that day. I asked Pedro to give you that specific job. Anyhow, Mr. Burns' various companies employ about ten thousand people—many of whom are immigrants—and those companies purchase materials from other companies that employ thousands more. He's been my mentor and my role model since I was twelve. In addition to employing people, he gives millions every year toward scholarships, replenishes food shelves, offers matching grants to nearly every charity you can imagine. He does tons and tons of good, most of which nobody ever knows about. Anyhow, his wife wanted a big house so they could have lots of foster kids during the summer when school was out–at last count, I think he and Effie have had more than eighty kids live with them at one time or another. Many of them were from broken homes and had serious behavioral problems."

Hector finished by explaining, "Every person has a story. And, I believe, every person will be given a final opportunity to tell that story to the One person who makes all the difference. We are, each of us, accountable to God for the life we lead. I can't judge anybody by any human standard—the house they live in, the car they drive, the yacht moored at their dock…any of the conspicuous material things. Nor do I judge the poor man or woman in the tough neigh-borhoods of any American city that you can think of—or the addict, or the prostitute, or the bank robber. The food stamps and entitle-ments that keep poor people from starving come from the people who pay the taxes. Mr. Burns and others like him pay lots of taxes."

Trevor nodded, "You make lots of money and pay lots of taxes, too. But you ain't got no fancy house. Why's that?"

"That's just me."

"And you don't wanna have any big house to explain in that last story you gotta tell some day?"

"I think you got it, Trevor."

"You're a lot like this Burns guy, aren't you?"

"He was my mentor and my friend. He's given me lots of good

advice over the years."

"Like what? Tell me the one that's most important."

Hector contemplated, "I'll never forget something he told me on many occasions. He said, 'never aspire to be *good enough* at something'. That's selling yourself short. *Good enough* will never get you to the top of the ladder."

~

It was the day following that conversation that Hector introduced Trevor to Johnny Aquilla, a former first round draft pick of the Houston Astros baseball team back in '84. Aquilla, who worked in Hector's accounting office, had agreed to come by every other evening after work and 'play catch' with Trevor. Aquilla, like many other pitching phenoms in the eighties, had never recovered from arm surgery. Johnny Aquilla and Trevor hit it off from the start.

51/ SHOWING HIS STUFF TO THE TWINS

On Monday, the morning after talking with Marella, Hector informed Trevor that the two of them had another appointment in Ft. Myers. "This one really counts, son…" Hector only realized his reference after saying the word. He covered the word quickly by adding, "Johnny Aquilla is coming along for the ride."

Trevor smiled at the idea of having his new mentor come along, "he'd be great moral support," he said. He might have guessed what the appointment was about but chose not to venture his speculation. Aquilla had worked with him on his pivot and release point, stressing what the old veteran called 'muscle memory'. The finger and palm grip on the ball for a changeup pitch was something Trevor couldn't do very well—it frustrated him to know that some form of changeup pitch was something he'd have to master.

On the drive down to the Twins training facility in Ft. Myers, Hector explained: "There is a simple and absolute protocol for our meeting, Trevor. I will do the talking—all of the talking. I want you to speak only when I ask you to—and when you do, be brief." Hector grinned, "Can you be okay with that? Being brief, I mean?"

Trevor was in his own world of thoughts and not paying close attention, "Yeah," he said without catching the humor at the end of Hector's instruction.

"I'm not patronizing, Trevor. But there might be some contract and money conversation—that's my game. Your game for now is throwing a baseball."

Trevor offered a rare smile, "Right boss...right *jafe!*" Aquilla nodded his approval at the Spanish choice of words. Hector laughed again.

After parking his vehicle, Hector told Trevor and Johnny Aquilla, "You two guys take a run and do whatever it is you need to do to loosen up. I'll be back in half an hour or so." Trevor's eyes widened when he saw a man giving some pointers to a uniformed player in a batting cage off to his right. "That isn't...?"

Johnny nodded, "It is. And who's that over there?" he pointed toward the infield where two players were working on double play footwork, near second base. "That older guy wearing number twenty-nine?"

Trevor shook his head in disbelief, "Rod Carew! Can I get autographs? And, wasn't that Tony Oliva with the bat on his shoulder near the batting cage? Number six?" The two former Twins greats were in Ft. Myers for a charity golf event and a spring training planning session, along with former manager Tom Kelly and hall of famer, Paul Molitor. Trevor felt as if he had awakened in the middle of an impossible dream—a *'Field of Dreams'* experience. His friend Johnny was equally enthralled, "Think of all the die-hard Twins fans that would give their right arm to be here and see those greats together in one place. Too bad Harmon couldn't be here." Aquilla's reference to Harmon Killebrew drew a nod from the younger man at his side.

Hector was gone for nearly an hour. The morning was turning hot and Trevor had taken off his shirt after working up a sweat running around the perimeter of the training fields. Johnny found a shaded spot to lie in the grass. Hector approached from the stadium with three men. None of them were talking, all of them had serious expressions on their faces. One of them was wearing navy wind-pants and a t-shirt under his catcher's gear, another was in casual dress clothes, the third was Rick Anderson. Anderson was the Twins pitching coach. Trevor had seen him many times on television and realized that, in person, he looked exactly like he did on TV—maybe a tad taller. Trevor's mouth went suddenly dry. This was big time stuff! "Jeeze!" he mumbled under his breath. "Rick Anderson!" The man in catcher's gear was Drew Butera.

Hector made the round of introductions. Trevor didn't get the last name of the guy wearing the red polo shirt. Rob something? Anderson recognized Johnny Aquilla and the two men small-talked from past experiences about pitchers they both remembered. Anderson was curious about what Johnny had been doing these past many years, Johnny wanted to know what Andy expected from Kyle Gibson and the new guy, Vance Worley from Philadelphia, this season. Gibson was an Aquilla favorite since being a first round draft pick by the Twins: Worley a potential ace this coming season.

Trevor edged closer to the conversation as Hector visited with the man in the red shirt. Anderson turned away from Johnny, gave Trevor a puzzled look. "What's that, young man?" he asked as he stepped closer and pointed to the scar tissue on the young man's left arm below the screeming eagle tatoo. "Surgery?"

Trevor looked to Hector, he wasn't going to say anything without permission. Hector moved behind Trevor, put a hand on his shoulder. "The boy's had some remarkable surgeries as a matter of fact. I've got the names and addresses of his surgeons up in Duluth. I'd expect you folks to check out everything with a Dr. MacIver at St. Mary's."

"What kind of work was done? How long ago?" From Rob, whose pleasant smile of moments before had vanished. "Let me see." Rob took Trevor's left arm in his hand and traced the conspicuous line of scars. "Lower arm and wrist? Nothing done with your elbow?"

Hector spoke, "I've got a full report in my folder. The surgeon did an incredible reconstruction of the wrist. I've got the *JAMA* story from last October's issue in the folder, too. We'll get into all of that later."

Rob Antony—the man in the red shirt– looked to Rick Anderson, then to Drew Butera. "Well, let's have a look guys. See if what we've heard about the kid is true."

The group walked back toward the stadium where a bullpen with five pitching mounds was located, Trevor and Johnny trailing the others by several yards. "What do you think they're gonna want to see?"

"They'll tell you what they want you to do. Just relax. Imagine that yer throwin' to me back at the house. If you get too uptight yer gonna be high with every pitch. Try and shut everything out of yer mind."

After soft-tossing for a few minutes, Butera asked Trevor to let him know when he was ready. Trevor nodded, "let's do it now…I'm ready to go." His shoulder was loose, and his wrist as flexible as he had hoped it would be.

"Let's see some heat first." Butera pulled down his mask, crouched behind the plate, and offered a target. Trevor cut loose a fastball that hummed high over Butera's shoulder to the backstop. "Whoa…hold your horses, amigo," Butera called out as he threw him another ball. "Rub it down, and don't grip so hard," he suggested. The next two pitches were on target making a crisp pop in Butera's mitt. Trevor's delivery, Anderson noted, was smooth for an eighteen-year-old, and he wasn't letting his arm lag behind his body nor was he overstriding in his follow-through. Anderson, behind and off to the side, held a *Bushnell* radar speed gun. He smiled approvingly, called over to Rob Antony: "Scale six," was all he said. A scale six fastball was in the 90-92 mph range—a scale eight would read over 98.

Butera held up his arm, turned to Anderson, "You want to see the other pitches?" Anderson nodded and Butera went back into his crouch. "Let's see a slider."

The ball bounced off the hard clay behind the plate and struck Butera in the groin. "What was that?" He stood up wincing and adjusted his cup. "The ball dropped two feet! Straight down!" The catcher turned to Anderson, "That was something!"

When Trevor was able to demonstrate that the first pitch wasn't a fluke, Butera asked him to throw a few from the stretch position. Trevor did as asked and had the same results. Anderson called over. "That's enough, guys. I think we can go back upstairs to the office."

Butera ran up to Trevor, smiled, "That was some awesome stuff, kid. I haven't seen anything quite like that before. I could tell when you were trying too hard…the ball was high in the zone. When you were relaxed and natural, you had some snap." He shook Trevor's hand, "Good luck with the brass upstairs."

Trevor returned the smile and nodded, "Thanks" was all he could say. He was trying to come up with a question or two for the veteran catcher when Anderson walked up to him, "That was impressive, Trevor. Very impressive!" Anderson didn't say it but he was equally impressed with the eighteen-year-old's size and could only imagine his future growth potential. The Twins' pitching coach liked to see raw speed, good junk, and a killer instinct in his pitchers.

52/ THOUGHTS OF EACH OTHER

Marella was pleasantly surprised to see Hector Munoz' number on her caller ID. She had just arrived home from work and tossed her Columbia ski jacket on the sofa. Her heart thumped an extra beat. Hector had told her the night before that he was expecting to hear from the Twins front office early on Monday morning. She hoped that he had some good news. Or any news, for that matter. Just hearing from him was nice. *Nice?* Mickey's chide of her use of the word *nice* brought an easy smile. She cleared her throat before picking up her cell. Her "Hello Hector" offered more enthusiasm than usual.

For a man more comfortable listening than talking, Hector gave a lengthy and detailed account of their day in Ft. Myers. "They, both Mr. Ryan and Rob Anthony, were impressed. They were comfortable with the conditions you wanted me to express. Before they do anything, or make any offers, you can expect to hear from them."

Marella imagined Hector sitting in a recliner, wearing a starched white shirt and khaki slacks, his face clean shaven, and his dark hair combed neatly on the sides…that image was more than nice. His ears were big and his nose had a slight bend, but his features all worked in a combination that most women would consider handsome. She certainly did. As she listened, Marella regarded herself in a reflection from the kitchen window in front of where she was brushing a few toaster crumbs from the counter into the sink. She was attractive, too. Her dark hair was stylishly cut, her eyes large and expressive, her lips full. When she smiled, which wasn't often enough, her white teeth were even and her cheeks slightly dimpled. In the back of her thoughts for the past several weeks were feelings she didn't understand. For years, countless years, she had developed an instinctive 'block' in her mind when it came to men. To her, they all had one thing on their mind and she wasn't going to have any of it. Her wariness had evolved into something almost phobic—she distrusted all men with the two obvious exceptions of her sons. Why hadn't the red flags waved when she first encountered Hector Munoz? Marella could not discern any good answers to that question.

The two of them talked longer than usual. For the first time, Hector asked her to be more specific about the job she had in Hibbing and her interests in other areas. Her work was mostly clerical and routine she admitted. Other things: she enjoyed reading—novels mostly–watched the news on ABC, did volunteer work at the local hospital on Tuesday evenings, belonged to a prayer group, and enjoyed her flower garden in the summer. Marella did have a unique hobby that had given her mild acclaim over the years. She asked Hector if he knew what a 'dream catcher' was. He didn't. "I'll try to give you a short explanation of what they are. Trevor can tell you more if you ask him to. I sent his down in the first package I mailed. I'm sure that it's hanging somewhere in his bedroom– probably in a window or over his bed. I made his dream catcher when he was small—four or five. His is very special– I might even say *sacred* to him. He's much more connected to his than Travis' is with the one I made for him at about the same time. As you will come to learn, they are my night and day twins." After saying that, she wondered how Hector might take her reference *'as you will come to learn'*.

Rather than dwell on the thought, Marella explained the lore of the Ojibwa and other Native American's cultural values regarding dream catchers. "It is believed that our dreams are messages sent by sacred spirits, the Ojibwe call them *Manidoos*—some are good and some are bad. The good ones pass through a hole in the center of the web, the bad ones are trapped so that they do not come through. A dream catcher is shaped like a hoop– they can be small or large– and they consist of a web made of strings and often are adorned with feathers and beads. Every item in their construction has an important meaning: An owl's feather, for example, is wisdom, an eagle's feather is power—and masculine. Gender distinctions are very significant to our people."

"Did you say that you made them yourself?"

"Yes. And, I might add, mine are quite in demand." Marella would give herself some deserved praise. "People think that the ones I create are more potent than most. I've made special ones for my sons, for Ben, and a few very close friends. I've never made one to sell—I think that would be wrong."

A long moment of silence hung between them. Marella wasn't certain if she should offer…Hector wasn't quite sure if it was proper for him to ask. "I'll make you one," Marella finally said. "I'll ask an elder at Fond du Lac, that's where Ben lives, if he will give me an eagle feather and some other things I will need."

"How about an owl feather, as well?" Hector said.

"For sure. What colors do you like, Hector? For the beads."

Hector gave the question a few moments of thought: "Earth brown and flora green…oh, and what I call *Gulf Coast*, of course. That's a special blue-green…"

"I know, it's beautiful—I love being near the water, walking the shoreline on a sunny day. Are you familiar with turquoise? It's blue-green like the Gulf and it's a sacred gemstone to us. I mean 'us' as in Native American Indians 'us'."

"I got it the first time, Marella. But, I like the *other* us, too." His timely and clever comeback surprised him. After putting away his phone, Hector pondered the mystical, even magical, paradox of 'chemistry'. He was a businessman and an intellect, a man who prided himself on understanding motivations, attractions, and com-pulsions, and their practical consequences. Logic. Reason. Com-mon sense. There seemed to be no rhyme-nor-reason for having these feelings toward Marella Windsong…except that they were real. Her beauty, her rare smiles, her voice…each held a magnet-ism. Was it her unmitigated spirit, more than anything else, that had first caught his notice? Over the years, Hector had dated many beautiful women: successful women, women of culture and prominence. But they were simply interesting or fun to be with. How was it that this woman from the a thousand miles away, living in the frigid north of Minnesota, and so different from him in so many ways…was so alluring? Hector could only smile at himself and admit there were things beyond his comprehension, and that it felt good just to go with the flow of feelings for a change.

53/ TRAVELING WITH THE BISHOP

Marella had goose bumps after putting aside her phone. Hector had offered several hints of affection, whether intentional or not, for her to dwell on. The giddy feeling was something wonderful, strange, and frightening—all at the same time. One thought, more than any other, lingered…when would she be able to justify another trip to Florida—maybe to sign Trevor's contract papers; maybe to see her son pitch, maybe something altogether different…?

Father Mickey also had an unexpected phone call on that Monday night, his from Bishop Bremmer. The bishop moved quickly through the small talk of the recent arctic blast (wind chills near minus forty) the upcoming Super Bowl (Bremmer, a disappointed Bronco fan who loved the intricate game plan strategies of pro football) and his favorite pictures from the trip to Florida the previous month. "I'll be picking you up about nine tomorrow morning, so make whatever adjustments necessary to your schedule. You'll want to pack some things because we'll be out of town overnight." Bremmer enjoyed the authority structures of his church bureaucracy, reveled in any opportunity to exercise his will, and more than either, to hang a bit of mystery onto his intentions. "I'll tell you more about it when I arrive—be ready to go. God bless."

It was all that perfunctory. Mickey didn't even have an opportunity to reciprocate a blessing to His Grace before the line went dead. Ten minutes later, Father Mario called. "Hey, Mick, I just learned that we've got a road trip scheduled for tomorrow—an overnighter with Beamer…how's that for a real treat?" Mario giggled. Mickey could picture his friend's silly expression at the other end of the line. 'Beamer' was a nickname the two priests held secretly for their bishop. Bremmer rarely smiled and kept it slight whenever he did. His surname lent itself to something altogether contrary to his nature: 'Beamer' was a perfect antithesis.

"Yeah, what's it all about, Mario? Beamer wouldn't say. All he told me was to be ready for a pickup at nine tomorrow morning. Fill me in."

"Can't do. I'm in the dark as much as you are. He complained about the weather, Denver's OT loss to Carolina a week ago, and all the catch up work he still had to do because of his taking those three days off to go to Florida. Then…"

"Then he said be ready to go, am I right?"

"That was about it. So, like you, I haven't got a clue. Overnight? I can't think of anything going on up here on Tuesday or Wednesday. I even checked Bremmer's calendar on line and it looked pretty routine to me. Something must have come up earlier today—but what that might be I have not a clue."

~

Elderly Father Leon Graham, a retired fill-in priest, unexpectedly arrived at the rectory door just after seven that evening. "Bishop said I'd be here for a few days, Father." No 'hello', 'how are you', or any other pleasantry. Graham hung up his heavy coat, picked up his satchel, and made his way to the stairway. "G'night, Father."

Mickey laughed to himself. Graham had been Mickey's substitute while he was in Florida and knew the parish well enough. "You can sleep in if you'd like, Father," Mickey said. "I'll be saying the eight o'clock in the morning." Father Graham probably wasn't wearing his hearing aids because he simply plodded up the stairs, one painfully arthritic step at a time.

~

The bishop's black Lincoln Navigator arrived precisely at nine. Mickey, dressed in his priestly blacks and collar, ran the fifty feet from the rectory to the car with his winter jacket slung over his shoulder. He felt the north wind's bitter sting on his cheeks and its burn in his eyes. The Navigator's back door was locked. Mickey rapped on the window for Mario to open up…Mario only smiled. "Password," he said. Mickey thought quickly for something clever to say, "God bless northern Minnesota…" he shouted.

"Sorry, pal. Not even close."

Mickey could see that even stoical Bishop 'Beamer' Bremmer was enjoying the tease. "Praise the Lord!" Mickey tried. Again Mario shook his head.

"Com'on, Mickey. What did your mother teach you to say when you wanted something?"

Mickey's fingers were getting numb, "Please?" The door opened and laughter escaped.

As they pulled away, Bishop Bremmer told the two priests that they were going to St. Paul—to the Cathedral there. "Now, can either of you tell me who's in the Twin Cities for the week? For heaven's sake, it's been in our *Northern Cross* (the diocean monthly newspaper) and the local papers enough."

Mario was in a witty mood this morning, "That guy from the NBA, visited North Korea…the one with all the tats and piercings…Dennis Rodman?"

The bishop wouldn't dignify the comment; his frown said enough.

Mickey racked his memory, it must be someone important; someone everyone would know. Hibbing's own, Bob Dylan, was doing a concert at the Ordway—but that was the following weekend. Obama was probably on vacation and golfing somewhere warm…and he would be the last person on earth that Bremmer would drive to the Cities to see. A politician, or an entertainer, or some celebrity. Stumped, Mickey would test the bishop's humor. "I've got it, Your Grace…how very thoughtful of you to take the two of us along with you."

Bremmer craned from his front passenger seat, "You've seen it in the papers then, Father?"

"Yes I have," said Mickey. "Britney Spears!"

Bishop Bremmer had very little humor but a giggle escaped his lips. Mickey's jest, like that of Mario's did not warrant a reply. The giggle was quickly suppressed, as Bremmer mumbled something barely audible. "Maybe I'll keep you two clowns in the dark until we stop in Hinckley." He turned to Henry, the ancient diocesian 'man of many hats'; "please turn on the Catholic radio station, Henry."

Both priests, Mickey and Mario, had heard the name Charles Chaput many times, but didn't know that much about his ministry. Bremmer, despite his office as Bishop of the relatively remote Duluth diocese, was quite well known in Catholic academic circles and had many friends in high places. He was a young 'middle age' at fifty-four, and was expected to rise much further in the hierarchy of his church. Bremmer knew Archbishop Chaput on a first name basis as the two of them had attended many conferences together over the years. Chaput was a Potawatomi Indian born in Kansas. His ascent within the Catholic Church was nothing short of phenomenal. Pope John Paul II, Mickey and Mario's favorite Pope ever, had named him the Archbishop of Denver years ago; Pope Benedict XVI had named him Archbishop of Philadelphia only months before. Chaput's career touched on matters close to Mickey's heart. The well-traveled priest had cofounded the National Association of Latino Leaders (CALL), helped found ENDOW (Education on the Nature and Dignity of Women), and had won the distinguished Canterbury Medal for work advancing religious freedom in 2009. "He's going to be a saint one day,"

Bremmer said. "I've never met a more spirit-filled human being. In my book, I'd put him right up there with Cardinal Tim Dolan. And, speaking of books, he's written a couple that I suggest you read at your earliest opportunity."

Bremmer went on to say that he had arranged a private meeting with Chaput for later that afternoon. "Chaput is aware of what we want to accomplish in our diocese," the bishop said as he craned his neck to make eye contact with Mickey sitting behind him. "And, I've told him something about what you've accomplished." He turned to Father Mario, "He's willing to travel up to Duluth next fall and would like to speak to students at Scholastica and UMD—I trust you can make all the necessary arrangements, Father?"

Reverend Father Charles Chaput was warmly congenial and smiled often for a man with a mountain of financial, sexual abuse, and other political stresses to deal with—all of which he had inherited with his Philadelphia ministry. He spoke openly of his heritage and philosophy, "My Potawatomi name means, *'the wind that rustles the leaves of the tree'*, he divulged. My Sioux name means *'Good Eagle'*; apparently my father and mother had incredible insights." He lamented that the Church was 'tied to management rather than mission'. "I just wanted to be like any loving father to his family, but learned that in order to be a loving father one had to pay the bills and be responsible for a hundred other things."

Their hour with Chaput and St. Paul Archbishop John Nienstedt was among the most inspirational of Mickey's life. Mickey was convinced that his church would rise above its controversies with people like these two men in positions of authority. After closing with a prayer, Bishop Chaput invited Mickey and Mario to the upcoming 'World Meeting of Families' in Philadelphia. "I'll find places for you to stay at the seminary where I am living. Oh, and Pope Bendict has told me that he plans to be staying there along with us." One of Chaput's first acts as Bishop of Philadelphia was to put the bishop's mansion up for sale in order to help alleviate the huge diocesan debts that came with his appointment.

On the trip up I-35 North, Bishop Bremmer commented, "We have just met a man who talks with our Pope on a regular basis."

~

Marella had promised Mickey on Sunday that she would call and let him know if Trevor had been given another tryout. The line was busy both times she tried to reach him at St. Gerard's. She tried again on Monday. A Father Graham answered but couldn't tell her where Mickey was. "He's with the bishop," was all that Graham would divulge. On Tuesday morning, Marella got the same response from the substitute priest. When she called Father Mario's office to see if he knew where Father Mickey was, the secretary with a youthful voice said that Mario was unavailable: "He's with the bishop, but I'm not quite sure where they were going."

54/ WOLVES

After work on Wednesday, Marella called her brother-in-law, Benjamin Little Otter, to see if he had any idea what Father Mickey had been up to these past few days. No answer. She tried later that evening; again, no answer. Marella knew that Benjamin would often choose not to answer his phone. She left another message on Father Mickey's voicemail before going to bed: "Trevor had a good workout with the Twins. I'll call after work tomorrow with more details."

On Sunday night, Benjamin paid another visit to the casino. He had five dollars in his pocket and eleven dollars left in his checking account. He'd lost more than fifty over the past few weeks: the last of what Benjamin considered to be the 'Bishop's Money'–money from his failed employment with the Duluth diocese. It was money he didn't deserve, money he'd told Mickey to send back, money he wasted without conscience. He had already sent fifty to Trevor in Florida and another fifty to Travis. He missed the boys terribly. He played with the last of his credits on a slot machine for nearly an hour before he was flat broke. Just another failure, he reasoned to himself, but a dose of shame went along with it. The fact that Ben had sworn off gambling and booze made him wonder–was his failure in one thing leading to failure in all the others? Being alone and feeling hopeless had Ben teetering on the brink of a deep and dangerous depression. He knew what was happening, knew he had to get some help, call Lester Hicks or get over to the AA meeting in Cloquet. He'd go to the meeting.

As he was about to leave the casino that Sunday night, he bumped into Brad Tomkins and his wife Lila quite by accident. Brad was the man that Benjamin's wife 'Nella' had been involved with years before. Brad's wife Lila was the woman whose gun had 'accidently' discharged, killing Ben's wife. Brad had been drinking most of the day and drinking made him obnoxious: "You find another woman yet, big guy?" he taunted. Benjamin wanted to hit the smaller man, but knew that if he did he wouldn't be able to stop short of doing serious damage. Then he would end up in jail. He pushed past his tormenter and left the casino without responding to the taunt. Outside, the brutal wind caused his eyes to water, and as he walked toward his car, he realized that he was crying. Rather than go the Sunday night AA meeting, Ben went home and cried himself to sleep.

~

On the previous Friday morning, Benjamin had spotted tracks from a small pack of timberwolves in the area where he had been cutting wood. So on Monday morning, he took his .22 pistol along with him when he trekked into the woods. The memory of his confrontation the previous Sunday night lingered like stink on a skunk in his thoughts: the taunt 'Find another woman?' still churned bile in his stomach. What woman could possibly want a big, dumb Indian who doesn't have a pot to piss in? While he should be at the Indian welfare office this morning signing up for financial assistance, he was tramping around in the woods looking for some birch trees to fell, an axe in one hand and his .22 in the other. He decided to turn east, toward an area he hadn't cut since the previous winter. After nearly an hour, he realized that his angry thoughts had taken him well past the area where he wanted to be. Ben wasn't overly concerned as he had his Sorell bootprints in the snow. It would be easy for him to backtrack to where he started. However, if the wind or the light snowfall that was growing thicker got much worse, he might have a problem.

Coming over a ridge, he saw a wolf pack stalking a doe in a clearing a quarter mile from where he stood. He counted five, then a sixth. The wolves were still too far away for a good shot, so he moved off to the cover of some pine trees up wind and to his right. As he waited and watched, he realized that the snowfall was getting thicker and being whipped by the westerly winds. His thoughts, however, were on the wolves below the hill from where he was crouching. He crept down the slope, using the brush for cover. When he was fifty yards from the circling pack, he took aim at the alpha, pulled the trigger.

The missed shot startled the wolves, allowing the small doe to dart toward the cover of a copse of aspen some thirty yards away. Ben shot twice more, both wildly inaccurate, then charged the pack yelling "Get outta here!" at the top of his voice. His third step caught the edge of a rock covered in snow, his right ankle twisted inward...he screamed in pain as he dropped his pistol and fell forward, rolling over on his side. "Oh no...oh no!" Ben loosened the leather lace on his right boot. He could already feel the swelling. He sat for a long minute, watching the wolves move to a position on the hillside where they could watch him. The doe had apparently escaped into the woods, and the hungry pack eyed the downed man with more than casual interest. Ben crawled a few feet to where he thought the .22 might have fallen…pushing snow away with his gloved hand. He couldn't find it. The snowfall was thickening as he searched in vain. As the minutes slipped away, Benjamin prayed and the wolves spread out in an encircling pattern, sensing opportunity, slowly inching closer. He counted again, there were six in the pack. He turned from where he was sitting to gauge how far he was from the hilltop. At least a hundred yards…then, from the spot where the doe had disappeared, Ben spotted two more. His ankle throbbed. He rolled over, got to his knees, lifting himself, and putting his weight on the left foot. Awkwardly, he managed to stand on one leg for a minute. The wolves backed away, eyes riveted on him.

When Ben tried to put a slight weight on his right leg—the pain was blinding. He took a step, then two, fighting the pain with every fiber of his being. After only a few steps, he stopped and sat back down in the snow. The two stray wolves had joined the other six, and all were circling less than a hundred yards away. Ben was seized with a fear he had never known before. Looking behind from where he was sitting, he noticed that his footprints were gradually becoming obscured by the fresh, blowing snow. He had traveled at least two miles from the Rez: two miles that might just as well have been two hundred. Reality was settling on him with an unbearable weight. Ben prayed, and cried, and prayed some more. His feet and hands were becoming numb from the subzero cold. He was becoming tired, very tired. He laid back in the snow and closed his eyes. The flakes were like tiny needles dancing upon his face. He thought of trying to walk again but…he was too tired to get himself up. As he lay there, a profound thought eased across his mind like a dark cloud in a clear blue sky…Benjamin Little Otter didn't want to live any longer. Life no longer held any promise for him. He smiled inwardly, closed his tearing eyes, and said his last prayer: *"Giiwewinishin Gichi-Manitoo…Ningiiahiitaanji-gaagige-giiweyaan…"*

~

Early on Thursday morning, Mickey returned Marella's call. He, Bishop Bremmer, and Mario, had stayed an extra day so they could attend a conference on 'Secular values' at St. Thomas University. Mickey took the opportunity to visit with some former professors at the St. John Vianney Seminary, which bordered the St. Paul campus to the east and the great Mississippi on the west. Father Mario had lunch with his sister who was a nurse at the Abbot Hospital. The three of them had returned to Duluth late on Wednesday evening.

"We all had a great time. I can't believe how old my teachers have become," Mickey said.

"What? You're getting younger?" Marella was in good spirits.

The two spoke briefly as Marella had to be off to work before eight. "Hector will be calling tonight so I'll know more about what's going on with Trevor and the Twins next time we talk," Marella said. "Oh, one more thing. A guy named Hicks, Lester Hicks called last night. Wanted to know if I knew where Benjamin was. He claimed to be Ben's AA sponsor. Have you heard anything from Ben? I've tried to call him several times with no answer. This Lester fellow sounded concerned."

"I'll check on Ben later, as soon as I'm caught up here at St. Gerard's."

Mickey soon realized that Father Graham must have said morning mass and then taken a nap for the remainder of the day. Nothing had been accomplished in his brief absence except for a pile of return call slips on his desk. Thank goodness for his housekeeper. Mrs. Murray must have tended the phone while Graham slept. The contractors had a million questions, the weekly bulletin needed his column by noon, the women's guild had a bake sale scheduled for Saturday and needed someone to give the event some publicity, and Millie Johnson, a devout parishioner, had passed away on Monday.

Millie's family was in panic mode over funeral arrangements. Late on Thursday evening, Mickey got a call from Lester Hicks. "Nobody's seen Ben since he left the casino on Sunday night. That's four days now. I thought he might be doing something with you. It's not like him to go more than a day, or two at the most, without calling me."

At the urging of Mr. Hicks, Mickey promised that he would drive up to Fond du Lac the following morning after mass.

55/ SEARCHING

In the week following his visit to the Twins training camp, Trevor worked on weights at the TriPalms community center gym and did sprints around the soccer field. Johnny Aquilla emphasized developing greater leg strength so that when pushing off the mound in his delivery, he could get 'more mustard' on the ball. In addition to his professional instruction, Trevor was learning a baseball lingo that would enable him to effectively speak in the clichés of professional ballplayers. He knew that he needed to pitch *lights out*, and to *pitch out of a jam*, he also needed to be able to *go the distance*...to do that he needed to refine a *payoff pitch*, and—if he didn't *mix things up* enough, he'd get *shelled*! In the evenings, Trevor and Hector watched baseball movies. Hector's favorite was *Bang the Drums Slowly* with Michael Moriarity and Robert DeNiro; Trevor's favorite was *Bull Durham* with Kevin Costner and Susan Sarandon. "I don't think my mother would approve of me watching this movie," Trevor said in reference to *Bull Durham*. "Let's just keep it between you and me...keep the weekly reports upbeat, okay?"

Hector received a call from Twins President, Dave St. Peter, from the Twins Minneapolis headquarters. "Mr. Munoz," St. Peter introduced himself, "I just got off the phone with Terry Ryan. He's been telling me about that young man who created quite a stir down in Ft. Myers a week ago. I can't be there, but Terry would like to get together with you and the Windsong boy again. Hate to have you running back and forth to Ft. Myers but…let me assure you…we're interested. Terry has the purse-strings, we pretty much give him a free reign on personnel matters. Mr. Pohlad (the Twin owner) has complete confidence in Mr. Ryan." Hector agreed to a second meeting on the following Saturday afternoon. Smiling to himself, Hector opened his iPhone directory and pressed Marella's cell phone number.

Marella had just finished a conversation with Carleton County Sheriff Talbot Ames and Fond du Lac Tribal elder, Lon Burkett, about the searching party's failure to find any traces of Benjamin the day before. "From what we can determine, Ben has been out cutting wood recently," Talbot said. "Once we locate where there's some freshly hewn tree stumps…well, then we'll have a better idea where to concentrate our searching."

A number of volunteers would resume their search on Saturday and continue through the weekend. Several inches of fresh snow had drifted and swept across the many open areas, making their efforts almost futile. "We might not find anything until spring," Burkett told a *Duluth News Tribune* reporter. "There's a thousand square miles of wilderness out there," added Talbot. The locals had mentioned that Ben had been going into the woods most mornings for the past couple of weeks. "He's usually gone most of the day."

Hector's call came only minutes after that of Sheriff Talbot, and Marella's first words were "Did you find something?" Hector paused, "It's me, Marella…Hector." Marella caught her breath, apologized, then explained what was happening. "I'm in Fond du Lac right now, visiting with a neighbor of Ben's…he's disappeared and we're all worried that something tragic might have happened." She explained the dire situation in detail. "It doesn't look good at all. Father Mickey and Mario have been out on snowmobiles all afternoon, along with thirty others from the reservation. It's subzero with the windchill and we've got a foot of new snow out there."

"What can I do, Marella? I'll be in Duluth later tonight if I can be of any help." Hector had access to a Learjet at the Venice airport with ten minutes notice. Marella told him that they had plenty of people involved now. "I've been debating whether to call you and Trevor…Travis already knows—he first learned about Ben's disappearance on the TV news of all places and he was really upset about that. I told him not to tell his brother or his girlfriend yet." Marella paused. "Trevor was the closest person in the world to his Uncle Ben. The two of them had a special bond—he will be absolutely devastated when I tell him." She began to cry, "What should I do, Hector? I'm a basket case."

Hector's throat went dry. Marella was asking him 'what she should do' and he—the consummate answer man– had no idea of what to tell her. His mind processed slowly, "He's got to be told, Marella. He'll be upset that he's getting the news a few days after the fact, but I think it's important that he be told—probably now that we're on the phone."

"You're right. Before I talk to him…is there anything new I should know about? He's on my mind all the time."

Hector explained the meeting he had scheduled in Ft. Myers for the following day. "I can cancel that meeting and the two of us can be up there tonight or tomorrow morning at the latest."

Now Marella had a difficult task. "Is Trevor around? If so, I'd better get this over with. I think I'll leave any decisions up to him. Wish me luck, Hector—this is going to be very hard…on both of us."

She could hear Hector call Trevor and then the whispered conversation between the two men. "What's up, Mom?" Marella's knees nearly buckled…"Some bad news I'm afraid…" She explained.

Hector watched Trevor's face, saw the jaw muscles tighten, the heavy eyebrows drop. For two long minutes Trevor listened without speaking. "Just a minute," he said, then turned to Hector. "Mom said you can fly us up there."

Hector nodded, "Tonight if you'd like."

Trevor shook his head, "Mom, we'll be up there on Sunday. I've got some business down here tomorrow." He listened for another minute, "He's gone *home*, Mom. I can feel it in my bones. Uncle Ben's spirit has left our world."

~

Although exhausted from their day of searching, Mickey and Mario took Marella and Travis to an early dinner at the Pickwick Restaurant in downtown Duluth. Nightfall came early in January, and with it a sharp drop in temperature. Thoughtfully, Hector had reserved rooms for mother and son at the Radisson Hotel for the next few nights, and reserved another room for himself and Trevor when they arrived on Sunday. "It's like a world of white out there," Mickey said. "My optimism is fading."

"I've never been very optimistic," Travis was candid. "I agree with Trevor…Uncle Ben's journey here is over."

"Have you told your brother about his uncle?" Mickey asked.

"No. I just have that feeling—whether it's my own or Trevor's being transferred to me, I'm not sure." Ravenous, the young man ordered two burgers, an extra order of fries, and a chocolate milk shake.

Despite attempts at small talk about everything imaginable, conversation at their table always returned to Benjamin Little Otter. "Our Arctic Cat got stuck in some of the drifts," Travis said as he tackled his second hamburger. "The guy that rode with me this afternoon said it's a hopeless waste of time. Sad as that sounds I know he's right."

Travis' observation brought a long two minutes without conversation. Marella changed her son's gloomy prophecy to something more optimistic, "I got some good news from Hector today," she went on to explain Trevor's next meeting in an upbeat voice. "Hector thinks there might be an offer of some kind from the Twins management people. If so, he'll be able to tell me about it on Sunday when they get here. He's so smart about business things."

Mickey smiled to himself as Marella's eyes brightened for the first time that day. "He told me that whatever the Twins have to say, he'll insist that there is a provision for college tuition, just in case Trevor fails to move up through the system or if he should decide to quit baseball. I didn't even think of that. Trevor's lucky to have a man like Hector looking out for him."

In her next breath, "Isn't that something…Hector can get a plane—a jet plane!—just by calling the airport. Amazing."

"Quite a guy, I'd have to admit," Mario offered, catching a wink from Mickey across the table. "I liked him immediately when I met him—Mickey had told me quite a bit about him on the trip down, so I already had good vibes. You're both lucky—you and Trevor…" he said in Marella's direction.

Mickey couldn't resist, "Yes, I'd second that. Hector's a very *nice* man."

Marella blushed slightly but Mickey was the only one at the table who noticed the tinge of red in her cheeks.

56/ MEETING THE TWINS BRASS

Major league pitchers and catchers report to spring training camps a few days before the other roster players, usually in early to mid-February. With this season's World Baseball Classic taking place, teams were reporting a week earlier than normal. Young prospects who had not been 'invited' to the big club's camp often arrived even earlier in order to get in shape and, hopefully, catch the eye of someone on the coaching staff who might be lurking around. Odds remained, however, that very few prospects would get much notice in Ft. Myers as they were probably already slotted to play on one of the Twins minor league affiliates.

Every organization's technical and scouting people have a thorough book on all the players in their system—their strengths and weaknesses, their competitiveness and temperament, and numerous other intangibles. Their computer files are not only thorough, but they are constantly updated. The Twins, for example, know that player Jones has certain aspects of his game to work on: swings at the first pitch too often, lacks plate discipline, struggles with off-speed pitches low in the strike zone, is not a good base-runner or effective at hitting behind a base-runner, and maybe has a higher than is acceptable strikeout to walk ratio—the lists are extensive. Defensive skills are analyzed as well. A player that can hit for average, has some power, has both range and speed along with a 'cannon for an arm', is referred to as a 'five tool player'. Terry Ryan and Mike Radcliff and other staff spend countless hours evaluating their talent and the talents of other prospects in other organizations. In many respects, the future is today!

Hector, Trevor and Johnny Aquilla arrived early for their Ft. Myers appointment at eleven. Several non-uniformed players were playing catch, stretching, and running on the three back lot fields reserved for minor leaguers. Hector had studied the newly released Seth Stohs 2013 handbook on Twins prospects that week and was looking for familiar faces among the eight to ten ballplayers. He recognized Joe Benson, a highly touted outfielder who had battled injuries the past two seasons, but none of the others.

The three men walked along the cinder pathway toward the stadium where they were to have their meeting in the third floor Hammond offices, when a burly young man in a sleeveless T-shirt with 'Rock Cats' stitched across the front, hustled up to join them. "Hey guys," he said as he brushed his longish hair back and wiped perspiration from his forehead, "I'm Chris Herrman.," He looked up at Trevor who was a few inches taller, "You must be the kid from Minnesota I'm supposed to meet this morning." Herrmann offered his hand.

Trevor, who hadn't said three words on the trip down I-75 from Venice to Ft. Myers, nodded, returned the firm handshake. "Nice to meet, ya," he mumbled with restrained enthusiasm.

"I know you've got some meetings upstairs, but I'm going to be catching you later on this morning. Drew isn't around today." He looked for a response from Trevor, turned to Hector and Johnny "…Well, just wanted to introduce myself. See ya'all later."

Hector wanted to tell Trevor to lighten up a bit and at least offer a smile, but knew the boy was still suffering from yesterday's tragic news about his uncle. Instead, he said, "Pleasant young man. He had a 'cup of coffee' with the big club last September." Johnny smiled at Hector's lingo, a *cup of coffee* referred to having a few games or at-bats with the major league team before returning to the minor league club. Trevor got it, "Did this Chris Herrmann guy hit much?"

"No. He was still a bit overmatched at the plate, but he's pretty good with the glove," Hector said with some measure of pride in his baseball lingo. Being Cuban, Hector Munoz had baseball in his DNA.

~

Terry Ryan's secretary, a pleasant young woman named Katie, welcomed the trio and offered coffee or juice, "I'll let Mr. Ryan know you're here." The Hammond Field conference room was small, a bank of windows looked out over home plate below, the walls were naked and the atmosphere bland. Hector had expected a bit more pizzaz for a major league club's primary meeting room. "The offices here at Hammond belong to the Ft. Myers Miracle (the Twins 'Class A' affiliate) most of the year; we kick them out for spring training," Katie said from her desk. "Back home at Target Field is a different world altogether." Hector mentioned to Trevor that the entire stadium, and training facility, would be undergoing major improvements the following year. Lee County was subsidizing the overdue renovations.

Dressed casually in a red polo shirt and olive colored slacks, Terry Ryan entered the room wearing the same expression he might have when attending a wake. The Twins General Manager had been under some fire for not bringing in any big name, big salary, pitchers over the winter. Two terrible seasons weighed heavily on the organization's personnel boss. Along with Ryan were his assistant Rob Antony and Mike Radcliff, both dressed casually in chino slacks and long-sleeved shirts. The morning was a cool sixty degrees and overcast. Before taking chairs with their backs to the windows, Ryan made the introductions with a poker-player's smile: "Rob does most of the talking, feel free to interrupt with any questions." Antony was in his late forties, about six feet, had short blondish hair. His smile was engaging. "Nice to meet you both…especially you, Trevor. Welcome to our posh facilities," he jested.

When all were seated, Antony slipped into a more serious expression, fingered a folder on the table in front of him. He rifled through several papers: "Just want to go over a few things with you, Mr. Munoz, and then we can have a brief workout with Trevor afterwards." Antony shifted his gaze from Hector to Trevor and then back to the older man. Hector had hoped to hear 'If all goes well we are prepared to make an offer'. He didn't. Anthony finished what he had to say. "How does that sound?"

Hector nodded, looked at Trevor sitting to his left. "Pretty much as I expected. Sounds okay with me—how about you, Trevor?"

Trevor nodded, "I gotta loosen up first—before I throw. Do you need me for any of this paper-work stuff?"

Antony shrugged then looked to Terry Ryan as he cleared his throat, "Terry, anything you want to add before I go over the files?"

Ryan shook his head, "Nothing right now—just go ahead. Trevor and I have met before," he smiled for the first time.

"Remember…the whole thing got off on the wrong foot but turned out rather well, I'd say."

Expressionless, Trevor nodded at the memory.

Antony explained that it was standard procedure to get a full medical evaluation from the team's physicians before initiating any contract discussions. "I've spoken with Doctor MacIver up at St. Mary's in Duluth, Trevor. I wanted him to explain exactly what surgeries were performed and how they have healed."

Trevor met his eyes without speaking. "He's amazed at your recovery." Antony went on to say that he also received a full report form the hand specialist and from John Morrison, Trevor's physical therapy specialist. "That was quite an accident you had back in June. Your apparent recovery is nothing short of phenomenal." He noted that the medical people in Duluth were confident that his arm was significantly stronger now than it had been before the injuries. MacIver, however, claimed that the wrist repairs were unlike anything he had ever performed before, and that he had no idea if the stress of twisting a complex figuration of ligaments with *'more than usual frequency'* would result in any further or irreparable damage. "We're in a world of uncertainty here," Antony quoted from the MacIver report. Included in the package were MRI photos of the wrist—palmar and dorsal views.

Some of MacIver's observations were highlighted in yellow. Terry Ryan was following Antony's presentation with his own duplicate file. He interrupted for the first time: "When signing pitchers, regardless of their medical history, it's always a gamble. Half of our top prospects have already undergone Tommy John surgeries on their elbows." His eyes narrowed as he sat back in his leather chair, "And…" he picked up another sheet of paper, squinted at the print, "Then there's the matter of your concussion. That's become a big concern in sports, all sports…I'm sure you know about some of our own players, namely Justin Morneau and Denard Span." Span had recently been traded to the Washington Nationals for pitching prospects. Ryan's expression was grave: "Do you ever get headaches or dizzy spells?"

Trevor looked at Hector who nodded, Trevor said, "Never. I was unconscious for a while, that's all, sir. Nothing since the accident."

The men looked at each other around the table, Rob Antony slipped the doctor's papers into the envelope, "I think Mr. Windsong can go now, don't you?" He looked toward Terry Ryan who nodded.

Trevor said, "S'cuse me," and left the room. Johnny Aquilla was waiting outside the door, sipping a red Gatorade. He tossed an unopened bottle to Trevor, "It's starting to warm up out there…don't overdo things."

Trevor punched Johnny's shoulder, "Let's go stretch out for a while."

Inside the conference room, Ryan slid a different manila folder across to Mike Radcliff, who had not said a word since entering the room. "Mike's got a few things to say," Ryan said.

"Thanks, Terry," Radcliff first explained his role in assessing talent within the Twins organization. "I had a long conversation yesterday with Mark Wilson, he's our main scout in Minnesota and the Dakotas." Radcliff briefly described the scouting system, "it's not quite like how that movie, *Moneyball*, portrayed the talent scouts." All had seen the popular movie and laughed at their recall of a meeting similar to the one they were having at the moment. Let me be candid, it's not like the Windsong boy slipped under the radar before the June draft—and before the unfortunate accident– it's just that no teams were very interested. I've got his report if you'd like to look at it," he said to Hector. "He was rated good—nothing to get excited about."

"Maybe I'll take a look later, Mister Radcliff."

Radcliff looked to Rob Antony, "For now, that's all I've got, Rob."

"We often do profiles…I mean like, psychological evaluations, on our players." Antony said. "We've talked to Trevor's high school and American Legion coaches." He turned to Terry Ryan again, "And some friends of Terry's up in Hibbing who have seen the boy play." Antony frowned, "They all saw flashes…fine fastball, better than average slider, but nothing like that 'one-in-a-million' rave that we're always looking for." He swallowed, looked at Hector, "Please don't take this the wrong way…but they all seemed to describe the Windsong boy as a loner, not particularly well liked by his teammates." We talked to a couple of guys he played with, too. They said Trevor never hung out with any of the kids at school, never went to dances…aside from the locker room and the fields, they hardly ever saw him anywhere." He looked up from the report, "They even thought, some of them anyhow, that Trevor was a much better football player than a baseball player. No one, however, ever questioned his determination or passion for the game."

Antony smiled, "I must share something highly positive in our estimation, Mr. Munoz. Trevor has been clean, I mean no drug history, no trouble with the law. That's a real positive these days."

Hector's icy expression never changed. He was taking copious notes as each man spoke, turning one yellow page after another. When Antony was finished, he stood and walked to a corner window looking out over beautiful Hammond field. "First, I expected you to do a complete medical investigation and I compliment your thoroughness. I talked with Doctor MacIver shortly after you did, Mr. Antony, and to Crosby, the PT guy, and Morrison, as well. I couldn't agree more with what Mr. Ryan said, with prospects it's always a crapshoot—that's a reality that will never change. Whether its analysis from your scouts, or the use of sophisticated computer data, Trevor has undergone every possible analysis. He was passed over in the spring draft for good reason—he wasn't outstanding!" Pacing and gesturing as he spoke, Hector went on to explain that Mr. Wilson's scouting report was probably very thorough.

Looking at Radcliff, he said, "No disrespect, but I really don't need to read what he had to say."

The three officials nodded, impressed by Hector's demeanor. Hector continued, "Trevor's pitching before and after his surgeries are night and day; of course you must already know that. You're staff, Mr. Anderson included, has already seen his slider and timed his fastball. That's why were all sitting around this table this morning. If I remember correctly, you called us—not the other way around. When we go back outside, you'll all have another opportunity to see what Trevor brings to our discussion."

He looked at his notes, smiled for the first time. "I must tell you that I find your psychological profile a bit over the top, gentlemen. Trevor's a quiet kid. Always has been. So were Jim Thorpe and Chief Bender for that matter. By the way, they were 'half-breeds', too." He glanced at Antony, Radcliff, and Ryan for any reaction to the *half-breed* reference—Antony touched a finger to his chin, the General Manager remained as stoic as ever, Radcliff nodded. Hector continued, "His twin brother is outgoing and highly social, articulate, extrovertish. These are mostly nature-nurture and cultural things that you and I aren't properly wired to fully understand. What difference does it make that Trevor didn't go to high school dances? Neither did I. Travis, on the other hand, is quite a dancer. Go figure…What his teammates had to say doesn't amount to much more than opinion. Travis told me that the kids he played with were jealous of Trevor's natural ability. Whatever." Hector put his tablet back on the table, leaned over and said, "Enough! Let's go take a look, gentlemen."

When Ryan stood, the others rose from the table. "Fine with me," Antony said. "We can discuss things further after we 'have a look' as you suggested, Mr. Munoz. You ready, Mike?" Radcliff was the talent technician in the room, Antony the administrator, Ryan the skeptic who held the pursestrings.

Before turning for the door, Hector added, "Just a couple of things I want you to know before we go downstairs." He slid in next to Ryan, "I will present several conditions for your consideration, if you are still interested in signing Trevor to any kind of contract with the Twins organization after we're finished." Hector, in order to add some extra weight to his position, would play his trump card before leaving the room, "I have good friends, business assoiciates as well, in the Tampa organization." (The Tampa Rays were an American League East team known for developing remarkable pitching talent.) "I could call Matt Silverman or Brian Auld right now and have a meeting with them on Monday morning. Just thought you should know..."

"Let's go out and take a look at the Windsong boy," Ryan said impatiently as he held open the door, "We're still getting heat for the Delmon Young trade with Tampa a few years back. I'm never going to sit and do nothing with Matt Silverman waiting in the wings a few miles up the highway." Antony and Radcliff nodded agreement, the Rays brass were not only good at the job of developing talent, but also in making wise trades. "We always like to keep our Minnesota kids close to home if we can," Antony said. "I don't think I have to mention that Joe Mauer and Kent Hrbeck lived within biking distance from our ballpark...so did some we let get away—like Dave Winfield and Paul Molitor." He didn't have to add that the two St. Paul athletes that got away have been enshrined in Cooperstown's Baseball Hall of Fame."

57/ 'POTENTIAL PHENOM..."

Earlier that morning, Rob Antony had sent a message to the Twins equipment manager and ordered a uniform with 'Windsong' stitched to the back of the jersey. Rod McCormick had the uniform, along with a Twins cap and new Adidas spikes ready when Trevor and Johnny left the office. As he escorted the two men to the locker room, where Trevor could change, he wished the young pitcher

'Good Luck'. Ten minutes later, after wind sprints and various other exercises, Trevor's new uniform was damp with sweat.

The main practice field was located to the south and east of Hammond Stadium. Chris Herrmann, the catcher who had introducd himself to Trevor earlier, was waiting when Trevor and Johnny arrived. At a batting cage twenty yards away, some other prospects had gathered for batting practice. Trevor's eyes were wide as he watched Miguel Sano put three consecutive balls deep out of the park. Terry Ryan and Hector, with Radcliff and Antony trailing behind them, were joined by a fifth man named Marty Mason. Mason, formerly with the Cubs organization, was the new pitching coach for the Twins AAA affiliate, the Rochester Redwings. He was in Ft. Myers for an afternoon meeting with Ryan. Everyone was introduced to one another; Kennys Vargas, Max Kepler, and some other promising rookies watched from the sidelines. Herrmann put on his full catching gear and gestured for Trevor to take the mound, "Let's warm up a bit, okay? Tell me when you're loose."

With an audience of several players and management officials, Ryan asked Eddie Rosario, a 19 year-old and one of the Twins' highly rated young talents, if he'd like to take a few swings. Rosario grinned, "Si, boss". Kepler was swinging a weighted bat behind the cage, waiting his turn to hit some balls off the big Indian kid. "Can I bat next, Mr. Ryan?" Kepler's German accent was thick. Ryan nodded without speaking.

Marty Mason had his speed gun focused behind the screen. Left swinging Rosario made himself comfortable in the batter's box, fixing an intense gaze on Trevor. Rosario was not a big man and Trevor smiled to himself; he should be able to blow his fastball past him. Herrmann signaled one finger for the fastball Trevor was hoping for. Rosario lined the first pitch deep into the left field corner. On the second fastball, high in the strike zone like the first, Rosario hit a towering fly ball over the outfield fence. Mason looked over to Terry Ryan, "eighty five and eighty four" he said, referring to the speeds of the first two pitches. Mason had told Chris Herrmann beforehand what pitches he wanted called. Trevor's next three pitches would also be fastballs—'put some fire in'em," Herrmann called.

After watching Rosario's long ball, Trevor wiped his brow. Maybe he hadn't loosened up quite enough. He'd reach back and add a little more to this next pitch. Rosario fouled it back. "Ninety-one," Mason said. The next two pitches, low in the zone, also hit ninety-one. Each had a breaking movement in on Rosario's fists. For an eighteen year old, the speed and rotation of his pitches were exceptional.

The next five pitches were Trevor's 'drop balls' and Rosario could only shake his head after each one. He had swung and missed on four of them. Max Kepler hit two of Trevor's five fastballs into medium center field for what would have been easy outs. The five dropballs that Trevor threw next were untouchable. "The ball just disappeared," Kepler told Mason watching from behind the batting cage. "I thought I had it when I swung and all I got was empty air."

A young outfield prospect named Angel Morales, from Puerto Rico, also had five swings and the results were about the same as Kepler's. Morales, like the other prospects, shook his head in amazement.

Standing off to the side was Mike Radcliff, the Twins evaluator of player talent. Mike's impressions were critical. On Radcliff's clipboard he had misprinted 'Wind Song' and below the name some of the specific qualities he would be looking for. When Morales came to the plate, Radcliff moved to a location behind the batting cage. What he saw from there had him scratching his head. At the bottom of his page of notes he wrote two words: *potential phenom*! Before leaving for his car, Radcliff passed his report to Mr. Ryan without so much as a handshake.

~

The search for Benjamin Little Otter on Saturday was futile. Another weather front was adding two inches of fresh, powdery snow, and covering the tracks of the previous day. Mickey's sister Meghan had organized a busload of Hibbing people to travel to Cloquet and assist in the widespread effort to locate the missing man. Family friends of Marella and classmates of Travis and Trevor also had joined the search that day and would stay through Sunday. The more than one hundred searchers were served coffee, hot chocolate, rolls and fried bread in the Fond du Lac community center. Hopes of finding Benjamin—alive or dead– were fading with each passing hour. Marella and Travis left early to check in at the Radisson where Hector had reserved rooms for them.

~

Hector called Marella in mid-afternoon and gave her the glowing details of that morning's meeting with Twins officials and how impressive Trevor's workout had been. "We're flying out of Ft. Myers in half an hour and will arrive at the Duluth airport somewhere around four." Marella and Travis would pick them up, and the four of them would go out to dinner at Grandma's in Canal Park. "Mickey can't join us tonight, but he'll be back at the reservation after Sunday masses tomorrow."

Trevor, wearing his personalized Twin's jersey, a new pair of yellow Nikes that Hector had bought for him, and designer torn Levi jeans, marveled at the sleek Learjet waiting on the tarmac. In the past two months Trevor had packed in more life-changing experiences than he had had in the previous ten years. The flight to Minnesota would be his first flight ever. At times he felt like giving himself a pinch—was it all real? Dreams that he had never dared to imagine were coming true. The teenager had come to like Florida, and had developed a deep respect for Hector Munoz. Yet, happiness remained elusive to the gifted teenager. He would give up anything and everything to have his beloved Uncle Ben safe and sound. Yet, he knew in his heart that that was not going to happen.

58/ TRAVIS' DIARY

Marella and Travis arrived at the downtown hotel just after two in the afternoon. Marella had a mild case of anxiety over the clothes she had brought along for the weekend and was tempted to find a shop and pick out something new. Never overly conscious about how she looked to others, regrettably, she was today. Being nervous about something so irrelevant as an outfit bothered her. With so many things on her mind she hadn't given much thought to what to pack. She had left her snowsuit in the car and was wearing jeans, an oversized T-shirt, and black New Balance shoes that went with her leather jacket. Maybe she didn't even need to change? What would Hector be wearing? She giggled, that was a no-brainer, he'd be in khakis and a white shirt!

Her open suitcase rested on the bed next to Travis' backpack. Looking over her choices, she selected a pair of rust colored dress slacks, a beige v-neck sweater, and the brown fashion boots she had purchased at Kohl's before Christmas. That'll do, she said as she headed into the bathroom for a quick shower. As her hair dried, she ironed the slacks and wondered if Hector was overly concerned about fashion and appearances…she was trying to imagine what kind of women attracted him? How foolish. She smiled to herself, "I am what I am…I'm past my prime and getting used to living alone."

Then came a fleeting thought that she hadn't processed before: A thought that should have been up front from the very start of everything. What if Hector was in a relationship now? What if all the vibes were nothing more than his curiosity and her fantasy? 'What ifs' bounced around the room like idea bubbles in comic books. What if she let go of all this nonsense?

Despite her uneasy mood of the moment, a Willy Nelson love song came to mind…she hummed the melody to *'You Were Always on my Mind'* softly…*'…little things I should have said and done, I just never took the time…but you were always on my mind…you were always on my mind.'* She felt choked up for a moment, but didn't cry. "You are a strong woman, Marella—never forget that," she needed to remind herself of that reality every so often. Aparently, today was one of those times. She should be looking foreward to a reunion with Trevor more than anything else. Her son brought a glower of melancholy to her face—her lost son. Her grown-up-too-fast son who had chosen to live away from her…"Onward and upward, Marella…" her frame of mind had her absently talking to herself.

She unplugged the iron, called to Travis through the open door to his adjoining room: "Anything you need ironed?"

Travis, wearing his *Bose* headphones, was nestled between two pillows on his bed and playing an iPhone game. Quite obviously, he was temporarily lost in another world. She walked into the room he would share with Trevor, shook his shoulder, and repeated her question. "Did you pack anything that needs ironing before I put the ironing board away?"

"I dunno. Maybe the shirt in my backpack—I think I left it on your bed."

Marella shrugged, returned to her room and checked Travis' backback. As she pulled out the pinstriped dress shirt he had stuffed in with socks and underwear, a notebook tumbled onto the bed. She puzzled, opened the cover, squinted at the small, tightly written text. A diary? She had no idea that Travis journaled. A pang of conscience struck her…was it right for a mother to snoop? Her first impulse was to return the notebook to the backpack, but mild curiousity tugged at her scruples. Just a quick glance she thought. Thumbing through the first few pages she noted that some paragraphs were dated, others random: *'Freshman Week'* headed the second page…skipping on she found the date 9/22…*UMD had beaten Augustana in football*, Marella wasn't interested. An undated page from October… *'Trevor was awesome! The Scholastica coach was so impressed that he offered Trev a scholarship to pitch for his team this year.'* What was that all about? She read further that he and Mickey and Trevor went for pizza after what he called a 'workout'.

Marella sat on her bed in puzzlement, her sons had private lives that she had no clue about. She understood that the bane of parenthood was letting go of a loved one when their time had come, but she didn't like it one bit. She couldn't help but remember a quote by Kahlil Gibran from a book of his philosophies that she had enjoyed years before: *'Your children are not your children. They are the sons and daughters of Life's longing for itself. They come through you but not from you. And, though they are with you, yet they belong not to you…'* A tear formed in the corner of her eye. Gibran's words were more profound than she thought imaginable. If *'They do not belong to you'*—then they belong to the world that you opened to them.

Ready to return the notebook to the backpack, she hesitated when noticing something written on a page toward the middle of the tablet: *'had coffee with Father Mickey again…the date was October 24… 'We argued about religion—good naturedly, of course. I respect his spirituality very much. And, Mario…he's a BMOC!'* In November he mentioned Mickey again…Marella skipped a few pages. Thanksgiving, 2012, *'we all enjoyed having Mickey over to R house—OMG, this time he was actually invited by mom. Yay!'* Further down the page, *'So excited for Trevor, we're all going to make a trip to Florida over Christmas break—even mom. How is that going to be?'*

Marella skipped over December's travelogue and the Florida adventure, turning instead to the more recent pages. Maria Olivio! And more Maria Olivio. It appeared as if her son was either in love or in a state of serious infatuation. She remembered the lovely girl from the picnics at TriPalms only months before. She wasn't surprised. The two of them were almost inseparable for their entire time there. Both were college freshmen and Travis enjoyed an opportunity to show off his limited Spanish. Obviously, there was more than language practice between them. She smiled at thoughts of young love. She flipped beyond those many pages– Maria and Travis was private stuff. As she was about close the cover, she saw a line… *'I'm going to go down and see Maria over spring break– come hell or high water!'*

'We'll see about that', she mumbled to herself. The last page was titled, Uncle Ben…Travis wrote: *'Both me and Trev know that our uncle is gone. We think differently about most things but the same about his fate.'* Further down she read: *'Hector called me again tonight. He's pleased with Trevor's attitude and stuff. But, like last time we talked, he was more curious about our family and things like that. Says it helps him get a handle on Trevor. I think he's more interested in mom than he'll admit. I teased him about that…'*

Marella's mouth went suddenly dry. Hector? She hadn't made any connections between Hector and Travis. But—nothing more was writen about their conversation. He did use the word *'again'*— what did that mean? Were the two of them—Travis and Hector, like her coffee-drinking son and Father Mickey, were they all buddies? On the next page, Travis switched to a nice compliment he received from Dr. Venziano, his Spanish teacher. *He told me that I was his best student. Maria will be delighted when I tell her that.*

59/ "...JUST A TWINGE," TREVOR LIED

Trevor sunk into a plush white leather seat in the cabin of Hector's rented Learjet 60. One of the two uniformed pilots spoke respectfully to Hector before closing the fuselage door, "Should be a smooth ride with little turbulence, sir, in a little more than two hours we'll be in Duluth—I'd estimate about sixteen hundred hours at the latest. Linda will be your attendant." Linda was a petite brunette in a navy blue suit and her smile matched the sun beams from the window, "If you'll please buckle up, sir," she gestured toward Trevor who was looking out the window..."In a few minutes I'll get you gentlemen a sandwich and beverage if you'd like. Or some snacks if you'd rather...just let me know once we're on our way."

Wide-eyed, Trevor showed a glimmer of enthusiasm for the first time that day. "Yes maam," he said as he buckled. Then, turning to Hector: "How fast does this jet go?" he asked. "Duluth in a couple of hours? It took us three long days to drive down here."

Hector, sitting across the narrow aisle from his young friend, smiled in anticipation of some rare conversation. "We'll probably cruise at somewhere around five hundred miles an hour at...just over thirty thousand feet." The engine purred as the jet began to maneuver on the runway. After a brief pause, Trevor was thrust back into his seat and the jet shot down the runway. In seconds the plane banked inland, then swept out over the blue-green waters of the Gulf below. For Trevor, everything–the plane, the feeling of flight, and the sun-reflecting water below– took his breath away. Hector realized that Trevor had apparently exhausted his topics of conversation with one question and one observation. He settled back in his seat and closed his eyes: A smile of anticipation crept across his face as a picture of a dark-haired woman crept into his thoughts.

~

Marella watched the runway from the large terminal window at the newly expanded Duluth airport terminal building as Travis, sitting on a chair behind her, played a Backgammon game on his iPad. Her tired face creased into a smile as she saw the sun glint off the sleek, silver jet coming to a stop on the tarmac below. The door opened, stairs dropped down, and Trevor appeared wearing a light blue jacket over what looked like a Twins jersey. He looked larger than she remembered, and older. "I hope he brought some warmer clothes," she said to Travis who wasn't paying her any attention. She felt a lump grow in her throat as the second passenger descended the stairway. Hector was wearing Khakis and a heavy green jacket over his white shirt. He pulled the collar of his jacket up over his neck as he walked down the steps. A wind gust mussed his hair and billowed his slacks—welcome to Minnesota she said to herself.

Marella's eyes began to water. Hector looked a few years younger than she remembered, and even more handsome. 'My family is together again,' she thought to herself. *My family!* The thought came so naturally it was almost scary. "They are here," she said to Travis who shut down his iPad tablet, stood, and joined her at the window.

Hector watched from behind as Trevor and his mother embraced, then he shook Travis' hand. He felt an unusual awkwardness when Marella met his eyes, "Well? Do I get a hug?" she asked him as she opened her arms and stepped a few inches closer. As Hector held her close, he inhaled the subtle scent of cherry blossoms in her dark hair. He wanted to tell her how wonderful she smelled, and how breathtaking she felt in his arms but...

After long moments, Marella stepped back, took his large hands in hers, and said, "I needed that, Hector. You feel so very special to me."

Hector didn't quite know how to respond. "I'm glad...you feel special, too." On after-thought, he knew that he could have said something much more inspired or unique or profound. Marella's *special* was meaningful, his special was only ordinary at best. Why hadn't wonderful or incredible or exquisite come first to mind? Was he too uptight?

As they headed toward the outside exit, several steps behind the twins, Marella gave his hand a squeeze. "How is Trevor doing? Whenever I talk to him on the phone all he says 'okay'. Getting him to say anything more than a word or two takes a lot of probing."

"I know. I sometimes wonder if that's any different than when he was living at home with you and Travis?" Hector was curious about Trevor's life before Florida. "I'm kinda reserved myself, so I'm not bothered by that same quality in others. Over the years I've become pretty good at reading what's not said."

"He's always been...reticent? Is that the right word...reserved, inside himself? Anyhow, Trevor keeps most things bottled up. Has he said anything about his uncle? His feelings?"

"No, surprisingly, he hasn't said anything...but I can see a lot of pain. I think he expects the worst," Hector said.

"We all do."

~

Grandma's restaurant in Canal Park on Lake Superior was especially lively on a Saturday night when the UMD Bulldogs played hockey at the nearby arena. The University of Denver Pioneers were in town for a three-game series. Marella had asked Travis to treat his brother to some games in the Adventure Zone arcade nearby, so that she and Hector might have an hour or so to themselves. The boys took the twenty she offered and headed down the street.

Marella and Hector were seated in an upstairs window booth where they could look out at the Aerial Lift Bridge, one of the port city's more famous attractions. The two of them ordered: Marella a Chablis, and Hector a Corona Lite. After ordering, Marella met Hector's eyes and smiled…it seems much easier to talk with someone on the phone than to look them in the eyes and talk. After a long few moments, "It's been a long day—for all of us, I guess." She detailed the futile search efforts, "At some point, probably after the weekend, the efforts will be scaled back. I'm doubtful that we'll have any closure until the spring. I think everybody feels about the same—even if they aren't willing to say so."

Hector asked questions about the area being searched and inquired as to where he might purchase some winter clothing. "Should I purchase a snowmobile?" Marella laughed, "Clothes yes…snowmobile…not necessary. We can share the Arctic Cat I've borrowed. I got it from a man named Hicks, a close friend of Ben's."

After ordering a second round, Hector detailed that morning's session with Terry Ryan and other Twins officials. When the two major topics had been exhausted, Marella began to flounder with small talk: "Were you prepared for this kind of weather? I noticed that you winced when you stepped out of the plane and got a blast of arctic wind in the face."

"It did wake me up, that's for sure." Hector, having investments in a petroleum exporting company in Anchorage, added: "It's probably very much like the interior of Alaska this time of the year. I've been to a remote place called Glennallen in the center of Alaska a few times. The change from the seventies this morning to a minus ten this evening, however, is rather drastic–be it here in Minnesota or somewhere in Siberia. In a weird way, I find it almost refreshing. It certainly gets your attention when you step into it—your immediate and total attention!"

Marella wanted to contest the word 'refreshing', but didn't. Shocking might have been a better word choice. From the weather, they returned to Trevor, then to Travis' straight A's for the first semester. "My life has really changed…that 'empty nest' stuff is for real. I've always enjoyed my space but this is something altogether different." She laughed, "With all the empty time—no ballgames to go to, no helping with homework, no meals for a family to pre-pare– I've become a daydreamer of sorts. I know my dreams are failing to fill the void…but…"

Hector measured the risk in his mind and decided to let go of his troubling inhibitions. The beautiful woman sitting across from him had dropped some subtle hints of affection—he had done the same. "I've been daydreaming myself, Marella. That's really something new for me—I'm a workaholic to the nth degree. Anyhow, with Trevor around, I can't help but think of you. I mean…" Now, he felt stuck—what exactly, did he mean by adding the 'I mean' to his think-ing of her? He cleared his throat. "I've been alone for all of my adult life. That's made me independent and self-sufficient—almost too much so. Would you believe that I've always done my own laun-dry and ironing?" He laughed at himself, "I've never admitted that to anyone else before. Some would say that's getting in touch with my feminine side—I'd say its more being fussy and frugal."

Marella laughed. "Thanks for sharing. That makes me feel spe-cial" she said as she reached across the table and found his hands. "You starch and iron your own shirts? That's impressive resume material, Hector. I'll bet that you do a better job than I could."

Hector, mentally analyzing his every word, wondered how and why he had strayed from his intentions to something so meaningless and mundane as his domestic habits. Was he, however uncon-sciously, trying to communicate a resume?

When Marella's delicate hands found his, the touch was just what Hector needed to pull out from his depths what he really wanted to say. "You've become very special to me. More special than I ever thought possible. " His face reddened a bit but nothing more needed to be said. This time *special* seemed to be the most honest word in the thesaurus of his vocabulary.

~

Two frigid blocks off of Lake Street, the boys were engaged in a fierce sibling competition at the Adventure Zone entertainment center. The video games ended in a draw with each scoring better than the other three times. When playing mini golf, Travis was given a five stroke handicap, and beat his big brother by two. Then on to the Foosball tables. "I don't know why I even try," complained Travis after being shut out for a second time. Trevor was hot, "One more, Trav. Best of five– I'm goin' for a triple shutout." Determined not to be shut out another time, Travis gritted his teeth and refocused. To Trevor's surprise, Travis got the first goal on a cheap ricochet off of a defender and past his brother's goalie.

Angry at himself, Trevor bore down; he saw an opening and spun his middle handle with all his strength. The ping-pong ball shot like a bullet between the defenders and into the hole Travis was guarding. "Ouch!" The pain shot through Travis' wrist like a bullet as Trevor's hand left the handle. Trevor grabbed his wrist as he bent over the game surface. "God, that hurt." For the second time that day he had tweaked his wrist. This time it was sharper than when he threw his second drop ball to Angel Morales during his piching session that morning. Johnny Aquilla had seen him grimace at the time, "What was that?" he had asked Trevor after the workout. Trevor brushed it off with a lie, "I bit my tongue, that's all."

"You okay, Bro? Trevor saw his brother writhe in pain. "You felt that one, too—didn't you?"

"Yeah...I did...pretty sharp. Did you do something to your wrist earlier today? I spilt a cup of hot chocolate all over the magazine I was reading this morning."

"Sorry, Trav—for both times. Did you feel anything in your elbow, or just the wrist?"

"Both actually, but mostly in the wrist. It's gone now." Travis' expression was grave: "That's your pitching arm, Trevor. What did you do?"

"It's nothin'. Just a twinge. Not to worry," he lied. "Don't say nothin' to Hector or Mom—okay? Not 'til I figger some things out for myself."

60/ CONVERSATIONAL TENSION

Exhausted after their long and eventful day, the group moved from Grandma's to the Radisson Hotel on Superior Street in downtown Duluth. The boys went to their room to watch some TV before turning the lights off on their day. Hector and Marella decided to have a nightcap in the hotel lounge overlooking the glittering bayfront below. From her chair by the window, Marella pointed out different sites: the new arena-convention center where the UMD hockey game was in progress, the historic lift bridge, the long narrow ore and grain docks, and the needle of peninsula that was Park Point. "You've got to visit us up in Hibbing this summer, Hector. I'll give you the grand tour of the famous Hull Rust-Mahoning mines, the incredible high school, and the house where Bob Dylan grew up. Did you know that Hibbing is the home of the Greyhound bus line? There's a museum near Bennett Park that gives visitors a sketch of the history. Actually, there's lots of things to see and do in the summer—in the winter, well…that's something all together different. I love to cross-country ski and skate on a pond only about fifty yards behind our house. That's when the boys are around to shovel off the snow; so, as you might imagine, I haven't done much skating this winter."

Hector nodded. As with everything else, he had done his research on Hibbing, as well as Duluth, and the mining and shipping that both cities were noted for. On the two-hour flight, while Trevor was absorbed with the views from his window seat, Hector was Googling information on the landscape and attractions of an area he had never seen before. He could have explained in considerable detail what Marella was mentioning in her passing commentary. He could have told her about the Belgian cut glass chandeliers in the Hibbing High School auditorium, the complex taconite mining process from blasting the rock to pelletizing the ore, and he could have noted that Hibbing's most famous son, Bobby Zimmerman, was actually born in Duluth– not too far from where they were sitting. Or, he might have mentioned the little publicized fact that Roger Maris was born in Hibbing before moving to Fargo. What purpose would adding these bits of trivia to their conversation serve? He disliked people who came across as 'know it all's' as much as he disliked people who always had to 'one-up' everybody else with a 'well, that's great but I…' More importantly, however, he thoroughly enjoyed listening to Marella talk, watching her animated gestures, gazing into her dark flashing eyes.

Marella could see that Hector had slipped into some inner place for a moment. "Well" she said ". . . can I get a commitment, Hector? A date or a timeframe for a visit sometime this summer? That is, if all this snow goes away before August."

"Absolutely! Maybe we could do a tour of all those things you've told me about and then, if you and the boys would like, we could rent a cabin at some resort on one of the many lakes up there. Maybe even Lake Vermilion, I've heard that it's quite a lovely area." He looked for approval in Marella's eyes, but found a sudden dark cast he hadn't seen before. He let it slide for the moment, and continued: "Do you and the boys enjoy fishing? Walleye fishing? Boating?"

Marella's sudden frown was defensive. Did Hector know that a large part of the Lake Vermilion shoreline was Bois Forte Ojibwe Reservation land? The place where she and her sons were born and spent many years? Marella's spirit was roused, "What do you know about Lake Vermilion? I can't remember ever telling you anything about it. Has Trevor told you about it…? Better yet, please tell me what gave you the resort idea anyhow…" Her jaw tensed, eyes narrowed.

Hector read the threatened and suspicious reaction in Marella's eyes. He would have to mitigate an obviously sensitive topic. However well-intended, his suggestion had touched upon a nerve. She released her hand from his. He swallowed, "Marella, I was born on a farm in Cuba. My folks were poor farmers, and when Castro came to power, they lost what little they had. My mom was killed in a freakish hurricane when I was six; she was only thirty-one at the time. My father had me and my sister smuggled into Mexico with an uncle who defected from a Cuban baseball team. From there, we were stowed in a bin of fish on a trawler that was headed to Miami. We had only the clothes on our back and a plastic bag with our birth certificates when we landed in America. I lived with relatives I'd never met and from that day on I never saw my father again. My sister met the wrong kind of man and was deported."

Hector paused, his next words would be risky. "We, all of us, have our own unique story—and each story has something bittersweet buried inside of it, something we feel—rightly or wrongly–is best secreted away, protected from anybody's scrutiny."

Marella didn't relax the hard expression on her face, "And...? I know we all have a story." Her stomach tensed, she wondered if he knew anything about *the secret* locked so deeply inside that even her sons didn't know about it. She bit her tongue; what Hector knew probably came from conversations with one of her sons. She would have to keep that theory to herself. "Go on..." she encouraged.

Hector cleared his throat. "I like to think that life deals us a hand of cards to play with. We draw and we discard, some of us play our cards well, others don't. Even others fold altogether. Most of us simply stay in the game, hoping for that elusive full house or straight flush. Hoping to cash-in at the end of it all with something more than we started with."

Marella nodded, "Clever analogy, if that's what it is—or philosophy—I'm not really very much into cards or fate or things like that. I'm more into the gut stuff of life. I asked you a question and

I think I got fluff for an answer. I'm sorry, what's happened in your life is important to me...but–" She looked away.

"You asked, what do I know about Lake Vermilion? Well...not that much. I do know that you were born there. I'd like to see the place one day...I'd like to breathe the air and get a feel for the land you grew up on. That would be more relevant to me than the taconite mines or the Zimmerman's house on Seventh Avenue—or Bob Dylan Avenue as it's been renamed..." He leaned forward, took her hands back into his and stroked the back of her hands with his thumbs. "I'm a very curious man. I've always had a compulsion to know things, little details that most people could care less about."

Marella's face softened a bit. Hector continued, "I know so little about you and yet, at times, I feel so very close to you—spiritually more than anything else–even when I'm two thousand miles away. This attraction is all new to me. Please don't ask me to explain my feelings—they just are. I even feel close to you now...even when I can see anger and confusion in your eyes. I feel close to *who* you are. Is it wrong for me to want to know *why* you are what you are. . .? I mean, that sounds awfully convoluted, but it might help me to understand my attraction."

Marella looked down at their hands clasped together on the table, "I don't know. What's happened in the past is...is just that, I guess. The distant past. I own it all, for sure, but I don't live it–not anymore. Time has been a convenient eraser." She smiled, "I've learned to like what I've become—not always, but mostly." She smiled.

Hector chose not to disclose that he and Travis had been emailing each other on a regular basis. Travis knew that Hector 'liked' his mom—and suspected that she was fond of him–so he was at ease in sharing things about his family. "We've never been told who our father is," Travis had confessed. "That really bothers us— Trevor and me. I've, well both of us but me more than Trevor, have tried to find out. We've traced high school and college yearbooks from, we think, June of '93—when mom was about our age, eighteen. Secretly, we've talked with some of her classmates in Tower and Ely. We've been down a thousand dead-end roads. Uncle Ben—he married mom's sister—he told us that Auntie Nella might have been able to help...but she's dead."

Marella seemed to have relaxed her emotions as Hector's honesty was disarming. The way he had just explained his feelings touched her deeply. "I'm very proud of my Native American heritage, Hector. My Anishanaabi blood. My sacred Ojibwe name is *negamowaad*, which means something like singer or singers, and *noodin* which is the wind in our language. We are very spiritual people. Maybe one day I'll be able to share all that, my tribal culture and traditional beliefs, with you. Maybe?" The trace of a smile went away. "For me to do that...I'd need to feel a spiritual connection...I hope for that, but–" Marella was a skeptic in many ways; she didn't buy into the popular cliché of a 'soul mate', preferring candor and stability to things intangible. It was reassuring to her that Hector had both qualities.

"I'll hope and pray that you do feel that connection, Marella. One day in the not too distant future. And please...I'd like to wade into your culture rather than gulp it down in huge swallows. Maybe when I next visit we could attend a powwow together. Somehow, that intrigues me. Mickey has told me that the ceremonies are awesome. I've listened to a drum ceremony on my computer and found it absolutely powerful. Like you and your people, I am also quite spiritual—more than simply Catholic-religion spiritual."

Marella was tempted to tell him about her traditional Ojibwe ceremonial costume, and a 'jingle dress' that her mother had made for her...and about being named powwow queen on two separate occasions—but she chose to save that for another time.

Hector was happy to be over the glitch and didn't want to start any more fires. He had hoped for an opportunity to tell Marella that her sons were having an identity crisis of sorts. And, that Travis in particular, was both persistent and skilled in the research he was doing. That issue, however, was a road he would not travel.

"So, you like birds," Marella moved the subject to lighter ground.

"Where did that come from?" He didn't add 'did a little bird tell you?'

"I know some personal things myself," Marella teased.

"Okay. I do like birds—and flowers, too. Did Father Mario tell you that? The two of us were talking about birds a while back."

"No. Trevor told me. He said that you have a favorite cardinal…lives in a tree outside your bedroom window. I'm told that you talk to him in the morning. Is that really true?"

Hector smiled, "Did he tell you that I've given the bird a name?"

"He did. The bird's name is '*Blue*'…is that right?"

"Can you think of a better name for a cardinal?"

They both laughed and gave each other's hands a squeeze.

61/ SUNDAY MASS AT ST. GERARDS

On Sunday morning, Marella and the boys met Hector at the third floor elevator of the Raddison Hotel. All had slept an hour or so longer than they had wanted and only had time for a light breakfast of coffee, juice, and donuts, before driving out to St. Gerard's Church in Benton Park. Marella's hair was still damp and fell straight over her shoulders, her face without makeup. Hector's 'you look lovely this morning' gave her day a much better start than the rich, black coffee. She would happily take a compliment like that every morning.

"And you look quite handsome yourself," she said as they sat at a small table in the hotel's restaurant. Hector was wearing a flannel shirt that Trevor had loaned him the day before. "It might help you fit in with everybody better than if you wear a white shirt," he had suggested. "Plaid becomes you, Hector," she couldn't suppress a giggle. "It might be a size too large...but I like it."

Trevor laughed from across the table, "It's mine, Mom. Don't you remember...last Christmas...?"

"Oh, sure...a gift from your uncle." As soon as she said it, her expression changed.

Hector suggested that they finish up and get on the road. "I'll drive around to the front door," he said. Trevor was on his feet and offered to go with him to the ramp. Their plan was to surprise Father Mickey at St. Gerard's. Mickey wasn't expecting to see them until they all met at the Reservation later in the day. The temperature had moderated, and the morning was laden with a thick fog that crept up the hillside from Canal Park to the college campuses and then westward toward Spirit Mountain. Hector found Grand Avenue going west to be free of any of the downtown fog and took the old highway to the Benton Park turn off a mile west of Riverside.

The four of them were two minutes late for the ten o'clock mass and had to split up to find places to sit—the boys found seats on the side aisle, Hector and Marella near the back of the sanctuary. The smells of fresh paint mixed with incense wafted an exotic fragrance. Watching Mickey celebrate the mass was something special to each of them for different reasons. Marella could actually feel a potent spirituality in his every word and movement—he was a uniquely holy man. Knowing him as a person, outside of his priestly garments, gave her deeper insights than most.

Hector saw some of the same qualities in Mickey, but he was more in touch with the priest's deeply felt compassion for others. Travis found the priest to be 'cool' and having both Mickey and Mario in his life was 'neat'—especially when he wasn't particularly Catholic. Trevor's feelings were mixed and mysterious. Maybe he'd get his head around them when his heart was in a better place. Trevor's thoughts had wandered several miles away from the mass and into the forests surrounding the Fond du Lac Reservation, and then back again to the church. In both places his thoughts were intense.

Father Mickey sat with hands folded in his lap to the side of the altar while an elderly female parishioner with a high-pitched voice read the Epistle. While most were listening to the reading, Trevor's eyes were riveted on the priest. Although Mickey's eyes were closed, Trevor saw an almost imperceptible grimace on the priest's face. Trevor felt something– some essence or depth or inner truth– that deeply moved him at that same moment. Having had less opportunity to be around the priest than the others, his perception was more distant and impersonal. Father Mickey, he discerned, was troubled with something. When the priest stood and walked slowly to the lectern to read the Gospel, Trevor could see a dark cast in his eyes. Like himself...Father Mickey knew.

Mickey's homily was a poignant portrait of a St. Gerard's parishioner who "very few in our parish community ever really knew." Mickey spoke in general terms of the man's many battles with life, his few successes and his many failures. "A man like me and you—imperfect in so many ways. Yet, possessed of an inner goodness that could touch one's heart if one only allowed him to do so..." Mickey's intention was to encourage everyone that could, to join the search efforts for Benjamin Little Otter in the Fond du Lac reservation area that afternoon. His words, wearing the cloak of many past tense references, betrayed any realistic hope of finding his friend alive.

Mickey first saw Trevor Windsong on the end of a pew near the back of the sanctuary. Then, Travis two rows forward. A trace of a smile crossed his face. Marella and Hector must be somewhere. As he was about to speak on Luke's Gospel message, he saw the two of them in the very back, crunched between the large bodies of Marjorie Farley and Nancy Danich. "Following mass we might all take a moment to offer some words of support to Benjamin's family members who are worshiping with us this morning," he said.

"Now…where was I? Yes, remember Luke's Gospel last week? Jesus had just proclaimed that He was *'the One'*: a proclamation that was well received by the Jewish elders—until! If you're older, you'll remember Paul Harvey's *'and now you know the rest of the story'*. . . well, some loud mouthed buttinsky in the synagogue shouted out, 'Aren't you the son of Joseph? The carpenter?" The St. Gerard's congregation laughed at the 'loud mouthed buttinsky' reference. "The galoot went on to shout 'Joseph's a nobody…how could his son ever claim to be somebody– much less the promised Son of God?' That was all it took," Mickey gave an emphatic gesture, "Jesus went from a Jewish super-star to a quack Rabbi. In fact, after Jesus left the synagogue, the mob was about to push him over the cliff until he escaped from them. Thus the saying: 'You can never be a hero in your home town!'"

Father Mickey concluded his sermon with a post-script of sorts, "After an afternoon of searching for our friend, with all the fresh air and exercise, you'll be ready to kick back and watch the Super Bowl." Before stepping away from the lectern, he added: "Please put the money you might be tempted to bet on the Ravens in the collection basket instead. The 49er's will win by six."

62/ SEARCHING IN VAIN

When Mickey finished saying a Sunday mass he felt spent. As always, he had put his entire energy and spirit into each and every element of the sacred ceremony In concluding the mass he signed the cross over his congregation: "My friends, walk always in the peace of Christ."

Travis Windsong was the first to greet Mickey in the crowded foyer, "Great sermon, Father," he said before giving the priest an awkward hug. Hector and Trevor, more reserved than Travis, offered a handshake. Marella, emotional from the kind wishes of support from many passing strangers, said "Thank you, Father. Your mass was inspiring..." she began to tear, then stepped into the priest's embrace."

After Mickey had untangled himself from the post-mass crowd and changed into outdoors clothing, everybody piled into the spacious Chevrolet suburban that Hector had rented for the weekend. During mass the foggy drizzle had turned into a wet snow, making the roadways slippery. Hector spun his wheels as he drove out of the St. Gerard's parking lot; then -for a split second- lost control of the big vehicle, sliding into the curb and blocking the street. Everybody laughed at the bemused Floridian. "Now what, Hector?" Mickey teased from his seat next to the wide-eyed driver. "How about giving us all another spin and a good bounce off the curb. That was really fun."

Hector, serious as always and entirely missing his friend's humor, looked over his shoulder and asked, "Is anybody hurt? Marella...are you okay?" Picking up on Mickey's ribbing, Marella moaned: ". . . I think I broke something...my back or my neck– the pain is unbearable!" Hector leaped from the suburban without turning off the ignition. "Don't move...Mickey, or somebody, call an ambulance." In his rush to help Marella, his feet slipped out from beneath him, but he broke his fall by grasping the handle of the open door. As he regained his balance, Hector saw that Marella was doubled over with laughter. "Hector...my dear Hector. Won't you please sit back here with me? We'll let the other Florida guy drive— Trevor, will you kindly take the wheel?"

When Hector 'got it', the red blush left his face and he could laugh along with the others. His recovery line was splendid: "What all of you don't know is that I did that spin move on purpose." He looked at Marella, "I knew that you'd ask me to quit trying to drive and sit in the back seat next to you."

~

It was nearly noon when they arrived at the Fond du Lac community center. The parking lot was filled with cars, trucks, snowmobiles, and trailers. Lester Hicks, Benjamin's AA sponsor, greeted them at the door, "We've got nearly two hundred people out there this morning," he told Marella and her party. Hicks had been coordinating the search efforts for nearly a week. "This new snow ain't gonna help none, but…I think that maybe…just maybe, we'll find him today." Lester had reserved three Arctic Cat snowmobiles for the group of five. "Why don't each of you take a thermos of hot chocolate and some cookies along with you. I've packed some signal flares with each machine. Good luck and God bless and thanks."

Mickey looked at Hector, "You wanna ride with me?" Hector looked at Marella, shrugged…"I suppose?"

"He's riding with me, Father. You can have a snowmobile all to yourself."

Believing that Marella was the one person who was most familiar with the area, Hicks suggested to her that their group head north, "When you get to Bart's Pond 'bout two miles up there," he gestured, "Then spread out and go east to the Makis' farm. Then double back to the pond, and try again. We wanna cover every square foot if we can. This might be the last major effort we'll be able to put together." Lester had a large, detailed wall map with pins and yarn marking the day's planned coverage. "Over here's a layout we put together."

Trevor looked toward his mom, then spoke to Hicks. "I think I know the area better than my mom does. I been to Jimmy Maki's place a few times before." He offered to take charge, "I know a short-cut from here to the pond, you guys follow me. Let's go." Trevor would lead the search and direct the efforts of his group for the remainder of the afternoon.

After nearly four hours of combing the two miles from Bart's Pond to Maki's farm, the daylight was already fading. The earlier tracks back to the reservation were barely discernable with the fresh snow cover. "We gotta head back," Trevor's tone was that of an officer to his troops: "Follow me and Travis, okay?"

~

Lester Hicks shook his head. The Windsongs were among the last searchers to report back and only a few cars remained in the parking lot. It was Super Sunday. "We ain't gonna have many folks back here tomorrow. Monday's gonna be ten below with a wind besides." He rubbed the side of his large nose, "Matter'a fact, most guys are sayin' we'd best wait 'til spring. We've had almost a foot of new snow since Ben disappeared."

63/ BUFFALO BURGERS

Rather than eating leftover sandwiches and chili at the Reservation's community building with a handful of remaining stragglers, the weary group headed back toward Duluth, "We'll find some place to eat along the way," Marella suggested.

"Buffalo House," the shout came from Trevor in the back seat. "I played in a softball tournament there in May of last summer. We camped out, had a blast." That was the first time Trevor had tasted beer—he didn't like it, but joined the older guys in polishing off a keg. Travis, buckled in next to him, looked up from the game he was playing on his iPad. "Let me count the words, bro…eighteen, I think. That's some kind of record. You must really be high on this buffalo place." Trevor gave him a punch on the shoulder. "Shove it!"

"Eighteen," Travis persisted, "that's two days worth of words in less than a minute. What's with all the talking lately? People back in Florida where you've been living got lots to say? You catching this virus from them? Or is Mr. Munoz teaching you how to string words together?"

Hector, back at the wheel of the suburban on a dry highway, ramped up to I-35 south and merged into the string of traffic returning to Duluth and the Iron Range from the Twin Cities. Every weekend there was a southern migration to the Cities for one venue or another: Pro sports were huge in Minnesota, the Mall of America was an international magnet for shoppers, and cultural events of every ilk –the Guthrie and the Ordway were nationally recognized theaters—these and countless other attractions could be found in Minneapolis, St. Paul, or the many suburbs ringing the two mushrooming cities.

Marella called Mickey on her cell phone, "We're stopping at the Buffalo House up the highway near Spirit Mountain—hope you and Father Mario will join us." Mickey was riding with Mario, who had recruited some twenty UMD students and joined the search in mid-afternoon. The priests were only a few cars behind Hector. "Will do. We've both got stuff to do back home so we can't stay long. Maybe a cup of coffee," Mickey said. "And pie…" Marella heard Mario's voice in the background.

Hector saw the huge buffalo on the right side of the highway, nearly a quarter mile ahead, signaled an exit, and pulled into the large lot. Cars were packed in and it took minutes to find a place to park the big vehicle. Travis teased, "Good job, Mr. Munoz. You kept us on the highway for nearly ten miles without an incident."

Marella giggled, "like a tried and true Gopher. I knew when I saw him in that flannel shirt that he had some hidden potential."

"What's a gopher anyhow?" Hector asked. "A harmless, little rodent? How can you brag about Minnesota when you have a gopher for a mascot?"

Trevor pretended to be irate over the put-down, "The Gopher's play Big Ten ball—if Florida played our schedule in any sport they'd give it up or go home beaten to a pulp."

"Touché," said Travis without looking up from his iPad.

The Super Bowl crowd inside was boisterous, but Marella

found a booth that would seat four in a corner away from the bar and the bank of big screen TV's. Hector surveyed the room; about a fourth of the revelers wore Raven's black, another quarter were in 49er's red. The remainder were eternal optimists or impossible dreamers wearing the Viking's purple and gold. "Can you tell that they like football up here?" Trevor whispered into Hector's ear.

Conversation was nearly impossible: "Are you sure you want to stay, Hector?" Marella shouted above the din. "We can find another place where it isn't so loud."

Hector was enjoying the ribald atmosphere of a Minnesota bar. "Do they really make hamburgers with buffalo meat?" he asked Marella. He had no more than asked the question when he realized its absurdity. Apparently nobody seemed to catch the blunder. . .

"No, my dear," Marella lightly punched him in the ribs. "But they do make buffalo burgers. I can tell you wanna stay."

Hector shrugged in a noncommittal gesture, but smiled quietly inside–the 'my dear' had a wonderful ring to it. "It's up to you." Then he paused, "No," he corrected, "I mean yes. I'd like to stay and try one of those burgers."

When Mickey and Mario found them, they both shook their head…"We're gonna pass on this," Mickey said. "I'll call you guys in the morning. Okay?"

64/ *A FEAR OF WINDIGO*

Mickey's bedtime prayers were of the 'catch up' variety. The past few days had been so consumed with out-of-the-ordinary matters that his prayer life had suffered neglect. On this Sunday, he mentally ticked off the intentions that came most clearly to mind. Although he believed that Ben had already found his heavenly reward, Mickey prayed for the recovery of his body. He prayed for his all-too-often neglected parishioners, his family members and his friends—each by name and with a specific intention attached. And, he prayed for his suffering ministry.

In recent weeks there had been no tangible successes in his diocesan Indian mission, so with the bishop's apparent blessing, he was settling as comfortably as possible into the routines of his re-energized St. Gerard's parish. It seemed that when the bishop wanted him to do one thing, Mickey was of a mind to consider something different. Despite all the 'ego food' of recent months, Mickey was disappointed with himself as a servant of God. His obstinate spirit did not cope well with failure or consession. That reality was a constant displeasure, so he prayed for deeper resolve and a renewed dedication to his mission. Somehow, he realized that his friend Benjamin was the key to any success he might find. . . and, Mickey was certain, Benjamin was in a better place now. "I know you're up there," he spoke to Ben. "Send an angel or some kind of miracle to help me out down here. Please, don't let me flounder like a doofus, Benjamin."

When Mickey prayed, he often sent his petitions to Jesus through an intermediary of sorts. "Dear Saint Joseph, patron saint of a 'holy death', take my friend Benjamin into your companionship and help him to help me as I search for a way to serve our Lord as I have been called to do." As he prayed he found serenity, and from that serenity he found a new confidence—his prayers would be answered. The how and the when were not Mickey's to discern.

Mickey's cell phone rang, interrupting the quietude of his thoughts. It was nearly one in the morning. The caller ID read the Radisson Hotel—Hector or Marella—trouble of some kind? Or, news about Benjamin? Calls at one in the morning were never good...he answered, the voice was Trevor's. "Father...I'm sorry; I know it's very late...but I couldn't sleep." Mickey assured the boy that he was fine with late calls—"No problem; like a good father, Mickey is there." He smiled at his mimic of a familiar insurance commercial on TV. "I get them all the time, Trevor. What's on your mind?"

Trevor went on to make a confession of sorts beginning with his Uncle Ben. "Is it wrong to believe—even to hope– that he's already dead?" He explained that he knew his uncle better than anybody else and that Ben was a very unhappy man. "Not long ago, he told me that he often wished the Great Spirit would take him away."

Mickey had also sensed his friend's melancholy for the past several months and had often tried to get Ben to talk more about his feelings. Ben, however, rarely allowed his feelings to escape what he called his 'dungeons' inside. Once he had told Mickey that a *Windigo* was relentlessly pursuing him.

"Today I had a vision or something…it was strange, Father" Trevor confessed. "I don't know how to describe it…but I'll try. My people, the Anishinaabe, believe in *manidoos*, they are good and evil spirits. Anyhow, one day last summer when my uncle was visiting me in the hospital, he told me that soon he would meet his evil tormenter and break free from its grip on him. Today I knew, without a doubt, that he had escaped that evil spirit…once and for all."

"Did his tormentor have a name, Trevor?"

Trevor swallowed hard. "Yes. It was *Windigo* that he feared."

At that moment, Mickey felt a strange peace come over him. He smiled to himself– both he and Trevor had been blessed with an assurance that Benjamin Little Otter was in heaven. "If I tell you that I have the same feelings as you do, will you be able to get some sleep now?"

"I don't know, Father." A longe pause…"There's something else." Trevor explained what had happened to his wrist—his incredibly reconstructed left wrist. "I tweaked it pretty bad…it's been like an abscessed toothache all day. Mr. Munoz has a contract offer from the Twins in his suitcase…he's planning to discuss the details with my mom tomorrow." Another pause and an audible sigh…"My conscience is bothering me—terribly! If I tell anybody, like Mr. Munoz, or the people with the Twins…well, it's like they might all get very upset with me."

Mickey listened patiently through many lengthy pauses. "What do you want to do, Trevor? Have you ever tried praying when you're confused or frustrated about what to do?" Trevor, wanting to be honest and open, admitted that he never prayed for himself: "In my own way, Father. I ask the Great Spirit to do things for others quite often."

"Did you ask your Great Spirit to take your uncle?"

"Not really. I've always prayed that my uncle would find peace. That's all."

Trevor returned to his injury: "I want to tell Mr. Munoz...but–" He couldn't finish the thought.

"There's more, Trevor?"

"Yes. Lots more."

"Go ahead."

"I'm not going back!"

"Back where? I don't get it, Trevor."

"To Florida. I'm not going back there."

"Why? Something between you and Mr. Munoz?"

"No...he's a wonderful man. It's not the Twins, either. It's me. It's things."

"Keep going. I'm on the same page."

"I can't go back until my uncle's found. It wouldn't be right. And..."

"And..."

"I'm afraid." He cleared his throat. "Afraid of failure. I don't think I can pitch anymore. And, what's worse, I don't even know if I want to."

"And signing a contract with the Twins would be deceitful?"

"It would be...but that's a cop out."

Mickey would allow Trevor to finish his thoughts without offering advice.

"I know my spirit is here, Father. My Ojibwe spirit!" He spoke with passion about something no one, not even himself, could fully comprehend. He explained that he respected Father Mickey's deep faith. "I feel your spirit whenever I'm around you—it was very strong at mass this morning. Yours is a very good spirit, but I don't think that it's...well, it's not mine." Trevor's words conveyed his deep and honest torment.

The young man was struggling to untangle a conundrum that had him searching through thoughts that confused and mystified so deeply that they became a spiritual paralysis. Mickey wanted to pray for discernment with him, to give him every assurance that whatever decisions he made would be the right ones, if he allowed his heart to lead him.

Marella had seen a blinking phone light from the next room where the boys were sleeping. She went to the adjoining door and listened. Trevor was speaking in hushed tones but she could hear his every word.

65/ FINDING BENJAMIN

The second weekend of February saw a welcome thaw to the long stretch of cold and blustery weather. Only Marella and Trevor Windsong, Hector Munoz, Father Mickey and a handful of searchers were continuing their search for Benjamin Little Otter. Travis had a research paper to complete and was glued to the computer in his dorm room. Nearly every square foot of five square miles had already been canvassed, and few held any hope of finding Benjamin before spring.

On Monday morning, the eleventh of February, a young man named Billy Grivette had the day off from his job at the Sappi paper mill in Cloquet. Billy was snowmobiling to his fish house on a remote lake east of the reservation when he discovered what appeared to be a fragment of red cloth caught in a shrub near the edge of an aspen stand. Curious, he got off of his Yamaha, stepped into snow that was nearly knee deep, and kicked around. Several steps to the left of his machine, his foot felt a lump of something. He kicked more snow away...What Billy Grivette discovered beneath the snow made him sick to his stomach. What remained of the body he found was a sight more horrific than any his eyes had ever seen. On his day off a week before, Billy had searched along with a group that included some of Benjamin's family and Father Mickey. Billy's first thought was to call the priest at St. Gerard's from his cell phone. It took only a minute to locate the church's phone number...

Mickey was meeting with the architect and two contractors on an amendment to the original remodeling plan. An anonymous donor from St. Francis Church (Mickey's former parish) in Brainerd had contributed a sizable sum for the remodeling project. "The family wants the money to be used for an addition that will offer some needed seating and a 'crying room' for small children." Mickey said, "I never thought that I would see the day when this parish had such a need...but, thank God, that time has arrived. Crying babies at St. Gerard's...who could have..."

Mickey excused himself to take the call. The name Grivette was not a familiar one. He listened to the heartrending description with tears forming in the corner of his eyes. "Thank you, Billy...our prayers have finally been answered." Mickey asked the young man to contact Lester Hicks at the reservation, "Give him your location and tell him that I asked that nobody notify the family just yet—I plan to do that right now. Have you got that, Bill? I don't want Mr. Hicks to contact the family. Tell Hicks that I'll call him as soon as I can. Okay?" When he put his phone down, he apologized to the contractors, "Something has come up and I really can't continue our meeting just now. Keep doing what you're doing—it's all going well."

The men nodded their understanding, the plumbing and heating contractor—a man named Galatz—said, "Bad news from your expression, Father. I'm sorry."

Mickey forced a smile, "Thanks, Reid." Reid Galatz was a parishioner of his. "Bad news wrapped in relief, I'd say. Ben Little Otter's body has been found."

As Mickey closed the door behind the three men, he crossed over to the rectory. In his office he regarded a small wood-carved statue of St. Joseph on the bookshelf. He said a prayer before pressing Marella's number on the land phone resting on his desk among a spread of blueprints. He caught himself on the fifth number. No, a phone call would not be the way to pass along this news. Checking his wristwatch, it was 9:40, in half an hour he could be in the Radisson parking ramp downtown.

As he reached for his jacket, the phone rang...the caller ID read, Mario Morelli...before he could pick up the phone, Alice Murray, the housekeeper, raced into the small office with a vacuum attachment in her hand.

"Father...Father, have you heard the news?"

Mickey had just picked up his phone, "Just a minute Mario, Alice needs to tell me something." As he turned to Alice he heard Mario say something about the pope...

"Pope Benedict has resigned, Father. It's on the TV now. I can't believe it! Resigned! What's gonna happen now?"

"Mario, you still there? Were you going to tell me about the pope?" Mickey listened intently as Mario explained what was happening in Rome. "I'm sad, of course, but I'm excited, too. This kind of thing never happens...its been—how long, do you know?"

Mario, nearly out of breath from his own disbelief answered: "Just two minutes ago the commentator said it been more than six hundred years since a pope resigned. You've got to turn on your TV..."

Mickey was stressed. He wanted to go to the TV and watch the evolving news, but he had to contact Marella. "Mario, I'm sorry, I'm not processing all this very well. I've got a dozen balls in the air right now. Benjamin's body had been found. I'm on the run right now…I'll get back to you as soon as I can."

Mickey thought to call Hector before getting out of the door. Making every effort to speak in his normal voice, he asked: "What are you guys up to this morning?"

Hector's voice had a rare excited edge, "We're all watching the breaking news on CNN. The pope…"

"I know. It's unbelievable, but…what plans have you guys made for the day?"

"The three of us are going up to the campus and meeting Travis for a late breakfast, then we're going back to Fond du Lac for a few hours. Why?"

Mickey thought quickly, a 'white lie' came automatically: "Nothing…I'm free this morning and thought I'd join you all—if that's okay."

"For sure. You're welcome to join us any time—you know that." They agreed to wait for Mickey to join them at the Griggs Hall cafeteria. Hector wanted to talk more about the news, but Mickey had already hung up the phone. He shrugged, that was strange. Something else was on Mickey's mind—it wasn't the pope.

Mickey drove east on Grand Avenue, going close to sixty as he passed through Norton Park and found the I-35 ramp going north and east. Priests and other clergy had been afforded an 'unofficial' leniency from the city police and Mickey was prone to taking advantage of his privileged status. Passing the huge grain elevators off to his right, Mickey proceeded to Mesabi Avenue, and ran two yellow lights on the hillside leading up to UMD. Mickey's mind was in turmoil, how was he going to break the news?

News! Mickey finally thought to turn on his radio. Both KDAL and WDSM were covering the pope story. Already scandal allegations were surfacing from the Roman media. The reporter was saying that old age—Benedict was eighty-five– and an inablitly to continue the necessary travel or to govern the church effectively were the stated reasons. But there were malicious 'back stories'.

Mickey's mind switched from one concern to another and then back the Windsongs again. He turned off the radio. When focused on his mission of the moment, he found himself more worried about Trevor than any of the others. As he reran their late conversation the night before about spirits and prayer and baseball, he felt a knot work its way from his lower back to the nape of his neck. His stress always seemed to settle in his neck before shooting into his head. How was he going to frame the news? He scolded himself, "Mickey, you've been the messenger of sad news a thousand times, don't beat yourself up over this. You know that whatever you say doesn't change the reality. Just be as upbeat as you can. As an afterthought, as he crossed over to Arrowhead Road, Mickey called Father Mario at the Newman center on campus. "I'm going to need some prayers, my friend…" he explained the gruesome discovery only an hour before. "I think we're all on overload at the moment, but…"

Mario agreed to meet him at Griggs in ten minutes. "I needed something to get me away from the TV," he said. "Why is it that whenever the Catholic Church becomes newsworthy, the media jackals revert to sex scandals…it's like they think that's what defines us. Makes me sick."

66/ COFFEE ON CAMPUS

Mickey passed the sprawl of campus buildings, turned off of College Street and onto Kirby Drive. He parked in a 'Faculty Only' space in Lot W and rushed into a stiff hilltop wind toward the red brick dormitory complex. Inside, students with their stuffed backpacks and laptop cases were milling about the Griggs lobby. Mario was surrounded by a cluster of students who appeared to be engaged in an animated conversation about the morning's news. At UMD, Father Mario was the foremost ambassador of the Catholic Church. Seeing Mickey, he broke away from the group with an apology,

"C'mon over to the Newman Center this afternoon. We'll have a good discussion about everything going on now." Several students recognized Mickey as he approached, and one coed said, "With guys like the two of you, there's hope for us Catholics."

"Sorry about your friend, Benjamin. What can I do, Mick?" Mario said. "I can't stay too long. I'm giving a lecture at eleven thirty—that's just over an hour from now."

"I really don't know what to say. Just having you with me means a lot." He gave a sigh, "I'm going to focus on Trevor...he's the one that's going to take the news the hardest."

"Or...maybe not. I think there's going to be a collective sigh of relief. The ordeal of the past couple of weeks has really drained them all. Now everybody's lives can begin to head back toward normal."

The foursome was sitting at a table near the bank of windows looking south into the frosty, gray morning. The room had two big screens and most of the people in the room were watching the set with CNN news from Vatican City, a few others were glued to a sports channel. They all stood when the two priests entered the spacious room, "Hey Mario, c'mon over for a minute," from a tall kid at the CNN set. "We wanna get your take on all this." Mario, it seemed, knew most of the students on campus by name, "Later Kent," he said in passing by. Lagging a few steps behind Mickey he stopped briefly at nearly every table and wished the students a 'good morning'—each by name.

"What a pleasant surprise to have you join us," Marella said when Mario took the chair beside her. Hector, looking more comfortable wearing a freshly starched white shirt and khakis than when clad in plaid flannel, was seated on Marella's other elbow. He reached across to shake Mario's hand and offer a pleasant greeting. Mickey moved a chair in between the two brothers, gave each a hearty slap on the back, "Mind if I interrupt whatever you two guys have been talking about?"

Travis smiled, "Trevor talking? You've got to be kidding, Father. Contrary to what everybody else is talking about this morning, I'm more into the Drones controversy that the networks put on the back burner to cover the pope stuff. No disrespect, Fathers." Trevor ingnored his brother's banter, nodded a greeting to the two priests without showing any interest in what anybody was talking about. Apparently, however, Trevor wasn't in his 'leave me alone' zone this morning. Looking up, he rolled his eyes at Travis, "I ain't talkin' because I could care less. I don't believe nothin' the TV people say these days. Everything has so much spin on it that it only makes your head swim. You have no idea what's really true." He looked at Mickey, "I mean, the pope stuff is true...but now we gotta hear all the spin-off junk."

Mickey nudged Trevor, "Good observation."

Hector Munoz sensed a hidden agenda from the moment the two priests arrived. He read Mickey's eyes and demeanor, and despite his effort to be affable, his friend appeared to be a little off this morning. The quick hangup of the phone had triggered his concern. He decided to open the dialogue, "To what do we owe the pleasure...?"

Mickey looked to Mario, then to Hector and Marella, and turned in his chair so that he could focus more on Trevor who was at his elbow. "Truth be told...some bad news, I'm afraid."

"Benjamin's been found?" Marella's sudden blurt was more question than statement. She breathed deeply, leaned toward Mickey, met his eyes: "That's it...isn't it, Father? He's dead."

Mickey nodded, chose his words carefully: "His spirit has returned to the Great Spirit of his ancestors. His body was found this morning."

Trevor's expression was deadpan—not even an acknowledging nod. Travis reached behind Mickey and gave his brother's arm an affectionate squeeze without speaking. He could feel the same knot in his chest that Trevor was feeling.

"There's more isn't there, Father? I can tell..." Marella had pulled a packet of tissue form her purse. She sniffled, "What else should we know?"

Mickey explained that it was assumed that wolves had discovered Benjamin's body. "From what I've been told it's not a pleasant sight." He went on to say that Lester Hicks would retrieve the body and bring it back to the Fond du Lac Reservation. "You will probably have to make an identification of the corpse for the Medical Examiner, Marella. I don't think the rest of us need to see...whatever remains of Ben."

Mario took Marella's hand in his, "Can I lead us in a prayer?"

Marella nodded, closed her eyes...the others at the table joined hands as Mario prayed: *"Eternal rest grant onto Benjamin Little Otter, our Lord...and may Your perpetual light shine upon him. May his soul, and the souls of all the faithful departed, rest in peace..."* The others offered an *'Amen'*.

67/ JOSEPH

Marella Windsong, the closest living relative of the deceased, made the funeral arrangements through Dougherty of Duluth. It was her wish to combine traditional Ojibwe rituals with those of Benjamin's Catholic faith. The funeral mass would be celebrated at St. Gerard's in Benton Park, with a reception following the ceremony at the Fond du Lac community center. Interment would wait until spring. At the Reservation, celebrated author/poet, Jim Northrup, would offer a special welcome and tribute. A friend of Benjamin's, Northrup would compose a special verse for the occasion. Fathers Michael Moran and Mario Morelli were asked to concelebrate the mass along with an Anishinaabe spiritual leader from the Mille Lacs reservation. Bishop Bremmer would offer his blessing and condolences, along with a special invocation referencing Native American Saint Kateri Tekakwitha .

Marella, along with Trevor, identified Ben's ravaged body prior to sending it off to the funeral home. Trevor's insistence to join his mother would not be denied. Neither cried. The casket was sealed forever. The funeral date was set for Wednesday.

As the sanctuary filled for visitation prior to the mass, Marella and her sons greeted friends and many others she had never met before. Those who knew Ben had kind memories to share with the family, those that did not offered appropriate words of support. Fond du Lac Reservation chairwoman, Karen Driver, along with members of the FDL tribal council were to be seated in the front pews opposite the Windsong family. FDL's radio station, WGZS, was equipped to cover both the funeral mass and the reception.

~

Early on the Wednesday morning of the funeral, Father Mickey sat at his desk with his third cup of coffee and a stale cranberry-orange scone, trying to fill in some anecdotes for the skeleton of a homily. The blank yellow page of his legal pad stared at him as if pleading for something tangibly written in ink. Nothing was working—Mickey was stressing. The harder he thought the bigger the blank between his ears. What could he say about Benjamin Little Otter? This wonderful man…this dear friend? He needed first to put aside any guilt over the reality that he had not seen nor spoken to Ben in the weeks before he died. Instead, he needed to recall their good times together—that was the conundrum! In their last conversations, Ben had told him that he no longer wanted to be a part of the Ojibwe project that the two had been struggling with, that he had nothing of worth to contribute, that he was beginning to feel like a 'doofus'. Nothing positive there! Yet, Ben's credibility within the Native community was the most viable foundation that Mickey, and Bishop Bremmer, had planned to build their program upon. He scribbled…'Ben's goodness is heartfelt and can't be properly…' he crossed out properly and struggled for a better word: 'fully', 'accurately', 'entirely'. The word 'finally' crossed his thoughts and he discarded it. He dismissed the heartfelt idea he'd started to pen as both trite and irrelevant. Why was it so much easier to characterize someone who wasn't so close to you, someone you only knew from a distance?

Mickey got up from his desk and began to pace the small office space. The heart and spirit of his friend had slipped beyond his ability to characterize…under his breath he said a prayer. The digital clock on his desk flashed 6:42. He stopped and stared in futility at the legal pad resting only feet away, snatched it up, and tore off the sheet he had been working on. Crumpling it up, he tossed it toward the wastebasket several feet away. He missed. "Damn!"

Frustrated, Mickey grabbed a light jacket hanging on the coat tree near the rectory door. He needed to get out of this space if he was going to contemplate, or meditate, or formulate any workable ideas for his homily– now only a few short hours away. Stepping into the lingering darkness and biting chill of the early morning, he began walking along the deserted back streets toward Blackmer Park on the eastern edge of the aging blue-collar community. Mickey had hoped to be able to combine the Christian concepts of death with those of the Ojibwe, but Lee Staples of the Anishinaabi people, would probably draw those comparisons himself in making his address. Staples, he had been told, was a man of deep passion. Should he contact Staples? Inquire about what the man was planning to cover with his remarks? The last thing he wanted to do was to say something that was, in his Catholic vocabulary, sacreligious. No…that should have been done yesterday or the day before; it was too late now. "Damn!" Mickey cursed for a second time. He couldn't possibly 'wing it' for the most meaningful funeral of his priesthood—he'd risk looking like a fool! Father Mickey, the miracle priest, stumbling and stammering…the thought only added another layer of stress. The 'miracle priest' needed a miracle!

The first extremities to feel the numbing cold were his feet. When Mickey turned back toward St. Gerard's, he realized the mistake of beginning his walk with the wind at his back. He began to jog along the snowbanked street when a car pulled up beside him, stopped, and the tinted window rolled down. "Can you tell me where the Catholic Church is located?"

Mickey stepped closer to the window, smiled: "I would think so."

"I'm a *doofus* from out of town…here for a funeral later this morning," the stranger said.

Mickey's eyelid flicked at the stranger's *doofus* self-reference: "If you'll give me a lift, I'll take you right there and offer you a cup of coffee besides. I'm Father Moran." Mickey offered his hand through the open window. The stranger appeared to be an Indian man, yet his features were hard to categorize. His coloring was copper, his hair blonde, his face narrow. He wore a buttonless white shirt and white slacks which was unusual for the winter season. Somehow the man looked familiar. Vaguely familiar. Yet, quite unlike anyone Mickey could place. The man's smile was radiant.

"Hop in, Father Mickey. I'd enjoy a cup of coffee."

Mickey frowned, had he introduced himself as Father Mickey, or simply, Father Moran? His mind was so full of things that he wasn't sure. Inside the car, Mickey was further perplexed by the posh, but simple, features of the car's stark white interior. The dashboard had few displays; none of the instrument panel gadgetry he was accustomed to seeing were evident. Soft, ethereal music played, but no radio controls could be seen. "What kind of car is this, sir?" The man had not identified himself.

"A hybrid of sorts. I'm only borrowing it for the day." He smiled, "By the way, I'm a close friend of Mr. Little Otter—my name is… Joseph…just Joseph."

Before Mickey could tell the stranger to turn left on 88th, Joseph was already turning correctly into the intersection. "I can see your church up ahead…"

Mickey strained his neck but couldn't see his church about two blocks ahead on the right side of the street. The stranger must have remarkable vision.

Joseph pulled to a stop in front of St. Gerard's. The engine went silent and the doors opened by themselves. Mickey was amazed, "I've never seen anything like this before. Where on earth did you find it?"

Joseph chuckled at Mickey's question, but ignored it. "Let's go inside for that coffee you offered me." Mickey took one last look at the white car, shook his head in disbelief and followed Joseph, who was already walking a few steps ahead of him toward the rectory. Joseph opened the door in front of the priest and stepped inside as Mickey hung up his jacket. Rather than wait, the stranger walked through Mickey's small office, around the dark dining room table in the adjacent room, and into the kitchen. As Mickey watched from a few steps behind, Joseph opened the cupboard door above the range and took down two cups. "You take yours black…don't you Father?" Joseph poured two cups of coffee.

Mickey stood dumbfounded. He remembered turning off the burner on an empty pot earlier that morning…yet? Strange was becoming stranger! The man had said he was from out of town: "Sir…I mean, Joseph…have you been here before? In Benton Park? In this rectory? Somehow, you seem to know…"

Once again, Joseph ignored the questions. "Let's sit down and visit, I only have a short time. We can talk about Benjamin if you'd like."

The two of them sat down, "I've known Benjamin all of his life…" Joseph began.

68/ 'MIIGWECH'

Mickey noticed that the legal pad that he had left on the desk in his office was resting near his empty coffee cup on the kitchen table. At the top of the page, in his own handwriting, was the name: Benjamin Little Otter. Below the name were some biographical notes: details of his friend's life that Mickey had never known about and had no recollection of having written down. On the next page were a few personality characteristics, which could be summarized as confirming Benjamin's simple but virtuous nature. The page held the very same thoughts, but in much greater detail, that Mickey had contmplated while walking to Blackmer Park earlier that morning. Earlier! He checked the kitchen clock, an hour had passed. Where was Joseph? The second cup, a green 'Erin go Bragh' match to his own, was gone from the table. Mickey got up and checked the sink...nothing. The coffee pot was empty and the basket was devoid of filter or grounds, exactly as he had left it on the stove the night before. More confused than he had ever been, he returned to his tablet and turned to the third page. A simple note in perfect cursive was addressed to him:

Father Michael:

Just wing it. The perfect words are in your heart. Let's keep our brief time together this morning between the three of us. Hope to see you again...

Miigwech

Joseph

'Just wing it?' The expression was one of Mickey's favorites. Yet, he couldn't remember ever sharing his tendency to simply 'shoot from the hip' with his homilies with anyone else except, possibly, Father Mario. And what was *'Miigwech'*? Strange! Even stranger was the reference...*the three of us*!

~

The ceremony opened solemnly with Sherman Obey drumming and chanting an Indian 'Honoring' song. Lee Staples, the spirtual leader of the Mille Lacs Band was dressed in traditional Ojibwe clothing and spoke eloquently of 'the sacred duty to keep the native Anishinaabe language, native traditions, and spiritual ways alive' to an audience that was almost equally mixed between red and white faces. He tailored his eulogy to *'Nahgahchinwanong'*: 'The people at the far end of the Great Lake', referring to those of the Fond du Lac Reservation. He reminded his bretheren: "We have our Anishinaabe spirit within us during our lifetime…a spirit that will return to our Creator when we die." His talk was relatively brief and ended with *'Miigwech'*, the traditional 'thank you'.

Mario, sitting beside Mickey as Staples spoke, whispered, "You're up next, pard. Where are your notes?"

"Back on my kitchen table. I'm just the voice…whatever words I speak are going to come from somewhere else." Although tempted, Mickey didn't add an honest, 'At least that's what I'm hoping!' As Staples walked from the lecturn, Mickey cupped his hand over his mouth and said to Mario, "What you are about to hear will be a small miracle. I'll explain later, please just say a prayer that I can pull this off."

Mickey stood for a long moment and peered out at the crowded sanctuary. Folding chairs had been placed along the side aisles and people were crunched together in the back of the church. He smiled, opened his arms, spoke in a calm voice: "Welcome to Benjamin's church, and mine. Six months ago our dear friend told me that he would do anything, I must emphasize *anything,* to make our assimilation project work. As some of you know, that project was an effort by my Church– and the Catholic Disocese of Duluth– to bring our two peoples and cultures together in the praise and worship of our Lord, Jesus Christ." Mickey went on to explain that the two men were waiting outside the emergency room at St. Mary's, praying together for Benjamin's nephew who had just suffered a serious accident. "Benjamin's heart was heavy with sadness that day. He told me that he couldn't continue with our project...I remember his words as if he spoke them this morning, '...it's like a pair of pants that's too big and make me look like a doofus and I don't wanna be a doofus'. In his own unique thinking, I believe that being a doofus meant he was losing face with those he cared for: That would be each of you who have come together this morning to honor his spirit and memory."

Mickey looked to his right, nodded toward Bishop Bremmer, seated near Mario. "At that very moment, I let go of our project as well. I gave it completely to God. In these past months nothing of any consequence has happened—that is, until a winter morning nearly two weeks ago. . ."

In Mickey's mind a picture of that morning was as clear as if he were there; he felt the snowflakes touch his face, the chill was in his bones. "I can see the shadows of the aspen along the nearby hillside. I can see Benjamin lying in the snow, looking up to heaven, a smile is on his face—not only can I can see him...but I can hear his words: *"Giiwewinishin Gichi—Manitoo. Ningiizhiitaanji-gaagige."* Mickey's eyes closed as he continued speaking in a language he had never learned. Staples stood in astonishment. "He's talking to my people in our words—and to Benjamin who is standing at the side of our Great Spirit," he whispered to Bishop Bremmer at his side. "His words are perfect Ojibwe!"

The Indians in the sanctuary all stood, bowed their heads and listened with reverence to the priest's conversation with Benjamin. Jim Northrup, in the front row, who always kept a small notebook in one of his pockets, began writing everything down as rapidly as he could:

"My dear friend, your death has given life to our dreams. Here, in this church, are your people and mine, together in worship. Your Great Spirit and my Divine Father are one and the same God, just as we are one and the same flesh. Just as you are with us in spirit

on this day, so is our Savior. Our spirits will be forever joined with you in this world and in the world of our ancestors."

When Mickey opened his eyes he was physically drained and perspiring. He had spoken for nearly ten minutes. A brief glint of light radiated from the entry door as Joseph left the sanctuary. Mickey looked toward Mario, whispered…"What did I just do?"

"Another miracle, my friend."

the end…

EPILOGUE:

September 2013

In conclusion, I'd like to let the readers of *'The Sons of Marella Windsong'* know that several lives have been changed in the telling of this story. Mine included. After leaving St. Gerard's church, following that remarkable funeral, I took a few months off from any serious writing. I have been prone to that dreaded author's malady called 'writer's block' and hoped that it wouldn't revisit me. I do have another story lurking in the back of my thoughts—another Father Mickey story—but I don't want to force it out just yet. Like a fine wine, I must give that new voice enough time to mature and come to a proper age, before indulging in that next writing adventure.

I will be brief in this story's epilogue.

Trevor Windsong took months to emotionally recover from the loss of his Uncle Benjamin. After the funeral, he told his mother that he wanted to live for a time in the Fond du Lac house that Benjamin had left behind. He believed that he needed to be on the Rez to get more deeply 'in touch' with his Ojibwe spirit. This meant, of course, that the Twins minor league contract that Hector Munoz had brought along with him would go unsigned. Trevor did have the civility to contact Terry Ryan in person and explain that he had 'tweaked' his injured wrist and that he was taking a needed rest from baseball. Doctor MacIver and the rehab team that had worked so remarkably with Trevor found no permanent damage and encouraged the young man to keep up with his conditioning regimen. Trevor's competitive drive would eventually be rechanneled to golf where the Black Bear Course was an easy walk from where he was living. His innate athleticism would serve him as well on a golf course as it had on a gridiron or baseball diamond.

Travis, along with his mother, did go to Florida during UMD's April spring break. In that Trevor was no longer living with Mr. Munoz, an extra bedroom was available for Travis if he chose to relocate to Florida. After watching the 2013 NCAA basketball tournament, Travis, along with millions of hoops fans across America, learned something about Florida Gulf Coast University in Ft. Myers. Travis was glued to his TV as the 'Eagles' of FGCU stunned the basketball world by upsetting two major college powers. Ironically, Maria Olivio was a student there when all the "March Madness' hoopla was going on. Travis has since transferred his college credits to FGCU where he will be a sophomore next year; both he and Maria will graduate with the class of 2016. His twin brother's bed at Hectors house would by his for some time to come.

Marella...I saw in the *Hibbing Daily Tribune* that a two-bedroom, two-bath, home on Anderson Road was for sale. On a visit to Hibbing over the Fourth, I drove out to take a look, and found that it was the Windsong place and that it was empty of any furnishings. The old widow across the dirt road told me that Marella had moved someplace in late May. Mrs. Berthuame wasn't sure where. "Not surprisingly, she didn't tell me anything. I sure have missed those boys of hers this past winter," the old woman said. The winter of 2013 had been a brutal experience for her and those thousands of other northern Minnesotans who shoveled snow from one blizzard after another.

I wish I could tell you what Hector Munoz is up to these days, but I don't know for certain. We haven't been keeping in touch with each other as much as we had before the christening of St. Michael's Church. I plan on traveling down to Florida this winter and stopping by his place in TriPalms to say 'hello'.

The 'inclusion project' that proved so elusive to Father Mickey and Benjamin Little Otter has born fruit since the February funeral. Elders from the five reservations in the Duluth Catholic diocese met with Bishop Bremmer and Father Mickey in March of 2013. The discussion centered on the '*The Year of Faith*' which had been proclaimed by Pope Benedict XVI in an Apostolic Letter in 2011. The resulting commitment was promising. On Sunday, July 14, a special celebration of St. Kateri Tekakwitha's feast day was held at the

Cathedral of Our Lady of the Rosary in Duluth. The bishop celebrated an afternoon mass and a 'fellowship' picnic followed at the Catholic school across the street. Perhaps that event, more than any other thus far, will establish bonds that promise a stronger Christian brotherhood in the future.

I have been told that Father Mickey Moran is enjoying his time away from the limelight these days. The bishop has scaled back Mickey's speaking schedule and has 'graciously' accepted the corresponding decline in revenues. Would you be surprised if I told you that Mickey is struggling with himself and his priesthood? Again! The remodeled St. Gerard's has been a comfortable place for him to be these days, but he isn't nearly as inspired as he would like to be. He does, however, want to write a book—a memoir of sorts. I can only wonder if Mickey isn't much too young to pen a memoir...or, maybe...could there be something down the road that I don't yet know about? I guess that we—you and I–will have to wait and see. God bless...

OTHER WORKS BY THE AUTHOR...

'The Mesabi Trilogy'

To Bless or to Blame (ISBN: 978-0-9724209-0-7)
> An historical drama, romance, set on the early
> Mesabi Iron Range.
> Ruthless and driven, entrepreneur Peter Moran is bigger than
> life in the rowdy mining hub of Hibbing in the early 1900's.
> A "compelling debut novel" and NEMBA award finalist.
> Trade paperback (2002). $18.95

A Blessing or a Curse 978-0-9724209-1-4)
> Sequel. Ambition runs in the Moran bloodlines. Obsessed
> to achieve what his unscrupulous father never could, Kevin
> Moran plunges into a political battle against the established
> Iron Range power structure. An historical drama, romance.
> Trade paperback (2003) $19.95

Blest Those Who Sorrow (ISBN: 978-0-9724209-2-4)
> Sequel. A psychological thriller completes the Mesabi
> Trilogy. Kevin and Angela Moran are swept far from their
> familiar Hibbing roots in a page-turner of deceptions and
> delusions. "A deftly crafted drama!"
> Trade paperback (2004) $16.95

Other novels

The Hibbing Hurt (ISBN: 978-0-9724209-3-8)
> Murder mystery set in Hibbing, 1956. A racial
> abduction/homicide stirs the conscience of the ethnically rich
> Iron Range community. Pack Moran is hard-nosed cop
> who unravels the complex conspiracy.
> "There are no heroes in this tragedy."
> Trade paperback: (2005) $14.95

'Flag' (ISBN: 987-0-9724209-4-0)

Angry and conflicted, 18 year-old Amos Moran is a runaway who ends up in Flagstaff, Arizona. Connected to earlier novels, this forth generation Moran is a compelling character. Amos witnesses a murder, falls in love with a spirited coed, and risks his own life to save that of an innocent Navajo man. "Action packed!"
Trade paperback. (2006) $13.95

Saint Alban's Day (ISBN: 987-0-9724209-5-2)

The consummate political thriller with a wide Minnesota scope. Amos Moran accepts a controversial political appointment while coping with a psychopath from his past. The prison escapee had threatened his family. Drama builds in McGauley's most provocative story.
Trade paperback. (2007) $14.95

A Passage of Redemption   (ISBN: 978-0-9724209-7-6)

Mickey Moran is a misunderstood and disillusioned priest in search of the passion that once inspired his calling. Brian Slade is a destitute young man searching for any thread of hope. The two men aare a contrast in every conceivable way except in their appearance—they have a doppelganger link! What happens to both is a creative masterpiece.
Trade paperback: (2012) $14.95

Children's books

Mazral and Derisa: An Easter Story (ISBN:987-0-9724209-9-0)
A spiritually uplifting Easter fantasy involving a mouse and a dove in ancient Jerusalem. A Resurrection miracle occurs in a cave on a Calvary hillside. Trade paper. (2004) $12.95

Santa the King (ISBN: 987-0-9724209-8-3)
An incredible fantasy in which one of the Wise Men is spiritually led to the North Pole where he becomes Santa Claus. The story combines the 'real' Christmas with the delights of Santa. "A delightful story for young and old alike." Hardcover. (2005) $13.95

The Midnight Hour (ISBN: 987-0-9724209-6-9)
A mischievous elf named Nathan almost ruins Christmas for all of the children of the world when he puts a sleeping potion in Santa's hot chocolate. A story that provides a positive message of redemption, and a story that will not be easily forgotten. Hardcover. (2011) $14.95

*Autographed copies of all titles can be ordered directly by emailing the author at **shatiferin@aol.com**. Check his website for more information: **www.patmcgauley.com**

Minnesota author Pat McGauley is a former Hibbing High School teacher. Born in Duluth, Minnesota, McGauley grew up in Hoyt Lakes. He graduated from Winona State University (BS: '64) and the University of Minnesota (MA). A former political candidate, iron mineworker, regional historian, and state agency commissioner under Governor Albert Quie, McGauley resides in Hibbing and Naples.

'The Sons of Marella Windsong' will be available on Kindle and Nook on November 1, 2013.